To Charles

Lucian

Allan Ward

Lucian

A NOVEL

By Allan Ward

Design: H. K. Stewart
Cover illustration: Linda Carol Butler

Award Press
6609 Sherry Drive
Little Rock, Arkansas 72204
award@ualr.edu

ISBN 0-9748636-2-9

Printed in the United States of America

"Without freedom,
no one really has a name."

—Milton Acorda

1

"Think how many stories that we have studied deal with cultures that froze individual greatness into a series of social roles," Dr. Fenwicke lectured. "The emerging works to which I have alluded will not be about those roles but about individuals *escaping* from roles. Individuals performing societal functions without *dehumanizing* into a role."

Five hundred and forty-three students in the paint-peeled university lecture hall, in the Boston winter, sat before her. Dr. Fenwicke thought of the Charles Addams cartoon of a theater full of people watching a horror film on an out-of-view screen, all cringing and shocked at what they saw, all but one, the one sitting smiling in ghoulish fascination. Here, five hundred and forty-two faces sagged in varied degrees of mental disengagement. But one feasted on every word, as distinct from the others, in his intensity and concentration, as the cartoon figure had contrasted with those who surrounded him.

Dr. Fenwicke: "Notice, in all countries there was a hierarchical pattern that had built up over time. Leaders of these, as they swept along in pageant and conquest, became the stuff of what they considered to be their culture's great literature. Nor..." and she held up a warning index finger, "...did that change in America. Intruders came by the hull full, smallpoxing the inhabitant tribes to smithereens, a cacophony of contending peoples..."

Watches foreshadowed the hour's end, and figures began wrapping their quilted coats around them, anticipating the outside.

"The difference is that the emerging works will not be about this clatter and clash of contending classes and roles and representatives of cultures. It will be about the ones who fall through the cracks, the ones who exist between the turmoils.

"The non-hero will be a quiet, inward-turning observer, who walks in solitude among the jabbering crowds. He is the new creation. Freed from the caste system of every other culture, she is neither suppressed nor relegated to a menial role. He is freed to be a non-social entity while performing projects beneficial to societal needs, an observer, a new perceiver, with a perspective frequently impossible and seldom achieved. She is an individual."

Five hundred and forty-two quilted shapes were exiting. One remained in place, the one with the focused, wide-pupiled eyes.

"And even if written, would it ever be read, this pending tome? Because among the oil barons and the dynastic tycoons, the popular culture droids, and the attention-deficited readers of pulp, the true individual and his story are virtually invisible and can scarcely be heard."

Lucian sat motionless. Dr. Fenwicke engulfed herself in a winter coat and headed for the cold. Beneath her earmuffs, she did not hear the solitary remaining student ask hesitantly, "Are you writing that story?"

Alone in the dismal chamber, Lucian pulled his calendar-book from his pocket and wrote in the space of that day's date, *final class*. In a space for the following week, he wrote, *graduation*. Across the week following that, he wrote, *oblivion*.

2

"You are self-destructing, and there is no…," the psychologist paused and sought for a word, "…*release*."

"Release?" Lucian leaned forward, his eyes unblinking.

"Release, relief, recourse, solution." Her hands reached habitually, unconsciously, for a cigarette.

"But when we started, you said there was…hope of…something," Lucian said, his voice trailing off, ending in a cough as the smoke reached his nostrils.

"Hope?" she said, standing and pacing. "There's always hope. I wouldn't have a profession if there wasn't hope, okay? You came six months ago. You had money to put into the process, so we could take tests, and explore and the rest. Now you tell me you've used up your savings...." She blew a cloud of smoke at the ceiling. "When you're out of quarters, the bed stops vibrating, okay?"

His hands made small motions with the fingers as if they were about to generate a word, a question.

"Look," she interrupted, "you've got fifteen minutes left. I've been straight with you, right?" She picked up a folder and fanned the air. "Okay, Dr. Kellerman sees you for allergies and plows your back, and checks out a thousand substances, and you're allergic to everything in the city." She flipped the folder back onto the desk. "He refers you to me to see what's at the other end of the body-hyphen-brain continuum, okay?"

She sat down at the desk across from him and stared into his eyes for a moment. "You know I don't believe in all this lead-a-patient-to-his-own-insight crap you studied at the university. Your ancestors in the jungles didn't survive by waiting to be led anywhere. Those that did had their genetics end up in a tiger's digestive tract. The others saw, responded, and left, and passed their genes along to another generation."

She could not stay in one position long and paced again with another cigarette. "The tigers don't come in stripes anymore. They're invisible to your senses. That's my job. And Kellerman's. He makes visible the things that creep in the air and water. And he gives you extra teeth and claws like tetracycline to fight with.

"I show you other invisible tigers and give them names so you can picture them. And..." She banged her left palm on the folder on the desk, "...there they are—stress, despondency, unrealistic expectations, and all, *all* of the rest."

She walked away from him, talking as she went. "See, you have this TV version of life, where people care for other people enough to sacrifice themselves." She turned and faced him from across the room. "But have you found any of those people? Huh? Have you?"

He looked down at the table for a moment and back up and said simply, "I don't watch television."

"Movies, then, *movies!*" she blurted out. "You have a *movie* version of life. You even *talk* like the movies. You don't sound like you were ever in Boston. Or anywhere else real. You have *stage diction.* You sound like you were *born* in a movie."

He looked at her with those clear, unblinking eyes, the face otherwise expressionless.

She waved her hands. "You're a foreigner in this world, Lucian. It's like you were raised on another planet and adjusted to that, your habit patterns, and everything, and then transported here, and—pow!—nothing fits anymore. All your reactions are—they're useless!"

She sat across from him again, ground out her cigarette, and without stopping the movement of her hands, lit another. "Useless! See, we know—you and I—we have explored enough of your background. We know part of why you're like this, okay? You have older parents who never really wanted a child. They're benign, but basically ignored your existence. They spent their time gallivanting around supporting various political candidates. They collected photos of themselves with the candidates, like some people collect matchbook covers. You existed in their eleventh floor apartment like a vase on a table. You have never had a conversation with your father. Your mother—to her, talking is synonymous with consciousness. She never talked *to* you, she was an environmental noise like the refrigerator motor. So you never had a conversation with her, either. You went through all your imprinting years relating to rugs and lamps and sidewalks and traffic lights and buildings. They are your role models."

She stood and blew a bellow of smoke above her. "My god, Lucian, you have the social awareness of a piece of bathroom tile. You read everything…but…" She came close and leaned over, her upraised palms gesturing, "…but to walk into a new room, to have a rudimentary conversation with *anyone*, and your stomach starts to consume itself. Listen to me—you're allergic to people, to social occasions, to decision making, to anger, to assertiveness. For godsake, you've never *argued* with anyone. Don't you know you haven't *lived* until you've argued? Life is a conflict. You haven't lived until you fight."

She paused and walked away. From across the office, she said, quietly now, "Your ancestors evolved a defense for firing up their systems with adrenaline to face catastrophic dangers and then fought and fled and survived. But the things *you* are conditioned to react to as if they were catastrophic dangers are saying *hello*, or asking for a cup of coffee."

"I don't drink cof..."

Her voice rose and interrupted his effort. "Your phobias have all run together like overlapping pancakes on a griddle, and you can't tell where one ends and another begins."

"Pancakes on a griddle?"

"That's part of it, there." Her index finger aimed at him. "I'm trying to get you to focus on the base of this, and the one word you choose to react to, the one word you respond to is—*pancakes!*"

"Foreigner?" he suggested as a substitution.

"Foreigner!" she seized on it. "Yes, even a foreigner has a home somewhere. He goes back to it and fits in. You can't go back to your parents end-table and set there."

"*Set* there? Sit there."

"No, *set* there. You're a lamp. Oh, god, I can't believe we're getting lost in metaphorical grammar. There's no place on earth where people behave like in the books you read. Straight A's in school, personable under the rare conditions, when everything is just right..."

She was pacing again. "If ten people came in that door, didn't make small talk with you, sat in a circle around you, and said they wanted to explore life, and they were wondering how the ethics of the Ming Dynasty related to Donald Duck, you would be interested, knowledgeable, articulate, at ease." She turned. "You could do that, couldn't you?"

He shrugged slightly.

"You get out of college, you get a job based on those grades and the perfect things some of the teachers, who adored you—if they could even remember you—said about you. Of course, in a large lecture class, they wouldn't even know you existed. But in the smaller classes—you were the one who asked them about the cruddy little professional studies they had to publish in journals no one reads, for promotion and tenure, that no one else cared about, that, by god, you really *were* interested in. Now the job. You're afraid to get up, to leave the house, to walk into work, to decide anything, to take responsibility, you don't have a friend in the world, and not the remotest notion of how to get one."

She looked at him squarely. "You're damned handsome in your own way, and so polite and courteous and patient. You want therapy?"—her voice taking on the tone of a comedian moving toward a punch line—"you come home with me and I'll give you therapy. I'll teach you the step by step process of intimacy. Oh, god, don't die on me now. Consider it a psychologist's joke." She glanced at her watch and daubed out another smoldering butt.

He looked at her and said softly, "If I can ask—if I have a couple of minutes left—uh, how do you—and I mean you the *individual*, not you *generically*—how did you decide to be a psychologist, and how do you keep from getting torn up inside by the things you have to deal with professionally?"

Her hands behind her back, she paced slowly now, nodding. "Yes, I should have suspected it. You're in the process of self-destructing, and yet you have a curiosity about *that*." She looked at him. "You don't even see the irony in that, do you? But what the heck, a freebie.

"I was marketing director at my father's clothing business. My mother had a kind of mid-life crisis. She wanted attention, and she was getting older, was all it was. Anyone knew that. But she went to this psychiatrist. And when I realized what he was getting for telling her that! She was paying for someone to talk to. Our society had gotten to the point that you go to a vending machine to buy anything, even a surrogate friend. I figured up the money I could make, and invest, and I knew I could be rich in ten years.

"Psychiatry would take a medical degree and too much time. I got a Ph.D. in psychology and here I am, right on schedule. I hear the anguish of the world pass through this office. And I can't solve any of it. I listen, I collate, I name people's tigers, I give them fair share, and what they do with it is their own business. I'm not their keeper, I'm not responsible for their behavior. I sell them information about themselves, and I go home and sleep like a baby, a very rich baby, and that's what life is all about, Lucian."

He said, "I know Dr. Kellerman already told me I would probably not get along if I stay here doing what I'm doing. He said it had to be a complete change of lifestyle. That's a very high abstraction, and I find it difficult to relate to."

"You have the lifestyle of a doorknob. Go find a door."

"I don't understand the analogy."

"*It's a joke.*" She rummaged through a desk drawer and flipped him a small business card. "Here's a travel agency my sister owns. Find a place as far from a city as possible and a job you can do all alone, like… like…let me think…like a *worm farm*," she laughed, "and maybe you'll heal up some, and…" She looked at her watch. "Time's up, and that's the real world, Lucian. That's the real world and your time is up."

"Thank you," he said, looking at the rug as he walked toward the door.

She ran her hand over her eyes like she was suddenly very tired and motioned him back. "Sit down," she said. She faced him silently for a moment, with no cigarette and no movement.

She said, "I have two patients now who have genetic defects. They're trying to decide whether or not to have children. If people who have conditions like theirs keep having children and passing these defects into the gene pool, the time will come when the strength that evolved from natural selection will be lost in weakness and deformity. The weak used to be separated naturally by death, before they could reproduce and pass on their defective traits. Now they're pampered and prolonged and breed their problems for another generation to face. It's one thing to make a defective individual comfortable and as long-lived as possible. It's another to let him debilitate society.

"Think about it, Lucian. You'll probably never get close enough to anyone to breed anyway. But take a long thought before the occasion ever arises as to whether you want to perpetuate your maladjustments, whether they're genetic or imprinted, for anyone else to go through."

He looked puzzled and said, "What is a worm farm?"

3

Worms. He watched them probe a grey-purplish end out of the soil and then coil back into the loam. Baskets full of dirt. Dirt full of worms.

A worm farm. A worm farm in the desert. The cottonwood

trees shaded the back yard. The desert beyond rippled in the light of the unblinking sun. Basket after basket of dirt, row after row of baskets. Not neat. Not orderly. Every conceivable size and shape of container. A garbage dump of a farm.

Lucian slowly walked along the rows looking at each container, each one lovingly pointed out by the ancient Gitano beside him. Gitano, whose formless clothes hung like ship-sails in the doldrums, had despaired of finding anyone to take over his worm farm. Fertilizers, mechanized methods, pesticides increasing, he was the only wormer in the region, and no one had shown interest in the decaying farm he wanted to leave.

Then, out of the blue, out of the east, out of a far city, had come this young man with the gaze of a deer buck, who wanted to buy the place. Gitano, with strings of white hair streaming down his cranium in all directions, blowing over and away from his eyes in the desert wind, had at first felt elated at the prospect as they toured the grounds. But as he talked to Lucian, he began to feel sorry for this youth with gold-green eyes, who walked like a shadow. Gitano found himself trying to talk the young man out of isolating himself in this scorched heap of timber, tending worms. It seemed to him not right, somehow unnatural.

"Well," Gitano said, trying to disinterest him, "this is just a lonesome house beyond the farthest edge of town, by the foothills here that lead on into the arroyos and desert canyon country, godforsaken as a…," and then he said it, "…a tomb."

"Good," the young man had nodded.

"And the nearest town is on the edge of nowhere, itself. Wouldn't be nothing if the space agency hadn't put that little research center a ways over yonder. But they're not using worms."

"That's all right," Lucian said.

"Well, the house is falling apart, here and there, and there's work to be done on the tin right over there where it joins, and a loop's been knocked off," said Gitano.

"Uh-huh," Lucian said, not knowing what a loop was.

Feeling some urgency he did not understand to *unsell* the farm, Gitano said, "I done a lot of things before I settled down here, and this was kind of peaceful, but, the truth is, a bit lonely, and you're such a young man, and I don't know what kind of future there is for you here…"

But the young man, by that point, was tapping on an old cottonwood tree and began to tell Gitano about the approximate age of the tree, how its root system differentiated it from other trees, how it served for kachina carving, and the pattern of tree migration in North America since the last ice age.

Gitano made a sound that was not quite a word. He could not think of a word to say, and the sound occurred down in his throat.

. . .

Gitano sold the place for less than the amount he first named. He had expected some bartering. There was none. When he made out the papers he lowered the price without saying anything. When the arrangement was completed, the youth just looked at him with the bright eyes and said, "Fine. Thank you."

The little bank in the desert town gave Lucian a loan, payable over thirty years. He had no credit rating. He had never bought anything on credit. He had never bought much of anything. He had no references, no visible means of support, a humanities degree, whatever that was, and a letter of reference from a corporation in New York that concluded, "This young man is different from our usual interns. It was mutually agreed that he did not at present fit into the corporate structure of the company."

The bank gave him the loan because no one else, not a single person anywhere, wanted the worm farm except him. And as soon as he defaulted on payments, as they assumed he would, the land would be theirs.

. . .

On Lucian's first Sunday after he had moved into the house, an arid mid-morning, five black-clad men, without knocking, filed through his unlocked front door. He had been sitting on the floor, knees to his chin, arms around the knees, wrapped only in a sheet, staring at a wall, mummified in silence, when they walked in.

He said not a word, nor did they. They sat on the four chairs, and one on the floor beside him, and all stared ahead in silence.

An hour passed. "Praise the Lord God," erupted one with such vigor, breaking the silence, that Lucian's muscles jerked him into a standing position.

The five rose and moved in linear unison toward the door. Lucian, draped in his white covering, made his rusty voice say toward the back of the last one, "Uh…who are you?"

That man turned stiffly and said, "Did Mr. Boswell not tell thee? This is our meeting place. His departure reduces our attending members once again, though he would never fully abide by our ways. Thank thee for joining us."

"Mr. Boswell?" questioned Lucian. "*Gitano?*"

"Oh, thee almost makes me laugh, young one," said the man, without his expression changing at all. "He would have been the Steinbeck character could he have managed it. But Boswell he was, and the old gypsy wandering off into the hills, he was not."

"But he wanted to be?" said Lucian.

"He wanted to be," said the man, turning and departing, to where the others waited silently for him in a row in the sharp sun outside. "We will see thee next week."

Until the next Sunday, Lucian fretted over the expectation of their coming with waxing discomfort, nursing an upset stomach from the apprehension. A week later, the hour came and went, as he sat stiffly in the darkest clothes he had. The people did not reappear.

4

A back door to the prehistoric world. Lucian stood and stared through the screen. He had never heard silence before. This absence of familiar noises deafened him. Sound had always existed in the city, human sounds, garbage cans, sirens, traffic wheels and horns.

Boston and New York were human-made. Three-dimensions of space, curbed, rented, bartered, all occupied. He had never seen a sunrise or sunset, except in pictures. Sun had appeared over building tops in mid-morning, if at all, and disappeared in mid-afternoon over the opposite buildings. Street lights blazed all night.

Now he had reached some kind of line of demarcation. Gitano's house, or Boswell's house, now his house, was at the edge of the human world. Lines of demarcation marked things,

separated them, warned of change, transition. Here, outside of his back door, lay a line of demarcation.

Beyond the door, human beings had not seemed to have parceled or plowed the land. Land untouched by homo sapiens' hands or feet, he thought. Or if touched, left undisturbed. Unaltered. Land, evolving. Prehistoric land. He looked at it in strange fascination. For a long time, he could not prompt himself to walk out into it. He looked. He sniffed the unfamiliar fragrances. He saw dried, uprooted remains of plants rolling across the desert in the wind.

But he had to go outside into the yard to tend his worms. As he walked this new territory, he picked up a stick from time to time and scratched symbols in the sand at its parameter. He made the Sanskrit symbols for the word *boundary*, and at various times, the same word in other languages.

Lucian savored the prolonged moments of standing at this imagined border. He stood in the mornings, wrapped in his sheet, peering out past this boundary, until he shivered.

He imagined something calling him, the wind, the sounds, the animal howls in the vague distance. And then, one night, as the full moon shown upon the vastness beyond, with the sheet around him, he went out to the edge of the yard where all the words were written and shuffled through them with his bare feet until none remained.

At dawn, he went outside, and over the places where his feet had erased the markings, he now wrote *frontier*.

At the next dawn, he stood at the same location. And then, past that threshold, past the pots and containers and tools, past the scraggly growth and trees in the yard, he placed one bare foot on the seemingly unaltered desert. And withdrew it, and put it forth again. And then walked forward across the *frontier*.

Each morning, he proceeded further out into the dawn, wrapped in his sheet, in a haze of feeling. As if not fully conscious, as if something was being communicated from the desert floor upward through the soles of his feet.

Then dressed in faded garments that Gitano had left behind, he wandered further still, onto this land devoid of people. Wandered directionless toward the encircling horizon, the edge of the world, sensing the wind, the dust, the sage-scented plants. He walked and sometimes moaned and sometimes his eyes teared uncontrollably.

5

Lucian stood one night, at the edge of his yard, where it blended with the desert. The moon shown full round. He walked back inside and savored the sense of timelessness that continued from the desert into the house. This building with bare walls, bare tables, an absence of clocks. An absence of calendars. Humans measured time. Here time simply *was*. Or *wasn't*. Or *never* had been.

No adornments on the walls. The cracked adobe formed its own patterns from which his mind generated stories. The few pieces of ancient, styleless, unstained furniture remained where they had been the day he arrived. The desert appeared somehow to be reclaiming the house, its contents, and Lucian.

One room had a single unshaded light bulb. Another had a kerosene lamp. The third had been illumined, as if from some prehistoric time, by generations of candles of multiple colors, each succeeding the other, on top of a buffalo skull, the horns of which protruded from the mass of drip-wax that had congealed around them.

Lucian sat by this stalagmite of many colors, by the solitary flame, in the midst of night, with a ragged, leather-bound volume opened before him. He had found it in his grandfather's attic years before, saw it as a treasure for reasons he could not explain, for which others laughed at him. No one had wanted the volume with its dry and flaked leather, its yellow and crack-edged pages. No one knew what it was nor how it came to be there, for its cover had no title, and not a mark of any kind adorned its blank pages.

Into this volume, Lucian, as he read the poets of the world, had begun in high school to place his own thoughts in forms as various as those he read. One time an ode, another a sonnet, later a verse in an ancient Indus form. These moments distilled the clutter of his thoughts and raging feelings. Almost in a collapse of all strength, he would sink into stupor after penning the last word that had urged itself outward and onto paper. The unmeasured night. The buffalo skull. The mound of wax. The flame flickering periodically from a desert breeze through the open window. Lucian writing. Wrapped in his sheet, kneeling on a lopsided chair, hunched over the table, the scarred leather volume before him.

what lies there in the desert
what is it in the desert

all the sagebrush and dusty desert floor
  breath it
  in unuttered syllables
humans strive to capture it
  with the nets of their mouths
  as bigness
  vastness
  spaciousness
  quietness
but it absorbs the words
  as they are uttered
as the thirsty desert floor
  sucks in a droplet of dew

lonely night poets
and magazine-paid poets
  strive to dip their pens in it
  and ink their paper thus
    wild ridge-ringed vastness
    turquoise-domed immensity
    arid timelessness
    the impersonal caress of deities

  but it
    the great it
    dissolves the words into itself
    like the arid air

absorbs the stranger clouds
that glide from over the mountains
into evaporation

what lies there in the desert

what is it in the desert

He wrote and spoke aloud the words. He paced the room, his shadow huge upon the walls from the candle flame. He circled through the other rooms, with the single bulb, with the kerosene lamp, with no illumination except what seeped in from the other sources, reading the words aloud, changing, altering, gesturing. He ranged his voice around the lines, trying the shapes of sound until the fit felt right.

As the desert seemed to invade the house, so in reverse, his voice, through the open windows and doors, invaded the desert night. All of the turmoil that during the daylight bubbled inside of him, came out at sunset as words, onto the paper, and voiced into the darkness.

He gestured as he walked, arms moving out of his sheet like a tuniced Greek actor, posturing his whole body with the feeling of the words. Then hunching over the candled table, he poured out more words onto the paper.

late at night
yoga-positioned on my mat
the bubbling urge to communicate
spills over
anguished waxes
hardening into grotesque shapes

a worm is boring deep a hole
within my soul
inside my soul
and eats a morsel every day
upon its way
along its way.

20

And another night, when the wind gusted through open doors and windows of the house, making the candle dance and sputter, his sheet loosely wrapped around his lean frame, he wrote in the leather-bound volume and howled a duet with the wind.

Please, someone, tell me why I live.
What purpose have I here?
For all my worthless being knows
Is fear, fear, fear—

Fear of life and fear of death
And fear of some misdeed;
Fear that grows from thinking
That I never shall succeed;

Fear of never having friends,
Fear of being wrong;
Fear of never finding
Any place where I belong.

I mourn the past for my mistakes,
I fear tomorrow's troubles,
And watch my fruitless days go by
Like empty worthless bubbles.

He turned back to a poem he had written in high school. He remembered how, on the day he had written it, his mother had taken the book out of his drawer. He found her reading his verses to his father, who continued to stare at his newspaper, as he sat in front of a wall of photographs of candidates they had supported. She had said, *Isn't that nice the way Lucian makes up these things. I never understood how anyone could put all those words together like that.*

When she noticed Lucian, she said, *You should read your father one of these things you've written. I don't understanding them much. Wouldn't that be nice, father, that our son is talented enough to write things.*

His father had said, *It doesn't bring in money any more. Poets*

21

used to get paid for it. He had continued staring at his newspaper. She tossed the book on the table and turned on the vacuum cleaner. Lucian had gone up to the attic with the book, wrapped it in a towel, and placed it at the bottom of an old trunk.

. . .

A storm raged one night, webbing the sky with strands of fire, vibrating the house with its sounds. Lucian alternated between hunching over his old leather volume, writing, and then moving about the house and yard with sweeping gestures, his sheet flapping like a wizard's cape.

He wrote and intoned into the night, over and over repeating his lines to the punctuations of thunder:

entombed
in solitude
I watch people
I want them for friends
I shout
to explain my feelings
but my words mutely echo in my solitude

I feel the embryos of my thought
beg for life
pitifully grasping for nourishment
of purpose
they wither and die
for I have no one
no friend
to share them with
to be the purpose

my arms outstretched
to reach a friend
grow weary and numb
and to my agonized eyes
the people blur and fade
until I cannot remember what they were

I am an only being of creation
in a soundless lifeless place
I mumble my thoughts to the inanimate dust
I raise my head to the stars and the moon
and shout to them to be my friends
and so suckling the dying embryos
on distorted purpose
they swell into screaming things
to shapes
of red-veined madness
that burn my lungs
and with me shriek
to the mountains and the sky
until the screaming voices
echo from the moon
and reverberate throughout the universe
throbbing
pounding
until my fevered brain
explodes

He read the final word and ran out into the storm.

6

The books arrived.

Books. The one thing Lucian never threw away. The one category of possessions he sought. Every book he had ever acquired, he had kept. They had been lost until now. Not exactly lost. Displaced. Abandoned.

No regular movers had bought them. Back in Boston, he had made a *tag-on* arrangement for transporting them. He had read a small ad in a Boston paper: *Moving to LA, tag-on moving cheap.*

They were traveling from coast to coast, these two wilted flower children. Packing other people's objects in with theirs, dropping off the things along the way, helping pay for their own trip. This tie-dyed-clothed couple had a van, of sorts, and a truck, of sorts. Lucian was one of the takers of the tag-on ad.

One taker was an unemployed waitress who wanted to send westward, to her *terminally-cancered* stepmother, an old swish-and-swirl, wringer-on-top, washing machine. The stepmother had left it behind when she departed Massachusetts for *a better climate*. Now she wanted this remnant of her past.

Another taker, recently paroled, with a frayed canvas bag held together with mismatched belts, wanted it and himself delivered to a remote western town to build school bus motors, a skill he had learned in prison.

Lucian had headed west with this couple, the waitress, the parolee, the washing machine, and other assorted drop-offs, in the van that looked as tie-dyed as their clothing, and a lopsided truck of rust-spotted, robin's egg blue, that tilted toward the right side of the road. Things stuck out the glassless windows of the van like garbage through holes in an overstuffed bag.

Lucian had volunteered to ride in the enclosed back of the truck to perform a task for a reduction in price. Someone had to knot rope around boards spiked to the door from inside to hold it shut since the outside latching mechanism had long since disappeared.

He had ridden west in stifling, isolated darkness, risking extinction should the heaps of things all shift and emboss him on the inside of the door. His reassured himself with the thought that the door would break open, expelling him and the contents, before he was fatally crushed. He could endure this trek because it was the only affordable way he found to transport his boxes and boxes of books.

The waitress and her washing machine had been deposited by a puddle in front of a rural route shack, when the step-mother did not respond.

The parolee saw something in the distance at one roadside gas station in Oklahoma that made him shout to stop the van, and he dashed off on foot, not to return, his part of the journey unpaid.

Somewhere in the desert, Lucian had felt the truck shudder to a grinding stop. He had unwound the rope from the ties and emerged from his tilting enclosure, blinking in the desert sun. From the hood came smoke and fumes. Fluids dumped on the

24

highway beneath the motor. The truck was deceased. Lucian felt he might soon be too.

He had watched the pink-violet-yellow-green van sputtering off down the road without him, sounding like the automotive contagion of the truck had spread. Lucian stood in a vast landscape, with only the retreating van suggesting any presence of people. He stood and watched it disappear into a shimmer of road mirage.

He had not moved when some time later the Volkswagen Easter-egg reappeared through the highway shimmer and returned. The couple had at first forgotten that Lucian had been holed inside of the abandoned truck.

They mentioned something about *karma* and left the truck at the roadside with some of their own possessions inside that could not be compressed into the van, and all of Lucian's books as well. The van was stuffed to such capacity that it could hold no more, not even Lucian. He ended up squatting on its roof, between bulging plastic bags strapped in front and behind him.

As the van sputtered on down the unbending desert road, one of the plastic bags next to Lucian popped, ripping down the side, its contents of clothing flying like ragged birds that landed along the roadway. He hit the roof to get the couple's attention to stop, but they didn't hear him. *Karma*, he thought.

When at last they had emptied him off, it was miles past the crossroads closest to his destination. They had forgotten he was clinging to the roof. The driver had remembered only when he stopped to urinate by a cactus and looked up. "Oh," he said through the inner fog of whatever drug he had been ingesting, "this is as close as we get."

Lucian had never hoped to see his books again, picturing them in the truck, by the side of the road, with its back doors open to the wind and anyone who cared for the contents.

But then, weeks later, with no explanation, a note from a tavern owner outside of town came to the worm farm mail box. *Your boxes are here*, it tersely read.

And to the rooms of Lucian's house came boxes, and from the boxes came piles of books. And another of his containers on which was scrawled the word *zheng*.

7

His plan was simple. The arrival of the books had prompted it. He awoke one morning with the idea.

Of all that he had read, of all that he had studied, five books communicated more to him than any others. Each time he had reread them, there came to his mind the picture of himself sitting with another person, both reading the same books, and then a third individual and perhaps more. These imagined people felt as he did about the ideas in these volumes. Perhaps through the books, he and these individuals could somehow meet and merge together. His ideas of the imaginary people were vague. They were like mists, outlines of vapor.

Late into the night, he composed the message to these outlines of vapor, a message he might place in copies of these volumes in a library, in many libraries, awaiting the synchronicity of the right persons finding them. Could there be some, like himself, somewhere, who longed to meet others but did not know how nor where? He wrote and paced and read aloud and rewrote. He saw an image of himself, opening one of the books, of finding the note, an invitation to meet. How would such a person respond? What could convey what lay behind the words?

There must be no name on the missive, no address, no identification. There must be a rendezvous. A place for the *moved*, the motivated, to come. The careless, the disinterested, the dealer with daily details who might see these words would read them and not understand, would discard them, would not even seek these books in the first place.

But the others, the *some*, the *few*, who felt like strangers in the world, would know, would make the effort to go to the rendezvous. No name, just a place and a time. But go to where?

After the message felt generally *right-shaped*, he pondered the *where*. A spot, central in the country, easily accessible, where someone finding his message tucked within a library volume would come to meet him.

He opened an atlas and surveyed the map of North America. *Chicago*. Central, accessible. But where in Chicago? Opening the encyclopedia to the city's name, he looked at the page of photographs of landmarks. Which? Not buildings. Not inside. In the open. And there it was. Buckingham Fountain. In the middle of Grant Park.

And when? When people could be comfortably outside. The spring or summer. The date? He thought of the ides of March, when Julius Caesar died, which reminded him that Julius Caesar had taken the fifth month of the Roman calendar and removed its numbered-name, Quintilis, and replaced it with his own, *Julius*, July. Why not the ides of Julius, of July. *July 15.*

And how to recognize each other? That first fragile attempt at connecting. Something simple, but differentiating them from the others. A color of clothing? A flower? A book? *A book.* A copy of one of the five books, the title held where it would be visible.

He resurrected Gitano's old car that had been left in a shed in back of the house. A car that looked as scorched as the desert. With a stack of his reproduced messages, he drove off on his library odyssey, in search of lonely watchers of the world, who could understand each other.

. . .

His focus remained intense enough to force him past the sweaty palms, the stomach cramps, the loose bowels, that heralded the approach to each library in each new town. Into the library, trying to look casual, into the stacks. He knew the shelving numbers by memory. Find the books. Insert the…*the what?* What name could be given to the thing he had written? A note, a letter, a document, an invitation? A cry from a *within* to another *within*, who felt something, experienced something, agonized for *connection?*

Standing in the dim lines of shelves, the first time he inserted his pages, after having waited for someone else to leave the narrow aisle, sweat dampened him. His hands visibly trembled. Until that point, until that moment, this elaborate plan had evolved *inside* of him. He whispered to himself, *boundary.* Should he pass this boundary, the control of whatever happened would be irretrievably out of his hands, outside of himself, *out there.* The *out there* made him hesitate, until he heard footsteps. Then he audibly said, *frontier,* and with swift movement, he inserted his script, closed the book, returned it to the shelf, and walked away, his knees threatening to buckle under him.

When he walked outside of that first library, he went to the car and sat and tried to feel other than panic, but he could not. So he drove on. If panic must be felt, then let it happen while moving to the next location.

Across the states, random impulses moved him from city to city, to their libraries. Through the plains and hills, across the farmlands. *Where are they,* he kept thinking. *Can I feel their presence somewhere? Can I find the right towns where they reside?* He inwardly pictured his phantoms moving up the steps of the libraries he had visited, seeking something, a book with insight, a path, a goal, a connection with life, with real people, with a person, with *him.* They would check out one of the books, start to read, find his note. But was there anyone in the world who would want to know him?

It seemed as if, in these towns, he was not moving among actual *humans* on this odyssey. The people, these groups, crowds, pedestrians, drivers, seemed to merge with the fences, telephone poles, and street lamps as inanimate objects. Yet his phantoms felt real.

In St. Louis, he sat on a bench in a downtown park and watched the mass of people passing, wondering if one of the phantoms at that moment walked by him, both of them too enclosed within their crusts and shells to see each other. He pictured himself standing and shouting, *here I am,* and one breaking away from the others, also shouting, *here I am,* among a crowd which noticed neither of them. But all he saw were people as inanimate as *fences, telephone poles,* and *street lamps* rushing along the sidewalks, rushing toward—he could not name it— toward something he was not part of.

8

Boston. He arrived in Boston. Between ferreting out the libraries, he revisited the university building, the empty room, even the seat he had once occupied in Dr. Fenwicke's class. Before he could remove himself, a hoard of people burst in, flooding onto the seats around him. Before he could mobilize an escape, Dr. Fenwicke, herself, mounted the platform, speaking as she came, looking at no one, letting the mumble of voices dwindle as hers emerged.

"A general cannot be the hero of the novel of which I speak. Nor a minister, nor bishops, nor mullahs, nor rabbis, nor the members of any assemblage nor politicians. No..." her hand came up for a gesture as she looked at the mass of people for the first time. Something deflected her attention for a moment amid the crowd of several hundred facing her, and she did not know what, as she continued, "...any position that can be refilled, and go on, is only a story about a role, not the story of a human being. *The King is dead, long live the Queen* is merely the replacement of one actor with another, portraying the same part. But..."

Something kept distracting her, something in the rows of dull faces. "...if you say, my grandfather was a President, my aunt was a Senator, my parent was a Lieutenant, you have said nothing of the person, only of a social role." She squinted slightly at the first row.

"Great roles don't make great people. The great people are those who escape the roles and become themselves. And in doing so, they disappear from the awareness, the *perceptibility* of the role-players. They become as *nothing*." She scrutinized the second row. One mouth hung open. One gnawed gum. One was having a candy bar inserted into it. One drooled out of the left side.

"When role-players read novels, they think people come alive when they enter a *position*. Hence they write about *category-attainment* as if that role-assumption were the moment of their birth. In reality, it is the time of their demise. They have dissolved into a pattern of prescribed behavior, and their individuality perishes."

The third row, the fourth, fifth, sixth. People scratching, eyes starting to cross or roll up into their heads as interrupted sleep reclaimed the brain.

"The person who leaves the role seems to disappear to the role-players..." She was repeating herself, but something vexed her, something out of place. "...the disappearance spoken of in past tense as in *whatever happened to so-and-so; he just disappeared*. In reality the *disappeared one* had escaped, had been born. This is what the potential of the emerging narrative is all about.

"Most of life is about role-seeking, role-achievement, and role-loss, and most of the writing, likewise. But some escape, crawl out from between the roles, and survive in a polyglot society. The role-players could think the missing ones were in someone else's role categories, so the individualists could escape. In a strictly regimented society, they would tend to be discovered, halted, not permitted to leave their social mold in the first place."

Seventh, eighth, ninth, ten through fifteen. Writing, doing homework for the next class.

"Here, then, is the threshold of life. The writing of the real adventure is about the birth of the individual."

Sixteen through twenty.

"Mary or John Smith, Nobel Prize winner, awarded the Pulitzer, the Grammy, the Oscar, received a Rockefeller Grant. The human disappears under these spade-fulls of titles, like spade-fulls of earth covering a human and making it a corpse. Or spade-fulls of clay molded around the standing corpse, molded around it like a statue. Or bronze put around it, becoming a statue of a human being, not a person, but a pigeon toilet, a *thing*, a category, a cluster of categories, a statue to a category, a monument to a category. And that's what the role novels were about. But there remains that possibility..."

She was losing her concentration and the metaphors were bleeding into each other as it occurred to her that students were starting to look alike. That one, way back there, with the intense eyes and wide pupils, seemed out of place but vaguely familiar.

. . .

Between the library placements along the east coast, Lucian kept returning to Boston, and compulsively, to the campus, to the room, to the seat. He would arrive early, crouch down in the chair, and look at the floor as the others entered, and in that way could tolerate the vast urge to run.

Before Dr. Fenwicke entered, amid the babble, yawns, and coughing around him, a voice beside him said, "So what should I ask?" Lucian turned in that direction, more his eyes than his head, as if that would not precipitate as much notice. A student was looking at him. "I've got to ask something," she was saying, an expression of boredom on her face.

Beneath hair that flounced in all directions, she pointed a long painted index fingernail at an open paperback, topping her stack of books. "See, it says to get a good grade you got to ask a question in class about something, you know, to be noticed, and then you stand out as thinking and all, and get a good grade. And if I bum in this one, my dad will kill me. I mean, you know, he'll knot the hose."

Lucian's whole head had turned now. The first impulse, after she spoke and before he had looked at her, had been a momentary, a fleeting heartbeat of the possibility of that contact with one of the phantoms, someone who would look at him and recognize *something* and would reach out and...

"So what should I ask? All this literature stuff she talks about. What's her point anyway? I hate these required classes that don't have anything to do with anything. I can't think of anything to ask."

Lucian still wondered if Dr. Fenwicke wrote fiction, herself. Now that thought resurrected. Maybe this person could be his surrogate questioner.

"Yes," he started, and cleared his throat, and tried to speak again, and cleared his throat once more. He had not spoken to anyone for days, and the vocal mechanism had to be primed. He felt as if his voice might have atrophied from disuse.

"Yes," he managed. "Are you curious about whether she has tried to write such a novel?"

The girl penned painstakingly on a margin of her *Good Grades Mean Good Salary* book so she wouldn't forget it, *Are you curious about whether...*

"No," Lucian interrupted, "you might want to ask a question *about* that."

"Like how would I say it?" she asked, scratching though what she had previously written.

"Maybe: *have you ever written a novel*, or something like that."

Into the lecture, the girl raised her hand and read word for word from the book margin, "Maybe, have you ever written a novel, or something like that?"

Dr. Fenwicke focused on the back section of the auditorium

and lost the question for a moment as she noticed the person sitting next to the questioner, confirming that current students were starting to look like students from the past. "A novel? Write?" She stalled as if deciding whether to even answer or not.

"Of course," she finally said, and this was not her lecture voice. Several students looked up from their homework at the change in the tone. "Yes, of course. I had to do it. As an exercise so I could speak about it. How can a person teach something without doing it? As an exercise I wrote it, so I could know it could be done. So I could speak from experience. And that accomplished, I shall deposit it in some remote receptacle."

"You would throw it away?" Lucian whispered to the girl next to him. She said loudly, "You would throw it away?"

"I set small goals that I can excel in," said Dr. Fenwicke, in the strange voice. "Only those I can accomplish. I determined to write. And I achieved my goal. I never aimed at being a *published writer*. In our culture, that has become a role carrying with it behaviors which I am not willing to substitute for my own. I only set goals that are within my control, within me to accomplish. If I set goals that are under other people's control, if I internalize their expectations, there lies..." She hesitated. "...a condition that I do not choose to enter."

She concluded, "Some people are buffeted by failure, bewailing their inability to achieve; they need only change their goals to be constantly and totally successful." Lucian wrote the word *whimsy* on his note pad.

9

Spring break started on the day of that last visit to Dr. Fenwicke's class. Lucian felt foolish and guilty by what his intuition impelled to do next. He could not bring himself to leave the Boston campus yet. He watched the people with suitcases exiting.

The tone of Dr. Fenwicke's voice had reached him in some troubled way he could not explain. He sat on various benches and leaned unobtrusively against brick walls opposite the door of the building that housed her office.

When she emerged, with her briefcase and folio, walking with her head down, oblivious of any surroundings, he followed her. Followed her to the parking lot, and then, in his car, trailed her to her apartment. He sat waiting into the evening, like a stakeout.

Later that night, she reemerged with a suitcase, got into her car, and drove the city streets to the highway. He followed behind. He followed her all night.

He had placed enough of his pages within the selected books in libraries across the country. He felt the depression of a focus completed, like a sadness of something ended, of a project that had consumed him, that had become a kind of companion, but now the impetus was gone. In its place, transformed in the classroom, grew the resolve to track Dr. Fenwicke.

She drove along Interstate 90 through part of New York state, turned south on 84, intersected with highway 81 at Scranton. Then came the long sweep through the Shenandoah Valley.

Lucian had no idea nor concern where she headed. He followed as if by tractor-beam through the traffic behind her.

She crossed the Virginia line at Bristol, into Tennessee. Near Knoxville, she glided onto Interstate 40, straight westward. The night, the dawn, the day. She stopped periodically at rest stops and napped in her car. He did the same in his, attuned even in his shallow sleep to the sound of her reviving motor.

· · ·

They sped on westward, but with some side roads and stops now. She parked at the crater of the meteor that had crashed out of the sky ten thousand years ago and gouged a hole a mile across. Dr. Fenwicke walked its circumference and drove on.

She parked again and hiked for two hours on the flank of an ancient cinder cone. Northward she drove to the Grand Canyon, beheld it from a deserted point on its rim and headed back south, before going further west.

· · ·

Dusk approached when the hardened black lava beds appeared alongside the road. The ancient flows covered huge areas of desert floor.

Dr. Fenwicke stopped at a set of picnic tables beside the highway. She stood by a sign that explained the lava flows. A map marked *you are here* showed the relation to the long-extinct volcano and the extent of the blanketing lava, dark and polished-looking in the dwindling light.

She walked out on the ebony rock surface, then turned swiftly, went to her car, took out something, deposited it in the trash barrel, and drove on. Lucian watched from his parking place on the shoulder of the drive. At her departure, he moved toward the barrel, as several other travelers threw away their meal trash.

Beneath their rubbish, he found the packet, the discarded parcel, the *manuscript*. He opened it on one of the tables, dimly illumined by the the bug-satellited light globe that hung above the table.

His impulse to trail Dr. Fenwicke ended as he bent over the manuscript and looked at its opening lines. *In all that she said and did, the lady of the heart-stone knew a crack in time had appeared. She walked through and that made all the difference. Follow me, she beckoned...*

. . .

Lucian followed the lady of the heart-stone and read on into the night.

...intuitively, laconically, cat-like, ridges of mirth, realms of impressions welled up. 'Fear grows,' she whispered, 'as piece by piece one is disjoined and dissected, each part replaced by a prosthetic device from the limited parts inventory of patterns of a catalog of social roles.' She pointed her finger at his anatomy, item by item, as the silence lengthened. 'Tomorrow the final, crowning piece will be added, and you will be a thing. Critiqued in the thingness books, you will have an honored place.' She walked in a circle around his unmoving seated frame. 'If I seek to touch you, it is impossible for there is almost nothing of you left to touch.' As she spoke the final word, she seized his shoulders from behind...

As a hand grasped his shoulder, Lucian lurched to a standing position over the manuscript. "Is everything all right?" the highway patrol officer was asking, evidently the last of several things she had said to the oblivious reader. "Two in the morning is a little late to be trying to read in this light, alone in this deserted rest area, if you know what I mean."

Lucian did not know what she meant as he tried to return from the realm in which he had been immersed, from a story that already ranked with his five highly cherished volumes. He agreed with whatever it was she said, and she departed. He reentered the world of the manuscript.

10

When the complaining brakes of his car halted him in front of the worm farm, as the sun made long evening shadows across the land, the genie-like dust trail thrown up by the car tires caught up, blowing over him and the car, and onto the house. He had departed on his library odyssey leaving the doors and windows open, the screens unlocked.

Lucian felt a hunger of his whole being, like a starving of which he became conscious all of a sudden. He ran through the front door, through the rooms and out the back, through the back yard, past the tubs, and trees, and implements. Past everything that stretched from the Atlantic Ocean to the threshold edge of the back yard. Over that line he leaped and ran and dived onto the earth, into the earth.

Belly down, arms and legs sprawled, each part of his anatomy that touched the earth dug into it. His knees, his feet, his elbows, his fingers, probing into the soil, reaching downward like roots. As if roots sprouted at each point of contact and sucked up strength and energy. He lay and lay, churning the soil, revitalizing, resuscitating, growing strong, and with strength came a relaxation. With the relaxation, all thinking ceased, and he became joined with the ancient land. He relaxed into the earth, rooted in it, submerging into it, into a sleeping state, into more than a sleeping state, into a mind-melding, prehistoric state.

. . .

Long shadows swept the land from the opposite direction when Lucian reemerged into consciousness. He sat up in the dawn looking back at the worm farm. The *worm farm*. The

35

worms. He thought of them for the first time. Untended, what condition were they in? Even, were they alive?

He ran to the aisles of shaded pots, dug his hands into the loam, and found the plump inhabitants alive and well and living in earthy luxury.

Entering the house, which he had run through unobservantly the previous evening, he saw no expected layer of dust. On the table lay a pile of checks for varying amounts made out to *Worm Farm*, for *worms*.

His pondering was interrupted by the sound that Mr. Creps made when he appeared for a supply of worms. Not exactly a greeting nor a call, sort of a loud "*Eh,*" announcing his presence, after the noise of his arrival by pickup truck remained unnoticed by Lucian.

"Eh," Lucian said in return, basically repeating what anyone said who came to purchase, as if speaking their native tongue. Mr. Creps seldom spoke, at least not in whole sentences, but made simple gestures that Lucian, from their first meeting, seemed to understand, to his own surprise.

Their entire verbal exchange consisted of:

Mr. Creps: "Away?"

Lucian: "Yes."

Mr. Creps: "Here." This last word was accompanied by the check in his outstretched hand, before he departed.

Before his odyssey, they had been coming in this manner, the buyers of worms, at odd times, for varying amounts. New customers, coming at the suggestion of their acquaintances, sometimes arrived for the first time with the single question at the front screen, "Worms?"

Lucian's, "Uh-huh," and slight directional nod brought them to the back where they indicated some quantity followed by the question, "Made out to?" and since the bank deposited checks to his account simply saying "Worm Farm," that is how it had remained.

Others were talkative. "Look at the little fellers," one said, every time he came. Another was starting a new garden, hauling in rich creek bottom dirt, wanted worms to populate it, and described to Lucian's intense listening, every step of developing and planting it. He even invited Lucian to visit the worms in their new home.

But the stack of checks on the table now, accumulated in his absence, was another thing. It had not occurred to him to make any arrangement for his not being here. Had people helped themselves? A self service worm farm? But would they also clean the interior? Even the stacks of books bore no dust. Some now had new bookmarks in them.

The worms had been productive. And enough people had wanted them, and had left checks, to keep up the payments on the farm. *Payments on the farm.* He had made no arrangement for that either, during his absence. Nonpayment, overdue, repossession, did he still own the place?

He tried to rouse the car to life, but though it chugged desperately, it would not move today. Lucian ran to the shed for the old bicycle that Gitano had left reclining there, used the rusty tire pump beside it, and peddled toward town.

. . .

Clutching his checks to deposit, he asked how much behind were the payments, for he had no idea in human terms how long he had been gone. Many sun risings and sunsets, many roads, many libraries, but no clock time, no calendar time.

Gertrude, the teller, peered at the sweating youth before her, thinking how he looked like he had been sleeping on the ground, beads of water making lines down through the dust. She checked the record and said with the same voice that would have announced that *grass is green,* "The account is up to date."

"*Really?*" Lucian said.

"Really." Gertrude said.

"*Up to date?*"

"Up to date."

The disheveled customer turned and walked slowly out. Gertrude stared after him. A man looked up from his desk through the glass of his office in back and said, "Who was that?"

"It was the *worm person,*" Gertrude said, wiping off the counter.

The face. He did not see the face. For a long time Lucian stirred his scrambled eggs in an iron skillet over the wood-burning stove, staring up and off into the distance through the screen door. He was looking through the top half. The face was in the bottom half of the door, and he did not see it for a long time.

He became aware of it gradually. Imperceptibly. A difference, a presence, a *face*. The egg scrambler's amber eyes slowly focused downward and locked into the big brown eyes of the face.

They looked at each other in unmoving silence until the eggs smoked. Lucian opened a circular lid on the ancient wood-stove top and dumped the scorched yellow jumble hissing into the fire. He replaced the lid, put the pan on the sink, and turned to look at the face again. It had gone.

It returned the next day at the same time. It watched him fix breakfast. He watched it watching him.

The face was attached to a child. With a body. With legs. And arms and hands. Hands that made fists on the screen support. Lucian made a movement toward the door, and the legs carried the body off across the sandy soil.

Lucian stood watching as a lizard climbed in sudden spurts across the screen. In his mind he retained the after-image of the child. The features readjusted to transform into his own appearance at that age. At the same time, his own present features readjusted to become those of his father, as he had appeared years before. The *remembered self* looked at the *remembered father* in long silence.

A part of his awareness became like a movie director, guiding a scene between the two imagined people. He probed his own boy's mind for what he wanted the man, who was his father, to do. Not what his father *had* done; that would have been *memory*. But what the child *had wanted him to do*. The imaginary man began to share. Shared breakfast. Shared a book. Shared walking together and talking. Shared silence.

The imaginary father listened. Listened with complete concentration while the imaginary child struggled to tell a tale from the internal ocean of his imagination that only dripped out externally as tiny droplets of words. And the imagined man listened and understood.

The man was saying to the child in a series of scenes, *Tell me.... Go with me to.... Would you like to.... How nice you look... Come and sit with me.... What do you feel about....*

The real Lucian reached out, kneeling toward a vacant doorway, while tears as silent as the desert moved down his face.

· · ·

About the desert, Lucian had a sensation of entering it. Not of walking on its surface merely, but *entering*. Not as one enters a room, but of being enveloped, layered, buffered

In the city the stones were all someone else's. Now-dead people had put them there, stacked them. It was hard to breathe in the city.

Here: the scent, the rocks and arroyos, the ridges, the spikes and spires of prickly growth, the lizards, gullies, cliffs, and distance.

Lucian and the desert wind began to breathe in unison.

He walked in the long shadows cast by the morning sun. A long shadow came from behind, made by the child. They looked at each other, no screen between them now.

The child stopped a short way back and waited. When Lucian moved, the child moved. Always a few paces behind. When Lucian sat on a large rock, the boy sat a short distance away.

· · ·

The boy materialized from the desert on intermittent days and remained for varied lengths of time. When he appeared outside the door in the early morning, whatever Lucian cooked found its way onto two plates. They sat outside, then, the two of them, on nondescript chairs, under a cottonwood tree, surrounded by worm canisters, eating.

As Lucian made his rounds, tending his earth-housed tenants, the boy followed and did what Lucian did. Imitated. Watched, tried, adjusted his efforts. They began to move in unison.

When worm purchasers came, the boy shadowed Lucian. When one customer asked, "Who's your little helper?" Lucian looked at the boy, shrugged his shoulders, the boy imitating the movement, both of them looking back at the customer blankly, but smiled at each other.

Lucian read, selecting by impulse from the stacks of books. He sprawled wherever his lean form happened to be, adjusting to the curvatures of whatever chanced to be beneath him, as a cat seems to bonelessly assume the contours of whatever it lies on. The boy would follow, using Lucian's leg as a pillow, or curling up into some available curvature at his side.

Lucian was rereading the volume, *The Heartbeat of Humanity: Rhythmic Poetry from the Dawn of History to This Moment*. A singular feature of the book involved the several blank pages at the end, where the readers were invited to make truth of the title by inscribing a verse, *a heartbeat*, of their own.

The poetry translations from various languages had been rendered into rhythmic patterns by the editor-translator. Lucian liked to read the volume in sequence in its chronological order from ancient times. He felt the heartbeat of humanity pounding from the past.

He turned to a poem of Crete, about somersaulting over bull horns and backs. Though some scholars doubted its authenticity, originating as it did in a language still untranslated, this rendering from a later Greek form fascinated Lucian. On one page was printed the Greek, on the opposite the translation. He started reading the first silently, but the beating rhythm demanded to be heard. First a murmur in his throat, then a whisper, then a voice that made the printed symbols live again.

As his voicing of the verse in Greek concluded, he felt a hand on his arm. The boy was round-eyed, and his hand patted Lucian's arm in the rhythm the poem had started. The boy's lips were moving. Lucian read the first line again in Greek. The boy imitated him. Each line was thus repeated. Then the same in English. And then the next poem and the next.

Their bodies roused to the rhythms as they began to march around the room reading verses. When the sounds of translations from Saharan tribes rose, they emerged into the yard marching to its beat.

They read other books aloud. Sitting outside under the cottonwoods, as they read a selection about a tree, the child

40

slapped the trunk with the palm of his hand every time the word was repeated. Lucian took a stick and wrote on the dirt, *T-r-e-e*. The boy, with a stick, imitated the letters.

A game ensued, as the child pointed to objects and to Lucian's stick. Lucian wrote the name of each thing. The imitation followed. The boy raced from one word to the other, repeating them.

He plucked a lazy worm that was half exposed on the top of its container's loam and put it on the ground. He pointed to it and to Lucian's stick. Lucian inscribed beside the living tube that was starting to explore its new environment, *w-o-r-m*. The boy repeated the letters. The boy made a both-hands gesture from some inner delight, and said, "Herman." He circled the worm, pointing and repeating the name. Lucian wrote *H-e-r-m-a-n t-h-e* next to the word *worm*.

The boy ran to one of the sheds that was fringed by various forms of debris and ran back with an old jar. He pointed to it, then to Herman. Lucian scooped dirt into the jar and placed Herman in it. The boy had a pet worm.

. . .

Lucian used maps constantly as they read. He opened atlases to wherever in the world the writer had lived and to the setting of the story, or locales referred to. Soon, when they read, the boy would automatically bring an atlas and open it.

Increasingly, as place-names were repeated that he had heard before, the child selected the atlas and turned to the page and pointed to the spot. As Lucian read aloud inside, the boy made writing motions, pointing to the map.

Lucian went outside with him and the atlas. With a stick, they began to draw contours on the ground, the outlines of countries and continents. Lucian inscribed the place names and the child imitated them.

At one point, when they read a poem about a particular mountain, and had located it on a map, and had sketched the country's outline, the boy cupped up a handful of earth, plotted it down in the middle of the sketch, and pointed. Lucian wrote *m-o-u-n-t-a-i-n*.

The boy laughed and scooped up a second handful of earth

and placed it next to the first. *T-w-o m-o-u-n-t-a-i-n-s*, wrote Lucian. The boy gouged a line in the earth between the mountains with his stick. He ran inside and returned with a cup of water. He poured it into his little trench. *R-i-v-e-r* wrote Lucian.

By evening, a relief map of substantial size adorned the center of the yard. In its middle stood a jar full of dirt housing a worm named Herman.

12

"Longhorn. My name is Earnest Longhorn. I live out there." He motioned in the general direction of the desert beyond the isolated gas station.

"Not so much the saying that you live there, as *why* you live there," the partially-toothed man behind the counter smiled. "Why any of us do, in this dry, godforsaken..." His voice trailed off as he counted out the change.

Earnest Longhorn had come home. Again. Was always coming home. From somewhere. People saw him now and then. He must have been *somewhere* not to have been *here*.

His old dust-covered car moved off from the station, its lights projecting illuminated cones into the night. His hands moved the wheel more by memory than by sight. There was no pavement and even the ruts seemed to lack conviction of their own existence. For him they existed and led to his cabin, his haven. One of his havens.

Inside, he lay on what he used for a bed and listened to the sounds through the screened windows. Listened to things that sometimes leaped from the edge of the hillside and toe-clawed across the tin roof.

He saw the outlines of the records and books on his shelves. He listened to music. Eclectic listening. Into the desert air around his cabin sounded old Caruso recordings, Beethoven and Stravinsky, *Carmen*, the musical revue *New Faces*, Dave Brubeck, Johnny Mathis, Sting. The Sting album, *Synchronicity*, rested next to a book by Carl Jung, which had a bookmark inscribed with the words *synchronicity, always look for synchronicity,* inserted at a particular point.

And the other books. He knew their names, knew their stories, meditated on them. *They all have plots,* he said. Said or thought, he was never sure which. He never knew if he spoke aloud, or thought it, or just sensed whole clumps of ideas at once.

All have plots, he said, or thought. *But I can never be up there, never on the shelf, never in a plot. The fiction of fiction is that it reflects life. Fiction has a plot; life does not. Plot is a pattern imposed on a series of events. Rising action, climax, denouement, insight gained. Eat tacos, cough dust, watch a lizard, no plot. He who tries to live a plot destroys himself. It cannot be done. It is a fiction. Aptly named. I am safe from ever living again...*

Somewhere the sleep came as it always did. The part of the brain that thought gave over to the part that dreamed. Dreams without plots.

He had been, this man, around for as long as most people could remember, always going somewhere, always coming home. He turned up at Gringo's bar often enough for everyone to recognize him there. Always ordered something that whoever he sat with liked. Always ended up not touching it himself, but pushing if over in front of the other person.

His brothers, or were they his brothers, people did not quite remember, or particularly care, had died, both in the war, killed, by the Japanese in the Pacific, their partners had said. They had some kind of partners to work with them in the war, to look after each other. The partners had come to tell the family. Told them how bravely they had died serving their country, *making the world safe for democracy.* Or maybe that wasn't the story. It was too long ago.

He was part of a tribe, or something, or maybe nothing. He talked differently than others. Not so much how he sounded, though that too, but in what he said, or the way he said it. Others said *I did this,* and the next, *yeah, but I did that,* and the third, *but I did even more and better.* They told whatever story the first one reminded them of, and tried to top the one before.

But he asked questions instead. *What about this? How do you feel about that? Will you tell us about the time when...?* Things were different when he was there; people talked about different things and in a different way. Then he would head off, for a little while, for a long while, and then come back. Did odd jobs. Enjoyed meals if people invited him in. Walked a lot. They might see him almost anywhere, walking in the hills, walking in the arroyos, walking toward the mesas. Sometimes riding the old horse he kept.

He often walked at night, knew all the places, could see them in his mind from walking them in the day, knew where his feet had to go. Wandered.

. . .

Earnest Longhorn had helped Gitano pack up to go. He had disposed of the few things Gitano did not want to take or leave. But for a long time, Gitano had found no buyers for his worm farm. "Take it," Gitano would say to him, "Buy it, live here." Earnest Longhorn would neither nod *yes* nor *no*, but helped him tend the place.

They would sit long into the night, those two, out under the cottonwoods, listening and looking, memorizing the stars. Longhorn would ask questions of Gitano, questions about the days of his gold prospecting, of what it was like to pan all day, to dig all day, or how it felt to find the nuggets. Or not find them.

When Gitano had that youth contact him, then come, then buy the place, Longhorn had not gone to disturb the new tenant. But at night, his feet moved in their usual ways, and he continually found himself at the threshold of the yard, as he approached from his pathless ways in the desert.

And he would pause, realizing Gitano was no longer there.

And then he heard. He had not meant to listen, but he *heard*. The voice, the youth's voice, sounding from the house, sounding as one who feels he is alone, with distance between himself and any ear. The voice of one who talked little in the day, the time of people, but spoke much at night, the time of stars and moon and wind.

He had not meant to listen, but he heard, and with the hearing, listened. He heard the poetry spilling out into the desert, as the youth ranged about the house composing it. Saw the figure burst from the building into the outside night from time to time, shouting at the wind and sky. Stood in the shadow of a cactus so near he could see the youth's eyes casting looks at the milky way.

He had heard the voice speak not just from within the house, but from within the *person*, from the depths of the person, without masks, without alteration, the pure, unaltered nature of a person processing life. The pure expression outwardly of the inward, unguarded, unaltered. Longhorn felt himself transformed into the stars and moon and wind to whom the youth spoke.

The man had wondered all his life, and grew weary with the waiting and wondering, if one person could really ever hear another. He had once imagined that it could be. That there could be outward expression of what was within. And at last, he had given up ever hearing it, ever being a hearer of another speaking from within.

He thought of an animal he had long heard of in his own youth. *Out in the desert*, the old ones would say, *exists the creature which...*and they described a being so structured as to be a thing of legends. Yet he thought maybe such a thing did exist and in time he would see it and what a wonder it would be. But gradually, the tale grew tired in his memory, and he knew that never having seen such a creature, his hope was wasted on the expectation.

That people speak openly, that they speak themselves truly, this he must have heard of somewhere, too, in some legend, some ancient tale, heard that it once had been done. But the years had shown how people facing each other, making mouth sounds at each other, drew outward shapes with their tongued-sounds that did not reflect what was within. Screened. Filtered.

And then this. This youth telling the winds of himself. Thinking aloud all the things within. Holding back nothing. Describing the people, the places, the reactions, the feelings, the questions, the anguish. His poetry, his solitary conversations, unvoiced by day to any ear, released at night to the darkness.

Longhorn could not listen as *himself*, but he could not leave, and so became the *stars* and *breeze*, receiving at last, when every hope, every possibility had dried up, a pure message from within another human being.

His pilgrimage at night to this *oasis* carried him across the pathless places to this site where he fed, he drank, he energized on a nourishment that he thought extinct, never-existing. Fed and felt an energy never before experienced.

He came to know in this way the youth whom he had never met, better than those whom he had faced and spoken with for times uncounted.

Longhorn knew that when he became the *night wind* listening, he could not tamper with Lucian's flow of feelings by ever letting him know another ear had heard. It was too needful a part of the youth's life, an essential of his fragile personal ecology, to alter it by revealing its discovery. The oasis would remain unaltered.

. . .

Yet another night Longhorn waited again in the darkness after hiking the reaches of the desert, waited in the shadows of the night, and listened to the outpouring of the feelings from Lucian. The youth was searching for something, some thread of continuity, a vision of his childhood, seeking a connection with his present.

Lucian in his introspective searching, spoke aloud that night about how, in the city, as a child, from that attic of his grandfather, he had chanced upon transcriptions of every radio episode of the *Lone Ranger*. The *days of yesteryear*, as it had been referred to in the introduction of each installment, had lived for him in sound, long after radio dramas had ceased. He had listened to *the masked rider of the plains* and his *faithful Indian companion, Tonto*, riding into people's lives at the optimum moment and providing what the needful could not provide for themselves.

Lucian had pictured himself both as the masked man and as Tonto, interchangeably, always in the trusted companionship of the other. He had dwelt on that possible fusion of two personalities and their concern for everyone, until the characters had begun to live their own stories in his mind, after all the transcriptions had been listened to multiple times. He had no longer needed them, as he would lie watching dust motes in the sun shafts, and the stories told themselves. The faithful companions, when each episode had ended, had ridden off to...to *where?* His imagination, visual as it was, had only seen the streets of Boston and other cities. The pair he imagined moved on a landscape that was muted and indistinct in his mind. Until...

Until, later in his childhood, a set of books had arrived on *Indian Life and Culture for Children*, that an aunt had sent for one of his birthdays. He had opened the box. Each book in the set had a cover with children of a particular tribe in the foreground, and *typical elements of their culture* filling the background, which were explained on the inside of the front cover. The separate volumes had such titles as *The Plains* and *The Far West*. He had looked at each cover and explanation and moved on to the next.

Then he had came to *the one* and immediately knew where the two companions lived when they returned to *somewhere* from their wanderings. *The Mesas*, the volume cover read. The foreground focused on two fearless-faced children climbing the sheer cliff wall of the mesa, their hands and feet holding to little holes cut into the rock. They wore *typical elements of their culture*, as usual, as the explanation on the inside front cover pointed out. But in the background, in the vast desert region reaching to the horizon, rose another mesa, that showed what the one, the edge of which appeared in the foreground, looked like, nearly straight-walled, high, flat topped, reaching toward the sparse clouds in a sunset sky.

The child, Lucian, had longed to find it, because on it would be the other half of the pair, and he would not be alone.

Now, behind the worm farm, extended the desert, and somewhere in the desert, beyond the hills he could see, beyond the arroyos he had walked, beyond these must be the mesas, and among them must be the mesa of his imagination. But how would he find it? "Of course it is illogical," he at one point shouted at the stars. "Of course, the Lone Ranger and Tonto don't exist. So why must I search anyway?"

Longhorn heard him voice the question, "Where will I find this place?" as the shadow of Lucian paced in his candle-lit room and emerged from time to time to raise his hands to the stars, and ask, pointing in the four directions, "Is it there, is it there or there or there?"

And Longhorn, who had known imaginations himself long ago, imaginations that had blurred and faded, determined that this one of Lucian's could be given some kind of substance. Longhorn would find a way to guide him to his mesa.

13

Mrs. Burger bought worms. On a trip to secure them, she again saw the child trailing behind Lucian on his rounds. She kept looking at the boy out of the corner of her eyes. Before she departed, she squinted at the boy and pointed to the back of the house and spoke sharply, "Go back there and stay!"

Then she directed her finger at Lucian, "I buy your worms because you've got them, and I need them. But this is disgraceful the way you parade around with that boy. Why isn't he in daycare or kindergarten or something? It's perverse. His parents should do something."

She turned to leave. "And they will after I see them."

Her pickup truck created dust clouds into which it faded. Lucian stood looking after her. It had never consciously occurred to him that the boy had parents. Or a home. The child just materialized out of the desert. Lucian felt puzzled as to why he and the child should not tend the worms together and make maps in the sand, which now included all the continents, and stretched out into the desert, why they should not build the little earthen dinosaurs that stood beyond the continents, why they should not read poetry and prose, and create rhythms together, and write words in the dirt.
. . .

Lucian's always-simmering fear that he would violate the invisible rules around him boiled again, after Mrs. Burger's outburst.

His condition was exacerbated the next day when a large man stomped across the rickety front porch and vibrated the house with his pounding on the door.

Lucian looked up at the face of the over-sized man.

"You Lucian?"

Lucian nodded.

"I'm Dolphus' father. Come with me."

Lucian had never heard the child's name before. Not being able to get his lungs to push out any air through his throat to say anything, Lucian got into the truck. They drove to a house where a woman with tear-reddened eyes watched them enter.

The man motioned Lucian to a couch and then lowered himself into an old frame chair that sagged under his weight.

"His mother needs to talk to you," the man said grimly.

"Dolphus has been spending a lot of time with you," she began. She paused and wiped another tear from her eyes. "I can't begin to tell you how shocked..." She wiped away another tear.

Lucian's face froze as he searched hysterically inside himself for something to say. He opened his mouth, to force out some sound, but all his muscles were ready to spasm. He knew that one word, and he would begin to shake uncontrollably.

She rose, dabbing at her eyes, saying to her husband, "You'll have to do it." The man walked his wife into the other room and returned and stood, looming over Lucian.

"Our son," he began, "has formed an unusual attachment to you. He looks forward to going over to your place to see you. I don't know what you've been doing with him over there, but whatever it is, I can't tell you how grateful his mother and I are for your attention to him."

The man sat back down; the chair lowered again. "He's learning so much, I can't understand how you do it. He says you write in the dirt with a stick, and I suppose you know he can write all those words you write, and read them, and recognize them in books."

He went to see about his wife, returned, and continued. "We've been meaning to get over to see you, but both of us have been so busy with our responsibilities at the space institute, we've hardly had time for him.

"We knew Gitano, and he became like a kind of grandfather to the boy, letting him do the rounds at the farm with him. Gitano told us about how nice you were when you came to take over his place, and he was sure you wouldn't mind Dolphus continuing to make rounds with you. And what you've done is far beyond that. If it hadn't been for the fun he's been having with you, he would have been lost. Uprooted, you know, from all his friends where we were living. I hope he hasn't been bothering you."

Lucian was in no state to answer anything, as the woman returned and said, "We don't want to impose. I can't tell you how shocked I was to just get word that my grandmother has died suddenly, and we have to leave immediately and drive back night and day straight through. It would be just too much for Dolphus. He's too young for one of our funerals. They're so sad and long."

She wiped her eyes again. "We still don't know many people here yet and were trying to find someone at the center to keep him, when he said he wanted to stay with you. We don't want to impose, but would you consider keeping him while we're gone?"

Then, they thought it was touching, the way Lucian shed tears, for Dolphus' great grandmother, they assumed.

. . .

When the parents dropped Dolphus off, he came running with his cloth suitcase, the head of a teddy bear sticking out of an unzipped corner, and a purple blanket trailing behind.

If Dolphus had unconsciously learned letters scratched in the dust, Lucian was curious about the effect of labeling other things. During the several days together, Lucian printed names and taped them to the objects they represented: *wall, ceiling, floor, door, sink*.

Soon the outside had signs hanging on everything: *tree, basket*, then *limb,trunk*, and *root*. Dolphus cut out cardboard arrows and had Lucian write *up* and *down* on them, and placed them appropriately. They flew a paper airplane on which they had inscribed *wind*. Dolphus absorbed all of the words.

14

There was something in the colors of the moonlit desert night. Silvers, grays, blues. Shadowed colors unlike any other. Layers, overlaid. The illusion of sharp shadows, the blend of background and foreground together.

Lucian had many fantasies about the night, the light, and shadows. He pictured himself in this surreal landscape, sharp-shadowed yet vague at the same time. Just *there*, with no past, no future, an eternal moment. He pictured a figure that would talk to him, about everything. About whatever came into his mind. And the figure would have answers, wisdom like the ancient shadows. Lucian would feed on the communication, feel a merging with the silver darkness and the figure and his words.

He had talked to this figure in the imagination, talked to it since his days of the crowded rooms in the noisy clutter of the city.

It had developed, this image, from another picture in that set of volumes, *Indian Life and Culture for Children*. A volume with drawings of adobe ovens and cliff houses, and campfire shadows. About them were an air of mystery, of *something else*, as yet without a name. His imagined figure embodied those mysteries and had evolved into the form of an Indian shaman wearing turquoise and silver wristbands and rings.

Lucian responded to this memory of the campfire-picture by gathering dried branches that had dropped from the trees, took them into the desert beyond the yard, and started a fire.

The night now had the campfire. It had the silver moonlight. Lucian sat upon a rock outcropping and regarded the flames and the orb above. As the smoke rose from the fire, so it seemed to him the figure from the book had arisen like a mist, shaped in his mind.

He began to walk about the flame, speaking to the figure in his mind, who floated and shimmered somewhere before him.

"Why alone? Why must there be *alone?*" he spoke into the night. His eyes directed toward the flames.

In the darkness, Longhorn, as the night wind, heard. Heard and wanted to reply, but could not then. Tomorrow. Tomorrow in the light of day, when he could be himself and not the wind.

· · ·

When the noon sun shone, Lucian walked to the site of the fire of the night before, regarding the ashes. The image of his night reverie still lingered in his mind. He walked back into the yard, head down, looking at the ground and his steps upon it, and echoed from the night time, "Why must there be *alone?*"

Came the reply, "Those who cannot be comfortable alone cannot be comfortable together." For a moment Lucian felt as if the response originated in his mind, from the image of his nighttime reverie, but the words had a reality that reached his outer ear as well as his mind.

His head slowly lifted and turned and followed his memory of his own flickering shadow on the desert floor last night to where the voice originated. The image of his mind seemed to be alive.

Simultaneous panic and calm happened inside of him. The lingering memory-mood of the moon and flame and shadows prevailed. Lucian looked toward the dream materialized. He was looking at Longhorn, seated beneath a cottonwood tree. Saw the turquoise and silver he wore.

"I...I...have never met an...Indian before..." Lucian stammered, reacting to the image in his mind and not to the actual form before him. "To...a...native American...an *aboriginal*...I...you....your ancient wisdom...I had books about...could you teach me of the oneness with the earth...the peace with all life...the wheel...the great medicine wheel...the circle of life...how we fit...all things fit together...the flowing of the seasons...and could you...would you..."

Longhorn heard the halting words, the fragments of what must be *turmoiling* within this youth's mind. He felt a kinship as he looked at Lucian's eyes for the first time in the daylight and saw that which remained as undefinable as the night or day.

The former apparition said, "I'm sure the worms welcomed you on your return. They missed you. But we enjoyed each other."

15

A woman, slim and stately, appeared early in the morning at Lucian's door, tapping lightly. Lucian answered, with a pot of pinto beans in one hand and a spoon in the other.

"I seem to be lost," she said. "I'm trying to find the day care center, but the road ends here."

He said she must have the wrong road.

She asked if he knew where the *Lucian Day Care Center* was. "I am so impressed," she said, "with the way that the child of someone I work with at the space center, the way Dolphus is learning. His mother said that this Lucian person is dong it, and I want to enroll my child, Normita, in his day care center."

Lucian laughed aloud.

. . .

Now there was Normita, in accompaniment of Dolphus, trailing Lucian during his days, prodding into the desert surface looking for mysteries.

Normita the dainty, like a woodland sprite, who arrived each morning and danced her way through the day from one delight to the next.

The house and outside were heavy with signs naming everything. Little adobe dinosaurs plodded off into the desert. An arrow at the edge of the yard pointed into the distance, saying *roadrunner*.

He felt guilty for receiving money each Friday, when the children delivered the checks that the parents insisted on giving him. He deposited them into a new savings account. He served his own needs only from the bank account that Gertrude the teller referred to, on his visits to her counter at the bank, as *your worm money*.

. . .

As the Ides of July approached, Lucian, in the mongrel car of old Gitano, headed toward the east. The children both had gone with their parents for vacations.

His excitement as he drove expanded mile by mile. What if at the end of these roads that led to Chicago, to Buckingham fountain, what if no one came, holding a book? His heart pounded. What if someone *did* come? What would he say to them? What could he say, what could happen? His bowels were loose and his stomach churned.

Why was it, when he determined to do something, like the messages in books, it had seemed so clear, so obvious a thing to do, so promising a path to something else. Why was it that whatever he planned would warp and twist with passing time and seem a gnarled mockery of itself. Leaving him unsure and panicked.

No side roads on this drive. No stops but gasoline and toilets, and occasionally food, which he ate while he drove.

There it was, the fountain, Buckingham Fountain. The sea horses, the reeds of metal, the sweeping round of stone. Beyond, the grassy reach of Grant park. Further beyond, the tall rectangles of buildings that lined Michigan Avenue.

He arrived with the dawn, sat on a bench, watching the sun emerge from Lake Michigan, appearing through the crack that separated the farthest edge of water from the cloud banks near above. Then the sun continued its slow rise behind the clouds.

Pigeons flew and landed, surrounding early morning walkers, sitters, eaters, waiting for the crumbs. Lucian sat and paced and circled the metal railings over and over. He counted the hoops of the fence, counted each kind of unit in the fountain, counted the benches. But at the same time, he kept looking, always looking. Had someone come early, come walking, holding a book? How would they hold it, up in front like a sign, the title clear to viewers? Subtly, downward by the side?

How would they be looking for him, for his book? *Looking for his book.* That he had forgotten to bring. Yet would it matter? He would notice them, could approach them and make himself known. But what if they came without theirs, to scrutinize him first, walk around him, and then approach him? What if neither of them had their book, their badge of why they came, and passed each other, never knowing?

He bolted across the grass and streets, running down the avenue, running by the Art Institute, looking for a bookstore.

He ran down Adams Street, looking at the cross streets, turned on Wabash Avenue, saw a book store and rushed in. Gasping for breath, he blurted out the five titles. The person at the counter paused and looked at him, awaiting further instructions.

Getting none, she said, "Just a moment," and disappeared among shelves. She returned with all of the titles. Lucian grabbed one, tossed a bill for more than its cost on the counter. Not waiting for his change, he ran out the door, leaving the other volumes behind with the clerk, who made a face at his retreating figure.

When the noon hour came, he held his book before him, the title clear. He walked like a sentry on rounds, looking every person up and down for some sign of recognition. There were families, couples, loners, children, aged, a babble of languages, cameras aimed at the fountain.

"Here," a voice behind him said. "Here, you with the book. You're the one."

He spun around and faced an overdecorated puffy face. The overstuffed hands held out a camera. "Take us there, will you, by the fountain." She thrust the camera toward him and led her brood to stand before the waters, the smallest one pulling up between the fence loops.

Lucian snapped the picture, then another, returned the camera, and they ambled on.
                    . . .

The sun had set. The dusk. The darkness. The last pairs and groups of people leaving.

At last Lucian was alone, all alone, all night. Sitting on the benches, circumambulating the fountain. Thinking occasionally that he might be robbed, attacked, or whatever the warnings of being out alone at night were supposed to save you from in the urban landscape. He weighed which might be worse, those things or the depths of aloneness.

With the coming of the dawn, he walked away. Passing a man asleep on a bench, Lucian silently left the book beside him and moved on through the park.

16

In Lucian's absence to Chicago, Longhorn tended the worms and the customers. He usually wandered off at sunset toward somewhere, sometimes to his cabin.

At night, his habit often led him back, through the darkness, to where he used to talk to Gitano and, more recently, where he had become a shadow listening to the youth's nighttime unfiltered venting of his life, and where he now came in daylight, as himself.

Gitano's old car, that Lucian had driven to Chicago, had not returned. Longhorn wished the house not to be deserted, so that he might hear Lucian's *telling of life* tonight.

Longhorn thought of his *oasis* that way now, as Lucian's *telling of life.* Life happening within him. Guileless *telling. Telling* as the old ones did around the fires. Except their *tellings* had become ritualized. Those were the *tellings* of a *people*, not a *person.* Lucian's were the *tellings* of a person, happening in the present.

He wished, somehow, he could do the same. Could do a *telling.* Just once. He wanted to explain who he was to Lucian, as best he could, tell the tale that no one else knew. The fragments here and there that people might have heard were no more his *telling* than a leaf here and there is the forest. And no one knew the *inside* part at all.

With this thinking, he was pacing in the yard behind the house, and out just beyond its edge. His thinking became a whisper and then a voice. He circled around one of the chairs under the cottonwood, seeming to address it.

"If you were seated here, Lucian, there is a tale I would tell you. But if you *were* here, I could not say it. No one has heard it. But I would tell it once. Once and be done with it. Once to someone. To you. No, to the spirit of you, represented by an empty chair."

He adjusted the chair's location, as if he were positioning Lucian in the center of the yard, near the house, near the back door, where the screen separated the outside from the inside. The door, always open behind the screen, was like a black entrance of a cave.

"You wanted an *Indian*," he laughed softly, gesturing toward the chair, "you wanted a *Native American*," he gently laughed again, "an *aboriginal* who could guide you to the medicine ways of knowing, to the knowledge that you dream of."

He paused in his pacing and faced the chair and the house behind it. "You thought me to be that one. But Lucian, so much is not as it seems.

"Earnest Longhorn is gone, disappeared, probably dead. I am not Earnest Longhorn. In all the categories of people that abound, there are none for me, so I play the ghost of Earnest Longhorn."

He was walking in a long oval now, gesturing from time to time toward the empty chair, visible in the half-moon light that dissolved all colors into varied shades of gray. His circuit took him toward the seat and then orbited out toward the desert, and back, like a comet moving toward and away from the planet.

"I feel like an archaeologist opening an antique tomb, looking at the fragments of death and trying to do my *telling of life*. I came here as a child from a place I don't remember, with my parents. Devout, they were, in their particular faith. Better, they were, than all others because they had discovered the *truth*. Came as teachers to the reservation to guide the misguided. In the guise of education, they told of the one right way and felt superior to the listeners.

"I grew up with the children that they taught, who became my extended family, until I spoke their language as if born to it. But within our house, none of them were welcome. They only made good stories for the trips back east to the congregations of my parents' faith. There my parents told of waifs, waiting for the light. The collection plates rattled and rustled with money. The slides were shown of dusty children, caught in the plight of being themselves.

"My parents prospered on this charade. Financially. They assumed I shared their values. I learned to hate their perspective."

He circled silently for a while. "And then," he gestured toward the chair, "then came the war. All equal, right, in the service to their country? When I was barely old enough to draft, my father secured my deferment on religious grounds. My faith had set me free.

"And then, oh Lucian, then, do you know of the code-talkers? The Navajos the government called to service, to speak their native tongue into radios in islands of the Pacific, a living code that the adversaries never broke. Other codes were broken, during the battles, but not theirs. A living language. One Navajo here, one there, translating words into their ancient speech, broadcasting it for the generals.

"But the Japanese were trying, working to break the code. The Americans needed a backup code ready. A reserve code. So unknown to almost anyone, the authorities came again to another reservation. To the one on which I lived. Chose others, chose my friends. Another tribe, another language, another code with which to trick the enemy."

He paused with his palms to his face for a moment and paced on. "You see," he pointed a finger at the chair, "the Longhorn brothers were my friends. All of draft age, all were called to go. To talk their code. Punishment if they did not. Three brothers. Two were there to depart on time. The third, the youngest, my age, was afraid. He had trembled that night before. Shivered in our arms as we tried, his brothers and I, to comfort him. Just before dawn, he ran off, puking and crying into the gullies, never seen again.

"The military came to pick up the brothers. Violation if not ready. Punishment if not willing to serve. To take them to the camp. The officers came, saw the three of us there, looked us all in the face, looked me in the face, and told us, told me, the lieutenant said to *get your asses in the jeep*. But the Captain, he calmed the Lieutenant, whispered something to him, and then told us in that kind of condescending voice, that they were honored to have our services

"They wanted to see *Indian*. They wanted to see three Indians. They saw three Indians, they saw me as the third brother. As I moved toward the jeep, the wide-eyed brothers grabbed my arms on either side to hold me back. *You can't...*, they started to say. But I shook myself free, put my arms around their shoulders, and while the family, all the generations of it, stood with faces unmoving, but eyes alive, I put my arms around the two, and said, *Oh, my brothers, come, let us go together and serve this, our country*. I didn't want Earnest branded a coward and deserter. I didn't want the family to feel shame.

"In that instant, I became Earnest Longhorn, and no one ever questioned it. It was like a final divorcing from my parents and their faith and all the vileness. I became an *aboriginal* as you would say, Lucian. An *aboriginal*. To everyone, except to the *aboriginals*. From that day to this, I have never spoken my birth name since, and my parents never again spoke to me."

He dragged some fallen limbs together and made a small fire. "This *telling* calls for flame. This once-only telling must be done right, for when it is finished, it will blow into the wind like the ashes and be no more, no more heard, except within the echoes of the winds within the nighttime shadows." The flames flickered to life.

"Now where could this tale go? Onward to training. Each of us, and some others from the tribe, were all together for orientation. Actually they called it that, *orientation* for us, instead of training. Each of us had someone assigned to us. And that person was our *buddy*. That's what they called them. We had this *buddy system*. They were to help us, and assist us, and protect us, so we could serve our country with our talking of the ancient language.

"We speakers of the language, we worked out different phrases, different words to mean the things of war. After all, their—our—language did not include terms for *tanks*, *bombers*, and *aircraft carriers*. So we made the tanks into *turtles*, the bombers were *vultures*, and the carriers were *possums* carrying their young on their back. We practiced all this, writing down nothing, *nothing* that could slip out into the wrong hands.

"We practiced how, when we got into the battles, we would talk into the transmitters and say in the ancient language, the enemy has so many *turtles*, but one is *legs up*, and a *possum* with *fifteen young* swims in the water, and a flock of forty friendly *vultures* await their orders."

He made a circling motion with his arms. "We were dining on the best foods, pampered, treated royally. Our *buddies* always with us. We sat and talked a lot, and they treated us as equals. Every once in a while when one of our buddies asked what they called *an Indian thing*, my recently acquired brothers would look at me with sidelong glances."

Here, he stood at the point of his orbit farthest from the chair, beyond the fire, with the flames flickering on his front side, and the half moon etching his head and shoulders in white. He stopped and pointed to the chair.

"Now we were in battle. Each of us separated on different ships and islands, talking to each other through radio static about the *turtles* and the *vultures*. How our buddies laughed their narrow-eyed military laughs after we had spoken, saying things about how *the enemy would never decode this*. My buddy would clap me mightily on the back and say he had to take good care of his *secret weapon*.

"Even in the midst of war, I began to feel the hope for what could happen after the war. Maybe soldiers thrown together from all these backgrounds, on the battlefields, would begin to see each other as men, and not ethnic groups. Here was this person who guarded me with his life, protected me, practically served me.

"In the waiting times, between the transmissions, we talked a lot, about back home, him more than me, for I was creating a *back home* that fitted Earnest Longhorn, piecing together what I knew of him and embellishing where I wanted, and gradually created a *persona* that became my new self. I started to feel patriotic, part of something, a great cause, appreciated, united, part of the new vision that could come to America after the war."

His orbit continued faster now, his words more like a heartbeat in their rhythm. "And then it happened. Unexpectedly, a movement from the other side of the island, the Japanese were on us before we knew. My buddy grabbed his gun and was trying to aim, it seemed, at someone just behind me. The Japanese rushed into the radio hut, knocked the gun from his hand, and even with them there, my buddy tried to throw them off and get across the room to me, to protect me, it seemed, thinking of my life before his own. I remember even in the turmoil of those moments, the sweet wave of feeling that even if I died here, I had known oneness with someone else for a common cause.

"They knocked us around, him more than me. He was bleeding and unconscious. They seemed solicitous to me, somehow. Talking wildly as they went, they dragged us to a building that could be secured, and threw us in, pointing to me and jabbering excitedly.

"My turn now to help my buddy. I pounded on the door and asked for water, and they actually brought some, bowing slightly as I took the canteen. I sat there on the floor, cradling his head in my lap, and pouring water down his throat. He roused and looked at me. Finally I got him to a sitting position against the wall. And I even thanked him, told him that whatever happened, I could never express what his efforts for me had meant."

Longhorn now had picked up a flaming branch in either hand and was whirling them in circles as he almost danced his orbit now.

"He sat there in the shadows of that hut, my buddy, my protector, sat there in those shadows not knowing when death might occur. He fumbled around under his torn and bloody clothing. He found the small concealed gun they had not searched for when they had disarmed him of his rifle and side pistol.

"He took that gun and cocked it, lifted it up with both hands, aiming it at me, mumbling, *You understand you've got to die. I'm not protecting you. I'm here to protect the code. To be sure they don't torture you and get the code. It's not personal. It's what I've got to do.* And he shot me once, aimed quickly at another part of my body and shot me again, aimed a third place and fired again.

"The guards rushed in when they heard the shots and beat him senseless with their rifle butts. In my haze of semi-consciousness, I saw in etched detail that he never aimed his gun at them, even when they rushed him with their rifles lifted up to hit him. He fired off a fourth shot that entered by body. Faithful to his mission. Faithful to his cause."

He flung the fiery branches into the air. They arched and spattered sparks on the ground. He danced on.

"I died at that moment, Lucian. Became a dead man inside. Any will to live was gone. I sank into blessed unconsciousness, not wanting to see or to be with another human being again. Cursing the human race.

"Oh, how they tended me, extracted the bullets, nursing me, trying to keep me alive. My new benefactors. They saw no human there, but a means of breaking the code. They even spared my murderer, not knowing how he related to the code.

"They even gave me the four bullets they extracted. Placed them in my hand, saying in their broken English and pointing at him, that these were the bullets that he shot me with. And they laughed. They placed them in my palm and cupped my hand around them."

With this, Longhorn reached into his pocket and took out the very pellets and held them in his fist toward the chair. He came close to it and opened the hand with the four spent bullets lying there. "There, Lucian, do you see. I carry them with me still. I live with them. I sleep with them. Because I died from them. And they remind me I am a walking dead man who can trust no living person."

He produced a cry of anguish into the night, the sound of

which seemed for a moment to silence every other sound of every other night creature. He ran the orbit with the sound trailing out behind him, until no air remained in his lungs.

He walked again and said, "They even put us in beds side by side. With his remnant strength, my buddy, his collarbone broken, his arm hanging limp, tied by one hand to his bed, he wrenched himself around, throwing his shoulder completely out of socket, and tried to beat me to death with a chair as I hovered already next to extinction.

"They restrained both his hands then, but listened to us speak, to see if our emotions would reveal what they wanted to know. I had not uttered a sound from the bed.

"Then at that moment, for the first time, I pictured Earnest's brothers and the others, each with his *buddy*, and saw a jumbled, feverish nightmare of all of them being blown and hacked apart by their own comrades, their executioners, their *buddies*. And I screamed. It must have been a sound from hades, for even in my state, I saw the look on the faces of my captors reflecting some horror at the sound.

"Only my body survived. The rest of me had already died. The recapturing of the island, when it occurred, came quickly. Our captors used us as hostages to barter for their own lives.

"I finally was released from the veteran's hospital in Spokane, a dead man walking into the drizzle. None had come to see me, no one awaited me. I was a ghost named Earnest Longhorn now, unconnected to anyone.

"I came to see the Longhorn family one more time, to see what happened to my *brothers*, how they fared. While I was there, those people came, the partners of the other brothers came, their buddies came to see the family. Dressed in their crisp uniforms, shoes so polished that the desert sand slid off of them. They came and told the family how the brothers died, each on a different island, just as the enemy attacked. How they had been shot by the enemy. And how somehow, miraculously, these buddies had escaped.

"Until hearing their words that day, I had thought there was only one degree of death, but I found it was not so. I sank into some deeper substrata of my own death.

"*Wasn't there another brother*, they asked. *How is he?* They didn't even recognize me, the wasted frame of a dead man slouched in the corner. No one answered. No one looked toward me, the cadaver by the wall.

"*You would be proud*, they said to the family, *proud how they gave their lives for their country, for freedom, for democracy.*"

I walked out the back door as they spoke, walked into the desert and knew I could never return to the Longhorn's home to tell them any more, to ever see them again.

"Those two *buddies*, and the one assigned to me, mine has been in politics and now promotes his son's political career. Another is a wealthy televangelist who tells people how positive thinking and the love of God helped him survive the war and invites people to enlist in the army of the Lord. The third remained in the military."

The fire was dying now. His movements had subdued, and he walked slowly around his orbit. "I wander now. I am a piece of desert that has risen up and walked. I am a corpse, unclaimed by any one or group."

He stopped at the fire and stomped the remnant embers with his foot and scattered them about. A feeble smoke arose from them.

"Here then does my *telling* end, the one-time telling of this tale." He turned toward the empty chair, lifting up in the palms of his hands ashes from the ground. He scattered some at the foot of the chair.

And then he flung ashes in the four directions, saying:
"O, winds, now take the ashes of this tale
and mingle them with your elusive wail.
And take them to the corners of the night,
to east, north, west, and south by half-moon light,
this tale, how Earnest Longhorn once became
the walking dead man, lost, without a name."

And so saying, his shadow seemed to evaporate away, out into the desert.

What remained were the other shadows, and the leaves of the rustling cottonwood, and a silence.

There remained the central ashes where the fire had been.

And the residue of ashes scattered toward the four directions.
And the ashes by the chair.
And the empty chair.
And the screen door with the cave-like blackness behind it.

And just behind the screen, back in the darkness, seated cross-legged and motionless on the floor, a lean figure wrapped in a sheet. Wrapped in the sheet he had put around himself on his return in the darkness having walked far from where Gitano's old car had sputtered to a stop on a desert road. Who had walked the road home, sunk in the despondency of nothing happening at Buckingham fountain. Who had walked into the house without turning on a light, discarded his dusty clothes in the darkness, wrapped himself in his sheet and sat on the floor looking through the screen into the night.

His eyes had focused into that nighttime scene when the shadow figure had appeared. The moment when Longhorn first arrived.

When Lucian had heard Longhorn first speak, the youth had heard a voice talking to an emptiness in the way of a person who felt himself to be in a place where no ear listens. Lucian had not moved, not wanting to jar the fragile *telling* in the night.

And when it ended, and the shadow of him who was and was not Earnest Longhorn evaporated into the desert, the sheet-wrapped Lucian knew he had been present to a private moment and must never mention that he had heard. And knew, with an exhilaration unprecedented, that he had heard another human being speaking from his core.

He went, then, to the chair toward which all had been addressed and sat there. He softly said, "I have heard." Remaining there, he watched the half-moon in the sky.

17

Normita and Dolphus drew patterns in the sand. Two figures approached. One, Longhorn, and the other, a horse.

"Would you like to ride?" he asked them.

"Yes," they said in unison. Longhorn put them both into the

saddle, and holding the reins, walked them out and around.

Then he led them, each in turn, alone on horseback, holding the reins. Day by day, he would appear, he and the patient horse, and the children grew in confidence upon its back.

"Lucian?" he asked one day, indicating the horse's empty back.

"You ride!" chorused Dolphus and Normita.

"I'll try," said Lucian and mounted, moving around the yard. He rode, then, every day, along with the children. Longhorn thought, *This is the first step toward your magic mesa.*

All helped groom the animal. Longhorn said one day, "She likes it as well here as at my place. I'll be away for a while, and she needs somewhere to stay."

Together they constructed a makeshift corral adjacent to one of the buildings, and there the horse remained.

The children rode it now, each alone, in turns, and Lucian too.

In the dark hours, Longhorn, as the *night wind*, had seen Lucian when he stood with the horse and when he sat astride its back. Longhorn watched from the shadows, himself unseen. He saw Lucian communicating in his way with it. Saw Lucian mount it without a saddle. Saw him holding to its mane. Saw the movement of the two together.

Lucian felt at one with the horse, without the saddle, without the human-crafted thing between them. The horse walked slowly, responding to his guidance, into the desert and back.

. . .

"We have come to the little space agency outpost and have been deeply concerned with what that area provided for pre-school children. That is, with what was provided was doing to them, if you understand what I mean," said the parent. "I mean, the disinterested caretakers who are supposed to be doing something creative with them, just let them sit in front of television all day. They fight. Jhenaw is becoming unmanageable and doesn't want to go. Please, we understand that you…"

Jhenaw joined Normita and Dolphus. Jhenaw, the creative. Putting things together, taking them apart. Her attention riveted for a whole morning on the process of dismantling and reassembling.

For her, Lucian started a shelf with boxes, each containing something to dissect and repair: a flashlight, a stapler, old toys, a discarded camera. The number of boxes increased. She showed the others what she did, and they learned from her.

. . .

"Where did this come from?" Eriot said. "I never saw one of these at home." He was holding a curved piece of metal joined to plastic, with little projections, a dial, and a Y-shaped joint.

"It came from the junk pile in back of the fence," said Lucian.

"How did it get there?" asked Eriot.

Eriot, the curious, had joined the others. His favorite word was *why*.

"Someone put it there," Lucian said.

"Can we look?" said Eriot. They all went and peered at the junk pile off in a small gully way to the side of the house.

"Who put it here?" said Eriot.

"I don't know," said Lucian.

"What does it do?" Eriot asked.

"I don't know," said Lucian.

"How can we find out?" asked Eriot.

Lucian asked them, "How do you find out anything?"

"We ask you," Normita laughed.

"But what do we do when I don't know?" said Lucian.

"You look in a book," said Dolphus.

Lucian thought for a moment. "I don't know what book to look for this one. What else can we do?"

Eriot said finally, "We ask someone who knows."

Lucian said, "Who knows?"

They were all thoughtful. Normita said, "Let's just ask until we find someone who does."

They piled into Gitano's old car and drove to the crossroads gas station. This was the first time Lucian had taken the children beyond the yard.

In his mind's eye, Lucian could see, in public, his wall of panic beyond which he could seldom pass. But the children rushed ahead, and he passed through the hole they had made.

The garage man looked at the device, turned, twisted, pulled. "I don't know," he said, tossing it back at them, "but if you find out, come and tell me."

They drove to the place some called simply the *Junk Shop* but which bore the whimsical name painted across the full front outside wall: *Things You Didn't Know You Needed Until You Found Them Here And Knew You Could Afford Them.* The folks who ran the store seemed to know the name and function of practically everything. Except this time.

Lucian watched the undefined object turn into a *search*, turn into a *process*.

At the end of the day, they returned to the farm, hung the thing from a rafter, and stuck on it a sign saying *mystery*.

. . .

As the children watched, Longhorn made miniature landscapes on the ground. Three-dimensional models of desert topography expanded under his deft hands. He had started with a small area, explaining to the children that it was a model of the drainage pattern of the land around the worm farm.

"Here is the worm farm," he had placed a tiny square of wood on the ground to represent the house, "and here the ground slopes away, from higher to lower land, and here is the arroyo, where the water drains between these two higher areas..."

Longhorn's purpose was twofold in creating the miniature landscape for the children. They enjoyed it, and then, in other places, created their own landscapes from their imaginations. Lucian brought out maps, and showed them how the three-dimensional constructions could be represented on a page. Soon they were producing maps of their own of their landscapes.

But most important to Longhorn, in this indirect way, he was acquainting Lucian with an area ever more distant. For Longhorn noticed how, in the evenings, after the children left, and on the weekends, Lucian on horseback headed off into the desert, to see the reality represented by that growing and extending model.

Longhorn remembered the mesa of Lucian's fantasy and was gradually guiding him toward its location.

. . .

On a weekend day, Lucian rode the horse as he often did now, out into the vastness of the hills and gullies, guided by his memory of Longhorn's earthen maps. There were ridges beyond ridges. Each time, Lucian rode farther. This time, he dismounted in the shade of an overhanging ledge.

It did not occur to him to restrict the horse's movements in his absence when he wanted to climb to some outcropping. The horse always remained in the vicinity. Lucian felt they were equal partners in their exploits. He rode, guiding by almost unconscious movements of his knees on the horse's body and hands on its mane.

So while he left the horse to explore for itself, Lucian climbed up the stony slopes until he looked out on the rocks below and a dry stream bed far beneath.

He took a flute that dangled from a thong at his belt and began to play. Incan melodies floated across the sage and stones.

Music had burst into his consciousness all at once during a required course at the university. While others had spoken with sarcasm of the drudgery of the Introduction to World Music class, he had discovered Gregorian chants, African drumming, and folk music from the Pyrenees.

He had lingered after two traveling musicians had demonstrated *instruments of the world* in class one day, including bells, chimes, flutes, gourds, antlers with walrus thongs, and antelope ribs with monkey gut to strum. After everyone else had snickered out, he had remained, lost in the stories of the legends sung to the accompaniment of these devices, the plaintive melodies and exotic rhythms still echoing in his ears. The musicians, who were joining the Peace Corps and wanted to donate the instruments to someone who would appreciate the collection and keep it together, felt a kinship with Lucian, and gave him the entire lot. They had patted the *zheng*, saying to it, *Enjoy your new home.*

Then in a remote part of the record section of the university library, Lucian had discovered a seldom used series of folk records produced by some long defunct government project that had sent teams trudging into the remote areas of the world recording native chants and rhythms, and chronicling them continent by country by tribe by ceremony.

Lucian had listened and then tried to find the appropriate instrument from his newly acquired collection, and would blow, beat, and pluck, until it sounded similar like the recorded sound.

He liked the haunting Incan sounds. With his flute, he now sent the melodies from the Andes floating over the desert. Far below, the browsing horse perked up its ears.

The flute he played he had recently made himself, because he had found it impossible to transport his acquired collection of instruments westward. All but the zheng, which he had brought with his books. The others he had donated to the music department at the university. He felt a sadness at their loss and wished he had the collection for the children to use. He felt almost as if the instruments were sentient beings, and wondered how they fared now.

. . .

Orgol had joined the group. Orgol, often within himself, yet with active eyes.

He discovered Lucian's flute when he was exploring in the house one day. He asked Lucian if he could carry it around. He held it carefully. He sat under the cottonwoods looking at the carved instrument.

Then he held it toward Lucian, who took it and began to play. When he finished, he handed it back. Orgol sat, into the afternoon, playing a single note, over and over. His a face became a mask of concentration, lost in his one note.

. . .

"The children need a variety of musical instruments," Lucian told Longhorn as they sat beneath the night moon carving kachinas, and explained the acquiring and loss of those he once had. He mused on the *bawu*, the *dizi*, the *hulusi*, the *khaen*, the *guanzi*, the *ichigenkin*, and other music-making pieces he had once known and played. He pictured them in their show-room cases on display at the university, and again felt sadness at their confinement, when they should be free to be the channel for the creative sounds for which they evolved.

Unable to remove the image from his mind, he wrote a letter to the university department to inquire how his *friends* were.

Before he mailed it the next day, he showed it to Longhorn, who, after reading it, said, "Synchronicity."

"Synchronicity?"

"The impulse that has moved you to send such an inquiry at

this particular moment in time is synchronous with...who knows what, of which we are yet unaware."

18

Lucian had a rapid mind for relating dates, places, events—the panorama of history—making lightning connections that seemed to spark as they interrelated. Social interaction occurred more slowly.

Frequently Lucian did not know what people meant in ordinary conversation. It took mulling over for him to understand. He would listen and ponder and think of responses long after the exchange had ended, sometimes saying them aloud to his empty room.

When Mr. and Mrs. Pettkort came on a Saturday, when the children were not there, and said they had came *to enroll our child in your accelerated program, starting next month*, Lucian wondered why anyone thought he had a *program*, and an *accelerated* program at that, when he just talked with the children and answered their questions, and they all *did things* together. He did not even think of them as *children*, since he made no distinction between what others referred to as *children* and *adults*.

When the Pettkorts complimented him on excluding the *indigent natives* whose presence *would retard our children's innate potential* and *offer sloven associates best avoided at an early age*, he tried to untangle the phrases for a long time after they left.

He did manage to figure out that when they commended him on *developmental innovation* in *disguising the educational setting* with a *crude and rustic exterior* which by *hiding excellence in a pseudo-ruined setting*, the children would feel *unthreatened by feeling there was nothing they could further damage*. He laughed when he realized that they thought the worm farm was a purposeful camouflage.

It took him much longer to penetrate the other part, that they assumed the children that came, whom they had not seen, were of only one ethnic background, and that Native Americans, particularly, were excluded.

He sat eating his pinto beans at night, the darkness inside the house unrelieved except for the light of the moon seeping in from the outdoors.

In his mind, he perceived people as a cluster of concepts and processes, seeing them as a kind of attribual pattern. He could seldom remember the outer descriptions that other people seemed to notice. He had wondered what was wrong with him.

He tried to picture the children, to remember what ethnic backgrounds they actually did came from, but he could not. He knew there was diversity, but he could not place *what* went with *whom*.

The next day, he scrutinized their outward appearances. He remembered a sociological essay he had read on "the hyphenated Americans," and saw before him Euro-American, Afro-American, Asian-American. It occurred to him that if they were together as children, the first-hand experiences would neutralize the kinds of preconceptions that seemed to motivate the Pettkorts.

The children needed, he thought, experience with people of all the available backgrounds. Since Dolphus' face had floated from the desert to his screen door, he had actively sought none of the children. They had come to him.

But now he went forth to find....

"I'm looking for *Indian children*, could you tell me where Indian families live?" he inquired with a blank naivete that left people wondering if he was serious or joking.

He was finally directed several miles beyond the edge of the town to a cluster of adobe buildings. He explained to those living there the background and what he wanted—*children, diverse background, hyphenated Americans, real Native American*—with a candor that sent several of those who listened to him into loud laughter which they made no effort to hide, and which he somehow felt he was expected to join in, as if he and they were laughing at a third party.

"How much?" said one of the men.

"How much what?" asked Lucian, uncomprehendingly.

They laughed again, and one man had his arm around Lucian's shoulder as if they were again spectators enjoying a joke that had nothing to do with either of them.

"Money, for the child to attend," the man said.

"Oh," Lucian said. He still could not comprehend fully that the parents actually paid him; since he asked for nothing from the families. "Whatever," he shrugged, "or nothing."

They all laughed again.

"Are worms free, too?" interjected another man, pointing down at the ground.

"Oh, you know about the worm farm?" Lucian asked surprised, and the group laughed until some shed tears.

"Maybe, maybe, we'll see," a lady who looked like the matriarch of the family finally said. She patted his hand and arm and walked him back to the old car. As he moved off in a cloud of dust, he was not sure what had just happened. She said to the others, "Did you look into this eyes?"

. . .

"I am Reendo," the boy said. He had walked around from the front of the house and announced himself. He waved a hand in that direction and said, "My grandmother brought me."

Then Reendo said directly to Lucian, "My grandmother said to tell you I was an unhyphenated American." He paused and asked, "What does that mean?"

"It means," said Lucian, "that your grandmother has a sense of humor."

. . .

This *gathering of the children*, this coming together of these unique individuals, so unexpectedly, so unpredictably, somehow amused Lucian. He lay on the ground looking up at the night sky, thinking of all the tales he had read that began with the *gathering of the group*.

He relived *Robin Hood* in his mind. The finding of each member of the merry band. Each unique, each different, each entering into the company through some episode.

And he mused on the coming of Dolphus and Normita. Recalled the arrival of Jhenaw. The first words of Eriot and Orgol. And his own blundering look for the person that turned out to be Reendo. Like a merry band gathering.

He searched his books for the stories of those beginnings,

those descriptions of the *first encounters*, the *finding*.

The next day, the children found a sign saying *The Gathering* over a shed door. Lucian took them inside, seated them in a circle, and said, "We came together, each of us, from different events and places. But we are not the first. Others have come together before. And now we'll meet some of them."

With that, he read of Robin Hood, standing alone at first, and then one by one, the gathering of the merry band of Sherwood Forest. Each time a new person entered *the circle* in the story, the children cheered.

Thereafter, that day and those that followed, someone would remember, and say, "Another story," and they would run over to the shed where he had placed the appropriate books, and he would read that part of one more tale, of *the gathering of a group.*

. . .

It was on the first Monday of the month when the Pettkorts arrived to drop off their child. They were surprised and pleased to see, in front of the house, a long banner saying *Welcome to Worm Farm!* The children held the banner in front of them, in such a way that they were hidden behind it.

With the arrival, the banner lowered, revealing the group of diverse children. Reendo left his position at the banner, walked solemnly around to the car, and took the hand of the new child to escort her in.

The Pettkorts pulled their child back into the car, where she protested that she wanted to stay. They drove off.

. . .

"Permit? What permit?" Lucian asked the person at the door.

"To operate this," the precise man with a perpetual sneer said, with a gesturing turn of his head.

"To operate a *worm farm?*" asked Lucian incredulously.

"A *day care center,*" the man retorted. "You will either comply with the regulations, submit the necessary forms, or you will be closed. You have been reported by *concerned citizens.*"

After the sneering man left, Lucian looked at the volume of regulations he had just received. They specified the number of square feet of floor space per child, the number of children per adult supervisor, a lunch program if the children stayed the day, the size and nature of the stove and refrigerator, the mat space for naps, the type and nature of equipment available, the cleaning devices available. There were footnotes, addendums, references to law sources, to penalties....

The children recognized his depression the next day. "What's wrong?" Dolphus asked.

"You told us for every problem is a solution," said Reendo.

"Yes," Eriot added, "and that a group is better than one person for solving things."

So Lucian told them the rules, one by one. And one by one, they compared *what was supposed to be* with *what was*. Then they were all depressed.

"Problem solving," said Eriot. "You know how you've talked about how we all need to solve problems? Since we have a real one to solve, let's try it on these regulations."

First they paraphrased each rule into simple language. "Why didn't they say it that way in the first place?" asked Jhenaw.

After they had lined up a list of requirements on sheets on the ground, Lucian put a page with the word GOALS at the top of them. He wrote HOW THINGS ARE NOW on another sheet beside it, and they wrote out what the present circumstances were. They laughed at the disparity between each one.

Next came a column of NEEDS, to list what remained to be done. Practically everything. Followed by a column of RESOURCES, with PROCEDURE after that.

When those had all been filled in, they decided on *priorities*. They agreed none of the rest could be done until the required *covered/roofed square footage* had been built. They multiplied the number of themselves times the required square feet, marked off on the ground, in addition to the house and assorted out-buildings, the remaining square footage of housing that was needed. "Wow!" said Orgol.

Adobe had to be the material: cheap, accessible, and they could try to do it themselves.

They began to draw plans. They cut out paper pieces in a small scale to represent parts of the hoped-for building. This got all mixed in with other paper pieces they had been working on before, when they were studying the parts of the body.

"A body!" Normita exclaimed in delight. "Let's build it in the shape of a big body and then we can walk inside the body."

"We can build furniture like the organs," said Dolphus.

"We can have a table shaped like a kidney," said Orgol.

"We can make a rug shaped like a heart," smiled Normita.

Everyone started putting the building pieces together with the body pieces, forming a chimerical structure. That was the word Lucian used for it. They wrote *chimerical* in the sand underneath the tree for future investigation.

They piled in the car and went to the library. They checked out a book on *Building with Adobe*.

They built some trial frames and supports, improvising as they went. Everything they did kept collapsing.

Their best intentions kept mutating into exotic experiments with building shapes out of mud that had became a way of expressing anything they were interested in. They produced mounds of earth with a hole in the top for a volcano. They created an outline representing a big skeleton. Remembering the little dinosaurs they had previously created, with their new-found skills, they now tried to construct one that was life-size. It eroded into a great lump in a rare rain and was christened the *Mudasaurus*.

They brought themselves back with a *however*, every once in a while, to the day care regulations that had initiated all of this.

. . .

Lucian paced outside in the moonlight, wrapped in his sheet, pondering the adobe experiments and the deadline for closing of *the day care center*, if the regulations were not met. A sudden idea exploded in his mind. He ran back into the house and read the first sentence of the regulations again: "Any institution *operated for profit* engaged in the care, welfare, or education of children must meet the following...."

The next morning, he met each car as it came with the children, and canceled all payments. No payments, no profits, no day care center: *no regulations*. Just friends coming over to visit.

The parents complied. But it was remarkable how they suddenly began placing regular large orders for worms. And how, as the checks came in for the worms, notes would be appended saying something like, *I'm donating my worms to the worm farm for further research in your breeding program.* Sometimes a smiley face appeared beneath the comment.

19

A family that had heard about his non-existent day care center invited him to a Sunday afternoon meal. They were considering early education options for a child in their family.

On the day appointed, he arrived early so that he could circle the area and gradually approach the house. He tried going in four times but as his anxiety level spiraled upward, he kept retreating. On the fifth attempt, someone else drove up, and he was able to walk in with them.

The grandfather was an official in some denomination. The others even arranged their chairs to turn toward him. But there was a *distance* in his speech, for which Lucian could not think of a word. The grandfather spoke in high abstractions and not about the things around them.

The *moving force* was the grandmother. She marched from one grandchild to another, and with a pinch, a poke, herded them like a sheepdog, while her face perpetually smiling, frozen, like a mask, but her eyes did not smile. She inserted, "Oh, how *interesting*," and "Well, just imagine *that*," into the general conversation, whatever the subject and even if she had no idea what it was.

The parents carried on two simultaneous conversations constantly. One, smiling, directed toward everyone else. The second, in quick fluctuations, with narrowing eyes and lowered voices, to each other.

To the group: "Well, it will be about time to eat soon." To the spouse: "*I told you to get the cloth napkins!*"

"We'll eat soon, if any of you need to wash up first. *You said the ones in the drawer, and if you want some others, get them yourself!*"

At the table, the children became the brunt of the tag-end commands that sprayed out after more melodious public-voice conversation lines. The grandmother spoke *at* them, accompanied by a look and varied degrees of inflection and jaw tension, apparently used perpetually, to give them orders.

The parents' repertoire of asides to the children included *sit up, you're slouching; you're so clumsy; eating before others start is discourteous; wipe you mouth; you're messy as a pig; be quiet when I'm speaking; how many times have I told you…; you don't listen; you're always causing trouble; I don't know what I'm going to do with you.*

Lucian originally had thought that the dinner had something to do with him, but he found himself to be irrelevant to the process. They went through the motions of having a dinner guest on the first Sunday of every month. The process had become so stylized that it seemed unimportant as to the particular individual seated there.

He had the compelling urge to excuse himself and go to the bathroom to look in the mirror, to reassure himself that he still existed.

Their dinner ritual had been practiced so many times, that all knew their parts. As the drama proceeded, their script precluded any real communication. He looked at the children and thought of how free and open they still were, and then thought of them becoming ritualized, being turned into social zombies, performing the inherited routines.

· · ·

That night, Lucian paced the edge of the desert wrapped in his sheet. The dinner affair replayed itself in his mind. In that family, the parents had no doubt been ritualized by their parents, and they by theirs, with the same dull-minded platitudes, the same dismal assessments of each new generation, who internalized the assessments and passed them along.

Later, he sat on the bed by the light of a single candle. Children so treated would grow to dislike themselves, and then see the same negative qualities in others, and then pass on the same perceptions to their children. Unless there was intervention.

How could he help his worm farm children to understand this aspect of the society around them and help make positive changes?

· · ·

Under the cottonwood tree, they sat on the ground in a circle. Lucian said to the children, "Say the names of qualities that you think are bad." They called them out, and he wrote each word on a page and put it on the ground. The area was covered with paper.

Lucian read them aloud one by one. Each time, he asked the children to do something that demonstrated that quality. They ranted, raved, pretended to fight, grimaced, made faces, called names, made gestures.

"While we are doing other things today," he said, "any time you see someone doing anything that demonstrates any of these qualities, even in fun, I want you to call it out loud." The day was punctuated with outcries.

Another sleepless night for Lucian. They were so young. They were already so proficient in naming and seeing the worst of human behavior. They were experts. They could name, explain, and display. So can we all, he thought.

The next day, under the tree, he said to them, "Name the good qualities people have, and I'll write them down."

Silence, hesitancy. Strained effort. Uncertainty. They squeezed out only a few vague words, like good and nice.

As he read these back to them to role-play, there was confusion as they looked at each other for clues as to what to do. In each instance, they ended up doing nothing, sitting still, uncomfortably stiff and lifeless, with only their eyes moving to see what the others were doing.

"Let's try it today. During the day, call out the name of every good behavior you see." They tried, they struggled, but their effort stifled their exuberance, creativity, curiosity, and laughter. Trying to be good, they became nothing. Lucian called it off at noon.

. . .

The next day, he pulled out a big cardboard box he had disassembled and flattened into a large rectangle to draw on. He laid it on the ground.

"On the bottom of the rectangle here I have written the negative qualities you mentioned yesterday. When you get up here to this middle line, all the bad qualities stop. This is the line that is neutral. It is the absence of bad. It is our culture's definition of

78

good. It's a dead end. A dead zone. This is what you were trying to do yesterday. To define *good* in terms of simply not doing the bad things. Of being stagnant. Of being empty and lifeless.

"Beyond that line, it's largely unexplored territory behaviorally. It is familiar in theory, to some degree, but not behaviorally, on a day by day basis. This line between the two halves is like a boundary. People may stop there, thinking they have arrived at goodness, when, really, they've just limited the negative things. So they may not be doing much of *anything* positive.

"We're going to make the *boundary* into a *frontier*, cross it, fill it in, and live up there."

Lucian pointed overhead. A sign saying *kindness* hung on the lowest cottonwood tree branch. They discussed how kindness was expressed in behavior.

Throughout the day, Lucian tried to notice actions that demonstrated *kindness* and commented aloud on them to everyone. By the afternoon, others were seeing *kindness* and naming each other's behaviors that exemplified it.

The following day, the word *trust* hung from the tree. "I *trusted* you to come this morning," Lucian greeted them.

Day by day, the list grew: *patience, perseverance, truthfulness, honesty, helpfulness, concentration, sincerity, justice, humor, dedication, pleasantness, calmness, thoroughness, concern, mercy, courtesy, generosity, sharing, equity, integrity, tranquility, creativity*.... The list grew. And grew. And these spoken words punctuated the days.

. . .

An ant crawled along the ground through Longhorn's evolving creation. Longhorn the artist patted and molded, scraped and shaped the ground of his expanding model of the desert landscape. The tiny square he had originally placed, the landmark representing the worm farm house, lay far away from where he now worked.

He made his three-dimensional map from a memory of wandering. Hills and gullies developed before the eyes of the children. He coated his handiwork with a liquid that caused the clay to harden and remain little effected by the occasional rains.

Lucian had continued to explore the real land after each of Longhorn's additions. As Longhorn worked, he shared the stories of the land repeated by the generations of the people who had inhabited it. The ants and spiders that crawled across the model could have represented the spirits conjured by his stories. The spirits that bound the people to the land, that made it theirs. And now connected with his listeners.

Longhorn moved ever closer to his goal for Lucian. Longhorn knew where the mystic mesa would be in the model, could see it in his mind's eye long before he took the mud and began to fashion it.

"And here," he said, as that moment came, noting Lucian's intent gaze, which absorbed, always absorbed, "and here stands one of the pillars of the world. There are different pillars for different tribes and different peoples. And this," and he placed the first handful of mud, "this," he placed the second, "this is one of the pillars."

He pointed out further, to portions of the model not yet built, pointed in three directions, saying, "The other three of the four pillars lie out there. But this is the first we have now come to. This is the pillar of the spring equinox. The others," and he pointed again to where nothing yet stood, "are of the fall equinox, and the summer and winter solstices. And in the middle of them all, the central pillar."

He added more mud, shaping a mesa that he hoped would match the form in Lucian's fantasy. Nothing like it had previously appeared in all of the far-reaching landscape Longhorn had built, no shape like this one. It took the form that he had heard Lucian describe in his night reveries. A place of mystery and discovery.

"Here the power of the earth and sky meet at the spring equinox. When the sun strikes the distinct formations that lie on the top of this flat mountain on that one day, the connection is made. One can communicate with the spirits at that moment. And all the mysteries of the stars pour down that night upon that place. And then, that which lives within the human merges with the life that is the earth and sky, and they are all one."

When the children followed Longhorn back toward the house, Lucian did not move. His unblinking gaze stared at the new addition to the model. He stood looking as if his dream had taken miniature form upon the ground. And felt it calling him to come.

20

Dolphus handed the note from his parents to Lucian in the morning as soon as he arrived. *Important. Need to see you at seven tonight.*

In the evening, Lucian jogged the distance alone toward Dolphus' home, immersed in his thoughts about building a large walk-in model of the human heart for the children to explore.

Dolphus' father stood in the doorway and gestured with his head to come in. The room was dark. He led silently through the hallway to the back of the house. He opened the back door to the patio.

Lucian emerged to an explosion of sound and color. All the children and their families shouted *Yeah Lucian!* And the banner stretching across the wall proclaimed WORM FARM GRADUATION. Decorations and streamers hung everywhere.

Surprises froze Lucian. He did not assimilate events like this quickly nor well. Some time passed before the impact hit him of what was happening, and then it nearly destroyed him.

There were words of gratitude and kindness. There were refreshments and games, and everyone was caught up enough in them that they did not seem to notice that Lucian was dissolving.

A new consolidated school had been constructed through the instigation of the space center. Starting with the new academic year, all of the children would be bussed into the facility for their entry into the first grade.

The children would be gone. He would not be seeing them again.

The children from the district had been told to report, as the forms explained, for *processing, testing, orientation, assigning to tracks appropriate to their entry level of performance.*

Pain followed pain for Lucian with each new revelation. After the evaluations that were to start the following day, the children would then continue there for the rest of this school year, *to acclimate them to the new environment so they could be socialized to these surroundings.* The thought passed through his mind, *Processed for six weeks to be catalogued, put in rows, and warehoused?*

"Thank you, Lucian," someone was saying, "for preparing the children so well in your pre-school."

Only Reendo and his family were missing. No one seemed to know why.

The whole group gave Lucian a thank you card that everyone had signed. They gave him a gift certificate for The Junk Shop.

Then the children performed the songs and dances Lucian had been teaching them for the spring equinox, tomorrow. He had planned for them to have a day-long celebration. But they sang the songs and danced tonight, because tomorrow, they would be tested, evaluated, processed. And the next day, and the next....

Lucian left at the point when he felt he could without offending anyone and before he totally lost control. That happened somewhere on the desert as he walked toward the worm farm.

· · ·

He could not sleep. He could not eat. His head hurt and his stomach ached, and he was feverish. He roamed the house in his sheet and howled outside into the night. He walked aimlessly into the desert, watching the moonset and the sunrise.

He knelt on the ground underneath the cottonwoods, his body rocking back and forth, feeling almost delirious. He stared straight ahead, unfocused.

When, at some point, his eyes did focus, they were aimed out past the words on cards dangling from the trees, past the yard, past the adobe animal forms, past the model of the Mississippi River Valley, past the attempted building projects, out to where Longhorn had been constructing the ever-growing model of the desert area.

He walked toward the model, the end of the sheet dragging in the dust behind him. This, the time of the vernal equinox. The day when he and the children would have listened to and participated in music of the equinox of tribes around the world.

The equinox. What had Longhorn said? The mesa. *That* mesa. He walked to the the farthest extension of the three-dimensional map and stared down. *That mesa*. A pillar of the world. The mesa of the equinox.

He lay on the ground and peered at it. How it looked like the mesa of his imagination, the mesa of his fantasy, the mesa where the Lone Ranger and Tonto, *his* Lone Ranger and Tonto, lived.

Without changing into clothing other than the sheet in which he was wrapped, he went to the makeshift corral, to the horse, opened the gate, mounted, leaning forward until his head rested on the mane and his arms around its neck. They moved off into the desert.

He had seen the insects scurrying across the landscape of Longhorn's model, thought of them as little horses and riders making their way amid the hills and valleys. Now he felt like an insect, riding through the familiar territory he had explored with each of Longhorn's extensions of his model. Riding toward the undiscovered land.

Riding on into the new areas that he had never seen before, except in miniature, molded by Longhorn's skilled hands. Those same hands that had shaped the mud had shaped the means of finding the spring equinox mesa, and Lucian knew his destination, somewhere before him.

. . .

He saw it. The mesa. As it should be. As it should look. Amid the other landforms, each a work of eroded beauty that spoke silently of eons. Amid them, the mesa. No sign of human existence. No human hand nor feet seemed to have left their signs nor imprints.

Lucian did not pause on approaching the mesa's base, the base of the pillar that seemed to hold up the sky. He did not pause, as the sun continued moving westward. He let the horse roam, while he sought a semblance of a trail, and footholds and handholds in the rocks.

Upward, his sheet blowing in the breeze, he climbed the steep mesa face between the desert floor that now was a memory below, and the summit, indefinably somewhere above. He pictured in his mind the young figure on his own childhood book, climbing up the side of the mesa, suspended between earth and sky. This was the place, this was the moment, he was the child. He felt he had entered some ancient story, that every rocky foothold, every handhold, was part of a story that he knew, discovering it and remembering it simultaneously, as if he had entered a realm of synchronous time and no time.

He felt part of some rite, that this was where he should be at this moment, only him, and the mystic mesa, and the remnant sun. They existed together in a way so right that nothing, not a stone, not a feeling in his muscles, not a breath of sweet desert air, nothing needed to be changed, to be different. Its rightness was complete.

His fingers found the rim, the edge of the top. His feet felt their final foothold. He pulled upward and over, emerging into the rarefied air of his equinox world. The top of the mesa extended before him. He stood amid rock formations on its top like a gallery of prehistoric sculpture.

He sensed two horizons. One, the round rim of the mesa, and the second, the circumference edge of the world. On one side the red circle of the sun glowed, setting, while on the other side, the full moon, itself tinted with the sun's hue, rose. The mesa became their fulcrum and Lucian stood at the pivot of the universe.

In the haze of spreading dusk, over the rim of the mesa, far below, an indistinct figure moved. Walking. Moving toward the mesa.

· · ·

Time could not pass when no time existed. Lucian sat suspended in a condition of night, as motionless as the rocks on which he sat, beholding the ever-rising moon. Beneath it, over the rim of the mesa, appeared a hand. Then another hand. A head, a face, two arms, the chest and legs and feet. A youth of Lucian's age. Feathers placed in his uncut hair over either ear. His body unclad. Painted markings on his face and chest, back and thighs and calves. Around his shoulders, leather thongs that held upon his back a drum and flute, and a small leather pack. Around his neck, two thongs, each attached to a turquoise stone. Around his upper arms and ankles, around his waist, thongs with stones.

84

He stood and faced the red streaks that marked the location of the departed sun, raised up his hands, and chanted words that Lucian, unmoving and apparently unnoticed in the shadows, did not know.

The youth turned toward the rising moon and lifted up his arms again and chanted rhythmic words.

Then drawing a circle in the dust, he disencumbered himself of the drum and pack. From the latter, he took a small leather pouch and from it took powder in his hand. He flung puffs of powder in turn toward each of the four directions, chanting as he did so.

If the other figure yet knew Lucian watched, he gave no sign, but carried on the symbolic movements of the ceremony that he had begun.

Lucian could not say what each next move and sound would be, but at the moment that he saw and heard them, it felt not like the first time, but as if he remembered them, knew them, *was* them. His own muscles twitched in mimicking movements. Low in his throat he duplicated the tones, and his lips formed the sounds.

His being seemed to merge with the dancer until he could not distinguish in his perception between *observer* and *observed*. Is he sitting motionless now and watching the dancer or is he dancing? Does he hear the music or is he chanting? Does he hear the throb of the drum or is he now beating it? How is it now possible to hear the drum and flute together if only one is playing?

Is he the shadow of the other person? Are they each other's shadow's in the moonlight? Is their power coming upward from the earth, through the mesa's surface, flowing through their heels and soles, upward through every muscle of both of their dancing bodies, emerging from Lucian's throat in sounds as raw as wind and as impassioned as the cumulative howl of wolves since prehistoric times?

Is this prehistory, time removed from measurement, the darks and shadows of eons? Had he become an archetype of the night, the moon, the equinox, the movement of the earth, and spheres beyond the earth?

Is this youth somehow Lucian, himself, their synchronous movements beating rhythms in the night? Are their howls and sounds primordial merging with the mysteries within and around them?

The figures dance in unison in shadows of the night,
As pale and moon-etched outlines from the whiteness of its light.
The mesa is a drumhead being pounded by their feet.
The ancient pulsing heart of life now echoes in that beat.
The power of the earth beneath them surges through their frames
And howls into the night wind in the chanting of the names,
The names of all things blending in a deep, primordial urge.
With equinox and galaxies and eons do they merge....

The high cirrus clouds frosted the morning sky and chilled the pale sunlight that illumined the mesa's top and Lucian lying there.

He began to stir to consciousness, to open his eyes. He squinted into the cold light. He lay on his back on the ground. His sheet was folded, beneath his head. He slowly lifted his arms and saw the thongs of stones around his wrists and upper arms and the painted symbols on his skin. The rest of him was similarly adorned with thongs and rocks and designs.

He felt the feathers tied over both ears into his hair. He felt the thong and rock around his neck. Upon his chest, in ocher red, the print of a hand.

He peered to the horizon and nothing stirred.

. . .

When Lucian reached the worm farm, returning from the mesa, Mrs. Murdock stood amid the containers, digging out a bucket of worms. Without looking around at first, she said, "Getting them myself since you weren't here and..." She had glanced over her shoulder casually, then took a second look, as her voice trailed off. He walked by her without a word, the horse standing in the yard where Lucian had dismounted and left it free. It came over and nudged her shoulder.

She watched Lucian disappear into the house, patted the horse on the nose, and continued to get her worms, placing a small rock on her check which she left by the container, and departed.

Inside, Lucian was startled by his own reflection. The paint, the thongs and stones, the feathers, and more he could not define. He looked and wondered who it was he had become.

21

That night, he still had not removed the painted markings from his body. He still wore the thongs and stones.

He paced within the house and in the yard, speaking to himself, forming into words his dream-like memories of the mesa, jotting words on paper in the candle-lighted room, circling out into the yard and desert, shaping them aloud:

"The figures danced in unison in shadows of the night..." the words began. And no one heard the words except the night wind.

And when the night wind heard him say, *"With equinox and galaxies and eons do they merge,"* Longhorn smiled.

. . .

Lucian lay on the morning-lighted ground under the cottonwood tree, the paint and thongs still on his body. He lay looking upward at the dancing leaves of the tree between him and the blue sky. He hoped Longhorn would come. He closed his eyes. He knew how Longhorn somehow came on panther feet, so quiet he would not be heard until he suddenly seemed to appear. Lucian wished him to be there.

He opened his eyes, raised his head, looked over at the chair, and saw Longhorn, regarding him.

"You have been there, then." Longhorn said.

Lucian rested his head back on the ground, lay silent for a time, then said, "The mesa of your map, I found it. But what found me?"

Another silence, and Lucian said, "Who was that, there, and who am I now, a brother to a tribe?"

Longhorn rose and moved on soundless feet to where Lucian lay, knelt, leaned over and placed his hand on the ocher pattern of a hand on Lucian's chest. Longhorn said, "You are a brother now." And walked back to the chair.

"The tribe?" Lucian said at length.

"A tribe that never was." Longhorn replied.

"Hopi, Navajo, Papago, Laguna, Apache...*never was?*"

"None of them. All of them. None of us. All of us. Forbearers of us all." Longhorn said.

"Anasazi?" queried Lucian, raising his head for a moment, looking Longhorn in the eyes.

"Not the ancient ones," said Longhorn. "Nor the Hohokom. Older still. Before they were."

"His tribe, then, the person that I saw. You know of him?"

"I know of him," Longhorn said, "and of his tribe."

After a silence, Lucian said, "Tell me."

"He came from somewhere," Longhorn said, "alone. He came and talked with people of all tribes, though he was of none of them. He learned of dry farming and building in the oldest ways known to the oldest of the people in the tribes. He walked the desert with the old ones who showed him the places water could be found, the roots to eat, the plants to heal."

"And then?"

"He practiced near here, in the desert, staying on the land near by my cabin. Tried the times of day to be out and in what heat to rest. Looked for food, and tried non-irrigated growing. Learned the ways of animals. Constructed from the stones and rocks around. Only using materials that were there at hand.

"He sought out the old ones and learned the ways of the tracker and the shaman. And when he could survive by using just these ways, he walked off into the desert there, walked until he found a place remote from humans, to a place where no one came, way back in the cliffs and valleys like where the ancient nameless ones had lived and left their cliff house ruins."

Longhorn stood. "Tomorrow, with the dawn, we can ride to where he dwells. I can tell you more along the way."

Lucian nodded without words. Longhorn disappeared. Lucian, still unmoving on the ground, slept.

. . .

The horses found their own pace, carrying Longhorn and Lucian toward the canyon country.

Longhorn continued the story. "When he had found the cliff, shaded from the sun, with a stream bed in the valleys below, with desert growth of varied sorts, when the place felt right, he began. He called it his *sacred place*. I walked with him in the finding of it. For he would not use a vehicle nor horse. He was returning to a time before there were horses here.

"And when he found his sacred location, we sat on a ledge in a great indenture in the cliff, and he explained. He said he had found no place to fit wherever he had been. No people who behaved as he had hoped. And so, he would begin again. Go back to time before the cities grew, before the Anasazi, before the nameless ones.

"He cast dust in the four directions, held his hands up toward the sky, removed the garments that he wore, bundled them and handed them to me. *Go now, he said, and leave me here, with nothing but myself amid the earth and wind and sun. Amid the plants and creatures of the land. And I will start again, existing with the earth, as part of the earth.*

"He walked to where a pool of water remained in the drying stream, and picking up the liquid in his hands cupped together, held it high and let it run down his arms and face, and said, *Our blood is of the consistency of the water of the ocean.*

"He picked up handfuls of earth, and let the dust blow in the wind and fall upon his arms and shoulders and face, some sticking to the wetted skin. He said, *Our bodies have within them nothing not found within the soil. We are the sea and earth that has risen up to walk upon itself, the thinking, dreaming part of earth, but always part of earth. I stand here with only the parts of me that are the land and sea, to begin to live as what I am, a moving shape of earth that can make myths.*"

Longhorn remained silent for a time. They paused with the horses beneath the webbed shade of a desert tree. And then moved on.

Lucian said, "And so, he makes his myths?"

"He does," said Longhorn. "I left him there that day, standing alone. He would eat from what was there, plant in crevices and seemingly arid terraces. He began a tribe of one. Constructing structures, rooms, from the rocks, as he was moved to. Mixing colors from the stones to make paintings in the caves.

"He began to create a language unlike any other, developing

it as he moved through day and night. A language spoken by only one, spoken to the wind and stars by him alone. Developing his culture as he went. Devising rituals as the spirits of all things seemed to speak to him."

"And," Lucian mused, "making the land his by observing what existed there, and seeing in the forms the myths that he would voice."

They rode in silence with the sun.

"He found the pillars that hold up the sky," Lucian said.

"He found," Longhorn said, "the pillars of the equinox and solstice, the movement of the sun and moon that marked his time. He sings songs never sung before, in words not heard in any other place, in myths untold by any other tongue, and lives not only on the land but *as* the land. And lets it all evolve as it will. A primal tribe of one. A beginning. A first human discovering himself and all the environment around himself, and how they, that environment and himself, are a single entity."

Lucian, after silence, began to softly chant some words in rhythmic phrases as they rode, words remembered from the mesa. He turned to look at Longhorn looking at him. "I think I have begun to speak his tongue," Lucian said. He put his hand on his shirt over the place where the ocher hand print had been beneath it.

They rode on toward the canyon country.

. . .

The place existed as Longhorn had described. The ragged cliffs, the sometimes flowing waterways, with plants along their borders.

While the horses foraged below, Lucian and Longhorn sat on a ledge of rocks that overlooked the scene, itself overlooked by the canyon walls. Off to the side, hugging the cliff, barely discernable at first from the cliff itself, imbedded on the canyon wall-indentures and made of the same color stones, the youth's new cliff dwellings.

In time, looking around at the space that had been between Lucian and Longhorn as they sat, the third figure had simply appeared, silently, the figure of the mesa night.

He walked with them around his world in the cliffs, to the

plants growing in the crevices of the rocks, to the patches of terraces where plants of wide variety thrived. He described his experiments in growing them.

They walked among those cliff dwellings he had built and continued building, in his own designs, his own way. Down into the pits where food was stored. Into pits where jugs of water rested, vessels made by his hands from clay along the river banks. They saw the place where he experimented with weaving plant fibers.

They sat around the fire in the night, ate of the variety of plants they had harvested as they went. They slept among the dwellings of the cliff, with the breezes and the night sounds all around.

. . .

"The word?" Lucian asked for everything they saw. The other youth spoke in his new tongue the words he had created. With Lucian's facile way with sounds, he repeated them until they were his own.

Though darkness and light marked days and nights, nothing compelled them to count the number of the turnings of the moon and sun. Their silences and their words blended. They dug for roots, and watched the scurrying lizards, the patterns of the flights of birds that glided in the sky.

While they sat about the fire, eating roots dipped in flower-flavored mixes, Lucian, leaning back, supported by one hand on the ground beside him, felt a furry something suddenly resting on his hand.

"Taco," said the youth, looking at the creature.

"His name," said Lucian, "is not of the new tongue?"

"Not of the new tongue," spoke the youth, "but as a result of the way he was found." He nodded toward Longhorn.

"I found it," Longhorn said, "this baby desert fox, on the way here once, abandoned in a piece of log. I picked up the piece of log with it inside peeking out and brought it here. It needed to be cared for."

"He said it looked like *a taco*," laughed the youth, "a *fox* taco. The name remained."

The big eyes of the fox looked up at Lucian, its jaw still resting on his hand. The two big triangles of ears shifting like antenna toward the varied sounds.

"It has its world in the wild, but keeps its place here too, with me, coming when it will."

. . .

When Lucian and Longhorn readied to depart, the youth regarded them and said, with a small gesture to their environment, "The habitat of a tribe of one."

Lucian repeated brief phrases, which he did not yet know the meaning of, in the new tongue, that had imbedded themselves in his mind, from the mesa. He pulled the leather thong and stone from under the shirt where it hung about his neck, and brought it into view.

The youth placed his hand at the spot on Lucian's shirt under which the ocher hand print had been. Taking Lucian's hand, he placed the palm outspread on his own chest in an equivalent position. "Now two," he said.

Then both of them, simultaneously, turned and extended each a hand to Longhorn, both saying together, "Now three."

And the tribe of three stood together.

. . .

As they rode back across the desert, Lucian suddenly said to Longhorn, "His name. What does he call himself?"

"He has no name as yet. He said that names denote relationships to others. In a tribe of one, that one could have no name. The name must evolve as part of the language, must come from interaction, must come in interaction with another and himself."

"Then we shall name him," Lucian said.

As they rode, Lucian pointed to things around them, saying aloud the words newly learned in the canyons.

22

Lucian had slept he did not know how long and awakened in outer darkness, the inner despair of the loss of the children returning. He wandered from the house into the nearby desert at night.

There was a stir, a shadow, and a person suddenly walked beside him. The figure was Reendo's grandmother, who matched his stride in silence.

"I worried about him," Lucian said, "when he did not attend the..." he could not think of a word for the event at Dolphus' house that had disengaged him from the children, "...the meeting. Is he all right?"

"He needs you. Now. Come," she said.

Lucian followed her. Beyond a rise, around a rock formation, a horse stood. She mounted and patted the space behind her. Lucian joined her.

When they entered her adobe house, the only illumination inside came from a few candles. They walked through to a small room, where the windows stood open to the night air.

Small hands grasped Lucian and pulled him downward. A wordless Reendo clung to him for a long time.

"Don't leave me," the boy whispered at last. He held tight longer, then fell asleep, and Lucian laid him down.

His grandmother, who had been standing in the shadows, touched Lucian's shoulder, and they went back through the darkened house.

Outside, she began to walk, Lucian beside her.

"What happened?"

"He feels he is not *whole*. He is a part of you and you of him. He does not understand why the *growing* that began between you cannot continue. Why he must now go to another place. That school. And why you and he are not together. To him it is like a *dying*. Do you understand that?"

They walked in quietness for a time. "Why," she asked, "did you not prepare the children for this change to school?"

He searched for words. "I...It never entered my mind...I didn't know...that they were going." After a silence he added, "I am dying too," and tears filled his eyes.

She stood and faced him in the moonlight.

"Good," grandmother said, "good. You *feel*."

They walked again in silence.

"In Reendo," Grandmother said, "there must be no fences in his mind. At this new school, even now, even in what they call orientation, they are building fences. But you do not build them. I do not want them there, those fences."

After more walking, Grandmother spoke a word in her native language. Then in English, she said, "You know that some ideas cannot be formed in some languages. Cannot be transferred from one language to another. That word is such a one. Perhaps this whole sentence, *life-knowing, remains undividable but some dissect it and only the pieces of its corpse remain, unusable.*"

She laughed softly. "No," she said, "it does not translate well."

When they had traveled on further with only the sounds of their walking in the empty night, Grandmother said, "Die, then, so you can get on with your life."

She stopped moving and stood facing Lucian in the night.

"You have a college degree?" she asked.

"Yes."

"You do not have a certificate to teach elementary school?"

"No."

"Then you must get one."

They stood in the darkness. After a long silence, he spoke, "Say more."

"Get your teaching certificate. Start your own school. Would you do that even if Reendo is your only student? The only student you would have?"

"I am not a teacher," he said.

"You have not heard about Reendo's evaluation results?"

"No."

"They said that his tests were all mistakes, that he must take them all again. I told them, if it was someone else with these results, they would be pleased. I told them that they must now consider him as someone else, and then be pleased with the results. *Who could have taught him this,* they said. I said, *ask him for his words in Sanskrit.* They didn't ask. They didn't even smile."

She then added, "Find out what you must do." Then after a moment, "I will take you back."

"I'll walk," he said, scanning the darkness to orient himself.

The shadow of her arm pointed in a direction, and then she disappeared back into the darkness.

Lucian followed the direction she had indicated.

. . .

Lucian sat on the ground under the cottonwood tree. Much of the space above the earth was bedecked with clouds, flat-bottomed, billowing up into the heights, the contours marked by giant swaths of light and shadow. The sky visible between then shown a vibrant blue. Beneath the farthest clouds, a grayness blurred the space between the flat bottoms and the horizon. Lucian watched the distant rain and hoped it would come here. He tingled when the desert storms approached.

Longhorn appeared in the yard and came and sat cross-legged beside him. They exchanged a greeting learned in the cliff house in the canyon.

Lucian recounted the midnight talk with Grandmother, his phoning to inquire of courses, that they were available in the city at the university. Enrollment for summer was almost past, and the full program extended into the next year, and all at an expense beyond his funds available. Longhorn sat in silence, sharing the distant storm, then left.

The next day, when Longhorn returned, the clouds now filled all the sky, deleting any piece of blue. Lucian sat beneath the tree, watching the distant streaks of lightening and hearing the rolling thunder. The wind arrived in gusts, laden with scents from the secret places in the desert.

Longhorn, seated on the earth beside Lucian, produced three sacks. He emptied one on the ground between then. Chunks of turquoise lay upon the sand, as if the missing pieces from the sky had fallen there.

Longhorn told him where to take the blue stones in the city. "Three addresses are here," he said, handing him a paper, "and the minimum amount you must get for each sack. Tell them nothing of the source, nor anything about yourself. Accept nothing less than the amount listed, though more would also be a fair exchange. But let them set the amount. Accept only cash so they do not need your name for a check. Leave if they refuse."

Then he handed Lucian a ring. "Wear this when you make the sales. It will establish your awareness of quality. The third man will probably ask you to remove it so he can examine it closely. Do not. If he wants to see the central stone and the ones that surround it, through an eyepiece, let him, while you wear it."

"Even with the funds...to leave...the farm...the worms...if I am gone all summer..." Lucian could not put together his thoughts to express the impossibility he felt.

Longhorn patted the ground with the palm of his hand. "The worms have survived thus far. Perhaps they can endure for some months longer. Under my watchful care."

They saw the wall of rain approaching. It moved toward, into, and across the yard and house. They sat there in the falling drops of water, buffeted with wind, merging with the storm.

. . .

The new turquoise seller with his new reflecting sunglasses—who would have identified him as Lucian, the worm farmer?

The first two dealers looked intently at the ring. The third peered through an eyepiece and offered a sum for the ring, itself, that astonished Lucian.

Each of the three made their offers for a sack of turquoise. Lucian's silence, as he worked internally to formulate a response, the dealers took for dissent, and upped the prices several times.

Longhorn, when he learned the amounts procured, said Lucian had become a *barterer extraordinaire*.

"By default," Lucian said.

. . .

Lucian filled the forms and paid the application fees. When the day came for him to go to take the examinations to enter graduate school, he questioned his readiness.

Before he went, he said to Longhorn, who stood among the casks of worms, that all of this would be to no avail. He might not pass the entrance tests. He had no education courses in undergraduate study. Perhaps he could not do the advanced work. Even if he finished some courses, he would not have his advanced degree by summer's end and didn't know how he could be certified without it. But most of all, beyond those barriers, remained the major one. If the worm farm had been questioned as a day care center, there would be no way that it could be approved as a facility for a school. Even with one pupil.

Longhorn looked at him and spoke one word: "Go."

23

Lucian took the entrance examination and awaited the results. Time passed. When the examination results should have come by mail, indicating his admission or rejection for graduate study, the notification did not appear in the worm farm mailbox. A letter came instead, from a Dr. Pandra. Couched in formal, almost hesitant, phrases, the few sentences asked Lucian to appear at her office at the university on a designated day and time.

He drove to the city, found the campus, and walked toward the building in which her office was located. He started to enter, turned aside, walked around the building twice, stood looking at the entry once again. He took out of his pocket a leather thong and stone, pulled it over his head and hung it around his neck. Then he entered.

At the outer office, he half expected to be handed an envelope by the secretary with the outcome of the test. Perhaps they did not think *Worm Farm* an acceptable address to which to send such information.

After Lucian had waited in the outer office for a few minutes, the secretary told him to go in. Dr. Pandra met him at the inner door. She looked closely at him, in a manner beyond the casual.

Lucian, being focused on one thing, thinking of Reendo, asked immediately, "What were the results? Am I admitted?"

"Things are not always that simple," said Dr. Pandra. "No, would that they were, but they are not."

Lucian's eyes, hypnotized as they were by books, had uncontrollably wandered off down the shelves of volumes that lined two sides of the office. Light streamed in the window of the third wall. The fourth displayed framed posters of Delphi, Easter Island, a not-readily decipherable white-and-shadows photo with the small caption reading *The South Pole*, and above them all, attached to the ceiling, from wall to wall, was a telescopic panorama of the milky way.

"The entrance test..." she began and paused.

"I didn't pass it?" he finally filled the silence.

She pointed to certain test items on her desk. "Have you seen these kinds of questions, that is, done those kinds of questions before?" she asked, not saying exactly what she meant.

"Yes, they occur to me all the time." he said.

This was not the response she had expected. "*Occur* to you?" she asked. And then interrupted herself to be sure they weren't talking about different things. "These kinds that measure reasoning and perception with narrative questions like…" here she reached for the copy on her desk and started to read, "…If John left at eight o'clock from Denver to St. Louis on a train going seventy-five miles an hour…" Here she paused again, realizing how blurry the sentence looked to her. By the time she had reached in the drawer for her reading half-classes and had them perched on her nose, Lucian was speaking.

He was looking absently at the corner of the milky way, as if he were reading something written there, saying, "…and had to stop for refueling every sixty-two miles for twenty-seven minutes, and if Donald was traveling by a bus from Miami to St. Louis that left at eight o'clock, and the bus stopped at all towns en route with a population of more than twenty-seven thousand people (see the accompanying map and chart for population figures), and could go two hundred miles without refueling, and Cynthia departed from Winnebago by auto at nine that same evening, for the same destination, in a vehicle that got forty kilometers to the Canadian gallon, and a wind from the northwest blew uniformly across the continent of twenty-five miles an hour, considering the time differentials, stops and speeds…"

Dr. Pandra stood now, involuntarily glancing at the ceiling where Lucian's gaze rested, and interrupted, "Where are you getting that?"

Lucian abruptly came out of his quoting-reverie and said, "I wrote it as a joke, as a take-off on the kinds of questions that appear in…"

"*Wrote it!*" Dr. Pandra voice had an edge of exasperation.

"At the university. In Boston. One of my professors who did consulting work for the testing service that does those things. He saw my parody and didn't realize it was a joke, submitted it with his own, and the testing service used it. That's how I got a part time job writing questions for them."

She was standing now with the test in one hand, the index finger of the other hand pointing at the pages, her face distorted in a strange way, her voice now more to herself than to him, half question, half statement. "*Wrote it…*"

"Questions seven and thirteen, eighteen and twenty-seven, and the last three are all ones that I wrote," he added simply.

She sat back down, not with grace, but as a weight that no longer has support. "How on earth did you…did you…start to…" her voice trailed off.

"I always see questions like that as a whole pattern, and then I just write them down. I did that as a child. I would see things I was reading as a question like that. I remember one that occurred to me in grade school, *If the Lone Ranger rode from the high mesa at a point sixty miles distant from the giant cactus from the west, and Tonto, departing from Adobe Wells a half hour later from the southeast….*"

She interrupted, "You *think* like that?"

"I believe questions like that are not particularly relevant, but I do think of them. It's like a game. It used to occur to me in books where the authors hadn't thought things out very well. I was reading James Fenimore Cooper, and he had people leaping from trees into boats they were attacking as they passed along rivers below. But it was apparent to me that the heights were so great, they would have broken bones, and the movement of the boat so swift that it would have been way down the river by the time the people hit the water."

He was smiling now at the memory and continued with animation, "And in one he describes in detail the curves of the river and then gives the dimensions of the boat, which was so big it could never have negotiated the turns."

Noticing the look on her face, he abruptly asked, "Is something wrong?"

"No," she smiled. "No. We did wonder at your walking out of the test forty-five minutes before the others, the nearly perfect score, except for two answers, and the way you meticulously explained how those two test items needed to be rewritten because they didn't contain sufficient data to be answered properly. We checked that with the testing service, and grudgingly they concurred, and thanked us for the information. But other than that, *no, nothing's wrong.* You have passed. In fact, you are admitted, or will be when we can now complete the paper work."

"Good." he said, and assuming that to be all, walked toward the door.

"Lucian," she said. "One other thing. What kind of address is *Worm Farm?*"

24

The summer. The classes. Lucian was feverish and congested. He sniffed through lectures, clutching a box of tissues wherever he went.

"Excuse me," Lucian said softly, at the door of Dr. Snideker's office. I had a question about today's lecture on the text."

Snideker invited him in.

"Could you tell me," Lucian said, "why our text indicates the attention span of the first grader averages three minutes? I have some pre-school friends who have spans up to three hours."

Snideker looked at him strangely.

. . .

"For godsake go to bed," the voice snapped from the darkened doorway. Lucian glanced up from the desk in his university room to see one of his dormitory-apartment sharers looking in from the shadows.

"I'm sorry, but I can't," Lucian said. "We all have started learning at least by the time we were born. But *how* did we do it? Why aren't we aware of how we did it?"

After a strained silence: "You aren't seriously asking me that at this time of night! What difference does it make?"

"But we do it all the time. We learn. Why can't we explain how, examine it, and do in classes what we are organically organized to do?"

Two hours later, the pajamaed questioner exclaimed, "B'god, you've done it again. I said you wouldn't do this to me another time and you have. I've been sucked into another of your internal vacuums. I came back this summer to take a course because I'll lose my job in high school without it, not to have all night conversations. What do you teach, anyway?"

"It will be first grade. Maybe."

"You've got to be kidding....You're not kidding. How long have you been teaching?"

"I haven't been."

"How many students will you have?"

"Maybe one."

"For how much salary?"

"Nothing."

"What kind of facility do you have?"

"Facility?"

"A building! Forget it. I'm having a bad dream."

· · ·

Lucian started to write a hasty letter to Reendo's grandmother to repeat that there was no way to have the school, because if the worm farm was not acceptable for day care, it certainly would not be acceptable for first grade, whether or not he was paid for it.

His pen lowered in mid-air and settled back on the desk. He did not know an address for Reendo's grandmother. Nor her name. Nor had he ever asked Reendo's last name. He began to submerge in depression. But this time he laughed at himself. He wrote the letter and addressed the envelope to *Reendo's Grandmother, on the dirt road past the Junk Shop, Northeast side of town...*

The letter did not return to him.

· · ·

An envelope arrived in the mail. The note inside said, simply, *Reendo needs you. He comes Wednesday on 11:26 a.m. bus.*

The bus arrived, Reendo was the first passenger off, with the driver helping him down. Around the child's neck, on a string, was a tag with his name and address. Lucian approached.

"You Lucian?" asked the driver. "Got a parcel for you." He smiled and patted Reendo's shoulder.

· · ·

"You are here to make a school?" Reendo asked. "Show me."

Lucian tapped his forehead. "I'm putting things in here that will enable me to pass tests that will let the university give me a piece of paper that will enable the office of education to write another piece of paper that says we can maybe have a class together."

"You mean you're getting your teaching certificate?" Reendo asked.

. . .

Reendo looked up from his burrito. "Those classes you took me to were dull. Is that what you're going to do with me next year, instead of having fun?"

. . .

Late at night, Lucian slept on the pallet on the floor, so Reendo could have the bed. A small hand gently shook Lucian's shoulder. He awoke. Reendo whispered. "The papers. I forgot to give you the papers my grandmother sent for you. She said I was to remind you to sign them and send them back yesterday. And it's tomorrow already."

Lucian knocked over the lamp, trying to turn it on. He blinked at the complex document Reendo held in his hand. "What is this for?" he asked.

"She said you have enough to do, not to trouble yourself reading it now. Just sign it and send it back. She said I was to address the envelope. That the address I would put on it would be better than the one you would put on it."

His suite-mate appeared at the door. Coming in late, he had heard the lamp falling. "What's the noise? Can't you even..." Then he noticed Reendo. "Oh m'god, Lucian, what have you done now, kidnapped a kid for one of your projects? You take these things far too seriously."

. . .

"I wanted to talk about my project for class," Lucian said, standing in the doorway of Dr. Pandra's office.

"Yes," she said, and walked around her desk to sit at a chair in front, motioning him to another. They began to talk, when Reendo, who had been exploring in the outer office on his own, casually came in. Dr. Pandra observed this random child walking comfortably about her office, looking at the pictures on the wall. Lucian continued talking without seeming to notice this stray individual.

Reendo, glancing upward, saw the huge poster of the night sky, the milky way, extending across the ceiling. With a soft exclamation of pleasure, he spread himself out on the floor, face upward, to behold it better.

"Look," Reendo said quietly to no one in particular, "they're so clear." And he proceeded to point to and call the names of zodiac positions, ending, "that's the Roman ones." He began again, pointing, and naming the mythic figures in the sky as seen by Chinese, Arabs, Kenyans, and Hopis. He now had Dr. Pandra's attention. She made some rapid notations on a pad of paper.

She looked quizzically at Lucian, one hand extended toward him and the other to Reendo. Before she could formulate the question into words, Reendo rose and sat in Lucian's lap and said to him, "We need one for the worm farm." He thought a moment and added, "but there we have the real sky."

"Reendo," Lucian said, "we'll see if Dr. Pandra can tell us where to order it."

"*Reendo?*" questioned Dr. Pandra, standing and moving to her desk, and shuffling through a pile of folders. She picked up one, and read Reendo's full name, asking it as a question.

"Yes?" he said.

"Are you…" Then she looked from him to Lucian, "is he…" She sat back down, explaining that she had had been sent this folder of a pre-school student whose scores seemed questionably high. The school district had forwarded them on to her at the university for review and evaluation. "But now he's here, and we can administer our batteries of tests…"

"No," interrupted Lucian. "He is not an object to be measured and catalogued. He is Reendo. If you really want to know him, it should not be in this office where you are Dr. Pandra, and he is your case to study. It should be on neutral ground where both of you are equal, sharing as you will."

In the silence that followed, Lucian could not believe he had just said that.

Dr. Pandra looked him in the eyes and then regarded

Reendo's open gaze. She raised a finger indicating *just a minute*, and went to the desk and phoned. The brevity of her side of the conversation indicated that the person on the other end of the line was someone who knew her by voice and long experience. She spoke about *going up again, how soon, which day, two people,* and *I'll call you back.*

She resumed the other chair and said, "My husband Walter's hobby is ballooning. Would you both like to ride the breezes?"

. . .

They sailed upward in the mists of morning, with the huge reversed tear-drop shape, the silken envelope of air, above them. They looked down upon the landscape, saw the city like a map below them, saw the deer in the arroyos.

"Longhorn could build a model of all that," said Reendo.

At one point, Janice—she insisted on this as her *civilian name* instead of Dr. Pandra—said to Lucian, "I'm sorry, with the other things that came up in the office, I never got back to asking you what it was you wanted to discuss about your project."

"Not now," he said, "I'll see you on a workday for that."

"*Thank you,* Lucian," Walter said. "Perhaps between us we can convince her that there is life after work." Then to Reendo, "Pull the chain again to make more fire. Take us higher."

. . .

Reendo sat with Lucian in the class, watching a project presented by one of the other graduate students. She had a shoe box from which she took two solid geometric shapes, placed them on the table, replaced the lid on the shoe box beside them.

"This is a presentation on math for early elementary. This will acquaint them with two basic shapes," she said. "This is a cube, and this is a sphere."

Since she made no reference to the other shape on the table, the shoe box, Reendo, trying to be helpful said aloud, "And that's a *parallelepipedon.*"

The class all turned and looked at him.

"That's what Lucian told us," Reendo said.

"Your turn for the project," Dr. Pandra said to Lucian.

She had agreed when he had asked if he and Reendo could do it together. She had hesitated, until he had asked her, *If an* educational theory A starts in Europe, educational theory B starts in Africa, and educational theory C starts in Asia, how long will it take them to have an impact on a child in this city? She had given him a sidelong glance and had slowly asked, How long? Never, he had answered, until they are implemented with the child.

25

Clauda Lavender roamed the library stacks like a ghost. She felt disconnected from the Detroit streets outside, as if she had become some kind of permanent resident amid these rows of volumes. Hours, days, searching the books for her research paper on detailed aspects of African-American heritage in the urban setting. And the interviews. With the oldest in her family, with the oldest in her neighborhood, recording the oral stories.

She treated herself to other materials in the stacks to get away at times from the topic and the note cards. Today she had not taken a break at all. The deadlines were too close. Until the end of the library hours. Thirty minutes left. She browsed the shelves. Saw a title that attracted her. Remembered it with pleasure from some time before, she could not remember when. It was a time B-R-P, she mused, Before Research Paper.

She fanned through the volume. Her eyes scanned snatches of paragraphs. They called up memories from her earlier readings. She removed folded pages that some previous reader had apparently forgotten and left in the volume, glancing absently at them.

The first few words on these inserted pages alerted her attention. Then the soft voice from the end of the rows of books interrupted her. "Closing time. Check out now."

She placed the book back on the shelf but kept the folded pages she had started to read. Curiosity. Something compelling.

Back home in the small apartment where she took care of her grandfather, she read the rest of the message. What a strange and haunting manuscript to find, she thought. Her rational self wanted to throw it away as a scrap of someone else's life. Another part of herself knew that she could have written these words, herself. Knew that they came from someone else, breaking through all the improbabilities that brought it to her hand. Knew that if she could possibly arrange it, she would be at Buckingham Fountain in Chicago on July 15 to see who had written this poignant script that had come to her in such a impersonally personal way.

. . .

Clauda felt simultaneously excited and calm. She had arranged her complex schedule to gain this fraction of time to come from Detroit to Chicago. July in Chicago sweltered. A light shower had hit the concrete and asphalt skillet of the streets and walks, and hissed its vapors back into the air. The rising moisture seemed to mimic Buckingham fountain.

Clauda paced around the circle of the fountain, not thinking to hold the book other than casually at her side, the book she had checked out of the Detroit library, the one inside of which she had found the note. She had not thought further than that one person, feeling remarkably like herself, had left a note, and she was the only one to have received it. She looked at those who strolled and those who walked more earnestly toward destinations.

She found it hard to anticipate how this mysterious writer would look. But somehow the outer appearance seemed irrelevant to the *presence* she felt from the message.

Then she saw him. He held a book before him. He walked almost hesitatingly, looking at the faces of the people. She felt so moved by the moment that she ran a few steps, and he saw her. She walked rapidly the remaining space between them.

"You're the one," she said, "who wrote that beautiful message. I don't know what to say, thank you, and I want to hear about your background…" She let the sentence trail off unfinished because she could not think of more words, but simply smiled and made a gesture that gave a tentative punctuation to her remarks.

He looked at her, at her book, at his, and smiled. "You're joking," he said. "I was wondering what to say to you, and you've taken the initiative and said it for me. Really, I cannot tell you how moving your words were. It was like I had written them myself. And I wondered about a person who could sound so much like myself, or at least, like I *think* to myself inside."

Her expression of surprise surprised him. She said, "You mean you didn't write the message? I assumed you did."

"No," he said. "You didn't either?" They shook their heads and then simultaneously looked around them. Where was the third person, the writer of two copies of the message?

They sat together on a bench, talking, looking for the remaining member of their trio.

Clauda introduced herself, and he gave his name as Jarmon Trander. He had been born in Buenos Aires, Argentina. His father had been a musician and had come with his family to New Orleans as a member of an orchestra. Jarmon, himself, had debuted as a cellist at the age of seven, and now also played in the same orchestra. He had performed in Europe and had traveled in concert tours across North and South America. On his birthday, his thirty-second, he had roamed in the Louisiana city alone, as he often felt to do on occasions which other people considered festive, to which he felt no connection, and had wandered into the library.

There he had sought out a book that had been a favorite, one he had revisited in times when he seemed not a part of other people's events. There, as he read, he came upon the message that had brought him here.

Clauda told him of her studies, of her courses in the field of urban mythology of African heritage. Of her summer projects funded by humanities grants to interview the long-lived people and place their tapes in the special university library collection for researchers.

Simultaneously, as they shared their stories, they saw *him*. The third person for whom they had been scrutinizing every face. He had a book. He seemed not even to be looking for anyone, as if sure no one else would be there. He stood facing the fountain, holding the book behind his back.

They approached him, moved on either side of him, standing by the rounded fence. Clauda said, "We've been looking for you. We both found your messages."

He held his book before him and looked at theirs. "So," he said, regarding her carefully. "You didn't write the message?" She nodded no. He looked at Jarmon, who nodded similarly.

"Then," he said, "I am a third to read the writing, and I am not the author either. Where is that person then?"

They stood, sharing more of themselves. "Paygon Zelschmidt," the newest of the trio said. "Just like the character in the story."

They both looked blank. "Story?" Clauda said.

"*The Man Called* X. The sidekick. The only other time I ever heard the name. Wondered how it happened that they chose mine."

Their expressions still showed no recognition. "Radio. Of course," he said, understanding, "of course you don't recall. A radio program, when radio *had* programs. I knew them all. Brian Donlevy played the part of the title character."

As a child, he had troubled all his teachers, finishing his work before the others, asking questions beyond the pages of the books, wanting applications and connections. After he had dutifully enrolled to college, he sat through classes for three months and then walked out.

"Walked out a few decades ago. Wasn't what I wanted. Wasn't what I needed," he explained.

He had proceeded to work at odd jobs, mastering each, finding that he could most immerse himself in projects that involved him from start to finish. A craftsman, a builder. This *process of completion* became his satisfaction. He had built every kind of unit as they came onto the market. Had put together television sets and microwave ovens. But early on, doing carpentry work, he had apprenticed with an organ builder and had become known as a master constructor, traveling the country and to other countries, staying each place for the months it took to make and install the pipes and to adjust them.

He had signed them all, these organs, like artwork. On the largest pipe that produced the lowest note, he had always inscribed his name. His artwork in the sanctuaries of the land.

"You must have felt deeply about the religious ceremonies, to devote those years to organs," Clauda said.

"Oh, no," he said, "no, I figured with most of those congregations having to hear about being sinful and evil and facing damnation, about being inherently bad, that those poor souls deserved a little touch of beauty in their lives, if even for a moment while they sat there. And if my instruments gave pleasure and a passing sense of peace, then my part was fulfilled."

"And now? You still are building?" asked Jamon.

"Sort of," was Paygon's answer. He had decided that education may have caught up with his interests in the time since he de-matriculated. So he took a year and visited every university and college in the Chicago area, where he now lived, and received permission to visit classes. He did not want to hear what the admissions officers said, what the public relations personnel had put in slick brochures that all sounded alike. He wanted to see the faculty and classes in action.

He had gone in one day to a program for the *gifted learner*, and there he found his home. Though the special non-traditional classes were originally intended for people straight out of high school, he had applied. After some discussion on the part of school administrators about admitting someone of his age, they had given him a full scholarship. And now he was building an organ for the school in his spare time. "At seventy-two," he said, "I am non-traditional in several ways."

When it seemed of no purpose to wait longer at Buckingham Fountain, when none but themselves remained in the darkness, they moved toward the tall buildings along Michigan Boulevard.

They agreed that there was *something* in their coming together, some pleasure in the meeting, some tranquillity they felt together, even in this brief encounter. They could not just separate into the crowded streets, with this moment only as an anecdotal memory.

"I have a place," Paygon said, "in Oak Park, and if you feel comfortable in coming, there is plenty of space to stay. Then we can talk more tomorrow." . . .

Clauda and Jamon felt welcomed by the house, itself, designed by Frank Lloyd Wright, with surprises and moods built into the passages and stairways, the windows and positions of the rooms.

The next day, they agreed on a future date to meet, in December around the time of winter solstice, to make this house their place of meeting, to enjoy a comfortableness with each other. And to reproduce the message they had found. And as they traveled, to put it in copies of not only the titles in which they had found it, but others they agreed upon as well. And then, next year at this time, they would return to Buckingham fountain and see what would happened then.

. . .

Lucian had seen Reendo onto the bus to return to his grandmother. Felt the empty space where Reendo had been. Reread textbooks and prepared assignments.

He took a break and walked around the campus. A thought fluttered in his head. What was it? The time. *The date.* It was July 15. The Ides of July. How long ago it felt that he had made his trip across the land. How he had stood, solitary among the crowd in Chicago, waiting, hoping, his effort vain and futile.

He walked on to the library and read passages from some of the books of the same titles into which he had placed his messages in other libraries, though never here. He closed them and left. To him, the marathon journey to the libraries across the country had a reality only for the time of the journey and the following July. Only on that one day of that particular year, it seemed to him, could anything have resulted.

Somehow, in his mind, when no one had appeared at Buckingham Fountain, the slips of paper he had left in the books had ceased to exist. It did not occur to him that any cause and effect relationships regarding the messages could have extended beyond that moment. He assumed he had put a year as part of the date of meeting on the message.

26

Lucian returned from the university to the worm farm during a thunderstorm. Attempting to keep them dry, he shielded under his shirt the temporary teaching credentials, wrapped in plastic. His continued accreditation remained dependent on his continuing his course of study by no later than the second semester of the coming year.

He sat in the darkness of the room for a long time thinking

of the futility of the summer. He put the plastic-wrapped papers on a shelf in the darkness, lay on the bed, and wound himself in the sheet.

The next day, he saw no one. No one came. That night, as Lucian sat in the darkness under the cottonwood trees, Grandmother moved toward him in the shadows from the desert.

"Do you have the certificate?" she asked.

"A temporary one. Dependent on continuing the rest of the program by the spring semester. None of this will do any good." He held out his hands toward their surroundings. "This is not a school. It was not even acceptable as a day care center."

He could barely see in the darkness that she was laughing. "You bought a school," she said.

"Bought a school? No, I didn't. How could I?" Lucian said.

"By the application you made."

"I made no application."

"The one Reendo brought you, that you signed." She beckoned Lucian follow her.

They walked into the darkness. Behind the ridge, her horse waited. She mounted, with Lucian behind. In silence, they rode in the night.

They stopped at the shadow of a building. They walked to its front door. Grandmother unlocked it. They entered. She aimed the beam of a flashlight into the hallway and rooms.

"We have to use a flashlight, because you haven't paid your electric bill," she said.

Lucian started to say something, but could not think of a reply that made sense to a statement that did not make sense.

Grandmother said, "When the consolidated school opened, those who attended this little old one had to go there. The state has a stipulation that such structures, if still usable, are to be disposed of by priority listing to non-profit organizations. First priority, educational purposes."

"But the cost..." Lucian started to speak.

Grandmother said, "The federal government has a program related to financial services with fine print related to what they call *native minority populations* You qualified."

"*Qualified?*"

"Your entire student body is Native American," she said, "one hundred percent."

"*Reendo?* One student?" Lucian asked.

"The forms ask for percentages, not numbers. Statistics are wonderful when you need them," she said.

"But the equipment, appliances…" Lucian said.

"Enough came with the building," Grandmother said.

"But the standards…"

"It met standards last year. They can't say it doesn't meet them now."

"But the cost?" Lucian said.

"Given the native minority population of your student body, and the age of the building, and the non-profit nature of your organization, the arrangements are special for this, very special, only token. You pay over time in installments. And no taxes on the property or land. "

"But what about…"

Grandmother shrugged, "It's your school."

· · ·

It was a strange time. The school year began. Lucian and Reendo sat the first day in a class room. Traditional style. Lucian at the teacher's desk in front. Reendo at a student's desk in the middle of the room, surrounded by rows of empty seats.

They sat in silence until they both started laughing.

Then they left and locked the building and went back to the worm farm. They did not return from the worm farm to the school building until the preliminary inspection team came.

· · ·

The three inspectors were a quiet lot, with eyes that darted everywhere, who whispered among themselves. On the day they were scheduled, Lucian and Reendo went and sat in the school room again.

The inspectors mulled over their official forms and checked the books in the library. Checked the kitchen facilities to see if they were sufficient for the size of the student body. Checked the number of commodes to see if there were adequate numbers for the students.

They sat in the sterile classroom and observed Lucian

lecturing to his class of one about periods of Chinese history. They asked, with whatever meaning they intended, if this was not a waste of time, without explaining what *this* referred to. Lucian said he thought not, that a study of one fifth of the world's population should have some significance.

A lady on the team asked where the faculty women's restroom was, and they could not tell her, because they had never looked for it.

The team checked blanks on pupil-teacher ratio and looked oddly at each other as they did. "Grandmother would enjoy that one," Reendo whispered to Lucian, "she likes statistics like that."

They checked everything they could think of and left shaking their heads at the young teacher with the distant eyes and the single student whose standardized test scores showed that he was advanced beyond almost anyone else in his age group in the region.

Lucian and Reendo went to a window and watched the inspection team's car drive away. Then they also left and locked the door behind them.

. . .

Because of a teachers' workshop, the students at the consolidated school were free for a day. Dolphus wandered aimlessly about his house for a while, then headed for the worm farm.

At the worm farm, Lucian and Longhorn had gone off to get supplies, and Reendo was just handing Mr. Billus his three containers of worms for his new tomato beds.

Mr. Billus asked, "Why aren't you in school, young man?"

Reendo answered, "I am. I'm learning small business practices," and smiled.

When the man had left, Reendo looked out past the yard and saw his friend, Dolphus. The two ran toward each other, hugged, jumped up and down, and cheered.

Dolphus explained that school was a cage in which he was trapped and suffocating and that he must escape somehow.

"Why aren't you there, too, Reendo?" Dolphus asked. "Are you sick and can't go to school?"

"I'm in school here," Reendo said.

"Where?"

"Here, like always."

"But we're supposed to be in *real* school now," Dolphus said.

"We have a real school to go to when we want to, but we don't want to," Reendo replied.

They talked until, with a moment of explosive insight, Dolphus understood. The vision was too much to contain. He jumped straight up on the air, let out a whoop, and went sprinting into the desert, shouting something that Reendo could not understand.

The mind of Dolphus, the organizer, began to work.

. . .

A few days later, Reendo said to Lucian in an offhand way, "Let's go to our other building today."

They reached the deserted structure and entered. Reendo led the way to the nearest classroom. He sat at a desk in the center of the empty rows. Lucian stood in front.

"Write for me so I can see them, the emperors of China," Reendo asked, "while I try to play the melody that you taught me on this Chinese flute."

Lucian complied, enjoying the music. Then the sounds multiplied into many instruments. He turned around to see how Reendo accomplished this feat, and beheld, seated and grinning, Dolphus, Normita, Jhenaw, Eriot, Orgol, and one or both of the parents of each. And a new face.

The new face belonged to Pica. She had said matter-of-factly on introducing herself that the others had told her all of the things they had done at worm farm, so she was *all caught up*.

Pica, the gymnast, limber as a rope, who translated everything into body postures and movements. When her thoughts changed, her body moved. When she heard music, her body automatically twisted into designs. She defined everything by shape, saw ideas as if they were cubes and pyramids and rising wisps of smoke, and described them with her hands and torso. When she watched people walk, her muscles mimicked them. When she saw animals move, her postures duplicated them. Dolphus already called her *the shape-shifter*, and delighted in asking her to be a *tree*, a *post*, a *pelican*, the *color orange*, a *comet*, for immediately her gestures, posture, and movement transformed into a patterned response.

Pica had not been a favorite of any teachers, except in dance, because her shape never conformed to desks and linear formats. Her single-parent father had envisioned years of academic agony, until he had talked to Dolphus' father.

. . .

They were a group again. Lucian told the parents he wanted the children to learn economics and decision-making by discussing all finances with them. They, in turn, would share the information with the families. The families would pay what they wished. The contributions would be put into a *school use fund.*

The first priority became the monthly repayments of the loan for the building. He explained the amounts to the children. They talked with the parents and the parents contributed as they wished.

With Lucian, the children went to the bank to open their account. Thereafter, they helped keep the financial record book, wrote the checks, and, after Lucian signed them, mailed them.

The group's first decision was to replace the old sign at their school building with one saying *Worm Farm School: Campus Two.* The second decision was to lock it up again and move back to the cottonwood trees. There they hung a sign saying *Worm Farm School: Campus One.*

The Worm Farm School became solvent.

. . .

From where the banker sat in the glass-enclosed rear office, he could see over the front counter only the shoulders and heads of those who came in for transactions with Gertrude, the teller.

He saw the front door open but saw no head nor shoulders enter, until several moments later when the top part of Lucian appeared. The same routine occurred on exiting. The door opened, but no heads nor shoulders were visible, and then Lucian exited through the door, already opened, it seemed, by invisible hands.

He leaned back in his chair and called around through his door so Gertrude could hear, "Who was with him? Was it Harvey?"

"Harvey *who?*" she queried, without turning.

"You know, Harvey, the six-foot four-inch invisible rabbit," he said.

Gertrude turned slowly and looked at him over her half-glasses. "A *what?*"

He added, "You know, James Stewart...when he was still Jimmy...the movie..." Rather than pursue it, as he saw her expressionless face, he repeated, "Who was with him?"

Gertrude turned back to her counter and said over her shoulder, "The worm children are back."

27

Lucian introduced to the children, in quick succession, a variety of experiences, letting their interests guide them from one activity to the next.

Moving further out onto the flat expanse of nearby desert, they marked out a soccer field, and a field for a game of the Aztecs and another of the Celts. And they learned to play them all.

They returned to the outside of the Campus Two building to use the basketball court and also adapted a nearby area for tennis, volleyball, and badminton. They added related games from India, Brazil, and Kenya.

Orgol asked if they could also study the music of each place where the games were played. Lucian, with a wistful look, glanced at Longhorn, remembering their talking about the left-behind instruments.

When a letter arrived from his former university, Lucian panicked momentarily fearing they had discovered an unpaid bill or that they had made a mistake in past grades, nullifying his diploma. Under the music department letterhead was written, "Thank goodness you wrote us when you did. Your files had no current address, and we did not know how to make contact with you. The department has no plans for instruction on these instruments and no space to display them now since that area has been reallocated. We wanted to check with you first but did not know how and were about to look for some place to donate them to or give them away to students who wanted them."

Longhorn said, when Lucian showed him the letter, "Synchronicity two. Send for them"

When the crates arrived, they were marked with outside notations, such as *guanzi, hulusi, basu, dizi, khaen, ichigenkin,* and other terms that were to become the vocabulary of their *instruments around the world* study. Using them, the children began to became proficient in the melodies and rhythms of multiple tribes and cultures. Sounds of the zheng and dizi accented the days. They listened to recordings of every available kind of music. They experimented with related folk dances.

In order not to confuse where the music came from, Lucian first made sketches of the continents in the sand and pointed out the places of origin. Then the children wanted to build an outdoor relief map. They constructed a kiln and began to bake pieces of clay in the shapes of countries, fitting them together and taking them apart like huge puzzles.

Soon they could put together and take apart the world. They could sit in a circle in the Pacific Ocean, and pinpoint a clay-piece representing a Malaysian Island, while they listened to the music from the place. Then they attempted with their instruments to duplicate it. Music and geography, for them, had become inexorably linked.

Then came the food.

They wrote letters to embassies asking for information about the countries, including recipes, if possible. What came back, dutifully addressed to the Worm Farm School—although one was made out to *World Farmer's School*—included material on history, customs, clothing, products. And on food.

Together they prepared their lunch each day, approximating foods from one of the countries. They sat in their map while eating and listening to the music. Then they would take their instruments and try to imitate it. They sang songs in many languages, becoming increasingly multi-lingual.

. . .

Longhorn's corral grew. He acquired more horses, until there were enough for all the children, himself, and Lucian. He had places to take them, all the places he had explored alone.

At the worm farm, the children and Lucian squeezed into

Gitano's old auto, barely fitting, not fitting actually, on their way to Longhorn's cabin and corral. There they spewed out of the car like circus clowns. As they learned to ride horses, Longhorn took them to places at ever greater distances.

"To the Anasazi ruins," he said one day. And off they rode, out into the desert.

They left the horses by the water and the green plants of a stream among the canyons. They walked on from there, toward the places they could not yet see but in the direction of which Longhorn pointed.

As bursts of energy occurred in each, one after another, they ran ahead taking turns leading the pack. At one point, when Pica's moment of energy kicked in, she raced ahead of the others to the top of a ridge. She turned and motioned toward the others to hurry, walking backwards as she did.

The next thing that they knew, Pica disappeared. Not exactly as if she had walked on and been lost to view beyond the ridge. Rather as if a stage trapdoor had opened under her. As if she dropped into it, her upraised waving hands held above her head, disappearing last. Silence.

"The shape-shifter has just become *nothing*," said Dolphus.

"No," said Reendo, "she must have seen a hole and is imitating one."

"Let's take her to the Grand Canyon and see what she becomes," Eriot said.

They all rushed ahead, stood on the ridge and looked down on the sloping side beyond. Pica lay flat on her back where she had fallen, a short distance only, into a large, squarely-cut excavation.

Beside her, and looking up at the others as they arrived, knelt a young woman in Khaki pants and shirt, brimmed hat, with red hair, red like burnished copper, of a length to touch her shoulders.

About the excavation were piled and labeled pot shards, bone pieces, and assorted other objects.

They had stumbled onto a dig, and Pica literally *into* one, and the archaeologist looked momentarily startled by their entry, like one coming out of a dream. Or into one.

"What's your name?" Normita asked.

"My name…" the one with hair of burnished copper said, as if selecting one rather than remembering it, "…*Beth*, just call me Beth. I work among the remnants of the dead, to piece by piece, relive with them their lives."

"I'm Normita. Who are they?" She pointed to some bones.

"Those were animals that…" and here Beth removed a course cloth covering objects partly exposed in the ground, revealing remnants of human skulls, "…that these people ate."

The children grouped around the perimeter of the hole and began to question her as if this had been all planned and she had awaited their arrival. She began to answer questions with a smile that belied a look, perhaps of weariness, about the eyes.

They remained with her so long that the sun cast lengthy shadows. The children began to retrace their steps toward the place where they would camp, where Longhorn had remained with the horses. Lucian stayed behind with Beth and said, "I thank you for speaking to them as people, individuals, and not as some do to children. You have been kind and generous with your time."

She gave him a look as curious, and long, and penetrating, as if she tried to fathom all he felt behind those simple sentences.

Before she could reply, Jhenaw ran on back and said to her, "We have food at the camp and are going to play desert music at the campfire and Longhorn will tell the story of the ancient ones of the rock houses. Please come."

Beth looked as if a door had opened to her, more of release or escape than to a seat upon the sand at a campfire.

Yes," she said, "yes." She simply rose and followed as if she left her past and walked away without a glance behind, knowing it would all remain when she returned.

· · ·

Longhorn directed the building of the fire and preparation of the food, in the twilight. When they sang around the fire, Beth taught them short songs in Hindi, Parsi, Urdu, and Arabic.

Later, everyone else but Longhorn and Lucian already slept, including Beth, who lay between the forms of Jhenaw and Reendo. Longhorn said softly in the shadows to Lucian, as they unrolled their blankets, "She has deep sorrow in her eyes, as if she mourned the Anasazi, each one who had ever lived. As if they were only now departed, each a relative and friend."

. . .

They visited her now, with frequency, for Beth had included them in her dig. Showed them how to use the equipment. Showed them the photographs of the layers as they had been unearthed. Showed them how fragments of bone could be analyzed, how its place on the skeleton could be determined. How a certain kind of wear at a shoulder socket could identify the kind of action performed to cause it. How age might be determined. The nature of the diet from the evidence of refuse that remained.

When Orgol had joked about *where are the dinosaur bones*, Beth smiled and said, "Next time."

28

Lucian, on the weekends, often left on Friday afternoon to go to see the as yet nameless dweller in the canyon caves. Usually with Longhorn. The tribe of three. This weekend Longhorn was elsewhere. So two-thirds of the tribe gathered.

Both showed fascination in the development of the language. With the two speaking and experimenting, it advanced in complexity and richness. Already they determined that the parts of speech in English and most other existing languages should not be its pattern. Nouns disturbed them. Nouns, so concrete, so final, so unchanging. Yet everything in nature, in reality, changed and altered constantly.

They devised a simple way of saying the function of a thing that implied impermanence. *Temporarily, this is a woven piece of cloth,* their new word should say. Once, its elements were not cloth; in time they will not be again. The change is taking place before our eyes, but at a rate too slow for us to see it happen. So they experimented with words that implied *being cloth,* or *clothing,* or *now-functioning-as-cloth,* or *we perceive it as elements we call cloth.*

"Actually," said Lucian, "nouns are verbs in slow motion."

. . .

As they sat beside the smoldering coals of the fire at night, having eaten from the food of the land, they explored this *reflecting reality through language.*

Lucian said, "What of the olympic runner, who speeds to fame before the multitude? What is he when he is not running? Is he still a runner? The newspapers will identify him as a runner even when he is not running. Even years later, long after he has run, he still has that identity."

"Yes," his tribal brother replied, "and the scientist who plays golf. Is he at that moment a scientist? Or only when *sciencing?*"

"Or the comedian, is she still a comedian when she's serious?"

"And the astronaut when he walks the earth?"

Could humans have many designations depending on the actions at the moment, reflecting on their actions of the past, with potential for other kinds of actions in the future? She is *astronauting* now. He *scienced* in years past. She *pre-runs.*

They agreed that the forms sounded strange and unwieldy in English or in their other languages, because the structure, itself, was built on a different, static, model of existence. But in the New Tongue, as they tried it, explored it, created it, they felt a sense of rightness in its developing manner of expression.

They lapsed in and out, now, of English, other languages, and the New Tongue.

Lucian asked if he could bring the children.

His brother of the mesa said, in their new language, *yes.*

. . .

The dweller in the canyon guided the children through all the locations, the rocks and ridges, the secret places of his domain. They saw the growth of gourds and squash, of corn, and plants for which they had no name, springing out of places where it seemed no plants would grow.

He told them what to gather and directed their preparation of it. As they ate this produce, it was as if, in a way not previously experienced, they had come in contact with *the earth.* Here beyond the market and even the garden, in the wilds and rocks, they had harvested pieces of the earth that grew, earth formed into growing things. As they placed the leaves and fruits and roots, of various colors and textures, in their mouths, they seemed to taste the essence of the earth's products anew, as if for the first time.

With the tastes came the *scents*. Their noses caught the fragrances upon the wind, and they began to differentiate the sources. Found they could locate certain plants by becoming conscious of the smells. Could walk in the direction of a fragrance, overturn the leaves, and find the source. "It's as if," said Normita, "I can see odors like some twisting strands of yarn floating in the wind, and can tell them all apart, and follow one among all the others, right to where it comes from."

When Taco, the desert fox, came and sniffed them all, Lucian could not find a word for the look on their faces, the focused look of oneness with this creature of the wild.

When they had seen the rooms that the dweller of the canyons had constructed, he sat them in a semi-circle, and said, "Around you are the rocks and wood, the clay, the elements from which to build. When you come next time, I want you each to choose a place, and there, at your individual direction, we will build you each a small room."

The children's ears became attuned to hearing Lucian and Longhorn and their tribal brother speak in the New Tongue. They readily adopted all the words they heard and began to speak themselves.

29

"Reendo," Lucian said, as he and Longhorn and the children sat beneath the cottonwoods in the worm farm yard, "you're the only one that has met Janice Pandra at the university. She sent a letter to us all." He handed it to Reendo to read aloud to the others: *Dear Worm Farm School friends: My husband, Walter, has some vacation days due at work. I get time to visit educational centers in the state. Since yours is such a place, you cannot imagine—no, probably you can—how much I would like to go there. So, my question is this: if we pack up the hot air balloon equipment, would it be all right for us to come, and we can sail the skies together.*

In the momentary silence that followed the reading, a grinning Reendo said, "Say *yes!*" They did. In unison. Shouting. Reendo wrote the letter of response on their behalf.

. . .

When Dr. Pandra and her husband arrived, and when they stood for the first time in the midst of the expanding area that housed the containers of loam, she said, "So this is a worm farm. And this is Worm Farm School."

She knew much more about each of the children than a first meeting would suggest. All of their folders had been forwarded to her for evaluation, as their scores, when previously tested at the new consolidated school, had clustered in the highest ranks with Reendo's.

Walter found the conditions prime for ballooning. The morning after their arrival, with the first lights of the east, the balloon lay extended across the sands off to the side of Longhorn's model of the desert.

The tanks of fuel breathed their dragon's breath into the wrinkled silken envelope and swelled it to life. It bobbed on the ground, then lifted upright and pulled against constraints to be freed from earth.

The basket and balloon rose gently into the fresh morning air, lifting them up into the dawn. They looked down on the worm farm as it began to resemble Longhorn's model from this height.

Walter told them, while they rose on the currents of the air, how the wind directions would change as they went upward, giving them some control of the flight. They felt the change themselves and drifted one way, only to find themselves moving in a new direction, as the hollow cloth bulb above them pierced a new level of air, and then another.

On the ground, Janice followed in the specially equipped van and trailer. Longhorn drove with her, knowing the places they could navigate and which to avoid. Knowing where there were roads that did not seem to be there, even when driving on them.

. . .

Gertrude, the teller, on her way early to the bank, heard voices above her. Since that was impossible, she did not look up, until they repeated several times. "*Am I hearing things?*" she muttered aloud and looked skyward.

She saw children waving at her, the light of the newly risen sun illuminating the brilliant colors of the balloon. She waved in return.

Later at work, when the banker came in, Gertrude said simply, "Well, the worm children have taken to the air now."

· · ·

"There's a question I have," Lucian said to Dr. Pandra before she and Walter were to leave. The two of them sat under the cottonwoods, under the night sky, while Walter showed the children his telescope. Ballooning by day, astronomy by night, equally interested him. He had aimed the scope at several objects in succession.

Now, it picked up the light from Andromeda. "It was two million, two hundred thousand years ago," he told them, "when the light you see tonight left from that galaxy. The light you see is ancient."

Lucian said to Janice, "You know I have to continue classes next semester in order to complete the courses in time, before my temporary certification expires. That means returning to the university. I want to bring the children with me, somehow, so we can continue there. If you can suggest potential places, as inexpensive as possible—an unused room in the stadium, or houses bought up on the edge of the university for future expansion that may not be in use—any options you know of."

She looked thoughtfully at him for a moment. Then looked back at Pica at the telescope, with two million year old light creating an image on her retina. She watched the others staring upward, as they realized that they also could see the galaxy without any aid. That they would be able to look upward many nights and see the fuzzy spot that was a galaxy.

"It takes," said Walter, "more than a hundred thousand years for light to travel from one side of that galaxy to the other, from one side of that dot you see to the other side."

· · ·

They were in the store looking for a thank-you card to send the Pandras for the ballooning and the exploration of the night sky. Dolphus said, "I don't really like any of them. Let's do one ourselves."

Back at the worm farm, they each drew what they thought would be appropriate. Lucian circulated the cards to let the parents see the work before he planned to send them all off to the Pandras.

A note came back from Eriot's father: "These are good. Print them, and I'll buy several dozen for myself." Lucian discussed it with the children. "Let's be printers," Jhenaw said.

So began the search for means of printing that took them to the newspaper office, the printing firms, and finally, the Junk Shop, which had, out in a back storage shed, equipment adequate for the job. It worked and was cheap, the only criteria they had.

And so the Worm Farm Press was born.

. . .

Beth of the burnished copper hair took them to the dinosaur digs in the desert. She knew of people at the university engaged in these long-term explorations. Layers of bones at what had been a watering hole, millennia ago.

She guided the children through the excavations, had the paleontologists explain their process, let them brush away the dirt of ages, exposing ancient remains.

She took them to a nearby ridge, eroded down to an ancient streambed, where the tracks of seventeen creatures had been preserved in the rock. The contemporary humans walked parallel to the prehistoric tracks, looked at drawings of the creatures, and speculated on the events frozen in the stone.

"Lucian," she said, as the children made plaster molds of the tracks, "do you have any science equipment?"

"A little is still left at the school building we received. Not much."

"Microscopes? Slides? Chemicals?"

"No."

"Then let me bring them. I can get some supplies that the university is disposing of to make way for new equipment. And a huge dinosaur skeleton. At the university, they have an old model skeleton made of plastic they once used for study. Now they have actual bones and casts, and are running out of space. Let me see if I can secure the model. Would they like it?" She nodded toward the children.

Lucian looked at her and smiled, that she even had to ask the question.

. . .

Around the campfire, they still talked of the dinosaurs. Beth passed around pictures from a folder of the giant reptiles. Some names were mentioned without pictures, and when the children wanted to know their shape, Lucian asked Beth to sketch their outline in the sand.

After a while, Normita took a stick and sketched another form, the outline of a kind of fat and furry creature, standing on little legs, little arms outstretched in an exaggerated gesture. She said to Beth, "Do you know what this is?"

"No," said Beth, "but I think we've left the age of reptiles."

"It's a *Murlwump*," the children said in unison. They explained in overlaid voices that every once in a while when they were doing something, Lucian had absently drawn variations of the little creature in the sand. They had asked him finally what it was.

He had explained to them that in school, somewhere in the early grades, as he would sketch things in the margins of his notes, the little creature just evolved from the lines and loops. And once he had appeared, Lucian imagined conversations with him, had imagined once asking his name, and *Murlwump* was the answer. And there were two of them, but neither had an individual name. So their likenesses had adorned pages of his notes, doing fanciful dances, and making comments about the lectures going on in class.

Eriot said, "Tell us another story about the Murlwumps. Tell us one now." The campfire flickered underneath the stars, the circle of listeners waiting.

"All right," Lucian said, and began.

Since they were both Murlwumps, neither had a name, so their conversation might be difficult to follow. Of course, since they both look alike and sound alike, it really doesn't matter, does it.

"No, it doesn't," one of them says, overhearing what I was just telling you.

"I get confused at times myself and wait for you to speak, when

really, all the time, it was my turn."

"Actually we wouldn't need two of us, except you can't have much of a conversation with any less."

"Fewer."

"Fewer?"

"Fewer. Grammar, you know. But back to conversation."

"Isn't that what we're doing now?"

"Yes, and Socrates found this method very effective."

"Who's Socrates?"

"Wait, that's my question."

"Why?"

"Since I don't know the answer, I should ask you."

"But since neither of us knows the answer, we should ask it together."

"All right. One, two, three."

"One, two, three what?'

"Just one, two, three, that's all. I was just counting."

"Oh."

"Now then, together: who's Socrates?"

"You were right; no one answers, so I guess we don't know."

Lucian ended. His rendition of the dialogue, his facial expressions and vocal intonations as he shifted back and forth between the two improbable creatures amused something deep in Longhorn. "Of such are myths born," he laughed. "More, some more."

"More," the children chorused. Beth had the look of one who sat with others by the fire and simultaneously floated at a distance watching herself sitting with the others by the fire.

Lucian, by the look on his face and his gestures, was back in character, and the almost-British voices of the Murlwumps began again.

"It's wheat," one Murlwump said, indicating an imaginary wheat field.

"Well, I didn't imagine it was sour," said the second.

"Sour? What made you think of that?"

"What you said."

127

"That it's wheat?"

"Yes. How do you know it's sweet if you haven't tasted it?"

"I've seen pictures of it in a book."

"But you can't taste a picture."

"No."

"Then how do you know if it's sweet or sour?"

"It might be both."

"Both! How can it be sour if it's sweet?"

"Maybe it's sour wheat."

"What's sweet got to do with it?"

"Well, you're the one that first plunked 'sweet' into the middle of our conversation without even so much as a fanfare. You tell me what sweet has to do with it."

"Not sweet—wheat!"

"Sweet wheat! Sweet wheat! Just listen to that. Why, if it were longer, it would be a poem!"

"That's right. It already has end-line rhyme."

"You know, I wish we could work alliteration into it."

"Why?"

"Because then they would both be the same word, and the same type-setting could be used if it's published."

"Yes!" he said, hardly daring to think of the full potentialities of the idea. "Yes, that's right!" He repeated slowly a second time, "Yes, that's right!" He would have repeated it a third time, but he forgot just what was right. However, that really didn't matter. For as long as something was right, he must feel happy about it. So they sat for a long time just feeling happy and thinking Murlwump thoughts.

Lucian ended with his arms extended wide to all his audience at the conclusion. Beth smiled at this improbable picture of herself sitting here at the campfire listening to this animated telling of a story about Murlwumps.

30

The morning light shown behind billowing clouds, above the cottonwood trees at the worm farm. "The time has come to build," Lucian said to the children. "We each need time together and time alone. Each condition enriches the other. The *alone* space, the special space, differs for each of us. We'll each have a space here, just like our friend in the canyons will help you each build your cliff house rooms there."

His arm swept in a gesture out around the yard and desert. "There is space close and far to choose from. And..." here he indicated a pile of books he had brought from the house, "...here are the habitats that our human ancestors and relatives have designed around the world. From these ideas, from your own, we are going to make drawings, decide on the materials, and together construct as best we can a special place, a room that suits each one of us now. And when we feel like something suits us better later on, we will try another one."

They sat in a circle, passing around the books, pointing out designs to each other. They looked at desert tents, jungle branch construction, island thatch, space carved into cliffs. Structures made of sod, ice, bricks, stones. Buildings square, round, oblong, The multitude of adaptations based on available materials, climate, and myths.

They studied the societies from which the structures came. They talked about how some designs *felt* different from others, and what might cause those different feelings. Discussed the cultures that had buildings with no corners, because tradition said that evil lurks in corners.

They started with the pencil and paper sketches. Each did several and discussed them with the others. Discussed their feelings about each one. Structures that went down into the ground or that rested on it, that rose on poles above the land or resided in trees.

Next came the the models, the effort to see in three dimensions the pattern of the rooms that they might build. They gathered materials, straw and limbs and twigs and pebbles, with which to construct their miniatures. They positioned little doors and windows, made small things to put inside to get an idea of what the rooms could contain.

During one of the days when they worked on these ideas, Beth drove up the dusty road and brought some equipment for future experiments. She became intrigued with the matter of the rooms. Longhorn heard her say softly to herself once as they watched the children working on their models, "A private place, if only there were a private place."

The children urged her to build one too, and Longhorn and Lucian as well. They also agreed that they would make a rock house at the nearest rise of land to be like a cliff house for their friend from the canyon, when he came here just as they went to his area.

. . .

Dolphus decided on a kiva-like place, beneath the ground, roofed over at the surface, with an entrance by ladder from above.

Normita wished for a house on poles, like those in the swamps, that needed a ladder for climbing up to, where she could look down on the land.

Jhenaw planned one in the form of a little lighthouse, an ancient kind, in which a fire could be kindled in the top for a light at night. She planned for a spiral stair that would wind upward, with shelves along the way.

Eriot wanted darkness, silence, a retreat from light and sound and movement. He wanted a sod house with thick walls and roof, with no windows, and a door with a wall built a few feet in front of it, so the door could be opened without anyone seeing in from a distance.

Orgol wanted thatch. A bow house, such as those once built by tribes in central North America among forest dwellers, who constructed structures from the bow tree. Shaped like a hive, it would be round at the base and curved from top to bottom.

Reendo liked a hive design as well, but his, as the houses of Phoenicia, would have two hives, side by side and be made of clay. "Like the capitol letter B, except on its side."

"Observant," Lucian said. "The drawing for this house, flat on the bottom with two arches side by side, was the ancient sign for *house*, and became the letter *Beta* in Greek and *Beth* in Hebrew. But the Greeks turned it upright on its end, and it became the Roman B, the one now used in English. Cities in Israel that started with the sounds of *Beth* all meant *house-of-something*. Like *Beth-leham* means *house of food*."

Pica wanted sun-dried bricks to build a fantasy shape of rounded wavy walls. She had learned the word *chimera*, a *thing that never was*, and wanted hers to be a *chimerical* house.

"But," Orgol asked, "would it be *chimerical* after you built it?"

"And yours?" Jhenaw said, turning to Beth.

"Mine, I know already," Beth replied. "I want one perfectly round, central to all of yours, with windows all around. I want to look out at yours, always, all I can."

Of his, Longhorn said, "I think a houseboat in the desert would be what I want, built like a Chinese junk, like some people in harbors live on permanently, except mine would be on dry land."

Lucian said, "I want a castle, with turrets, walls, ramps, a moat, dungeons and towers. But since that's too much for us to undertake now, I'll be satisfied with the worm farm house as it is."

They agreed to start with the one for their canyon friend, so they could tell him, on their next journey to the cliffs, that he had a special place to come to. On the model of his house, they built a little annex. "That's for Taco," Dolphus said.

. . .

"What about some of the other letters of the alphabet?" asked Orgol, as they scratched symbols in the sand under the cottonwoods. "If 'B' was a Phoenician house, what was an 'A'?"

"The Phoenician's way of drawing the head of an ox, with horns sticking up, resting on its pointed end. *Aleph* in Hebrew, *alpha* in Greek. The Greeks didn't like it resting on the point, so turned it upside-down, with the horns on the bottom."

"'G'," said Eriot.

"The remnant of the hump and neck of a *gimmel*, or camel."

"How about a 'D'?" asked Normita.

"An ancient Egyptian wooden door. They built solid stone structures, but the wooden doors didn't always fit the doorway, so they rounded off the two corners opposite the hinges."

"Any body parts?" asked Dolphus.

"The 'K' is the extended hand. There used to be a fifth finger in the middle, but shorthand eliminated it."

"Or short-*fingered* it?" said Dolphus.

"But the single finger remains in the letter 'I' and the number *one* as well. The 'O' was the symbol for the eye, and in very ancient versions of it, the pupil and iris were drawn, but later left out."

"Sounds like shorthand again," said Reendo.

"The 'H' is fun," said Lucian, drawing an extended fence of upright poles and cross-pieces. "The 'H' is all that remains of the drawing of a fence, with two upright posts and one cross-piece."

"Water was so important, it had to be somewhere," speculated Jhenaw, and then as soon as she said it, drew a succession of waves on the sand. "I bet either the 'M' or the 'W' were waves."

"The 'M' for *mare*, meaning *sea*,from which we get all the word family that includes *marine* and *mariner*. The Romans even called the Mediterranean a form of *mare nostra*, or *our* sea."

. . .

The cards designed at worm farm sold to the parents as fast as the children printed them. Orders came from relatives who received them. First came the *thank you* cards. Then they created one for the Celtic new year, "the origin of Halloween," as Lucian explained to them, when they commenced their study of the Celts.

A card they sent to the owners of The Junk Shop prompted those two to come around to the Worm Farm School and ask Lucian if he would be interested in their carrying a rack of Worm Farm Press cards in their store.

Lucian, as usual, would not respond individually, but had the owners meet with the children in their circle underneath the cottonwoods.

Dolphus said, "We could do a series of Junk Shop cards, like *Junk is stuff whose virtue has not been discovered yet.*"

Lucian let the group work out the financial arrangements with the shop owners. The deal was on.

Normita came up with a card with her drawing of a dinosaur on the front and a caption that said, *Unless I see you soon...* Inside it continued, *I think I'll face extinction.* "My older sister's already away at school, and I want to send it to her."

31

The *naming time* had come. On one of the days in the canyons, their nameless friend had arranged the time for them to all return for the *ceremony of the names.*

He chose the night time and a site on a high bluff where they could survey the shadowed land below. Lucian, Longhorn, and the canyon youth could all converse extensively now in the growing new language. The children all were absorbing it in whole phrases.

Beth, who accompanied them, also picked it up rapidly. "It is like the skeletons from the digs coming alive, and I could speak with them in long forgotten ways. This new language you develop is not just a substitution of words. It is like a new way of thinking. You are restructuring your story of life in a manner that creates other ways of interacting. People tend to pick out of their environment what their words and stories call attention to. They tend to behave in ways for which they have vocabulary. This language is restructuring the whole perception of self and the universe."

Every once in a while, she would repeat some new way of saying things as if to savor it on her tongue like a delicious taste, unknown until the moment of experience. "Oh, yes, *yes*," she would say, repeating it again.

It was in the New Tongue that the names would be given. The moon lighted the night scene. The individuals sat on the ground in a semi-circle facing an open space between themselves and the edge of the bluff.

The youth of the canyons threw dust into the four directions and repeated phrases of unity for each of them. Then he took black powder and let it slip from his hand onto the sandy surface as he walked. When he completed his steps, a sizable circle had been drawn in the open space

Each had brought something that their *feeling* had suggested. Orgol brought crinoid stems he had excavated on one of their searchings for fossils. He placed them in the space near the edge of the circle and said, "It is ancient life, from even more ancient land. Seeing it gives me a feeling of being a part of something vast I can't describe."

Reendo had a pouch of red powder. "These are ground seeds that are red, like the fire. My grandmother says that when they are sprinkled in a little hole with other seeds you want to grow, it gives them the fire of life, and they grow better." He pulled out some pumpkin seed. "Since of all the things growing here in the canyons, there are no pumpkins yet, and since I like them to eat, and want to share them so all of us can enjoy them, then tomorrow you…" and he nodded toward the youth, "…can show me where to plant them. First the hole, then the powder, then the seed. Next year we'll have pumpkins."

After each had shared something important to them, the youth asked everyone to take a dried limb from those strewn about the bluff. They sat and faced the circle. The youth said, "Now the naming can begin."

He took his limb to the center of the circle and sprinkled wood shavings around its center. He gave Lucian a pointed stick and said, "It is for Lucian, from our interaction, *to bring to light* a name for me." He moved outside the circle. Lucian entered the space alone, squatted by the limb and began to twirl a small pointed stick on its surface.

As the first curl of smoke began to appear from the friction, Lucian said, "The name that comes to light tonight for him who began this tribe is…"

At the moment that the first small flame appeared beneath the curl of smoke, Lucian continued, speaking in the New Tongue, "…*Zoyan'qual, the earth that walks.*"

When Lucian stepped outside of the circle, the newly named Zoyan'qual stood within it and said, "Lucian, who by the hand print on the mesa became my brother, now is…" and in the New Tongue said the word that meant *chameleon-eyes.* "They change from green to gold to violet and hazel, reflecting outwardly the diversity of his feelings within."

Lucian placed his limb upon the one already there, and they began to flame in unison. He, too, now stood within the circle.

Zoyan'qual said, "And Earnest Longhorn's name is *he who shelters us.* In ways we do not know, he helps to make places for us to experiment and to grow like our fragile crops among the cliffs."

Longhorn entered the circle, placing his branch on the fire as Zoyan'qual continued the naming.

Dolphus. "*Explorer of the world*, for he would find out what is there and lead us all to his discoveries."

Normita. "*The dancing wind*, blowing free, causing us delight."

Jhenaw. "She is *visions animated*. For what she perceives within her mind, her hands compose."

Eriot. "*The finder of the pathway*. He looks beyond, to the hilltop, the goal, and does not stop until he knows a way to get there."

Orgol. "*Discoverer in the dawn*. Each day he emerges and excitedly finds new things he did not notice the day before."

Reendo. "Our *brother of the fox*. So quick and agile, both of body and of mind. Even in his repose, his eyes and ears miss nothing. He sniffs the wind and receives the story of the land."

Then Zoyan'qual said, "And Beth…" At the mention the name, she jarred as if some jolt had shocked her from within. "…is *moon behind the clouds*. We see its light on all it touches, yet it does not reveal itself."

She stood and moved into the circle, placed her branch upon the fire, staring at it as if seeing something for the first time, and as she did, tears moved down her cheeks, prisming the firelight. In the almost-silence, they heard the sounds of burning branches, the near sounds of small night creatures, the distant sound of coyotes howling.

They all stood in the circle, around the fire, beneath the moon and stars, to receive the tribal name. "Together…" said Zoyan'qual in the New Tongue, "…as a tribe, we are called *the part of the universe that makes myths*."

32

Walter and Janice Pandra's balloon had flown above the ridges and desert again, carrying the children on the wind. That evening, after the children had gone home, and Longhorn took

Walter walking to explore the twilight desert, Lucian and Janice sat beneath the cottonwoods in the yard.

"Since I must return to the university in January to continue with my courses," said Lucian, "I want to complete them as rapidly as possible. If I can write my master's paper at the same time the courses are underway, I can finish sooner. If there is any way the children can not only be in the city with me, but can attend the classes with me, I want to work with them on a *translation* of all the course work into writing and illustrations that elementary students, themselves, can understand.

"Instead of the teachers always having concepts that they keep like alchemic lore from the students, I want to produce a book so that students can be co-participators in the process. An empowerment for them to know the process and procedures behind the daily routine. So if what's happening in their class rooms does not fulfill the best of learning concepts, they can have awareness of this, a vocabulary with which to speak, suggestions they can make for doing it differently.

"I would like to end up with a study, co-authored by them, edited and supervised by me, illustrated by them, breaking down the educational concepts to make them available to the users, the receivers of the process. The children"

By the time Walter and Longhorn returned, Janice had approved of Lucian's proposed project and agreed to serve as major advisor.

"Have you already told him?" Walter asked Janice.

"No, I wanted to let you do it."

"Lucian, we started thinking that rather than trying to find some other location, you should move the Worm Farm School into our house for the semester. We have a U-shaped place with a patio and garden in the middle, that continues on its open side out into a fenced-in back yard. Our children are grown up and away now, themselves, and that makes their rooms available too."

Lucian looked at Longhorn.

Longhorn said one word, "Yes."

. . .

The children had shouted their approval when they heard the plans.

Longhorn already had been looking for some vehicle for road trips. Between him and the owners of the Junk Shop, who sometimes had unusual trade-ins, they secured an old school bus. It showed the wear of many years, many paint jobs beyond its school use, but solid, sound, reliable. Quaint, different, unusual, fitting in nowhere, a *one-of-a-kind*.

When it was parked at the worm farm, beside Gitano's old car that they had outgrown, the bus looked right, somehow. As if it had been sitting there all along, weathering in the desert. Customers coming for their worms felt something different had been added but were not sure what. The bus seemed camouflaged, disguised, matching its new surroundings so exactly, it called no attention to itself. It *belonged*. The children called it that, *the bus that belonged*.

In this vehicle, with the children and their baggage secured inside, Lucian sat in the front seat, opposite Longhorn in the driver's seat.

The parents came and cheered and waved at the improbable departure, the bus heaving off along the dusty road.

"I wish I were Normita's age," her mother said, "I'd rather be on there with them." .

Eriot's father said, "I have a hard time explaining all this to our friends."

"I've stopped trying to," Dolphus' father shrugged. "Heck, they can't explain to me why they watch Monday Night Football. Why should I try to explain why my son, who they think should be in *regular school*, is taking off with the worm farm proprietor, in a dilapidated bus, to stay with strangers in the city, miles away, and go to university classes or whatever."

. . .

The Pandras welcomed the arrival of the bus and its occupants and took them to the patio, where a sign on a tall stick, in the middle of a cactus bed, proclaimed, WORM FARM SCHOOL, CAMPUS THREE.

Janice introduced someone she had brought for the others to meet. Kayla. Living in the same county as the space center, she had been sent to the new consolidated school.

Kayla lived at the orphanage. A *found child* as those at the orphanage described her, she initially had no known connections of family. Later they pieced together some background. *Mother on drugs, on the street, sometimes involved in prostitution for survival. Father of Kayla unknown, mother now disappeared, probably deceased.*

Her short time at the consolidated school had not been pleasant, either for her or for the teachers. While she had bursts of enthusiasm and output, most of the time she withdrew in a morose mood.

Dr. Pandra had been contacted and the copies of the records forwarded to her for evaluation. As consultant, they awaited her recommendations. She had scheduled the week of Kayla's evaluations to coincide with the arrival of the worm farm group.

"Could Kayla join in whatever you're doing this week?" Janice asked the others.

Of course, was the response. Thereafter, Kayla asked endless questions. *What is Sanskrit? What is a Zoyan'qual? The letter 'K' is a picture of a what?* And she absorbed the other children's bundles of responses.

. . .

Housing arrangements for everyone at the Pandras evolved rather than being allocated. Janice and Walter walked them all through the house as he explained, "Here is the guest room space, and other bedroom space, and a sort of storage area. Any spaces that you find that you want are yours to use."

Some people started out in beds, others in sleeping bags. Some inside, others outside in tents. Some together, some alone. They created *nests*, rather than formal areas of living.

The *superstructure of their time management*, as Orgol called it, centered around Lucian's graduate classes. These, Janice had arranged for him and the children to attend together. A new experience for the graduate students and the faculty.

Lucian had homework time. But that included all of them, to some degree, since the children were learning the same material, in their own ways.

To free up as much time as possible from actual school work, Lucian had purchased all of the textbooks back when he first registered for classes. Had read the material. Had requested and received the syllabus for every class by mail or on line, immediately after registering. Had completed all of the activities possible before coming to campus.

As a result of the pre-preparation, the time between classes, hours every day, provided spaces for trips to places unavailable in the desert. They started with the natural history museum.

In the evenings, events also evolved at the Pandra household. They continued with their discussions of the activities of the day, international songs, and their variety of sports from around the world at a local park. Walter joined in. He played, he sang, and he innovated.

Toward the end of the week, the Kayla question on her mind, Janice almost hesitantly approached Lucian, who was sitting out in the patio, completing an assignment. He let her make a few generalized statements which were obviously not what her mind focused on.

Then he said, in response to nothing she had verbalized, "Yes, the children are enthusiastic about Kayla. Yes, they want her to be part of the Worm Farm School. Yes, they want to visit her home, the orphanage. Yes, you did just the right thing to bring her here so they could get acquainted. Yes, she has already asked us if she can *belong to us*. I told her *no, no one belongs to anyone else*, but we can choose to share ourselves with each other."

Janice sort of looked around, with a little, "Oh." And then after a pause, asked, "Was I that obvious?"

She hummed for a moment, then said, "Okay, what else can I ask about? Is that your assignment for Pratt's class for tomorrow? That convoluted thing about…" She caught herself and stopped. "I guess I'm not supposed to say that."

Lucian said, "Actually, I'm working on an assignment due a month from now. We started on Pratt's material earlier. It *was* convoluted, and seemed difficult to apply, but…" And he dug down beneath the papers he was working on, "…look what the children did with it." He handed her a loose-leaf notebook.

She perched her half-glasses on her nose. "But this makes sense!" she said. "It really does!"

"Well," said Lucian, "as I go over all the material with the children, after they've heard the class lectures with me and I *translate* it, we try to divide it down to the *simplest-possible* component parts. A series of them.

"We layered out the names of the theorists, their theories, their dates, their contexts of place and social conditions, talked about each simple unit of the theory. Then, for example, here..." and he turned the notebook to a particular page, "...is the first one Dolphus did. Look how he took this from the abstract to the concrete. And look on the next page at the picture he drew to illustrate it. And then look at the kinesthetic activity for learning it he has outlined on the next page."

"How did they get this background material straight, you know, *organized?*" she asked.

"Have you looked in your yard lately? We sort of confiscated it like the desert area in back of worm farm. When we were talking about different artists one day at the farm, and trying to get some idea of when they lived in relation to each other, we wrote their names on flat sticks and their birth dates, then measured off a line where each year was represented by one foot. Then we stuck the sticks into the ground. Very quickly we had the beginning of our time line."

"Beginning?"

"Well, it grew from there. When we were listening to Bach and Beethoven, Reendo, without saying anything about doing it, just wrote down their names and birth dates, and trotted out onto the desert, and put them in place with the artists. Then came the other things. The date of first ice cream cones, when we were talking about that. With that one, they drew a picture of one, attached it to the stick, put it in the ground, next to the artists and musicians. Then the first radar, television, microwave oven, electronic computer."

Janice rose and walked toward the back yard. There, stretching from one end to the other, were sticks holding cards, with the names, dates, locations, and theories, from Pratt's material, untangled, spread out, visual, orderly.

"Lucian..." Janice began, in a tone that suggested she would never finish the sentence. Instead, she was on her knees reading the simplified history of educational theory stretching across her yard.

A package arrived from Longhorn. He had been to the canyons to see Zoyan'qual. The youth had given him some dried plants to forward on to the others. The note said, *Since all of you will be exposed to another environment, here is some echinacea plant to help preserve health. It seems to stimulate the immune system. Just prepare and use it as described here.*

A question in Zoyan'qual's note concerned the development of the New Tongue. *Since we are progressing with trying to develop the spoken form, it would be well to develop a written form as well. I assume no language yet in the world uses all the sounds that humans are capable of producing. Why not see if we can build it into this one. Has anyone ever studied this before? Could there already be a list of all sounds in all languages already existing and described?*

Lucian reflexively took a pen and paper and began to draw two diagrams of cross-sections of a human facial profile with exaggeratedly open mouths. Positioned onto these, he began to write symbols.

"What are those?" Kayla asked.

"One is for all the consonants and the other is for vowels of all languages, each showing the positions where a person produces them."

"Where did it come from?"

"The International Phonetic Association. They published the International Phonetic Alphabet first in 1888." He wrote the phonetic charts out in their entirety from memory, with a sample word for each sound from a variety of languages. Soon Janice looked over his shoulder, jotting down something in her notebook as the children asked questions.

Reendo asked what *phonetic* meant.

"One symbol for one sound. So that once we learn the symbol, it will always stand for only that sound. We could transcribe what anyone says in any language and be able to reproduce it, even if we didn't yet know what the meaning is. In contrast, in many languages, like English, letters can often stand for several different sounds, depending on how they're used."

Dolphus asked how Lucian had learned it. He had been fascinated when he had discovered it in a book once while he roamed the stacks of the university library and then enrolled in a phonetics course to deepen his understanding. After that, he had written all of his college class notes in phonetic symbols.

In his reply to Zoyan'qual, he suggested that the symbol for the first sound in the name *Zoyan'qual* be in the form of an "X" with an additional line starting at the midpoint and going straight up between the two raised arms. This, he suggested, could represent not only the sound, but with the suggestion of arms, legs, and torso and head could also stand for the whole concept of *human: the earth that walks*.

By the end of the week, the children had learned all of the phonetic symbols of the international alphabet. In addition, they had added the names of early association members Otto Jesperson, Paul Passy, and Henry Sweet to their outdoor time line. Lucian mentioned casually that Henry had been the model for the character of *Henry Higgins* in George Bernard Shaw's play *Pygmalion*. That began a series of related spin-off activities, including reading the play aloud together, watching the musical based on it, studying the life of Shaw, and exploring the profession of *linguist*. They delved into Greek and Roman mythology to explore Pygmalion, king of Cyprus, who became enamored of a statue of Aphrodite, and the story by Ovid, the Roman poet, in *Metamorphoses*, who wrote of the sculptor, Pygmalion, who carved an ivory statue of his concept of an ideal human figure, fell in love with his creation, and prayed to Venus to bring it to life, which she did.

. . .

"I have never had more fun, than with your group," Walter told Lucian one evening, after they had all eaten in the patio and the children were playing a game that Kayla had invented. She said it *combined agility of mind and body*, and that she had thought of it when Dr. Pratt's lecture had gotten particularly tedious, right after he had said that *we must be concerned with developing the combined agility of mind and body*.

As he watched the children leap through various parts of a maze marked off on the ground, answering history questions as they went, Walter said, "I've got a week coming up when I'm going to be conducting some evening meetings, but I'll have the days off. I can't think of anything more interesting than to do something with them."

"Could you get us into the power plant," Lucian replied, "the sewage treatment center, water purification system, the various utility services? We've just been talking about the *between things*, as Orgol calls them. He said that water comes down in rain, then water comes out of the faucet. But what are the *between things*? And that started a whole series of questions. Where does the *electricity* come from? What happens after you *flush*. They need to see the whole infrastructure of the city."

"I know someone in the water purification plant, if you want to start there. And we can network out to the others," Walter smiled. "I'm going to enjoy this myself." With barely a pause he added, "And tell me more about this Henry Sweet."

33

Operation Infrastructure got under way. Like most of their other activities, it soon found its symbolic counterpart appearing in the yard. In a corner appeared a strip of blue cloth representing the river; an old colander representing a well; little boxes representing purification plants and office buildings and homes; an old commode float with its stem end stuck in the ground, with the ball in the air, representing a water tower; assorted tubes, and pieces of hose that Walter scrounged out of various storerooms, that represented the water pipes. A tangle of other materials soon represented the return water and sewage systems.

They built the electric system model inside, in the hallway, operated with a little generator that actually powered a variety of little lights. As it grew, it moved from the hallway into the front room. Walter got out an electric train, and the children wound its tracks amidst the enlarging model.

Soon after that, they replicated everything from the outside model in a refined form on the inside, as part of the indoor model as well. They connected little tubes that actually carried water powered by a miniature pump that Walter found at a hobby shop. Tubes and wires proliferated. This village had a life of its own.

Daily, whatever they had seen became part of the infrastructure of their expanding model.

Kayla stood back observing it one evening and said, "It's starting to look like a miniature holiday village, *with its guts exposed.*"

Janice Pandra made a quick notation in her notebook that she carried with her all the time now.

. . .

They walked through power plants and sewage treatment facilities, went out on vehicles from the electric company to check lines and joined work teams digging out underground pipes.

The project spread to other services. Someone would notice another potential destination as they rode along the street and then call out the name. Eriot, looking out the window of the water system repair truck at a building they were passing, said, "*Fire station!*" And that joined the itinerary list. So with the police station, street repair crews, and garbage collectors.

With the law enforcement officers, they rode in patrol vehicles and cruised the city. The fire truck, during its practice runs to locate house numbers in their district, took the Worm Farm School crew with them.

There were certain underground walks overlooking the sewage flow below, in the downtown area, which their guides thought safe for them to experience. As a result, they went underground, walking the hollow corridors below the city. At various non-dangerous locations, the guides popped up the manhole covers and let them emerge into the sunlight before descending again below the streets.

"Are they *person-hole* covers now?" Dolphus asked.

. . .

It had happened that Gertrude, the bank teller, had business in the city. She was in the process of conducting her transactions downtown, when she noticed, at one of the corners, that some repairs were in progress, where orange-stripped wooden horses and barrels blocked off a section of the street.

As she passed by, absently watching the urban scene, her mind on her next activity, a manhole cover slowly pushed up from beneath, in the cordoned-off section. The emerging man did not particularly warrant her attention. But what happened next riveted her full faculties. Following the man came of series of children. That was curious enough. But not just any children. It was *those* children.

After she returned to her little town near the worm farm and to her bank counter, she said over her shoulder to the man in the glass-windowed office, "You know how they've not been in here recently? Well, I know why now. They are *migrating*. Here, they were on *land*. Then they were in the *air*. Now, there, they are *tunneling under the ground*."

"*Who's* migrating and tunneling under the ground?"

"The worm children."

A pause. Then from the office: "It seems appropriate, somehow."

Gertrude turned and gave him a perplexed look.

"Just think about it," he said. "It'll come to you."

. . .

Reendo's grandmother arrived. She brought with her a variety of foods that she felt they could not get in the city. The Pandras' house yielded yet another sleeping space for the four days she stayed.

Her visit coincided with their schedule for a trip to the mayor's office, where they were all made honorary citizens of the city. They sat in on meetings of several commissions and boards. One group discussed a diagram marked *City Government Organization*.

When one of the women on the council asked if they had any questions, Pica inquired, "Is the organization of this city basically like those of other cities?" The council woman answered affirmatively.

Then Pica asked, "Is it organized this way because it is the custom and just evolved like that? Or is it the most efficient system that you can devised and the most economical?"

When the woman expressed some of her own concerns about the points of efficiency and cost, Pica asked, "Could you consider starting again and designing a new organization?"

. . .

Everyone knelt, crouched, lay on their stomachs, peering at, worked on the expanding miniature city in the Pandras' front room.

Grandmother and Kayla worked with bridges. Reendo and Dolphus were adding parks. The others focused on assorted interests. Janice sat back and watched the whole enterprise, jotting occasional notations. Walter intervened at different building sites, asking if some materials from the workshop would help. If so, he and one or two others would move off to the place where they and his tools and all of their inventiveness produced more objects for the city. Lucian sat at a desk in the corner, preparing class work.

At nine o'clock, Grandmother stood up and called for everyone's attention. "Tomorrow," she said, "I must go back home. And I need to drive the bus back, because as many of your parents as can want to come and have the fun of riding the bus up, like you did. So I'm going to bring them back for a visit as soon as we can arrange it. But tonight, we need to celebrate this special date."

Everyone shifted enough to form a loose semi-circle at the edge of the city. Janice searched inwardly for some memory of what this *special date* was.

"This date marks the discovery of Europe," she began, "in 1493 of the common era. Our ancestors who lived on this continent now called North America, knew from legends of the probable existence of other places across the waters.

"A major decision they had to make was whether to expend all of the effort in constructing sea-worthy vessels to proceed on this great exploration, or to let others from the as-yet undiscovered lands take the risks and provide the transportation for us. This latter course of action was taken.

"So it was that a scraggly group of their people, mainly illiterate deckhands and currently unemployed mercenaries, headed by a man named Christopher, did that task, and brought the taxi-ships that we needed for transportation. They brought three, but owing to their poor training, managed to sink their flagship on a coral reef. The driver of this ship even cut down the mainmast to lighten the vehicle once it stalled on the reef. One mismanagement after another sank it. So that only left two vessels for us to sail on.

"No matter, we were ingenious and made do with the space available and some of us sailed back with them. It was on March 4, 1493, that we officially landed on and discovered that new world. Our people named the place where we first set foot, *the river of blue waters*, and claiming it in name of the tribe. The people who transported us called it the *Tagus estuary*, a few miles from a place called in their native tongue as *Lisbon*.

"We rested there briefly, and then went five days later to meet the chief of Portugal. He wasn't the chief who had put up the money for the transport vehicles for us, so we went over to the place where the next tribe of European aboriginals lived, and on March 15, met the chief of Spain there.

"These European aboriginals were not too strong and began to succumb to a disease our people had long known. It is now called *syphilis*. With us, it was milder and prolonged. Among them, it became a plague. At first, they called it *the pox*. Columbus' men had sexual activity with us when they landed in our land. Then, when we arrived in Europe, we had more sexual contact with their aboriginals.

"At first, in fact for about a century, they couldn't figure out how the pox, or plague, was spread, or where it came from. They just knew it came from somewhere outside of wherever they lived. So, at first, the Italians and English called it the French disease. The French thought it was an Italian disease. The Polish called it the German disease. The Russians called it the Polish disease. In the Middle East and India, they called it the European disease; inland China called it the Canton disease, while in Japan, they thought it was a Chinese disease. Some people called it the Jesuits' disease.

"Those people were all so sexually active, whatever their social class, or religion, or nationality, that syphilis swept across Europe, and on throughout Africa and Asia, and all in fourteen years, before Columbus died. And when you read about how he ranted and raved in his last days, it's pretty obvious that he had syphilis, and it had reached his brain.

"It killed enough royalty that two European dynasties

entirely died out: the House of Valois in France and the House of Tudor in England. Also Mary Queen of Scots and her two husbands, and Francis I, and Cesare Borgia. Some say even the Pope wouldn't let people kiss his feet any more because they were so disfigured with the disease.

"Shakespeare, one of their aboriginal writers, mentions it in his plays. Since for a hundred years they didn't know how it was being spread, they tried different things. They closed public baths, even kissing was discouraged, and shared drinking cups were discontinued. And when the real method of transmission was suspected, publications on *safe sex* appeared.

"Of course, in the meantime, our people were dying of small pox and pneumonia.

"These people of this new world we had discovered were not particularly exact with words. Since *we* had just discovered *them*, they obviously lived in the *new* world. But they were copycats and began referring to *our* land, the *old* world, as the *new* world. There was confusion for a time.

"We were able to observe their costumes, their native religious festivals and superstitions, their quaint customs, and their mythologies.

"The discoverers of Europe were from our Taino tribe, from the island that was later called Hispanola. So this day of the discovery of Europe, I call *Taino's Day*.

"In the kitchen, in honor of Taino's Day, I have prepared some of the foods of the new world we discovered. Such as pizza, from their Italian tribe. Follow me to the kitchen, and we'll continue the celebration."

They followed, chanting, *Taino's Day, Taino's Day,* and wishing each other a *Happy Taino's Day!*

34

When Beth came for the first time to see Campus Three and finally located the house where the Pandras lived, the hour was so late that she hesitated to disturb them and started to drive away. Yet there was a light showing around the edges of the window shades in the front.

She walked onto the front porch and heard no sounds from inside. She wrote a note and tried to stick it firmly on the door handle, when her efforts jarred open the unlocked door.

Through the opening, she saw the edge of a miniature city. Making a silent effort to see more, her curiosity aroused, the door swung open further. She glimpsed a child's foot and ankle looking like its owner was lying flat on the floor. Concerned, she quietly stepped inside and peered around the corner of the hallway, trying to see the rest of the child.

The foot and ankle belonged to Eriot, who lay fast asleep on the rug. His head rested on Lucian's leg as a pillow. Lucian, too, was asleep. Lucian lay, arms and legs splayed out in four directions, and all being used as pillows. Dolphus' head rested on one of Lucian's arms. Jhenaw rested on the other. His stomach served as Pica's pillow. Each had a headrest of some part of him. All asleep.

Whatever they had been doing, they had probably sprawled out on the floor to talk about it, and after a full day, had dozed off in the process. Nor did it take much imagination to see what the focus of their interest had been, for the city twinkling with tiny lights spread out in back of them.

Beth stood and stared. She wanted to record it, every detail of it, in her memory. She thought of pictures illustrating the story of Gulliver, staked out on the ground by the Lilliputians. In this case, the Lilliputians were using him for their pillows.

So intently did she focus on the scene, that it startled her when she became aware of a movement over to the side, from the doorway. A lady was beckoning her to come with one hand, while the other index finger up to the lips signaled her not to make noise.

Beth obeyed and found herself led to the kitchen. "You must be Beth," Janice said. "They were hoping you would come back onto the campus sometime from your digs and would come by before you left again. Do you have a place to stay? As you can see, we have all sorts of accommodations here," smiling and nodding in the direction of the room they had come from.

Beth started to refuse the offer, but the internal vision of

149

being *here*, instead of wherever the alternative *there* was, made her shift her words even as she spoke them. She would stay and wanted to be in the front room with the others. She explained that she had a sleeping bag outside and would bring it in and be quite comfortable.

Beth sat on her bed roll, in the shadows at the corner of the room, watching the sleeping forms and the city they had been building.

. . .

Breakfast preparation was a sight to behold, Beth thought. They had decided on an Indonesian breakfast this morning, and Dolphus and Kayla coordinated the kitchen preparation. The others orbited in and out, depending on how long it took them to do their parts.

Between the kitchen activities, they were vacuuming rooms, dusting, washing and drying clothes. All this they referred to as their *local environment infrastructure preparation.* They had analyzed the whole house and the area outside for each task of *basic life support,* as they called it. Everyone did some different aspect each morning.

Lucian had emphasized the importance of having private spaces here, so each had identified some corner of a room or the yard, for a particular meditation place, a quiet place, a place to be alone for a while.

Walter, who was enjoying the whole process of watching his house evolve into something quite unnameable, had brought home large packing crates. These, he helped the individuals organize into their unique spaces. The crates were big enough for one child to sit inside cross-legged or to lie down in comfortably.

It was to these places that each person retreated after the *personal infrastructure* activities ceased. At that point, Beth consulted Lucian and Walter about the content of her truck.

"I have it," she said. "The question is, what to do with it."

Lucian immediately knew what the *it* was, to which she referred. Walter did not, but grinned in genuine anticipation, saying, "I haven't the foggiest notion what *it* is, so why do I feel this is really going to be fun?"

"I have the boxes of the disassembled plastic replica, full

scale, of the dinosaur, that the university is disposing of."

Walter found this unexpected information irresistibly funny, and his unrestrained outburst of laughter brought Janice.

"What is it?" she said.

He cackled so hard, he couldn't get the words out, and Beth had to repeat her description. Walter looked at the look on Janice's face and vented another peel of laughter. This last brought the meditators from their packing crates, to surround them. Normita asked, "What's happening?"

Now Janice looked at Walter looking at her, and they both started to laugh. Beth had to repeat.

Lucian asked Janice and Walter if it would be all right to unload the boxes here at the house, and then see how much would fit on the bus for the next trip back to the worm farm.

"Or," said Jhenaw, "when our parents come back with Grandmother in the bus, maybe they could take some of it back, and we could take the rest later."

As they were unloading the boxes, a familiar sight came cruising down the street. The bus. *Their* bus. The *bus that belonged*. Longhorn driving. And hanging out the windows like schoolchildren on a field trip, the parents, shouting and waving.

They helped move in the remaining boxes, and, ready for anything, returned to the bus, with the children and Lucian, to set off for his Friday classes.

35

Dr. Rutledge watched Lucian arrive in class.

Lucian came in far enough ahead of the others that Rutledge had time to say, with a professional chuckle, "Where are your little charges today?"

Before Lucian could respond, the children entered.

Rutledge then just had time to remark, "What? Haven't you added any more since last time?" before the parents entered.

"Well, Lucian," Rutledge managed after a moment, "perhaps since you *brought* most of the class, you would like to go ahead and *teach* it today."

Lucian stood and moved to the front before Rutledge could say he was joking. Rutledge lectured straight from the book, and since Lucian had purchased the textbooks weeks before the semester started, he had long since read and organized all of the material.

He had started developing, at that same time, a notebook for each class. After reading the original major studies cited in the texts, he had summarized their findings along with his text notes, developed possible activities to illustrate each concept, and had tried them out with the children under the cottonwoods at the worm farm.

Knowing where Rutledge had ended his lecture last time, Lucian stated the heading of the next section and said, "Normita?"

She remembered the discussions and briefly summarized them in her own words with examples.

Lucian stated the next heading and asked Reendo to speak. When Reendo finished, remembering the next topic, he casually named it and called on Dolphus, who was sitting next to him, to cover it.

Pica, for her part, while speaking, transformed everything she said simultaneously into kinesthetic movements, until even Dr. Rutledge, after a particularly involved gymnastic-dancing sequence, asked her to repeat what she had said, so he could see the movements again.

Each one, in turn, dealt with a subsection. Lucian, himself, had only uttered those first words naming the section. The whole process took a few minutes, and Lucian sat down.

Rutledge rose slowly from where he had been watching and listening. He stood at the podium, cleared his throat, and with no additional comment, began his lecture with the section following the one Lucian and the children had addressed.

. . .

As Dr. Rutledge walked down the hallway after class, he saw Dr. Pandra walking in the opposite direction.

He stopped her, without even a greeting and said, "That boy...."

Dr. Pandra just looked at him, waiting.

Dr. Rutledge continued, "I wonder about him."

Still no verbal response.

Dr. Rutledge exclaimed, "Lucian. He comes to class with those children. I've accommodated that into the classroom. But the more I think about it, shouldn't they be *doing something?* Shouldn't they be *in school?*"

"This *is* a school," Dr. Pandra said, suppressing a smile. "Remember I sent you the memo, and you said all right..."

"I haven't had time to read all that. Actually the first time, he brought that whole bunch of kids, I thought it was for just one day. And they've kept coming back."

"Our understanding was..." Dr. Pandra started.

"Next," Dr. Rutledge interrupted, "not only them, today, in troop these other people. Did he say they were parents?"

"Steve, if you're having second thoughts..."

"And the children started talking in class today," Dr. Rutledge continued.

"Disrupting the lesson?"

"Summarizing the lesson."

"Isn't that..."

At this moment, Bill Elvan, the student work-study secretary came jogging from the office toward Dr. Rutledge, giving one of his condensed messages, accompanied by urgent gestures. "Phone. Dean. Project Budget. Immediately."

Dr. Rutledge called back to Dr. Pandra as he hastened behind Bill Elvan to the office, "I've got to talk with you about this. You're got to fill me in more. Can I drop by your house on my way home where we won't be interrupted so we can talk about this?"

"Steve, I..."

"Thanks. I don't know what I'd do without you. See you." And without missing a beat, turned toward the moving figure of Bill Elvan in front of him, saying, "How did he sound? Did he *sound* urgent? Did he say anything else..."

. . .

Walter Pandra had returned to his home, or whatever it was evolving into, which he liked better and better, than whatever it had been, before Janice returned from her office at the university, before Lucian, the children, and the parents returned from their sojourns.

The boxes of model dinosaur bones were stacked in the hallway and along the wall of the front room. He stood looking at them, running his hand over the exterior, as if to receive tactually some sensation of their contents.

He walked on by them to his room, changed into his *relaxing* clothes, and found himself again at the boxes, running his hand over their surface, trying to receive some vision of what their assembled contents might look like.

His curiosity increased, as he thought, *it will be erected at the worm farm in a few months. He could transport the balloon down again, and at the same time see the finished product then, but on the other hand...*

He walked on to the kitchen, poured a glass of water, and found himself again standing by the boxes, stroking them with his free hand.

Of course, he thought, *it may be a while before anyone returns. What harm would it be to open one box, just peek in it, see what some of the skeleton parts look like.*

He cut the tape on one of the large boxes, opened the four flaps of the top, and stared at the ivory-colored pieces within. He stroked them, satisfied with the authentic look of the casts. He cross-closed the four flaps, took his glass of water, and went sipping it down the hall.

A few minutes later, he returned, opened the box again, looked around without thinking, as if to see if anyone watched him, and lifted out a piece. It had a number written on it and little holes where something could attach it to something else. He held it in front of him with both hands, held it above his head, as if picturing the creature assembled.

He laid the first bone on the floor and took out a second one, laying it randomly beside it. Then a third. And a fourth. He noticed one that was cracked. He got a bonding material from the workshop, repaired it, and laid it outside to dry. He looked for others in the box that needed repair.

He opened a second box and then a third. He started taking the bones outside and laying them on the ground in the extensive patio area, in the U-shape of the house. In one of the boxes, he found the assembly plans. He unfolded it like a treasure map and found the diagram of where to place each numbered piece.

The rib cage began to take a general pattern as the separate bones lay in relationship to each other. The tail bones began to spread across the ground toward the back yard at the open end of the patio.

. . .

Longhorn had stopped the bus in front of the Pandras' house to let off the parents, because the children had been scheduled for a limited number of seats at a live evening television newscast, as they studied broadcasting. The parents had already made the rounds of classes, the library, and a tour of the highway department with them. Longhorn promised to return as soon as possible to drive them all to a motel.

The parents entered the house to find plastic bones strewn from open boxes in the living room out onto the patio. They saw the emerging pattern of the creature lying on the ground, and realized that Walter, beyond all hope of returning the bones to the boxes, was determined to see the whole array spread out.

Dolphus' father peered at the plans on the ground and looked up in the air as if he, too, could imagine seeing the creature assembled. "What holds it up?" he asked Walter.

Walter showed him the poles for the frame that formed the support. Soon everyone was participating in the process of assembling it.

. . .

The children, on their return from the telecast and a tour of the studios, arrived back at the Pandras' house to find their parents, under Walter's direction, with Beth's assistance—she had dropped by to see what was happening tonight—putting together the bones, attaching them to the upright mounts. They joined in immediately.

Lucian began naming each bone as it was put in place, and the children began to echo the names. It became a game of repetition, to start at one point in the partly assembled anatomy, and name them, to see how far they could go. The parents joined in the rhythmic chant.

Dolphus, like a circus-barker, gestured at Pica and said, "The shape-shifter becomes a dinosaur!" Pica's response to the assembled bones was a work of pantomimed gymnastic art, while

155

Normita danced in delight around her.

Janice arrived home to find this full scale skeleton of the Mesozoic Era evolving in the patio. She found herself making notes of the whole process. She joined in the chanted names of the bones and found, to her own surprise, that she was learning them, without any particular effort to do so.

She had gone back into the kitchen to think about supper for the dinosaur crew, when she heard the doorbell. She opened the door to see Dr. Rutledge standing there, true to his word, dropping by to discuss that strange student in his class, the diverse children who followed him around, and the new cadre of adults who had invaded his room.

"I appreciate your talking with me about this," Dr. Rutledge began. "You can't imagine what it's like to have that array of people invade my classroom and..."

Dr. Pandra took a deep breath as she motioned him in. She led him through the hall toward the patio. He glanced toward where the *city with guts* was evolving in the front room.

She said, as they arrived at the patio door, "We're having a little dinosaur party. Would you care to join us?"

She opened the door, and he followed her into the surrealistic sight of *those people*—*that* student, *those* children, and *those* adults—erecting a skeleton of enormous proportions, chanting the names of the bones as they did so.

36

Walter, Longhorn, Lucian, and Beth went out and accumulated enough food for the dinosaur builders. They laid it out on the kitchen counters, all helped themselves, sat outside around and under their new creation, and ate.

Beth said, "It never looked so good in the university museum. It's coming alive."

"Like your people in the digs, when you talk about them," said Normita.

"Lucian," asked Janice, "the naming of the bones. How did you ever come to know them?"

He reflected a moment. "When I was growing up, I spent time in the museums. In the natural history museum, I would make the rounds and read the descriptions. I liked the dinosaur hall. It was like entering a different world. One day, a small group came in while I was there, with someone giving them a tour. That was the first time I realized they had tours. I memorized the tour schedule and turned up for every one of them I could.

"I trailed them so much, the museum workers began to recognize me. One day, one of them was pointing out to a group the difference between the color on the dinosaur skeleton of the real fossil bones and the synthetic materials used to fill in the missing parts. In pointing to them, he casually mentioned the names of some of the bones.

"The next time I trailed him, and we got to the skeleton, and as he was about to make the same reference, he started sneezing. I didn't mean to, but found myself saying his next sentence, including the names of the bones. When the group had gone, he stood there with me by the dinosaur and pointed to some of the other parts, and asked me if I would like to know their names too.

"It was like the *magic of naming* in the old sagas. Naming was a kind of ownership. People who came and looked at it saw it only on the outside. I owned it *inside*, more and more, every time I could name its parts.

"The guide waited each time until the group had left, and then would ask me to name all that I had already learned. Then he would add some more. And then, one day, he took me back into the storage rooms where they kept the skeletons and the workrooms where they prepared them. He said I could be his assistant on weekends. And then he started letting me conduct the tours with him."

. . .

After eating, the parents asked where the nearest motel was. "Let you go to a motel?" said Walter, melodramatically. "Never. Just because people are strewn all over the place doesn't mean there isn't space here for more."

Some of the parents tried to make a lame protest that they really should get a motel and not impose on the Pandras, but their hearts were not in it. It was more fun here. Sleeping bags,

157

blankets, couch cushions, innovative improvisations emerged, until everyone had a place to sleep. Inside, outside.

In the corner of the front room where Lucian, Longhorn, Beth, and Jhenaw settled with their bedrolls, Kayla had come over and wanted to talk about something related to the orphanage.

Beth became all alertness. "An orphanage? An orphan? You are an *orphan*? Oh, Kayla, how fortunate you are. You should thank all the stars in the heavens for such a gift!"

The phrases outpoured with such feeling that all those nearby looked at her, including Kayla.

"Fortunate?" Kayla said. "Thankful?" She had never heard the words uttered before in relation to her circumstances. She had become accustomed to the wistful looks that people gave her, to the *Oh you poor thing* tone of voice. She had been made to feel by such people, by the responses she had gotten all her life, by what she saw on television and read in books, that she was deficient. She considered herself as a broken piece of something, of some whole that no longer remained. A discarded remnant at a discount store that people looked at but no one bought.

Her eyes became wide and focused at Beth's proclamations.

"Fortunate?" Kayla repeated.

Beth, as if she had no realization of Kayla's surprised reaction, spoke of what to her seemed a truism.

"Oh, yes!" said Beth. "To be so free. To be detached from the expectations of a family culture, and relatives, from people who prescribe your life, so you never can find it yourself. They take it away from you before it is ever yours. You are free! You stand in the midst of a world of wonder, of opportunities, with no ties to a tradition, no demanded duties."

At this, with emotion, she reached forward and swept Kayla into her arms and hugged her, rocking back and forth. "Oh, Kayla, I envy you. I envy you and would trade places with you if the stars above could grant the wish. Be joyful and be free!"

When they slept that night, just past the west boundary of the city with guts, there lay Longhorn, and Lucian, and then Beth on her pallet with Kayla snuggled at her side. Several times in the dark hours, each of them opened their eyes and stared upward toward the dim ceiling of the room and then toward each other.

37

Lucian rode the horse toward the canyon country on this spring break from the university, while the children spent time with their families, and Longhorn had moved off on one of his own pathways.

Leaving behind both the university and the worm farm, Lucian breathed in the air of the desert, feeling himself exist as part of its system of life. He inhaled the sage and other subtle scents from afar. When the sun set, he rode on into the night illuminated by the full moon.

As the canyons appeared on the horizon of the nightscape, amidst the sounds of the insects, the night creatures, the throat-thrown yowls of the coyote, and the huskier howl of wolves, amidst them all came another sound. A single flute, its notes dancing on the air, binding the other sounds in the web of its silvery tones.

Lucian, as he rode, took a flute, and in a lull in the tones he had heard, sent on the winds an answering melody of the desert night.

The messages wove back and forth in the winds, answering and blending. The notes from afar became louder. He followed them to a ridge. Left the horse by a thicket and stream. Walked upward along the flank of the rising land. Still hearing and responding.

He walked onward following the notes that led him toward the crest and along the serpentine way of the ridge.

The two flutes played together now, a dual harmony, blending, haunting the air of the desert with their audible shapes.

At the far end of the ridge, sitting cross-legged on a flat rock that jutted out into the space far above the silvered land below, Zoyan'qual merged his music with the winds. The lunar light etched his back and shoulders, his hair and two feathers above each ear, along with the furry peak-eared shape of a desert fox on the ground beside him, like a shimmering night mirage of the music he produced.

Lucian seated himself beside him, still playing in the harmonies of the desert, as the moon, above them both, measured the night with its ancient pace.

Beside Zoyan'qual were several flute-like instruments, various sizes and hollowed from different plants. He looked at Lucian and nodded downward toward them. They both tried them all, producing sounds, from the highest notes of slim reed flutes, to those low and mellow, of extended tubes carved from large limbs.

When the time felt right, and their last dual tones had vibrated into the breezes of night, they simply lay where they had sat, at the edge of this precipice, while the moon shone upon them and upon the desert fox that slept between them.

. . .

In the horizontal rays from the rising edge of the sundisk, they exchanged their dreams from the night. Taco trotted off along the ridge.

That day, they laid out with stones, about an extended circle, two overlapping calendars of rock, one for the seasons and one for the full moons. A central stone already stood, its rough-hewed shape rising from a broader base upward to a point. Throughout the phases of the moons and seasonal risings and settings of the sun, Zoyan'qual had marked with scratches on the hard surface, the locations where the shadows of the peak-stone fell. To these locations now, they levered large rocks.

When they had finished, Zoyan'qual led him across the rises and lowlands to another ridge where, centuries before, human ancestors had also moved their rocks into a circle, leaving the tale of their observations of the skies and its *eyes of day and night*.

. . .

They ran in the mornings. A sheer exhilaration in the running at the dawn time. Through the landscape, up the hills, over ridges, along dry arroyos. They ran, breathing in the sage-scented air. They practiced bounding up canyon sides like mountain sheep, from rock to rock.

They swam in the pools that formed in the rifts between

160

some of the canyons where water remained deep and clear. They sprinted around a rattlesnake sunning on a rock. They became a trio when Taco joined their chase of the morning wind.

They bounded in this way from one of the hidden food-growing places to another, gathering what they wished, settling where their feelings suggested, to eat from the bounty of the land.

Zoyan'qual introduced him to a lizard that would come to his hand and walk up his arms and across his shoulders. He showed Lucian a king snake, at the place where they sat eating their harvest, while the black and gold flecked creature wound its way among the rocks.

They stood so silently in a clump of trees near a water hole after a run along the canyon floor, that a bobcat lapping water sniffed at the air but did not see them.

Amid the pools Zoyan'qual pulled the reeds that grew. He wove them into flat pieces. He soaked them in water filled with minerals he had powered from a cave wall. With smooth-faced stones, they scraped the reeds into near pulp, the cross-grained fiber still intact and laid them on the clean rock surface to dry in the sun, producing a kind of parchment.

He showed Lucian the berries and bark that he boiled into liquid, thick enough to use as ink. Gave him a feather cut at the tip of the quill, to hold the ink to write with.

In the sun-dominated afternoon, when air wavered with the heat, they sat inside the *writing house* he had constructed in the deep shadows of the canyon. Breezes cooled by the pool below them rose through openings in the story beneath and moved through their room.

He showed Lucian the symbols he had made, sound by sound, from all the possibilities of making human speech. They practiced them, played with them, mixed consonants with vowels, and marked the reed paper with their ink.

They matched one sound with one symbol. Gradually their phonetic alphabet evolved. The New Tongue could be written. On reed papyrus. In ink of bark and berries. With quills from the birds of the sky.

38

The spring semester classes continued. Dr. Decke had ignored the children who accompanied Lucian. So far as he was concerned, this student, with the strangely luminous eyes, was baby-sitting a mixed brood for reasons he did not fully comprehend nor did he care to. The university faculty received notifications periodically *to fulfill the urban mission of our institution by meeting the needs of our diverse student body.* Dr. Decke followed directions as he interpreted them, so long as they did not interfere with his concept of class protocol. So far they had not.

On this particular day, soon after spring break ended, he felt expansive, even light hearted. For the first time he acknowledged the presence of the children as he introduced a sample of *name recognition in elementary classroom* practice.

"Here, in this sample lesson, we will imagine that we are in an elementary classroom," he said, "and we use the contextual names covered in the classroom exercises over a period of time. On an off day, such as a Friday, when everyone is restive, it can form a kind of diversion from the routine, while not straying too far from educational usefulness."

Then came his reference to the young observers in his class. "Children such as these might even find the exercise diverting for a time and could participate as we practice it, except..." He took square cards from a box and laid them on the desk. He held one up for everyone to inspect from a distance. "...except that I am using an advanced set that can even be appropriate in high school. We don't have one for the lower elementary levels currently available, but the process would be the same. So, although our little visitors *could* have participated if we had something on their level, it is not possible with these."

He pointed to the card. "On one side is a single name, like *Edgar.* In a hypothetical class, students would have to think of an historical figure who had this as one of his names. The exercise becomes challenging, because, as in this case, not always is the last name used, but sometimes a first, or middle, or even a title. So, let's try it out on ourselves, class."

Feeling included by the invitation, Dolphus said, "Edgar Allan Poe."

The teacher turned with a raised eyebrow toward him. "Yes. And then..." he flipped the card over, "on the other side are various aspects of the subject's importance that can be shared."

He had gone through several cards, with the children taking turns answering, and the university students in the class smiling at each other, as the children identified all of them.

Then came the name *Coleridge*. Reendo responded, "Samuel Coleridge-Taylor."

"You children are becoming a little eager with these," Dr. Decke said, "perhaps we'd better let the older people answer now. The answer is wrong, of course. It is Samuel *Taylor Coleridge*, and he's *not* in your children's books." He gave a knowing smile to the graduate students.

Reendo said, "Him, too," and picturing the worm farm time grid in his mind, continued, "he was born in 1772 and died in 1834, and wrote poetry. I like the *Rime of the Ancient Mariner*. But I was thinking of Samuel Coleridge-Taylor, who was born after that, in 1875 in London, and lived until 1912. He was the composer whose father was from West Africa and his mother from England. I remember he started playing violin at five. His *Ballade in A Minor* is beautiful. We listened to it. We're learning to play it."

"If you liked that one, can I do one?" Kayla volunteered. Before Dr. Decke could affirm or negate, Kayla assumed the teacher's role and said, "*Luther*."

"Martin Luther, theologian and orator," Decke blurted out in a kind of knee-jerk reaction. "Now I'll get on with our planned activity."

But Kayla, before he could continue, in a voice indicative of her fondness for and involvement in this new game, said, "The person I had in mind was *Luther Martin*, lawyer and orator, who defended Aaron Burr in 1807."

39

When the summer came, the children separated on travels with their families. Lucian had asked them to keep a journal of their individual journeys, along with photos to share. They were to record geological formations, architecture, plant and animal life, observations of behavior among people, conversational patterns and word usages in different regions, and their own reactions to what they saw.

They were to make a list of questions that occurred to them for which answers were not immediately available. He had urged the families to take along reference sources in the cars to look up information as they traveled. Each of them would return as a teacher for the others of the experiences of the summer.

Only Kayla had no family to take her on a journey. Dr. Pandra remedied that. She had received a Humanities Grant to conduct a summer project entitled *Cold-trailing the Appian Way*. She packed up Kayla and took her along to Italy, where, with camera and notebook, they would trace the remaining sections of the ancient road from Rome to its end. "Cold-trailing or cold-tracking," explained Dr. Pandra, "happens when the hound dogs come on the scent of the game too late for it still to be warm."

Beth was among those who saw them off at the airport. Hugging Kayla, she whispered, "Be free. Be free. And when you return, tell me what you have discovered about yourself along this Roman road."

. . .

A tap on the door. Lucian looked up from his thesis writing to see Walter looking in.

"Food," said Walter.

"Food?" said Lucian vaguely.

"You haven't eaten in two days," said Walter.

"Two days?" said Lucian, trying to remember what day it was.

His focus remained completely on the thesis. He needed to finish, to receive the degree to keep the certificate to continue the school.

Walter beckoned. He led Lucian to food in the kitchen.

While Lucian ate, Walter showed him a succession of post cards from Italy, from Janice and Kayla, tracking their Roman road.

Longhorn arrived the next day. Walter moved his own things aside in his office and made room for Longhorn to take over the desk.

Longhorn said to Lucian. "Give me the rough draft material as you finish it, and I'll do the best I can to double check spelling, grammar, continuity, the basics. And give you back corrected copy. In between, we'll take breaks, keep you fed, so you don't starve in the middle of the project."

. . .

On July 15, Lucian took a late break and walked the campus in the cooler evening air. The vague memory of his cross-country journey to place his message in books turned his steps intuitively into the library.

He browsed the stacks, gliding his eyes across the pages of those titles, long special to him, into which he had placed his messages. When a paper dropped from one of them, he started to put it back, then realized it was his own message, an anachronism of something that seemed ancient that had no place in the present. He crumpled in into his pocket and roamed further into the night.

On his return to the Pandras' home, he want back to his room and began once more to write. Time passed, as he transferred more material from his note cards into the rough draft. Contemplating more note cards, he walked down the silent hallway to the kitchen for a drink.

On the way back, the glass of pineapple juice in one hand and the note cards in the other, he freeze-framed in the middle of the shadowy hall. Through the concentration on the note cards, through the overall system of information he was organizing for the current thesis chapter in his mind, through the single-minded focus on his work, one long light-ray of a realization had penetrated from the outside. It penetrated through like a long streak of color and then exploded in a fireball of sudden realization.

He took the crumpled pages he had retrieved from the book in the library, smoothed them out and stared at them. One those messages which he had cast as if in bottles upon an ocean, for the currents to take to other persons waiting on their own private islands. But now came the realization—he had never placed copies of those pages in any book in this library. *How on earth did this...* His thought blurred into non-words.

. . .

At that same moment that Lucian stood unmoving in the hallway, others who had found his messages were together in Chicago.

The three who had met the year past came again to Buckingham Fountain. During the intervening months, they had met, phoned, written, finding a comfort in each other that they could not explain.

As they had traveled on their individual ways during the year, they had inserted copies of Lucian's message in books in other libraries, including the copy that Lucian had just found.

Jarmon Trander had been in Lucian's university city with the touring orchestra in which he played cello. Between performances, he had placed copies at the city library and also the one on campus. Lucian and the children had sat in the audience at the university auditorium and listened to the orchestra at the afternoon performance in which he had played.

On the afternoon of this Ides of July, the original three had strolled, circumambulating the Buckingham fountain again, each holding a volume, looking for others doing likewise. And one by one, they found them, fourteen more people in all, each with stories, each hesitant, each moved enough by the message to come, each feeling its resonance.

A fifteenth had arrived, but on finding out, as he told them, *that this wasn't something kinky*, he left.

They each, in turn, explained their coming. All had assumed they would meet the individual who wrote the note. All wondered about the person's identity and absence.

By the time the day ended, all seventeen had gone to Paygon Zelschmidt's house in Oak Park and talked into the night. They listened to each other's stories as they sipped mulled cider and Chilean chocolate.

Elaine Saynore, who came from the Broadway stage, had worked out a schedule so an understudy could replace her for the days she had planned around this Chicago journey.

"I was a reclusive child," she explained to the others. "Hid behind the characters I portrayed in school plays. Always looked for the mask of a part to hide behind, feeling that someday the right part would be like a doorway outward, that somehow what was behind the mask could enter the world. I go from one dramatic role to another, waiting for the moment to come."

Yanimo Yakamoto told about how he had never felt either Japanese nor American, but wondered if there was some other culture somewhere where he would feel comfortable. "When I read those words, on those pages, inserted in that book, it was like a message from that culture. I felt that I was journeying, not to Chicago, but to an unnamed land where I would finally meet my relatives."

The stories, as they unfolded, received the nodded recognition of the others. Not the outward events, which all differed, but the experience of seeking, of searching for something they commonly felt.

Harvey Krantz, an engineer from Los Angeles, jotted down some notes as people talked. Late in the night, he observed, "You know, I keep hearing recurrent words in our discussion, ones that I have a feeling for too. Listen to these. *Search, seek, quest, labyrinth, hidden, subterranean, shadowy, cavern, ancient...*" After he had read more of the list, they all nodded again, a strange sense of mutual recognition.

They talked until the dawn. Beavern Meedolay, a speech pathologist from Spokane, Washington, asked if the others had observed the same things she had. "Think for a minute," she said. "Don't most of you sit back and become the observer in most groups. Other people talk, you listen. You observe them interrupting each other, talking simultaneously, being louder than the others. By the time there's a lull and you get a word in, the subject has changed and there's been a whole evolution of ideas in the meantime, and you feel by then your comments are irrelevant to express. But did you notice *here*? In this room. The *listening*. I felt that I had never really been listened to in my life until tonight. There were silences, comfortable silences, between our speaking, thoughtful silences."

After their all-night marathon during which none had been aware of the passing time, they separated long enough to go back to their hotels and rest for a while. They re-gathered in the evening at the Oak Park home.

Sinston Baker, at eighteen, already a senior at an Oregon University, explored the organ pipes that lay everywhere around the house. "A dismantled organ," Paygon explained, "is *potential awaiting animation.*" He was in the process of repairing this one for a chapel near Starved Rock, Illinois.

"Here," Paygon, said, handing a six-foot pipe to Sinston, "blow." Sinston did, and a single swelling bass note filled the room. "Here," Paygon said, handing each a pipe and arranging them in a scale sequence.

They played melodies together, each using additional pipes of different octaves and different materials. A *group organ* evolved, as they blew into their pipes, and Paygon directed them.

Paygon hooked a blower to two of the longest pipes of slightly different length, that he placed a few feet apart. Their low tones vibrated the room. "Now walk around," he said. "The wave lengths will reinforce each other in places and be twice as loud, and two steps away, they will cancel each other out, and you will hear almost nothing." They tried and found it so.
. . .

When, after three days, the seventeen departed, they did not really separate. Although they returned to their parts of the country, as student, speech pathologist, actor, engineer, and all the other occupations and avocations, each had the names, addresses, phone numbers, and email information for all of the others.

No pause occurred following their return to their homes before they began contacting the others to continue conversations and share new thoughts.

Within a month, Sinston's university choir appeared in Carnegie Hall. When he said on the phone, before leaving for New York, in a call to Paygon, that he wished they could both be there to explore some of the dramas on and off Broadway, Paygon said simply, "Sure, I'll be there." They roomed together at a small hotel on forty-eighth street and immediately contacted Elaine Saymore, who was appearing at a theater two blocks away.

The three of them spent a week going to every show available and backstage at several of them. When one of Elaine's acquaintances asked where on earth the three of them—the actress, the teen-age student, and the organ builder in his seventies—had met, they all said in unison, "At Buckingham fountain." And added simultaneously, "On the Ides of July." And laughed.

. . .

When Jarmon's orchestra went on tour, he contacted the others along the way, and they gathered in two's and three's to do whatever their fancy guided them to.

When Jarmon sent Paygon descriptions of the places he had been and those of the group he had seen, Paygon added the accounts of his own journey to it and sent out a summary to the others. They all started sending him reports, and he compiled the information and shared it. A kind of newsletter evolved, a connecting link among them.

When Carmel Olbaga qualified for the national hang-gliding championship, and the up-coming event appeared in Paygon's mail-out, five others journeyed to cheer her on.

Small groups of them began to enjoy activities together that they had previously done alone. When they traveled, they put additional copies of Lucian's original message in books of the same titles in which they had found them and continued to add other volumes of their own choices that they found particularly meaningful.

They all began to work out their schedules in planning ahead for the next year in July, in Chicago, for two whole weeks together.

40

"This thesis writing is an exhausting business," intoned Walter to his wife on her return from Italy, as he, Longhorn and Lucian met her and Kayla at the airport. "It saps a person's strength, leaves him debilitated, weak-minded, demoralized, and susceptible to any manner of hallucinations. And that's me and Longhorn. *Lucian*, on the other hand, is fine, but I don't think *we* could survive another week of this."

With the thesis approved, the oral examinations followed close behind. Lucian requested that the children be permitted to attend, so they could also experience this final phase of the graduate study. They came and enthusiastically joined in the session, that, as Dr. Rutledge noted, *had no recent precedent, and on reflection, has no earlier precedent either.*

The August graduation came soon after. Lucian asked Janice to enable the children to march with him in the ceremony. She arranged it.

The children and their families came back to the city for the weekend of the event. The Pandras' house again looked like an oasis for a migrating tribe. People found locations everywhere. Once more, the patio and backyard were spread with sleeping rolls, as were the inside rooms and halls.

. . .

Late on Saturday afternoon, Lucian walked in the patio of the Pandras' house, pondering the sky, the clouds. Reendo enjoyed himself on a perch in a position that he and others of the group sometimes assumed. Reendo would come to where Lucian was walking or standing and put his arms around Lucian's midsection, put his feet on top of Lucian's feet, and just cling there for a while.

Lucian continued walking as before. Neither exchanged a word during this *clamping on*, as Reendo called it, or *docking procedure*, as Jhenaw named it.

It occurred with enough frequency that at times others were not fully conscious that there was a spare person clamped to Lucian. Janice came out the door and started to walk beside Lucian, oblivious of Reendo.

She said, "Dr. Rutledge really surprised me today. He said he thought you should become a paleontologist."

Lucian did not say anything but glanced up at the dinosaur skeleton that dominated the patio.

"He said," she continued, turning so she could see Lucian's

response, "that he had inquired about recommending you for a fellowship in anthropology."

"Another degree?" Lucian asked.

"A doctor's degree," she said.

They were walking again around the edge of the patio and the adjacent back yard.

Lucian said, "I don't want to be a paleontologist."

"I know what," said Reendo.

Janice looked down as if Lucian's leg had just spoken to her, only then becoming fully conscious that the familiar cargo attached to him was Reendo.

The attachment continued to speak, "I think Lucian and I should become *shamans*. Let's get a *shaman Ph.D.*"

. . .

When Grandmother appeared with miniature graduation robes for the children, the scene was complete. All of them awaited the ceremony.

The children marched in with Lucian, sat with him, and when his name sounded from the loudspeaker, with the announcement that his thesis had included the substantial contribution of the members of the Worm Farm School, they all strode on stage.

The children received, in their turn, small official-looking certificates, which read, *This entitles the holder to apply to this institution for enrollment upon completion of all preliminary requirements for admission.*

"Big deal," quipped Dolphis. "Everyone can do that."

. . .

Lucian had no idea of the extent of the construction that Longhorn had been doing at the worm farm. Returning now, Lucian found several new adobe buildings stretching out past the original perimeter of the yard. Longhorn ushered him into the first. It housed the *infrastructure city* that Walter and Longhorn had transferred from the Pandras' front room.

As they approached the second structure, Longhorn said only one word, by way of explanation, "Beth." They entered to find her there, unpacking and sorting supplies.

She indicated some boxes on the floor and, pointing to some

shelving, said simply, "Up there."

As they hoisted her boxes, she said, "This part is the chemistry building. The next is for physics. The third is biology. And the fourth is botany. The university cleans out all its things periodically and expands and replaces. They were glad these things could be used."

That night, she went over the forms for Lucian to sign as *Headmaster of the school*, for all the old supplies and equipment, so the university could show that they had been donated for educational purposes to a non-profit organization.

"They don't know how non-profit this is," said Longhorn.

"I have the opportunity to be here for a while," said Beth, "and if I can start on it tomorrow, I can work with them on all the new equipment. Then I have to be away for a while. But later I can come back and continue."

She began in earnest the next morning. Not actually because school was scheduled to start, nor because anything had been said to the children about being there, but because it was the day after they had all returned from graduation, and this is where they wanted to be. So they all accumulated and began to explore, on their own, the new structures and their contents.

Enter Beth. She arranged the children in an arc, outside, facing the buildings where the equipment related to scientific investigation rested. She stood like an orchestra conductor readying for a symphony. Intense, electric.

Her hand gestured as if it held an invisible baton. It pointed at Lucian. "Science." she said, as if the word alone began the introductory melody, and Lucian was the solo player.

"Science?" he responded.

"Science." she, in her turn repeated, with such emphasis, that he understood what she wanted. The introductory melody. The motif of what would come.

"Science," he said, rising, in some kind of synergy, with her, sweeping his hand in a gesture that encompassed the earth and sky. "There are all things. And there are ways of looking at all things. Perspectives. Science has become probably the single most influential perspective, the most widespread, that humans have ever known.

"It is a belief system that rests on three doctrines. First, whatever is investigated, must be available in some way to the human senses. Through the ears, eyes, nose, through touch or taste. Directly or through instrumentation—the extensions of the senses—like microscopes and telescopes."

This opening melody was what the conductor wanted to hear.

"The second doctrine," Lucian continued. "What is discoverable must be available to everyone. Given the same instruments and experience, all who try must be able to experience the same thing. A lone solitary vision may motivate an individual, but if others cannot experience the same, it is not within the science belief system.

"Third, what is discoverable must be repeatable. If the same elements are put together, the same result must be forthcoming.

"These are the cardinal principals."

"And," Beth swept up the theme, pointing to the new adobe structures, "in there are the instruments, the chemicals, the equipment, that will enable us to explore together, layers of information in our environment, making it available to the senses, to all of us, and we will be empowered to repeat the experiments as we wish."

She displayed stethoscopes. "You can hear the heart by placing your ear on someone's chest. But you can hear better with this." She gave one to each, and they listened to their own and to each other's hearts.

"We will use equipment that will magnify sounds too slight to hear without aid. And other equipment that will take remote sounds and bring them near. We will visually magnify small things, making them available to our eyes. We will make distant things viewable."

She gestured around her. "Select something from out here— a leaf, sand, anything, and bring it inside." She led the way to the first building.

Longhorn, who had been sitting also in the arc of listeners, picked up a leaf and said to the children, "Come, follow Field Commander Beth!"

Inside stood lab desks. And atop each, a microscope. "First," she said, "we will look into the realm of the very small."

She and Lucian and Longhorn helped adjust microscopes, until each person saw the magnification of the things brought from outside.

"Ah!" Pica exclaimed, as the miniscule world swam into view. She looked up, spread her arms wide, opened her mouth to say something, but all that came out was another "Ah!" and she looked through the eyepiece again.

Beth wanted them to have the impact of the very small and the very distant on the same day. So while the children bent over these windows into that tiny world, she went with Lucian to the house and phoned the parents to be sure it was all right to keep everyone for supper and then scan the night sky through telescopes.

. . .

As they peered at the fiery balls circling in the vastness of space, Pica again said, "Ah!" and "Ah!' again.

As Longhorn stood near Beth, both watching the children scan the sky, he said to her, "You are animated."

She responded, "Beth is truly alive," as if she were speaking of a third party.

"Tomorrow," she told them, "we start to look through the microscope at ourselves, at humans."

After the sky-watching ended, Lucian, Longhorn, and Beth drove the children to their homes. Coming back along a deserted stretch of barely visible road, Beth asked them to stop.

They parked by its side. She led them off between two hills and into a gully. On a rise by its banks, she pointed, in the moonlight, to a ring of stones.

"They lived here, you know. The ancient people. They saw these same stars and made these ways of measuring time. This is a site I worked on last year. Over there," she pointed, "are remnants of buildings, probably ceremonial. All the artifacts I found related to ceremonies rather than daily utensils."

They stood in the middle of the stone circle and contemplated the stars. She said, "Were they ever really conscious, or did they become so much a part of their myth, carrying out its routines and orders that spoke commands in their heads, that they never knew of choices? If, for any reason,

I am not able to bring the children here, be sure they have a chance to see it."

41

Field Commander Beth mustered her troops. "Napoleon marches on Moscow," announced Longhorn, as he joined the line following her into what Reendo had christened *the palace of microscopes*.

When everyone was seated, she explained, "We look at things from humans under the microscope, and we can see change, differences, over time. Lucian…" and she held both hands toward him, as a curator explaining an art object, which made Longhorn, also sitting at a desk with a microscope, laugh aloud, "…will provide the samples, day by day, that we will examine. I will feed him certain things during the day, and the next day, we'll see if we can see any difference in some of the samples."

Lucian had the *I will?* look on his face, being the first he had heard of this. "He will become for us," she continued, "the representative of all humans." The *I will?* look continued.

"Hair," she said handing him scissors. "Snip off a strand for each of us."

"Hair?" he repeated, and then followed her directions.

They proceeded, under her instruction, with a series of activities with the hair, comparing its width, under the microscope, with various other materials. Wool, cotton, threads, wires.

"Skin," she said.

"*Skin?*" he questioned, hoping she would not hand him the scissors again.

With a scalpel, she scraped painlessly some flakes of the layer of outer skin from his hand. Another series of activities ensued.

"Skin, hair, all aspects of the body come from…?" she said, her rising inflection asking for a fill-in.

"The *food* we eat," said Orgol.

"And the food we eat comes from…?" Beth asked, with that same rising inflection.

"From the *earth* it grows in," said Reendo.

"So," Beth said, "when we look at things from the human body we are looking at...?"

"A *part of the earth*," exclaimed Kayla.

"Next—expectorate!" ordered Beth, holding a beaker toward Lucian.

"*Expectorate?*" said Lucian.

"Spit!" said Beth.

She prepared the glass slides and handed them out. They examined saliva and discussed its chemical makeup.

"All the body's fluids," said Beth, "tell us something about the body that produced it, about that body's health, its nourishment, its relation to the earth from which it came."

She turned to Lucian, saying, "Run in place. Perspiration is the next fluid."

"Perspiration?" said Lucian.

"*Sweat*," said Beth.

She touched glass slides to his the moisture appearing on his forehead, and they all examined them. She talked about the purposes of this form of body product.

"But all liquids in the body ultimately are connected to the major liquid carrier," said Beth.

"Not..." said Lucian, "not..."

"*Blood*," affirmed Beth, in chorus with the children, readying the sterilized equipment. A prick on the finger, and Lucian's blood opened its secrets beneath the microscopes. "It is the sea of life to every cell in the body, which cannot survive without its constant nourishment. And of the other liquids on earth, blood is most like...?" Again the rising inflection.

A silence ensured among the thoughtful faces.

"The..." started Dolphus, "the...*ocean?*"

"*Yes*," said Beth. "The ocean nourished the single cells that developed there in ancient times. And when creatures emerged from the ocean to dry land, they had a built-in aqua-lung, in the true sense, *aqua*, meaning water, a built-in ocean system to nourish every cell within us."

"And now," she said, holding out a plastic container, "urine."

"Urine," said Lucian, and then, "*urine?*"

He dutifully disappeared while they continued discussion, and reappeared with the sample, from which she prepared the microscope slides.

Finishing with the sequence on the mysteries that reveal themselves from that body fluid, she continued in the same voice as before.

"Semen," she said, holding a glass receptacle toward Lucian.

There resulted a momentary silence, followed by Lucian saying, first softly, as if to himself, "semen," then louder, to Beth, "*semen?*"

"We need to study sperm, the transfer of life, itself, in the reproduction of the organism. It's a worthy sacrifice. You can do it." She continued to discuss this theme as he left with the container.

"You know how many times Lucian has said that roots of words tell us of their origins," she said. "What do you think the origins of the words *semen* and *sperm* are?"

Jhenaw said, "They were both from the Latin. They meant *seed.*"

"How do you know that?" asked Beth.

"Lucian told us," said Jhenaw. "Just like your name, Beth, means *house*, from the early Phoenician."

When Lucian returned, they studied the darting schools of sperm swimming in the minute sea of a drop, made visible by the magnifying lenses.

When their exploration came to its morning's pause, Beth said, "Tomorrow the same, and the day after, in fact, all week. We will take new samples of each of these substances from…" she pointed at Lucian, "…our human volunteer every day and study them under the microscope. We will see if any changes are detectable, and each day probe further into what we are. By the weeks end," she added, holding up the scissors, "he may be bald."

"But," added Longhorn from the desk where he had been looking through his microscope throughout the morning, "what a contribution he will have made to science!" and laughed while the children applauded.

. . .

The days continued as Beth had promised, with a sequence of explorations with the microscopes and other equipment that kept the children asking to stay and continue longer. Many nights, the parents did not need to come for them. They prepared suppers together and slept at the worm farm.

All of the small dwellings of their own design, their private spaces, were now completed, and they had ample room to sleep. But as frequently as not, they ended up in a kind of heap of sleeping bags, together, under the cottonwood tree, around the embers of an evening campfire, with Beth crooning melodies softly in her repertoire of languages.

One night as everyone was drifting into sleep, under the tree, Jhenaw suddenly sat up and said, "*neologism*."

"Neologism?" Beth repeated, coming to full consciousness and leaning up on an elbow.

"Yes," said Jhenaw, "Lucian said the other day he had a new word for us, and he gave us *neologism* and asked us to figure it out. It just came to me. *Neos* is Greek for *new*. *Logos* is Greek for *word*. It means *new word*." She rolled over along the ground to Lucian and hammered him softly on his reclining shoulder with her fist. "I like that. I like what you did. The clue was right there. That's what you gave us, a *new word*. All we had to do was open our mind and see it. But you can't exactly tell us how. But when we do, then we know how to do it ourselves, inside."

She rolled back to her former place. They all heard the sounds of the coyotes in the distance. And shape-shifting Pica, in her sleeping bag, assumed the form of a coyote howl.

42

Beth, one morning, said, "I must go for awhile," as if she had received some directive in a dream. She drove away from the worm farm and from the science projects.

Their momentum spun off into related interests. Orgol, who would ponder *things taking place*, often for a long time, turning everything inward, until it would erupt as a complicated plan, now had one *erupt*. He brought pages of a report he had written and illustrated in the form of a book that covered the idea of microscopes and telescopes and other devices that expanded human senses. The morning was his and everyone applauded when he completed his explanation.

Normita said, "Let's publish it." After the inception of the greeting cards they had first printed, they had gradually added more equipment. The cards, themselves, were selling regularly to the worm farm customers and also at the Junk Shop. The equipment that they had accumulated made Normita's suggestion possible.

So they transformed Orgol's work into a small book-form and distributed it to all of their families. Who gave it to friends. Who ordered some for themselves. *Science According to Orgol* became their first best seller, their *best seller* being defined as anything that sold more then one copy.

Dolphus, who enjoyed watching Pica translate concepts into shapes, said that her talent should be available to a wider audience and suggested that he and Pica work together to produce another book.

So was born *The Shapes of Life*, photographs by Dolphus, modeled by Pica. Dolphus became their resident expert on cameras and taught the others as he learned. He arranged the little volume with facing pages, the left side with a word, a quotation, or a picture of an object, and on the right side, the photograph of Pica *demonstrating* the word in her inimitable way. The book became their second best seller.

Kayla said, "If it takes half a million records to have a *gold* record, then I think, on that scale, with our sales, we have a *mud* book, on the way to becoming *limestone.*"

As with the school funds, the children kept the financial records for income and expenditures for the publications. To purchase supplies, they compared prices and quality and made their choices.

They sat in a circle with David and Essa Shimek, the Junk Shop owners, to discuss a fair profit for the items displayed and sold in their store and for the use of their binding equipment once the book pages were printed.

Most of the small profits from the sale of cards and books went into a Worm Farm School Travel Fund. The group could discuss any time the possible trips they would like to finance with this money. In addition, Lucian wanted each of them to receive a personal amount from any sales, that was theirs to do with as they would.

All of them, by now, had individual savings and checking accounts at the bank. They all also had their own college fund accounts and made regular deposits, however small they might be.

As Gertrude, the teller, had observed to her co-worker in the back room, after one of the deposit visits, "How can those worm children ever hope to go to college when they haven't even started *real* school yet?"

. . .

They often began the day by scanning newspapers together. The papers were always a day old, so each person could have a discarded copy and not have to buy them.

They would sit under the cottonwood trees, each with a paper spread out. When a headline, an event, caught someone's attention, that person would read it aloud to the others, and they would discuss it.

If the event involved a particular location in the world, they would all race out to the baked clay maps expanding out into the desert or to their map room. If the event involved a location within travel distance, out came the budget figures, as the children determined if they could afford to get on their bus and drive there.

"The tribal dances are next week, out in the mesas!" Normita exclaimed one morning. Out came the budget sheets, the calendar, the road maps. How many meals. What food to buy and pack for the trip. Whether the *bus that belonged* needed a checkup beforehand.

Essa Shimek at the Junk Shop was a mechanic who could perform remarkable repairs with wire and intuition. Jhenaw exulted in being around her. Their fingers understood that objects had a nature of their own that cried out to be put together and taken apart, that seemed to offer instructions as to what to do with them.

The children, Lucian, and Longhorn drove the bus to the Junk Shop and parked. "Ah-ha!" Essa said, at the sight of the bus, rolling up her sleeves. Everyone had their stool, chair, ladder, box, to stand on. These various platforms were kept in random abandon along the outside of the shop, where the contents of the inside of the shop overflowed.

"These are our levitation devices," said Dolphus, as they placed them around the open bus motor and peered in. Essa guided them again through the mechanical labyrinth. "What do we check first?" she asked. She went through second, and third, and fourth, each time with responses from her participative audience. "And next time, Jhenaw, you guide us through the checkup."

Jhenaw's fingers wiggled in anticipation.

"I have a favor to ask all of you," Essa said, after the bus had been pronounced in sufficient health for the journey. "David and I both have to go to Wyoming for a week on some family business. Now, all of you run the worm farm so well, and you do your printing business so well, we would like to ask you to take care of our shop for the week we'll be gone. We'll pay you wages for it."

"We're diversifying!" Reendo said.

"And," said Essa, "I have another favor to ask of you. While you're minding the store, will you take a look at some things that have been traded in, that need to be evaluated and cataloged."

She walked them around back, where David was sorting through what looked like parts of small-size cars. He explained that a carnival owner had unloaded these remains of several small-track children's autos.

"Maybe, just maybe," David said, "although none of the units is complete or works, in itself, maybe we could salvage enough working parts from each of them to put together a functioning vehicle. Will you take a look at them while we're gone and see what you think?"

"Yes!" Jhenaw said for all of them.

. . .

They worked at the Junk Shop for a week and explored its wonders. Orgol burst out one day with, "This is like discovering King Tut's Tomb! "

They had not only salvaged parts enough for one small car, but two of them. They had essentially assembled them by the time the Shimeks returned. When the finishing touches were put on the cars and the last paint coat dried, Essa suggested that they might want to consider accepting them in lieu of payment for their week of work. The vote was immediate and unanimous.

Longhorn guided them in constructing yet another adobe structure to house the small cars at the worm farm. In the process of assembling the cars, and then constructing the place to hold them, they had explored the history of automobiles. Shelves in the new *car house* now held volumes on internal combustion engines, battery-powered cars, designs, companies, alternative fuel sources and pollution problems and potential solutions. The inevitable time line began to grow out from the side of the building into the desert, with poles displaying pictures of cars and dates of their development.

While the extensive route of this new time line could be walked, there stretched a leveled way beside it, a car track, that they could drive, in their new vehicles, through the decades of time. "Our *time machines*," Eriot exclaimed.

Essa and David came, at the children's invitation, to see the building, the roadway, and the time line. The couple stood and watched Jhenaw take off on a demonstration drive into the distance, while others repeated for them, from memory, the information on the distant signposts. This included the dates and places of the first road signs and signal lights, the names of their innovators and who decided on which side of the road to drive in various parts of the world, along with the dates when manufacturers first began their businesses.

The children insisted that David and Essa stretch their too-long adult frames onto the two vehicles, balanced precariously, knees sticking up.

"This is like riding a dachshund," David shouted.

"You never told me you had ridden a dachshund," Essa shouted back.

The two drove off beside the time line into the desert. They finally returned, zig-zagging in and out of each other's path along an unmarked route, whooping as they came.

43

A blazing desert day. The *bus that belonged*. Longhorn driving. With Lucian and the children, fresh from digging for trilobites in the slate hills, singing and playing the assortment of primitive instruments as they traveled. Their sounds emptied out of the windows into the desert air.

By a pickup truck with a flat tire, on the side of the little-traveled road, a lean and weathered man stood, dressed in rumpled khakis, wearing what Eriot called *an adventurer's hat*, not even trying to flag them down, just looking at them calmly through the waves of desert heat.

They stopped the bus anyway, and its human cargo offered the man a canteen of water. Under Longhorn's direction and help, the children took equipment from the bus, jacked up the truck, and removed the flat tire. The spare tire was also flat. By the time they had gotten this far in the operation, they were explaining to the man the trilobites and other fossils they had unearthed and the place of their finds in the geological time frame.

They took him on the bus, with the tires, toward the far distance, to look for a service station. They shared the musical instruments they had brought along. Soon he was plucking away at a harp made of antelope prongs, and tooting melodies on bamboo pipes from China. He swayed in rhythm with the Indonesian drums.

Orgol moved down the aisle to Lucian, put his arms around his neck, and whispered that the man looked hungry. Why not take him back for a worm farm *special*.

They did. The special at the worm farm consisted of a mixture of international dishes they had been experimenting with, and the man sampled each one and listened to the explanations of the cultures from which they came.

With a bemused enthusiasm, he looked at the partly completed dinosaur skeleton being reassembled. It had been *deconstructed* at the Pandras, explained Eriot, and was *reawakening* at the Worm Farm School. The man asked if he could help with it for a while. They taught him the names of the bones as they assembled them.

In one of the small cars, he zoomed off along the time track of automotive development. He followed another of the time lines on foot, reading every placard, asking the children for further explanations.

They built a campfire. They peered at stars through the telescopes.

The man was leaning back against a cottonwood tree, the red of the firelight illuminating his profile. He clasped his hands together on his chest, the index fingers touching his chin. He looked at the group around him and said, "Who am I?" His eyes rested on Eriot as he completed the question.

Eriot, without pause responded simply, "You are a person with a sense of humor. You've made some of the funniest jokes about trilobites, which is not an easy subject to make jokes about. You could be a stand-up trilobitologist."

Jhenaw added, "And you're curious. You looked like you were really immersed in the time lines and asked some really interesting questions."

"You're helpful," said Pica. "You helped us get all the food ready for supper and then clean up."

"You're relaxed, and you treat all of us like people, instead of an age category," said Dolphus.

"And you're tired," said Kayla. "We're all staying overnight, because we didn't know when we would get back from the fossil dig and thought it might be late. We all have rooms here. They look like little houses—the one on stilts, the lighthouse, the round house, the rock house, the sod house, the Chinese *land* junk, the bow house, the Phoenician beehives, and the others," she pointed as she mentioned them, "and you could fit in any of them you'd like. We often end up in a bunch over here by the trees."

She led him to the various private spaces. He accepted a sleeping bag and space in Beth's place, since she had not returned yet. After a while, he migrated with the others back to the cottonwood trees.

. . .

As the dawn came, he said to them, "Breakfast is on me. Please. At a place you've got to see. In a roundabout sort of route, its on the way back to the service station where we left the tires. Cactus Max's Cantina."

Cactus Max opened for breakfast, or was still open from never having closed last night, it was hard to tell. How anyone located it for breakfast or any other time was also hard to tell. People did not *happen* to be passing it, situated as it was on the way from nowhere to nowhere. It had to be the *destination*.

Max gathered several tables together in the middle of the room, approximating one large table. Except that these were all different colors—turquoise, yellow, pink, purple—and of various shapes and heights.

Onto this hodgepodge table top appeared, without anyone actually ordering anything, an assortment of foods, prepared in a manner from *who knows where*, as Dolphus said, and probably indigenous only to this Cantina.

The side wall, unwindowed, a wooden overlay to the basic adobe structure, was splintered and pocked with use. The use being *knife-throwing*. An assortment of blades stuck out from where they had last been tossed. For throwing knives of every description was a way of life here. "We couldn't afford darts," shrugged Max, "and darts can be dangerous."

They all tried throwing the various shaped blades. Pica was the natural. In her *shape-shifting* way, she sensed space and distance, and flipped knives into the wall, as her proud fan, Dolphus, said with admiration, "like a pro."

When they left, no money seemed to change hands, but both the man and Max insisted that it was *all taken care of*.

They drove on and picked up the repaired tires, Lucian paying for them, because the man had no currency. They traveled the long road back to the truck.

"You know," said Eriot, "I think your truck and our bus are related. They're the same *genus*."

They returned the spare tire to its place in the trunk and mounted the other tire. The truck, which looked like it might never start again, did.

The man looked at them and said in a curious voice, "You have done so much. Is there nothing you want from me?"

"Yes," said Normita. "You need to learn to stay in rhythm

with the Indonesian drum next time."

"Agreed," he said, bowed his head slightly, got into the truck, and chugged off.

. . .

Lucian, wrapped in his sheet, opened the front door and squinted into the darkness of the front porch at the uniformed man who had knocked so late at night

Lucian could not identify the uniform except with the passing thought that it looked uncomfortable. While the individual's facial expression changed little as he entered the dim room, his eyes darted about and seemed surprised or disappointed at the setting.

He delivered into Lucian's hands an envelope and instructed Lucian to open it. Lucian took from it a cashier's check.

"The person," said the uniformed one, "whom you recently befriended in the desert wishes you to have this token of his appreciation."

Lucian stared at the remarkable amount. The uniformed man continued, "He goes out alone some to escape the pressures of his responsibilities. He found himself in a awkward and potentially dangerous position, and you aided him. If you did not recognize him, he wishes to remain anonymous. His solitary excursions are, of necessity, alone and without identification. An entourage calls attention to itself."

Lucian looked at the check. He thought a moment and handed it back.

"No, but thank him. Tell him the children enjoyed being with him, for himself, for what they shared together. They need to experience the effort to get funds to buy what we need. Learning that will be more valuable to them eventually than anything they could buy with this."

He rummaged around in a pile of things on the floor. "I didn't know how to get this to him, but the children said afterward they wanted to give him a fossil, and it's here somewhere."

The limousine drove off with the returned check and a five hundred million year old trilobite. Two, actually. One for the uniformed individual as well.

. . .

186

The uniformed visitor opened his briefcase and laid a document and check on the desk of the director of the state department of education.

"My employer, a philanthropist of some means, who does not wish his name to be mentioned, is interested in aiding your school system's environmental beautification and cultural enrichment."

The director had picked up the check as one who has been jaded by a succession of people with hidden agendas parading through his office. He nodded to the uniformed visitor to continue, while he looked at the check to see how much energy and time he would expend on this exchange. His eyes widened as they went over the amount five times, while his fingers began to follow across as well, as if the feel of the numbers could somehow transfer a confirmation of what his eyes saw.

The uniformed man continued, explaining that the agreement for the expenditure of the funds was very specific, and any deviation from the stipulations would result in the forfeiture and return of the entire amount.

A list of schools was included. For each of these institutions, *beautification funds* would be available for a flower garden. For the continuous revitalization of the soil of these gardens, and any lawn or landscaping currently in place, a substantial and ongoing quantity of earthworms were to be purchased for *soil quality improvement* from an organization known as the *Worm Farm*. For the purchase of these worms, a generous amount of money was provided.

For the cultural aspect of the bequest, students of a related organization, *The Worm Farm School*, were to be invited to present an hour-long assembly for each of the participating schools, on themes of their own choice, such as tribal music around the world, a comparison of the evolution of dinosaurs and automobiles, and other novel topics. Funds were provided to pay the Worm Farm School for these assemblies at *professional wages*.

All correspondence with the Worm Farm organization and the Worm Farm School was to originate from the Department of Education offices with no mention of the underwriting source. These and other details were covered in the legal documents which had to be signed to receive the monies.

When the uniformed one had left, the director said to his secretary, "Look up the location of the…" but he hesitated and added, "Bring me the list of all private educational institutions in the state." He thumbed to the back searching under "W."

44

Beth telephoned from somewhere. "You know the walk-in human figure you talked about building? Start building it now. It needs a walk-in womb. I should be there by the time it's finished."

The large recumbant hollow human form, in *creative adobe*, grew in the desert somewhere between the *poets of the world time line*, and *landforms of the earth*, where Longhorn continued to build his samples of geographical formations.

They were working on the lung room of the reclining figure, when Beth arrived. All of them left the various parts of the anatomy they were finishing and ran to her.

She entered the giant womb with everyone gathered around her. She of the burnished copper hair and the fragrance of sandalwood and myrrh.

"Yes," she said, "yes, this will do wonderfully." Her eyes scintillated. "How many of you were once in a womb?" she asked the children. They all laughed and raised their hands.

"All right," she said, "we need a model of an ovum and of sperm." She divided the children into a ovum group and a sperm group and told them to *be creative*.

They ran to the various store rooms, which had begun to rival the Junk Shop in interest and diversity. The ovum group came back throwing a beach ball back and forth. The sperm group carried small styrofoam balls, each with a streamer pinned on for the tail. They all stood outside of *the womb room*.

"Now," she said, "we've got to get the sperm in there," pointing toward the structure. The sperm group ran off and came back with a long hollow cylindrical wrapping for carpet, open at both ends, that they carried like a battering ram. They took it up to the womb entry and moved it partway in.

The ovum group placed their beach ball on the ground in the middle of the room. The sperm group took their styrofoam balls and hurled them through their large cylinder at the beach ball. The streamers trailed out behind the missiles. One of them made a direct hit on the large ball.

"That's the one," Beth said, "that made contact. That sperm will combine with that egg to become the baby."

There was no more time to talk about the womb room event, because they had to grab their musical instruments and head off in the bus to one of the schools that had invited them to present an assembly talking about and demonstrating tribal instruments.

Kayla said, "Beth, will you come too?"

"Of course," said Beth as she scooped Kayla up in her arms, and jogged toward the bus. "I haven't had a chance to ride on *the bus that belongs* for a while."

. . .

The Worm Farm School assembly presentation to the county school ended. As some of the audience moved to the exits, others moved toward the platform to talk to the presenters. Beth gathered up instruments, putting them in cases to carry out.

Lucian, in front of her, was packing up some of the song sheets with words in various languages on them, when the principal approached, a wry, thin woman over six feet in stature, with her graying hair swept up into additional height. She clutched in her arms that were crossed on her chest, in a gesture that looked perpetual, a clipboard with pockets on it, stuffed with notes. A pen, connected to the board by a chain, remained in a fixed position between her fingers, ready for instant note-taking.

She looked over her half glasses at Lucian. Her lips seemed permanently pursed, as if in speculation about whatever stood before her. Her head cocked slightly to the side as she looked at Lucian. "You want, I suppose, the check now?"

"The check?" said Lucian absently. "As you will."

She cocked her head in the other direction and continued staring at him. The tone of her voice had immediately arrested Beth's attention, and she watched the two, unobserved.

"Do you," the principal continued, "want it made out to you personally."

"No," he said, still gathering material, "to the school."

"You work with them at the school, then. You don't seem much like a teacher. You have a relationship with this group of children," she said, "like…" she hesitated, "…like a father? And they are like brothers and sisters? And that man that traveled with you, is like…" she hesitated again, "like a father to you?"

"No, I do not have a relationship with them as a group of children. Nor am I like a father, or even as a teacher." The intensity of his response riveted Beth's attention. "I have a relationship as Lucian with Dolphus, as Lucian with Normita, as Lucian with Reendo. They do not relate as brothers and sisters, but as Dolphus to Normita, as Normita to Reendo. I do not relate to Longhorn as father, but as Lucian to Longhorn, and he as Longhorn to Reendo, and Longhorn to Pica. We relate as individuals, each connection unique and dynamic. We have as many different relationships as we have individuals. Those family-metaphor categories are limited roles that others have prescribed. They mask the potential uniqueness behind the roles."

The principal pulled the check from one of the pockets of her clipboard, signed it, thrust it at him, and walked away, her heels clumping on the stage floor as she went.

Beth came forward, her hands filled with instruments, and said to Lucian, "Your response, where did that come from?"

He thought inside himself for a moment. Wzzzzzzith an expression of recognition, said, "Dr. Fenwicke." He repeated, as if an idea had just come to him, "*Dr. Fenwicke.*"

. . .

They returned from the assembly. Longhorn and Beth remained inside the bus, talking. Lucian and the children walked toward the front of the worm farm house. Mrs. Blargman came slowly around the side of the house, pushing a wheelbarrow in front of her. On it balanced an open cask of earth and worms.

She aimed in the direction of her parked truck, its back flap open to the ground like a ramp, with two casks already on its flatbed. She saw the others coming toward her and had the look of someone feeling she needed to say something urgently, but not being totally sure how urgent.

They clustered around her as she parked her barrow and said toward all of them, mostly toward Lucian, "I don't know how to tell you this, but there is a man wearing only two feathers above each ear, lying unconscious, sprawled in the yard where he looks like he has just fallen out of the sky or something. He looks like he's dead, or, inconceivably, sleeping..."

"There are two possibilities," said Dolphus in a moment of mock dramaturgy. "It is either Icarus, tumbled from the sky when his wings melted. Or..." and he paused for effect, "...it is Zoyan'qual!"

The children joined in a chorus, cheering, "Zoyan'qual!" They rushed around the house.

Mrs. Blargman watched them run off and then turned slowly to Lucian, "From such a description, they know this person? Or Icarus dropping out of the sky? But the other name, they actually know this Z-whatever person? A random substitute teacher, perhaps? Or possibly the inspector from the humane society, checking on the care and treatment of your worms?"

She hefted up the handles of the wheelbarrow again but did not yet push it forward. She took a kind of internal sighing breath and looked at Lucian.

"You know," she said, "I owe you a great debt of gratitude. Me and my son both do. He's about your age. And we've had a heck of a time getting along. I had such expectations for him, how he should grow up, how he should behave. But the boy was *strange*. He did such *weird* things. I just couldn't take it. He was just too *peculiar*. We were estranged from each other." She paused and tapped the air with her finger, in Lucian's direction.

"But," she continued, "now I've come to know you, Lucian. You and your worm farm, and your children, and your two-feathers-wearing friend looking like he dropped out of the sky. Your little adobe dinosaurs. What next, will you put up a full-size skeleton of one?" She bopped her forehead with the palm of her hand dramatically. "But how could I forget, that's already happening. Anyway, now, my son doesn't seem all that strange anymore. By comparison with you, he's really quite a normal person. And we're communicating again. We're getting along really well. And, Lucian, we have you to thank for it."

With that, she pushed the wheelbarrow on, Lucian beside her, and he helped her hoist the pot into the back of the truck.

He said, "Send your son over if things get too complacent. We can help him back to abnormality."

She turned as if to an imaginary audience, lifting her hands in a gesture of mock disbelief and said, "Listen to that! Lucian has made a joke!" She turned back to him, her hands now on her hips, her face adjusted to convey comic indignation, "As if my son needed any help to be weird!"

As she got into the driver's seat, she handed Lucian a few dollar bills, and said, "I left the check for the worms in the usual place. Here's some extra. Go get the guy who fell out of the sky some clothes."

Then Lucian closed the back flap of the truck and Mrs. Blargman drove away, her final words drifting back, "You're real people, Lucian."

. . .

Among the foods they ate around the campfire that night were those that Zoyan'qual had brought from the canyons. Grandmother had come and cooked a pot of *planetary stew*, as she called it, on the open flames. Longhorn had recently harvested some of the thirty varieties of potatoes he grew by his cabin, and they sampled those.

Beth asked them to sing *the song of life* in the new tongue.

"That is to commemorate," she said afterward, "the continuation for many months of what we started this afternoon. In that model of a human that you're building, in that womb room already constructed, we shall gather day by day to consider the progress of a developing child, of ourselves, of all human beings that have lived. "And…" She placed both hands flat on her lower abdomen, "…of this one. I am pregnant. I want you to follow with me, day by day, the development of life, of human life, within my womb. I want to have the birthing here with all of you present. I want all of us to be the first thing the child experiences on emerging into this outer world."

In the silence that followed, Kayla's voice entered. She walked over to where Beth stood and took her hand, becoming the personification of intentness.

Kayla said, "They told me at the orphanage that when my mother had me, she didn't have a husband and couldn't take care of me. And then she left. Beth, do you have a husband?"

Beth looked at the concerned face for a moment and said softly, "Yes, I have a husband. But he doesn't like digs and fossils and ruins and is far away now."

She looked at Grandmother. "When the time is due, will you help deliver the baby?"

"Of course," Grandmother said.

Beth turned to Zoyan'qual, "This will be the first child born into your tribe. What can we do, together, tonight, to celebrate the beginning of the journey of this new life moving toward birth?"

They created together a ceremony of song, of dance, of stories. A celebration of each other. A celebration of the new life. Into the night.

45

On the weekend, Lucian and Longhorn accompanied Zoyan'qual back to the canyon country. They began in the early dawn.

They took little with them. They knew how to eat from the land. How to find water.

They paused at a small spring surrounded by huge boulders. The water bubbled up into a little cup of land, nourishing a miniature ecosystem of green. They drank as they sat on the boulders for a time, watching the small creatures that darted in and out from beyond the rocks to partake of the liquid and greenery.

"There is a saying," Longhorn observed, "that there are three phases of insight. In the first phase, the land is the land. In the second, when the analysis of things begins, the land is no longer the land. In the third phase, when a kind of new insight is achieved, the land is again the land, yet never the same as before."

He looked at Zoyan'qual. "You live as people did before they knew there was a choice. All their rituals constructed a way to interact with the land. Then came choices, diversity, different ways, alternative possibilities. Now you have chosen this, you again live on the land, in some ways, to outward seeming, as the ancestors of us all did. But it is not the same really, for you know of options and have chosen."

. . .

At the entrance to the canyon, Taco greeted them. The sandy-colored fury form stayed with them, except for occasional forages for food.

An early morning, Taco pawed Zoyan'qual's foot, and walked away, making a whining sound, looking back. He, Longhorn, and Lucian followed. Taco led them down the canyon to a small cave, hidden from view by scrub plant growth. There, a female fox nursed her cubs. Zoyan'qual said in the New Tongue, "The lifeing forces proceed in all forms. Now they are Taco-ing."

Lucian smiled. "Humor in the New Tongue," he said. "The possibilities are limitless."

Also, Zoyan'qual had found a hawk chick, deserted in the nest. He had nourished it. Now it had grown strong and circled into the wild, but often returned and perched in the canyon near them.

When the time came for Longhorn and Lucian to leave the canyon to return to the worm farm, Longhorn said, "Here we have merged with the earth again."

Zoyan'qual nodded. He gave them many packets of dried leaves, bark, and roots, with directions for their preparation and use.

. . .

The beginning of each morning belonged to Beth. And the baby's development. As they arrived each day, the children rushed to the womb room. The rest of the walk-through adobe giant had been completed. Openings led from the womb to the the kidneys and bladder, the stomach and lungs. When Beth talked about changes in her body, she walked them through the chambers of the model.

Standing in the womb room one morning, Pica said, "It's pregnant with *us*!"

Beth accumulated charts, diagrams, pictures, models. "This will be a living adventure." She reviewed the beginning, the ovum.

"Here are the two ovaries," said Beth. "Kayla, Normita, Jhenaw, and Pica, you will start to ovulate at puberty. From the first time on, you will have approximately four hundred ovulations. If, at any of those times sperm is present, you could become pregnant. You have almost five hundred thousand egg cells, each. Most never ripen nor are used, though at first they all have the potential to."

While their gargantuan model was female, there was no corresponding complete male figure. Instead, right outside the opening to the womb existed what Eriot called *the almost invisible man*, or as Orgol said, the *penis and testes rooms*, for that was all that existed of the male.

They entered this trio of two round chambers and one tubular room.

Beth said, "Reendo, Eriot, Dolphus, Orgol, when you reach puberty, your bodies will constantly form sperm. This will start when your pituitary gland tells them to. You remember when we saw the hypothalamus in the other model? It releases exactly the same hormone in all of us, but the hypothalamus adjusts the difference, reacting to testosterone."

She pointed to the production areas of sperm on the testicle room sides. "The sperm are only about one six-hundredths of a millimeter long. But they are abundant. Each time they are expelled, there are about half a billion of them."

"We need to see half a billion *something*," Lucian said, "that are not microscopic, in order to appreciate what this number means." So they began their *sand-for-sperm* metaphor. They took containers and actually counted out one thousand grains of sand. They found a small container that these thousand grains filled. Then they took a thousand scoops of sand with that sized container.

Now they had one million grains of sand and found a box that this amount filled to the brim. They put five fillings of this container in something still larger, to see a unit of five million grains of sand. And then they lined up a hundred containers of that size and filled them all. And stood back. And sat down. In a circle. Regarding half a billion grains of sand.

"Wow!" said Orgol.

So they followed the process. A sperm and an ovum unite. They traced its path, in the model, for the four days in the Fallopian tube, the first cell division during the first twenty-four hours, the subsequent divisions. The passing of the ovum to the uterus. The shedding of its outer wall. The attachment of the blastocyst to the endometrium.

As always, with new words, the signs appeared. Everything was labeled. "Our insides has street names," said Orgol. It became familiar territory. "The *real* inner city," Kayla said.

They had a celebration party when they got to the description of the third week, and Beth said, "At this point, the blastocyst became an embryo." Everyone cheered.

In the center of the womb room were the models they were making to represent each stage of development. At this point, Eriot wrote *sibling* on a card and put it by the model of the new embryo.

Beth hugged him.

46

Lucian stood and looked at the reassembled dinosaur skeleton, in the early Saturday morning light. Quietude in all directions. Everyone gone.

The skeleton shown stark and clear in the sun's rays. The skeleton, standing in the desert, amid the time lines. Amid the house-rooms of the children. Near the walk-in human model.

All of this. In the desert. Extending in an array of *developments* from the house.

Into the desert.

Into the desert.

The phrase played in Lucian's mind as if talking to him, saying, *listen to me, into the desert, not by the house, not in the yard. Beyond the yard.* He realized he did not know how far out the property line extended into the dessert.

Into the desert... Maybe onto land that he did not own.

He thought of it for the first time. All of the things they were building, constructing, developing—were they on his property?

All of these thoughts coalesced into a single one: *Who owns this land?*

He bicycled into the little town to ask…to ask *whom?*

He peddled on beyond, out into the dusty stretches, to the Junk Shop and its proprietors.

"The land!" said Essa. "Isn't that true! What if some of that *stuff* is on someone else's land."

"The land office," said David. "The county land office, at the county court house." But not open on Saturday.

Monday next, while Beth modeled the continuous saga of life in the womb, Lucian drove to the county seat. He felt a sense of panic at the possibilities that passed through his mind.

The land office counter worker peered through her bifocals. She was cordial. Like a hostess inviting a guest to view a private collection in her home.

She directed him in the intricacies of the public records, how the books were arranged, how the shelves were ordered. She offered admonitions about not falling off the ladder when climbing it to reach the top shelves.

He searched for land plot numbers, deeds, land changing hands. He found the general area. The older owners, ranchers, departures, sales.

Then the volume that brought it all up to date. Top shelf. He balanced on the ladder. Brought the dusty ledger down. Spread it on the old oak work table with the green shaded light hanging on a cord from the vaulted ceiling.

There it was. The boundaries of his land. And then the land beyond. And the owner's name.

Earnest Longhorn.

Purchase after purchase of parcels of land over the months. One plot after another.

Acre after acre. Out into the desert.

All the land now being used. And far beyond. All was in Longhorn's name.

Lucian sat for a long time staring at the enormous map that dominated the wall. Not really seeing it. Thinking of Longhorn. Feeling bonded with him. Thankful to Longhorn or whatever name he had been given at birth.

When next Lucian saw Longhorn, it was at the end of the day. Longhorn had been building more of the three dimensional maps with the children, far out from the worm farm house. The children ran past Lucian toward the house and to families that had come to pick them up. Or some mounted horses and rode off toward home. Or bicycled. Whatever form of locomotion had been arranged that day.

Lucian watched them running toward the house and then turned to see Longhorn walking toward him, folding a geological map he had been using to explain the locations of the sites of his adobe landform models.

Lucian looked at him and Longhorn returned the gaze.

Lucian's hands made a kind of inclusive gesture of everything around them and he said, "Thank you."

Longhorn understood and said simply, "I traded earth for earth. It is a fair barter."

They both stood and looked around them.

Longhorn said, "I dig from the earth blue rocks and exchange them for this earth on which we play."

He walked over to an extensive configuration of bars he had erected for the children to climb on, in, among. A vast array that exercised every part of the body in navigating their heights and breadths. Longhorn hoisted himself up onto a bar, and began a nimble climb upward toward one of its circular towers.

Lucian followed into the complex, pulling himself up, and hand-over-handing his way into the labyrinth of beams, slides, ropes, swings, dangling from various heights.

Each attained a tower. Longhorn sat on bars bracing his legs on lower ones. Lucian hung by his hands, swaying back and forth dangling over empty space.

"You should see the blue land traded for this," said Longhorn.

"Yes," said Lucian.

"Let's go," said Longhorn.

"Good," said Lucian.

They swung their way down from the bars. Lucian left a note in the womb room for Beth and the children, that he and Longhorn would be gone for a while. The children knew what to do anyway. It was their world. They had adventures to ride, create, and share. They were empowered to learn. It was their environment. And Beth would be with them.

Lucian and Longhorn mounted their horses and aimed out into the desert evening.

. . .

They had ridden until they felt to stop riding. Ate from plants they found. Lay on the ground and slept. Rode on.

During the next day, they came to Longhorn's turquoise mine.

"No one else knows its location," said Longhorn. "In my desert wanderings I found it. Managed to buy the area. Took pieces of the *sky stone* to sell, and then bought more land. Always sold to a variety of dealers. Never wanted any to see how much I had. Never wanted anyone else to be too curious."

Its entrance was blocked from view by desert growth. Slipping through it, *carefully* through it, for many of the growths had spikes and needles, they entered a series of tunnels that branched out in several directions. These tubes in the earth gave echo to their voices.

Longhorn showed Lucian the veins of the rock. They extracted more and filled saddle bags.

"This is only one of the mines," said Longhorn. "I studied rocks that contained different stones that people valued. I found them here and there. I wandered and found them. Bought the places. Never did anything to make them noticed by others. I roamed the desert. The desert gave to me."

"Land for land," said Lucian, "Earth for earth."

47

Dr. Pandra's concern was evident in her letter. *The material in your thesis,* she wrote to Lucian, *contains the very information I need to cover in my advanced student adaptation class. Your study is the first one to thoroughly document lesson plans that include participation and direct input from students of this age, on the whole range of subjects.*

I took the liberty of contacting the university press, which prints speciality academic studies. I told them that if they would publish a book from your thesis, I would use it as a text, guaranteeing them a certain minimum number of sales annually.

They have just contacted me to say that they are financially strapped with cutbacks in funding and publications are frozen at current titles for two years. No new titles to be considered until then. They suggested three other university presses in other states that seem to be well budgeted and adding numbers of new titles.

What do you think? May I proceed to contact them?

Lucian pondered this late at night, wrapped in his sheet, pacing the house and the desert.

Then, acting on impulse, he rummaged through his university materials, finding the computer disks with the thesis content. He went to the leaning adobe construction that had the sign, *Worm Farm Press*, hanging lopsidedly over its entrance.

Standing, regarding the equipment, he estimated what more would be needed to produce such a full volume.

The next day he appeared at the Junk Shop. Essa Shimek welcomed him in. They went to where David poked through shelves of boxes.

"This," he said, "is what passes in our business, as inventory."

She said, "I was just telling David the other day how much I like to see you coming, Lucian. I have the same reaction a chocoholic has on seeing a triple-layered black forest cake covered with hot fudge."

Lucian looked quizzical.

She added, "I drool in anticipation of what ideas you've come up with next that we can get involved with. You're the light at the end of our junk heap."

"And you can put that on your vita," added David.

When Lucian explained his interest in publishing the thesis, Essa determined what else was needed to add to the equipment that they had already located. Not having it *in stock*, as David said, they hung their *Out to a garage sale sign* on the front door, and under it, the sign, *But take what you want and leave what you think we would think it's worth*, and the three took off to where they could locate the equipment. Used, and at bargain rates, of course.

With the equipment they acquired, Lucian began printing his thesis.

The Shimeks already did the limited binding service needed by the local school library on the old equipment that had been traded in long before.

They bound Lucian's volumes. Stacks of the *first edition* accumulated.

. . .

Beth's embryo classes continued. Every morning. With the beginning of every day. Orgol even developed a little song that started, *Good morning embry-o. It's fun to watch you grow...*

As they discussed the third week of development, sitting there on the floor of the womb room, they all took pages of newspaper, and rolled them up to duplicate the forming of the neural tube. They folded the paper to represent the way the embryo's skin thickens along the midline into two lengthwise folds, forming a groove, that closes up to form the tube.

They attached a ball of paper to one end, representing the swelling that is the beginning of the brain. Strings from this clump of paper running down the early backbone represented nerves.

They wrapped their constructions in two more swaths, representing the three layers of cells and labeled them *germ layers* or *cell layers*. They began to identify from which of these three layers each of the different body organs would start to develop.

"You notice," said Beth, holding up her own version of the paper construction, "how at this stage the embryo is not looking human." Calling attention to different points on the construction, she said, "Here we have the crude beginning of a head around the brain, with a large mouth opening, the bare start of the form of the heart, and the pointy end that is, for all intents and purposes, a tail. We are looking at a primitive tube of life, not unlike primitive tube life that developed in the early seas. We are not only seeing the development of a particular life form, an individual human being, but we are seeing the echoes of the forms of life through which our remote ancestors may have moved."

The days became a biological adventure. They were learning the vocabulary. They were learning about life in primeval seas and its resemblance to the stages of the embryo. They were learning about themselves.

They identified how cells from the outer layer become backbone, nerves, brain, skin, hair. How the middle layer becomes the dermis, muscles and skeleton, the lymph and blood vessels, heart, ovaries, testicles, kidneys. How the inner layer forms a primitive intestinal tube, lungs, and urinary tract.

Looking at a photograph of an embryo in its fourth week, Normita exclaimed, "It's a fish-like thing. It has gills." With a sudden leap of application she exclaimed again, "We had gills! *I had gills!*"

Eriot said, "I wish we could have kept them. It would have made swimming easier. Those ancestors were lucky."

They saw in the pictures, and then replicated on their models, the development of forty tiny blocks of somites, the bone that formed from the middle layer, thirty-two becoming vertebrae. They watched the six projections in the neck section move toward becoming a lower jaw, face, and neck.

Looking at the pictures in the next stages of development, Reendo exclaimed, "That looks like a prehistoric animal. Look at that tail and that bulbous head!"

By the fifth week, the beginning of eyes appeared on either side of the head, nostril holes that looked like those of a reptile, and a mouth like that of a snake.

As the backbone became apparent in the pictures of the sixth week development, the creature's rudimentary limbs looked like fins or flippers. "We're a frog!" exclaimed Pica. "A tadpole!."

They saw the hair that developed all over the skin, that would later drop away before birth. Dolphus asked, "Do you suppose that hair doesn't leave before birth in some babies, and that's how the legends of the wolf-men developed?"

. . .

Lucian's delayed reply to Dr. Pandra's inquiry about publishing the thesis took the form of a package containing the first copies of the book from the Worm Farm Press.

Don't tell me how you managed it, came Dr. Pandra's response. *Enclosed is the order form from the university for thirty copies. Since they needed a price immediately, and you hadn't indicated one, Walter* and I got estimates here as to what such a volume should cost, added a profit percentage, and made up an amount. Let me know if it's too little, and we'll make it up on the next order.

Lucian laughed at the amount. It was beyond anything he would have even considered. They had produced the volumes on dilapidated equipment *held together by bailing wire*, as David had noted, with no additional overhead.

Dr. Pandra's letter continued, *Since the university book store couldn't find Worm Farm Press listed in their catalogs of publishers, they need some information for their files. Could you prepare a simple flyer of some kind, or better, an order list with the titles you already have. What the children have already done will be quite sufficient.*

. . .

Among the book orders from the university book store came a request for boxes of the children's cards. Lucian expressed his surprise at this in a message to Dr. Pandra.

She responded that after his brochure and catalog of publications had arrived for the university book store files, she had gone in and asked to purchase some of the children's cards, expressing her surprise that a store at a university dedicated to education did not carry the line of cards *designed, produced and printed by children as part of their educational process.* The book store manager, after a moment of puzzlement, said that it must have been an oversight and immediately ordered them.

48

"This Dr. Fenwicke, who you mentioned after the school assembly," Beth asked Lucian, "who is that?" They walked around the chemistry room, helping with the mixtures the children experimented with.

"She wrote a book I'd like you to read." Later he gave Beth the manuscript.

Each night, after the children had gone and after she had prepared the next day's science materials, she read from Dr. Fenwicke's work.

"I have wept and I have laughed," she told Lucian. "I would

want my child to know these words, these ways, in its life journey. Why a *manuscript* and not a printed copy?" Beth volunteered to do anything she could to help that happen. *To make it available,* she said, *for her child and other children when they grew up.*

Lucian pondered: Dr. Fenwicke had discarded the manuscript, did not want to be associated with it, had disconnected herself from it. Since she did not wish her name connected to it, Lucian created another name, a Fenwicke *nom de plume.*

With Beth's assistance, he worked each night on preparing it for printing. The Worm Farm Press produced its first novel.

He thought of sending the first copy to Dr. Fenwicke but did not. Instead, he mailed copies to reviewers. One in Sacramento published an article that was more questioning than positive or negative. From that came five individual orders for the volume and a request from the library.

He included this review with copies of the order form and sent them to a small number of other libraries. Seven orders returned.

A reviewer in Pittsburgh produced a scathing analysis of it, in such vivid negative terms that Lucian felt it served as a kind of *magnificent opposite.* He remembered a culture that had the concept that certain things were so good that they could not be described except by their shadow opposite. Thus they created a description of derision and disgust that served as a kind of verbal mold. When the expressed words, the mold, were removed, what remained was the description of the masterpiece, exactly opposite of the now-removed mold. So, without a word being said in praise of the thing, it stood in all its pristine splendor.

Lucian felt the same about the review. And so, making copies of it, he mailed it out with order forms for the book to not only another list of libraries, but to selected book stores as well. He also mailed a copy of the blistering review and a copy of the book to reviewers in those same cities.

Seventy-five orders resulted. Every few days, additional orders arrived.

. . .

Lucian sat at midnight, in the room illuminated by a solitary candle, wrapped in his sheet, with Dr. Fenwicke's book on the table in front of him. He played an ancient melody on a flute from South America.

Then he penned a note to Dr. Fenwicke.

Enclosed is a copy of a book, published from the manuscript you wrote and then wanted to be disjoined from. Since you wished separation from it, I will retain the sense of distance by not detailing how the printed form came to be, nor my background nor connection with it, except to say it is now an important part of me. Any other details you wish, I will supply on your request.

I honor your desire to be distanced from the book by providing a pen name on the cover. I hope you find it an agreeable one. A modest number of copies have been sold. Additional orders come now in small numbers on a regular basis.

Though I secured the copyright, it is, of course, yours, and the adjustment of this can be made as you desire. Enclosed is a check from the Worm Farm Press for all profits.

I will continue to distribute copies in the manner already begun and forward the profits to you periodically, without further details, until I hear from you regarding your wishes.

In your volume, you have written about a juncture of periods of human consciousness for which I, and others who read the work, must be grateful, beyond our ability to express. For those of us who know the turmoil of thoughts in lonely night watches, to see those ideas that developed internally, solitarily, then made available and accessible, rewards us all.

He folded the note, bearing the Worm Farm Press address, placed the check within the fold, placed the note between the front cover and first page, packaged the book, stamped the package, and walked out into the dark night, placing it in the ancient mailbox by the road for pickup the next day.

49

Kayla had reported on the summer trip to Italy where, with Dr. Pandra, she had *cold tracked the Appian Way*. Each of the others had similarly reported on the travel with their families, wherever it had taken them. The pictures they took, their notes and journals, conveyed something the explosion of sensory input they had experienced. And how they had responded to it all.

Kayla, still in the mind-set of that experience, said, as they traced animal tracks into the desert, "Let's trail that." She pointed not at the animal tracks, but toward the arroyo. "I learned this summer that everything, whether human-made or nature-made, begins and ends somewhere. It's like a story. By *trailing* it, we *read* it."

"Organize," said Lucian.

"Well," said Kayla, "there are two ways the arroyo goes. That way and the other way. We could start either way."

"What would we need to take with us?" asked Lucian.

"Food," said Kayla.

"For how many days?" asked Lucian.

"We don't know," said Kayla, "so we should be prepared for several."

Orgol said, "We could cover more distance per day if we rode horses instead of walking."

By this point, everyone had ideas. They sat in a circle on the ground, by the edge of the arroyo and planned its tracking, from end to end.

They studied maps. First the ones they had, with roads and cities on them, but no arroyos.

"What kind of map has *arroyos* on them?" Kayla asked.

Lucian had them phone for information, starting with the university geology department. They secured, in this manner, the location of the state geological commission, where they could get topographical maps.

They loaded into the *bus that did not look like it could get them there but did*, as Pica sometimes referred to it, and drove to the commission office.

The officials responded to the inquiries and soon were on the floor, with dozens of maps spread out, one taking up where another left off, tracing the geographic features.

"So one of you traced the Appian Way?" a geologist said.

"Yes," Kayla answered.

"Boy, I'll bet that was really interesting," he said, in an exaggerated tone used by some adults with children. "And that's really old, too, huh?"

Kayla looked up from the maps and said, "It was built about 312 B.C.E., before the common era. Appian Claudius Caecus, the emperor of Rome at the time, ordered it built. It's more than three hundred and sixty miles long. It was between fourteen and eighteen feet wide." She returned to her scrutiny of the arroyo maps on the floor.

After intense discussions and explanations, the children, led by Kayla, decided on the maps they needed for their trek. These they purchased with a check from the Worm Farm School Adventure Account.

Orgol had moved over to one of the geologists desks, and stared intently at what looked like a clock, but with unusual features. He read the nameplate on the desk and asked, "Mr. Loggat, I've never seen a clock like this before. It has the time—hours, minutes, seconds—but it has another set of numbers that keep changing higher every second. What's that?"

Another employee said, "Now don't get him started on that. That's his biological clock, and you don't want to know."

Normita came over to look at it. "What's a biological clock? I thought it was something my mother referred to about herself, when she said her biological clock was running out."

Howard Loggat brought the two closer to the desk and held the device right in front of them. "It's really a population clock. This indicates how much the earth's human population grows every second."

The other geologist came over and put his hands over the eyes of the two children. "Don't look at his map, because then you may not get out of here for days."

They immediately looked at the wall map behind the desk. In many ways it looked like an ordinary world map, but color coded differently than they had ever seen one, and with small penciled-in numbers in each country.

"Is it a population map?" guessed Orgol.

"Yes, with colors indicated rates of growth, and the numbers I update every three months."

As they readied to go, one of the officials leaned close to Lucian and said, "That sure shoots to blazes the idea that kids don't have more than a short attention span. I'd like to go on this trip myself."

Kayla overheard him and turned back. "Can you?" she said. "You could help us a lot to understand what we were seeing. When we tracked the Appian Way, people who knew the area and history really helped."

The man just laughed and said, "Well, it sure would be fun, now wouldn't it. Yes sir! My name's Bob, so at least call when you set the dates, and if not, when you finish, come by and tell me how it all came out."

50

Beth stayed now most of the time overnight at her round room in the middle of the worm farm structures, from which she could see all the diverse rooms of the others. Her daily explorations in the development of the life in her womb with the children remained the pivot for all of her activities.

During an afternoon when she scanned publications that she had ordered on *pre-natal development*, it occurred to her that more might have arrived by mail. She rose from the piles of pictures she had sorted for assembling, in the middle of the womb room and walked toward the main house.

Lucian had taken the children to interview a woman who lived in the hill country, who today celebrated her one hundred and tenth birthday. They had taken note cards to do a time line of her life and the developments technologically that had taken place during the same period, and the impact of these, as she remembered them.

Beth liked these moments in daytime when all of the results of their activities stood like monuments to the rise of something unnamed, yet no people populated them.

She walked through the house, which she liked also, for it breathed of Lucian, his interests, piles of projects, his sheafs of plans for the children, the candles, the drawings, the sheets of music, the lotus-like scent of a plant that Lucian always brought back with him from the canyon country, the scent that clung to him and hovered about his presence.

She felt in a wispy, drifting mood, as if she had no past, no future, but wafted on the lotus-like fragrance that encompassed her. What she felt herself to be now, remained inextricably intertwined with Lucian, from the moment she had looked out of her archeology pit in the wilderness and saw those eyes, like none other she had ever seen of any other person. She felt that the *Beth* she was now had been born then.

One night, when she had returned late from a dig, as she looked out of the window of her circular room, she had seen him wrapped in his sheet walking from the house out into the desert, as if he owned the desert, or it owned him, or he and the desert were one.

She now noticed the sheet draped over the back of a chair where he had left it, in a room with a solitary candle on the mound of a wax-dripped stalagmite, in the middle of an ancient round oak table. She went in and felt she had entered somehow into the womb that had nurtured her present self.

She resisted not at all the temptation to wrap herself in the sheet, inhaling its desert herbal fragrance, and sat in the chair. She absently, driftingly, without meaning really to look at the material, turned over the pages on the table.

What arrested her attention on the pages that Lucian had written were the words topping the manuscript. Where originally he had printed the title, *The Night King Passes*, these additional words had been penciled in beneath: *Ah, Beth*.

She *glided* into it as she might into a spatial area, unaware of the pages and the words, but immersed in the content.

Of all the purveyors of the sad, late song, there had been no equal. He could write poetry that caused the inner tears to flow in empty people who elbowed bars after midnight. He could sing in a voice that embodied an ache for things unnamed. Things never discovered. And he had sung and talked across the airwaves, through his midnight microphone, his voice massaging their marginal existences through the radios in dim saloons, or in their cars driving nowhere in the night, or in their shadowed solitary rooms.

A lifelong of writing, and one theme exquisitely diversified. He had mourned lost life, or life lost, somewhere between the birthing and the long dying, where living had been misplaced or never defined.

His listeners sat by smoke curling from ashtrays, by the bottled deadeners ready to anesthetize the brain parts that thought too much.

He wrote the words and read them into the night airwaves, or sang them, that said to the all-alone, "I hear echoes from another so alone that he knows; I am therefore not alone."

Drifting in that zone of shadows between the sun's scarlet setting and its amber rising, he had been the king of night, the voicer of sentiments so private, they were universal. He was the poet of the night.

And how he died affected no one: ...singer, poet dead...last seen...found by...no sign of...remembered for...

Remembered for the sounds of night that gray-faced listeners never observed until he voiced them.

Found dead, and no one cared. Found dead and no one claimed the body. Found...and no living kin.

No kin at all. None. Not anywhere. Unrelated to anyone on earth.

Perhaps a thousand-year blooming flower not seen since...not to be seen until...Not parented, not perennial, but...a rare night flower.

When no kin came, and legal time permitted, he was interred. Only the diggers came. The diggers and the fillers. They were paid and did their work. And no one cared.

That was in the day, that no one came. That no one cared. There were flowers, a few that wilted in the closing technicolor world of day with reds and greens, then blended in the night's leaf-shadow shades of gray.

It was day and no one cared nor came.

But with the night came gray and purple figures, solitary, shadows among shadows. They moved past the marker and the gray and purple flowers, the remnants of the day.

One by one the shadows came. Shadow people from the bars, and night jobs, and coffin apartments.

They knew neither his visage nor a place related to his presence, when he had lived. But with the passing of the day and him, this place became somehow known.

Whispers in the night from lips his words had taught. Whispers of his words, uttering what they wished to say. They spoke his words by his grave. He had empowered them to speak.

No two came together. All came alone, to mourn his life they had not known, to mourn their own solitariness again.

And in the darkest part of night, one of them stood, a shadow in the shadows and whispered back the poet's words that rustled like the night leaves:
I sing, but not too loudly.
I move, but not assured.
And when they leaned forward, each, these figures, each alone, to read the words inscribed upon the marker, upon the stone that looked to have been placed there, not recently, but a thousand years ago, they read its two only words.
And they each whispered them alone into the wind. And knew they had been wordlessly repeating this phrase inside forever, but never until this moment knew the words, the words to say aloud. He taught them the final lesson, in the blackness of the night, in the core of blackness within, he gave them words to say:
Ah, Beth.

. . .

Lucian had dated his writings, out in the margins. The part up to *I move but not assured,* had been penned at an earlier time. But the latter part, the part that included her name as the inscription on the stone, that part had been written on the night she had returned and announced her pregnancy and being married.

And she who bore the name upon the stone within the writing, she cocooned herself within the sheet and lay upon his bed for a time, before returning to her circle of a room at the desert's edge. The pillow was damp on which her head had rested.

. . .

That night, when Lucian had seen the children home and had read passages from the Egyptian Book of the Dead and had charted more of the pharaohs of the dynasties of that land, preparatory to a time grid on its history, and played an ancient instrument pictured on the hieroglyphic walls of Karnak, he then proceeded to his bed.

There he found the scent of sandalwood and myrrh. He drifted into visionary sleep with the enigmatic statue of a Queen of the Nile becoming alive, turning her eyes toward him, and stepping from a pedestal, reaching out to him and he toward her, her hair of burnished copper glowing like a sunset in Luxor, as they merged.

51

"Do you think Bob from the geographical survey office might come with us?" asked Kayla. Plans proceeded for tracking the arroyo to its source. "I asked him when we were there."

"I remember you did," said Lucian, surveying the maps.

"But I don't think he will," Kayla said.

The two of them sat out under the cottonwood trees. Everyone else had left for the day, but Kayla's van from the orphanage was late.

"How so?" said Lucian.

"Some people are interested in observing what other people do, without getting involved. He enjoyed us visiting, in doing his job, explaining things to us. Then when we left, he could turn to whatever he needed to do next and concentrate on that and not think about us."

"What made you feel that?"

"There's a person at the orphanage like that. He concentrates on us when we need something, but then he goes on to the next person and concentrates on them. He's nice. But somehow, I don't know if he thinks of us as people, only part of his job. That's okay, isn't it?"

"Of the several people in the office with Bob, do you remember any who were different than that?"

"I think we were a diversion for them. They all seemed to know a lot about geology. Is there something different in knowing *about* something, and..." she searched for words to express her feeling. She often *moved* to think, and started walking. Lucian followed her, and they strolled out toward the dinosaur skeleton.

She climbed up the metal supports that held the center of the rib cage and looked out at Lucian through the ribs. "I like this view," she said. "If a dinosaur had eaten me, this is where I would be and could look out at the world from here. If..." she added laughing, "...it was a *transparentasarus*."

She thought more. "That opposite thing I'm trying to think of. It's like people can study dinosaurs and can know *about* them. But then, like we do, we really feel their relationship to *us*." She looked at Lucian for confirmation.

"I know what you mean." He climbed up on the supports and looked at her from the front of the rib cage. "Did you feel anyone at the geological survey office had that kind of connection to geology, relating *to* it instead of knowing *about* it?"

"Yes!" she sparkled, jumping down to the ground. "That Mr. Loggat. It was like…it was like…" She again searched for words. She started moving toward the automotive time line, climbed in one of the cars, Lucian got into the other, and they drove slowly through the decades.

"…it was like he *lived* it," Kayla said. "Like he felt he was a *part* of it." She circled back to the beginning and stopped. They sat their in their little cars and looked at each other like two people waiting for a traffic light to change.

"How would you describe it?" Kayla asked.

"People seem to get rewards or satisfaction from different things. For some, being busy and getting paid is their reward. For others, the knowledge or activity, itself, is the reward. For Howard Loggat, he seemed to lose track of time and place when we were there. Your delight in the material seemed to be his satisfaction."

"Yes!" said Kayla. "Let's ask *him*."

. . .

Lucian located the phone number so Kayla could call Howard Loggat.

The phone call from Kayla found him at the geological center counter rolling up maps for two hikers going into the back country. He listened to Kayla's invitation to join the worm farm troop in *cold tracking the arroyo.*

"I don't know," he said, even while thinking what fun it would be, remembering back to the first time of his awareness that the earth beneath his feet made up the composition of all animate beings. He forgot the two men at the counter.

He listed some options into the phone, asking if any of these would be all right: "What if I came along for just a day or two? Any problem if I didn't know until the last minute and just showed up?"

Then, in an impulsive and unexplained question, he suddenly asked Kayla, "What are the rock strata exposed at your place?"

Kayla named them in ascending order.

"How do you know that?" he asked.

"Lucian told us," she replied.

Howard chuckled. "And," he asked, "what are the age-equivalent formations in central Africa?"

Kayla listed them without hesitation.

"Who told you that?" he asked.

Kayla answered, "Lucian told us."

Howard chuckled again. "Oh, my," he said, "*oh, my.*"

As a kind of *threshold to epiphany* question, he queried, "And is one of your goals to know all of the strata in sequence, in all the continents of the world?" He half way expected silence on this.

There was only the slightest pause before Kayla responded, "Yes. Would you help us? If you come, you could show us the *real things,* just like you were showing us the places on the maps. But Lucian says that maps are only representations of reality and have no meaning except to guide us to the reality itself. You seemed to..." she did not know exactly how to express the feeling that came to her, "...to *like* the earth. And so do we."

"Oh," said Howard, "the endorphins are flowing."

"Those are brain chemicals that make us feel good, aren't they?" asked Kayla.

"Oh, yes," said Howard, "*very good.*"

He hung up the phone, with a grin of satisfaction on his face, and repeated aloud, forgetting he was not alone, "The endorphins are flowing." He turned to look into the faces of the two hikers who were staring questioningly at him.

· · ·

A letter came from the geological commission, from Howard Loggat. He did not mention more about the proposed arroyo journey. Instead, he said he had been recalling the focused faces of the children when they had been at the commission office. It had occurred to him that if field trips were part of Worm Farm School agenda, there was a place not to overlook. His note continued: *Half way between where you're located and the geological land office is an animal conservancy. I've become acquainted with the founder-owner, as he has requested our services concerning certain geological features of his extensive holdings.*

Once I started going there professionally, I came to like the place immensely. Among other things, he preserves animals that are rare or facing extinction. In my off time, I've even gone to help out with some of the newborns. I've worked with giraffes, zebras, and some exotic antelope. But he can tell you the details himself. I'm sure he would welcome your group. Enclosed is a map, phone number, etc.

52

Lucian and Reendo had been decorating Reendo's house. Not the room at Worm Farm School, but his home with Grandmother.

The place had begun to change under Reendo's influence. What he peered at under the microscope inspired its painted representation on the walls of his room in florid colors.

Grandmother had called Lucian for one of their night walks when they talked about the universe and Reendo's place in it. She had asked Lucian if he thought it was a good idea to let Reendo decorate, paint, diagram, on the walls of his room.

Lucian, in his turn, had asked her what she thought.

"The inside and the outside are one. Only language separates them into two. The walls of his room are the projection screens of his mind. On them can appear what is within."

"It is so," Lucian had said.

"You are starting to sound like me," Grandmother had replied, adding, "Then let the room evolve."

First there had appeared patterned visions from the world of the microscope. Reendo had taken Lucian to his room after he had painted these in profusion up the walls and onto the ceiling.

Pointing to the last one, Reendo had said, "And that's your sperm."

"I know," Lucian had said, "I recognized the portrait."

He then pointed to the corner of the room, saying "There's my biorhythms, when we studied those."

Since that time, the whole house was evolving into something else. The wall paintings had migrated out of the bedroom and invaded the hallway and into the kitchen. Starting at the dining table, a time line wound its way around all four sides. Pinned to the walls at the appropriate positions were pictures of events Reendo had been studying.

Lucian had taken the children to a library sales when discarded books were being sold for a few coins each. They had stocked up on dozens of pictured volumes. These they could cut up and use in time lines. So it was that two centuries curled around Reendo at breakfast.

Now Reendo had invited Lucian over on this Saturday to help him with the next project: a diagram of a dinosaur skeleton on the front room wall, with each bone labeled.

First he took Lucian to the kitchen to show him the continued development of the wrap-around time line. "This, and this, and this," he said, pointing to various pictures and notes along decades, "all of these Grandmother added. Here," he pointed again, "she put the first picture of me after I was born. And so here," he indicated a picture of another baby a ways back along the temporal route, "is where I put a picture of her when she was little."

Grandmother entered with some old sheets and spread them over the floor and furniture in the front room. Then she and Reendo and Lucian, together, created a representation of a skeleton, each bone identified.

"Next time," said Grandmother, "we will start a new time-line of tribal history."

The three of them sat looking at their handiwork, sipping a combination of celery and carrot juice.

Reendo said, "We need to invite him, the old truck man." He thought for a moment and adjusted, "The man with the old truck." And he added after another pause, "Unclear modifier. You know—the man who took us to Cactus Max for breakfast." Reendo produced a letter he had written and handed it to Lucian.

We are the people from the Worm Farm School who found you on the road, whom you took to breakfast. You have a kind face. You were interested in the things we did. You looked sad sometimes, not when we were together, but like there was a leftover of sadness of whatever you had been doing before we met you and maybe what you had to go back to. We're going to track the wild arroyo, following it to its source. We don't know how long it will take. But it doesn't matter. We won't miss any school. We take our school with us wherever we go. The school isn't the building but we are the school. We like the cottonwoods more than the building. We know that school is not a place but what we do. It is an attitude. So if you enjoyed the "attitude" you had, yourself, when we were together, you might like to track the arroyo with us. All you need is a sleeping pack. Longhorn has an extra horse. You can bring some dried food, but we'll have a lot of that too. I enjoyed things with you and hope you will come. And maybe if you do, when you go back to whatever you do that makes you sad, you won't be so sad. Your friend, Reendo.

"But I guess we can't send it to him because we don't know his name or address. And..." Reendo added with a grin, "...it's unlikely he'll still be by the side of the road with his truck."

Lucian said, "Come on."

He and Reendo and Grandmother headed out in Gitano's old car. They drove the back roads. They and their dust trail traveled alone on most of them.

Lucian's destination: Cactus Max.

They entered the gloomy interior. A few isolated individuals and pairs huddled at rickety tables at the edges of the room.

A man in clothes that looked like they had been inspired by the colors of the desert sand, with hair that had grown without interference, sprawled in a chair, caressing a guitar and singing in a voice like the desert breeze. He sang to himself, as if no one else existed. He sang of remote corners of life where no direct light had ever shown.

Max, himself, moved unhurriedly among the tables, and Dolphus later described him as *being like a personified slow-motion biorhythm.*

The three approached the bar. Max squinted at them. "This is a bar," he said. Indicating Reendo with a nod of his head, he continued with an expressionless face, "Is the kid eighteen yet?"

"Mentally," said Lucian, duplicating the expressionless face.

"Good," said Max, not breaking character, "cause I can't serve anyone under age. So what'll you have? For you..." he indicated Reendo again, "I suggest some citrus tequila, since you're of age."

Max poured and slid a glass of lemonade in front of Reendo.

"And for you guys," he said to Grandmother and Lucian, "a double C-T. For the road." He slid a lemonade in front of each of them. "With a worm," he said, dropping a cherry into each of their drinks.

Lucian held up the envelope that contained the letter. "Could you get this to *him*, when he comes in?"

He did not explain who *him* was, nor did Max need to ask.

Max kept doing things at the bar. There did not seem to be anything obvious to do, but he did them anyway. As if he never stopped. As if it was his dance of life, and he knew the choreography called for him to continue.

He looked at the envelope, as if sizing it up, as if it had been a character that had walked through the swinging doors of a bar in a western movie.

"Sure," he said. "Sometimes he comes in. Sometimes he doesn't." He took the envelope and with the other hand pointed to the knife area somewhere in the gloom on the far wall. To Reendo he said, "Okay, eighteen year old kid, go get me a blade."

Reendo complied. He handed it to Max and said, his own face taking on the expressionlessness too, "I got it this time, Max, but when you get to be my age, you'll have to get it yourself."

With this, Max broke character and laughed out loud. With the knife, he stuck the envelope onto one of the wooden supports near the stools at the bar.

53

There had not been much said about who would move out into the desert on the morning appointed for the start of this trek, this exploration of the usually dry water channel from somewhere to somewhere else. The children all knew they were going, and Lucian, of course.

Longhorn, who hovered around them all like a protective presence, helping things to be in place when they were needed, could simply not be anywhere else but on the journey into the desert, across the vastness that had become his exterior self.

The children had wanted Zoyan'qual to come. During their previous visit to the canyon country, he had said *yes*. Instead of coming to worm farm, he would meet them *en route*, when their arroyo led them into his terrain.

Already, he and the worm farm group had developed a system of carrier pigeons, which the children were now studying. They were investigating the means of animal navigation, of how creatures found their way across seemingly *unchartered* spaces, somehow *charted* to the animals. Zoyan'qual had told them of how such directional perception seemed to be related to iron deposits located in special magnetic sensing organs. Most intriguing, he had told them of speculations about the accumulations of minute iron deposits in the noses of human beings, that may be vestigial remnants of a directional sensory organ in people. Some people may still have it well enough developed to detect magnetic north, he had explained.

So, they had agreed to loose a pigeon with the message of the time of their departure, and somewhere along the way, Zoyan'qual would join them.

When the children had questioned Beth about making this unpredictable journey, while pregnant, she had given them all a look, what Jhenaw now called simply *a Beth look*.

Beth had said, "The trek is important. Also important, your keeping up on a daily basis with the development of this child. Of course I will ride with you. And every morning we will continue our progress report of life in the womb." So Beth prepared to go.

Neither the man for whom the note had been left at Cactus Max Cantina nor Howard Loggat had confirmed that they would go.

So the morning arrived. Lucian, the children, and Beth prepared their bedrolls and other equipment. Longhorn readied the horses.

Then he arrived. Howard Loggat. He drove up to the front of worm farm in a pickup truck pulling a double horse trailer. He went to Kayla and shook her hand. "Thank you for the invitation to explore the earth together." He turned to the truck as a child emerged. "This is my nephew, Lee."

"And wait until you see what's in there," said Lee, going

around to the trailer door.

Before they unloaded the trailer, Howard said, "Call it whimsy, if you will," as the group semi-circled about them. "You remember the animal conservancy I wrote you about? Well, it's one of my favorite places. The owner and I have become friends, and he lets me come after hours and wander the place. I go there to think things through, when I need to. He has one of the rarer kinds of zebra there..."

"Ahhh!" said Orgol audibly, jumping ahead in the story.

"Right," said Howard, "you've guessed. I went down for the birth of several of the animals, and Lee started going with me. Among them was a rare zebra. Born about the same time, another creature from a totally different part of the world, a reindeer. We hand-raised them together. Growing up that way, they're inseparable. In the process, we started speculating what it would be like to ride them like horses. Zebras are usually not considered to have the temperament for it."

Here he opened the doors of the carrier, and out stepped the zebra, ears alert, sniffing the air, and just behind him, the reindeer, both welcoming the petting hands of the children.

"Ahhh!" said Orgol again. "Do they have names?"

"Zee and Rain," said Lee. With the sound of the words, the animals turned their heads toward him and nuzzled his side.

Their attention diverted. Riding her horse across the desert came Grandmother. Prepared and ready. "I've always wondered where the water in that arroyo came from," she said. "And Beth needs her healer to take care of her."

Another cloud of dust from down the road, and another horse trailer, but of unusual dimensions, stopped in front of the house. The same uniformed man who had visited once before, with the check Lucian had refused, asked, "Is this where the *coal stacking an oriole*, or whatever it's called, is commencing?" he asked.

"Cold tracking the arroyo," Pica corrected.

"Whatever," he replied, in the manner of one often called upon to do things not fully understood, but who knows the sun will rise tomorrow anyway, whether he understands or not.

They all gathered around to watch him open the doors of the trailer.

The uniformed man coaxed out of the trailer's interior a camel. Orgol exclaimed, "Look, a Picasso horse."

"A desert ship," said grandmother, matter-of-factly.

"A *ship of the desert*," recommended Reendo.

"The same thing," said grandmother.

The uniformed man handed the reins to Longhorn and said, "Here. I don't know what happens next. I am only the messenger. Delivering this beast." He entered his vehicle and drove off in a cloud of dust.

From that dust cloud emerged another vehicle. The companion of the *bus that belonged*. The truck of the same vintage. The truck with a flat tire when they had first encountered it. It pulled up and stopped.

From it emerged the figure they had met on the road, who had breakfasted with them at Cactus Max. But he was not clad in ageless denim this time. A flowing desert robe of rainbow stripes, a headdress of the desert, its tails caught by the wind.

"Its Lawrence of the Rainbow!" laughed Dolphus.

The man stood for a moment regarding the diverse assemblage and said, "Ah, I see I fit right in. I have always wanted to do this. Except I didn't know it until you invited me."

He walked toward Reendo, extending his hand. "Thank you for the invitation, Reendo. Join me." Still clasping hands, they walked to the camel which now bellied on the ground, its legs folded beneath it. The man mounted and drew Reendo beside him. He tapped the camels side and gave a command. The camel rose, half of the front legs extended, then half of the hind legs, followed by the rest of the front legs, the remainder of the back legs, one segment at a time. Each partial rising threw the two riders first backward, then forward, then repeated, until they towered above the others.

"We are ready," the man said. Then noticing Lee, he added, "I didn't meet you before, young man, what is your name."

"Lee, and what's yours?"

Reendo said, "Since you never told us before, I get the feeling you don't really want to tell us your name, and that's all right. But we have to refer to you as something. What shall we call you?"

The man looked at the group, with a shrug of the shoulders

and raised eyebrows, as if to ask for suggestions.

"Camel-rider," said Reendo, without hesitation.

Hardly had Camel-rider been named, in this magnetic gathering that attracted participants, than they saw another rider coming across the desert. He reined in. "Good! I got here in time. I didn't think I was going to be able to arrange this."

It was Dolphus' father. Riding a Clydesdale. "What are you looking at?" he asked. "I'm a big man and I need a big horse. You know Dolphus has transformed our house into something cosmic. I've gotten so caught up in everything, that I wanted to experience this, too, instead of just hearing him describe it when he gets back."

He looked around, pausing at the camel and its riders. "So, are we all here? Ready to go?"

Lucian said, "Several times I would have said *yes* to that question, but I'm not sure any more."

"This is like another *gathering*," laughed Normita.

She jokingly shaded her eyes with her hand, like a sailor scanning the horizon for more ships. They heard a car stop on the other side of the house, saw the inevitable dust cloud blow over the house, heard the car door slam. Around the corner of the house came Walter Pandra, running.

"You're still here! Good! And I hope you have a spare horse. I couldn't bring one," Walter said, suddenly becoming aware of people he did not know.

Longhorn handed him the reins of an animal. "I knew you would come," Longhorn said simply.

"You did?" said Walter. "I didn't even know. Janice sends her *bon voyage*, but has to work. I had a bunch of time coming, because I almost never take off."

"Any more?" said Lucian, as if voices would answer from the desert.

"Oh, I forgot to tell you," said Eriot. "My mother said that since she had never done things like this, she wanted to ask if it was all right to come. I knew it would be. She'll be here."

And she came. Long hair tied back, wearing what looked like a comfortable adaptation of a bull fighter's garments, riding around the side of the house from the road.

And then another horse and rider came around the other side of the house. Astride her mount sat Essa Shimek, from the Junk Shop. "Wow!" she said, surprised by the gathering before her.

She said, "David and I both wanted to come but one of us has to stay with the store. But he's right behind me in the truck. He has something."

David Shimek appeared moments later, lugging coats for the children. Not just any coats. Down-sized replicas of old western coats, long, collared, rugged.

Soon the children stood looking like *the wild bunch* from a western movie. David disappeared back around the house and reappeared with the hats. Broad brimmed, low-crowned, a perfect addition to the coats.

"All we need are the side guns to look ready for the cameras to roll," said Kayla.

"We couldn't resist this," said David. "We had a trade-in of one of the coats and thought how great you'd all look riding off into the sunset in these. So we got the material and..." he gestured toward the finished products.

"Mount up," said Lucian, "and gather around in a semi-circle."

There they sat, on their mounts, the horses, the Clydesdale, Howard astride the zebra with Lee on the reindeer beside them, the camel, along with the extra pack horses that Longhorn led, with the additional supplies.

Lucian took colored powders that Zoyan'qual had given them on their last journey to the canyon country, for the initiation of the journey. Lucian spread them to the four directions.

He said, "Zoyan'qual has indicated that the *saying* must precede the *doing* of a journey. The *saying* gives the context, the binding of the people who will journey together. So here is our *saying* for what will come."

Howard Loggat smiled as if he had just heard something outwardly that had a resonance with something internal. As if on the hearing of this prelude, he had suddenly understood something about himself.

Lucian spoke. "We begin now the journey, but no true journey goes merely to a place. We are not going only to the headwater of the arroyo. Any more than those in India who

223

believe the headwaters of the Ganges to be a sacred place, a source of life. Yet, going there, they find only melting snow. What they see outwardly is a symbol, a metaphor, of something they seek within. But if they don't know this, they see only snow thaw.

"Such a journey as ours is not to a place. The place is a metaphor of the self. We set out into the desert, and we journey into ourselves.

"So a journey of place must be translated into the real journey. And we will each take part. Around the campfire every night, we shall tell where we have been. For though we all have traversed the same land, each will have had an individual journey that day of personal insights.

"The journey of no person is known to another until it is shared, and that we shall do with each other.

"We need, then, a singer of songs, to reflect in music the sights seen. We need a questioner, to voice the *why* and *how* of what we view. And we need the teller of the epic, who chronicles the narration of this exploration.

"We need a spokesperson for the earth, to interpret its shapes and colors, its textures and layers, consistency and contents.

"We need the viewer of the plants along the way to speak for them.

"And we need one to interpret the sounds of animal cries in the distance, and the tracks upon the surface, the nests on branches, the holes of inhabitants in the ground.

"We need the teller of the clouds and winds, who speaks for these to us.

"We need the teller of the tales of ancient ancestors who walked this land before and left their legends hovering over every hill and oasis."

Then Lucian released the homing pigeon with a message to Zoyan'qual attached, in the capsule on its leg, saying in the New Tongue, *We come.*

The bird flew upward and circled three times above their heads, describing a halo for the group, and then winged its way toward the canyons.

Lucian said, "The journey began with an idea voiced by Kayla. Now we continue onward towards *discovery.*"

With this, Grandmother said, in her other language, *"Discovery,"* and headed her horse outward toward the arroyo. The rest followed.

54

The areas of contribution mentioned by Lucian attracted particular sojourners to them. Howard became the revealer of the folds and erosions of the earth. He pointed to landforms and attached names to them, as they rode. The names empowered everyone to talk about them, ask about them, conceptualize them, think about them.

"Is this," asked Reendo, "what it means in the old sagas, when they said there was *power in naming?* Were they discovering that in names is the power to think about and discuss things?"

They would approach a *geological experience,* as Jhenaw began to call them, and Howard would have them speculate on what they saw. Then he would attach names to the kinds of rocks and the structures.

They saw rigid cones, rising starkly above the plain. "Once a volcano existed there. What we see is the volcanic neck, enclosed by a weak shale formation."

"The whole desert," Orgol said, "is like a time line. All these things happened *sometime.* Lucian, this is our biggest time line yet." Then with an additional thought, he looked up into the blue sky of day, thinking of the stars they would see there tonight, and how they had measured the time it took the light from them to arrive on earth, and added, "except for the time line out there."

"Look at that butte," pointed Howard. "Where it rises in relatively horizontal lines, you have sandstone. But look at the base, how it fans out at a forty-five degree angle. That is made up of weak shales that erode differently than the sandstone."

They rode by spires resembling painted columns, with strata-streaks banding them. "Those," said Howard, "are carved strata from the Eocene age. They were limestone beds laid down in an ancient freshwater lake, lifted up as a high plateau, and then eroded."

They picked up pieces of the rocks they discussed. Soon they could identify them by sight.

While Howard named the rocks and the shapes they formed and the designations of the strata and their ages, at the same time they also encountered the plants that grew on the land among the formations. Here, Grandmother and Longhorn served as the guides.

"Introducing us to the plants," said Pica, "is like going through a neighborhood. And you saying about the people, there's so-and-so, and telling us about their background and how long they've lived there."

Grandmother knew their names, and as well, their medicinal values. She stroked leaves from stalks, rubbed her fingers over them, releasing intensified smells for the others to identify.

"The juice of this leaf," she observed about a prickly plant, the green-gray leaves sprouting from the protective base of the thorns, "heals the skin. The plant will not only stick you with its thorns, but heal the wound." She spoke its name in her language.

"How does that translate?" asked Kayla.

"As the *irony* plant," said Grandmother. "Actually, that's my name for it. It seems to me an irony that it can hurt and heal, together."

Longhorn knew the plants' *distances in time*. He could describe the epochs of their development. "These two," he said, when they circled around two similar thorny, waxy growths, "migrated from opposite directions. "This one came from the north, this from the south. Both migrating into the desert region. The one is related to the rose family. The other to the legumes. But both adapted to the arid climate in the same way, to conserve their water, and not to be eaten by foraging animals. Now they closely resemble each other."

In the nighttime, Walter became the *teller of the stars*. When the campfire embers died and the panoply of stellar light spread above, he named sections and patterns, empowered everyone to talk about them, as they had the landforms and plants in the daylight.

Dolphus' father surprised them all with his renditions of songs. "Before my formal education, before my work at the space center, I went through a time I thought of being a singer. Of folk songs. I wanted to see the world as other people saw it. I figured they sang about not only what they saw, but *how* they saw it." He would pull from his memory songs with references to mountains, plants, and stars.

"You never sing at home," said Dolphus.

"I'm a closet singer," his father said.

"Good," retorted Dolphus in a Grocho Marx voice, "we'll clean out one so you can use it."

Camel-rider became the *connector*. He sat at the campfire and referred to what they had seen during the day, remembered random references people had made, taking phrases from the songs, and would say, "Think about how this relates." Or, "Look how the name for the Jurassic rock formation connects to the *sand song*." As others took the raw materials received by the senses and discussed them, he took these names and explanations and wove them into another level of contemplation.

Beth was the *curator* for the ancient people who had lived on the land, who had used the plants and viewed the stars. She entered into their perspective and theorized how they, the old ones who had lived here, related to this, their environment. During the day, she had seen a large circle of rocks. Dismounting, she had excitedly shown the others an ancient calendar. "Look at the alignment," she said. "Look at the placement of the stones toward the points of solstice sunrises and settings."

"What was your first clue that these weren't just random rocks?" asked Normita.

Beth started to explain, then stopped herself, remembering what Lucian did, and said, "Look. Think. Tell me."

"Ah!" said Eriot, as if something had just erupted before him. "Those are basalt rocks, and there are not others like that around here. So they had to be carried in. And only humans would do that. For a purpose."

Howard was at that moment pointing silently to a formation in the distance. "From there. They carried them from there," he said.

. . .

The campfire. The night. And time. Food eaten. The stars above. The quarter moon. Sounds of creatures in the distance.

"Lucian has been talking to us about how people choose careers," Reendo said to Howard. "How did you choose yours? How did you decide to go into geology?"

The burning branches on the fire sent a fragrance into the night air, the scent of promise and discovery that fires provide, the flames drawing the thoughts to *possibilities*.

"This trip was a remarkable kind of *opening up* for me," Howard replied, "and I didn't know why. That is, I didn't have words to explain it, until Lucian spoke at the start of it, at the *saying* for our traveling.

"He mentioned a journey into self. I realized that's what geology meant for me. Everything I studied about it opened revelations to myself. The whole professional study became a metaphor for *me*—my *layers, evolution, erosions,* and *eruptions*.

"It became clear why, or how, I used to differ from other students majoring in the subject, and later, from most of my co-workers. They studied information as if it existed outside of themselves. I was studying myself. Maybe that's the difference between a job and a passion. A finding of your own identify."

When he paused, Pica said, "More."

"I grew up, wanting to find my *roots*. Whatever, or wherever that might be. I thought it was in *ethnicity*. When I got to college, I majored first in African-American studies. I wanted to find my roots in *Mother Africa*. My family was delighted that I was exploring our heritage. Among other courses was one about the geography and geology of that continent. It was like something deep stirred within me. We all, in the department, could apply for a travel scholarship during the summer to go to Africa. I received one. I thought I was going to my ancestral *home*.

"What I found were diverse people, cultures, governments, all interesting, but not my *home*. One particularly long field trip took us out into the countryside, onto the *land*. And this guide, from a local tribe, loved the land—the land, *itself*. He kept making reference to the different tribes and how they each interacted differently with the land.

"Then it hit me. The land had helped *shape* them and their *food, houses* and *myths*. Their social contours were contours of the land, itself. And what was true *there*, was true *everywhere*.

"There was another student from my school with us. He was of Irish background. In *African-American* studies, mind you. He used all the phrases, about *Mother Africa* and *finding his roots.*

"*How,* I finally asked him, as we wandered that wild land, that piece of the African continent, *how* is this your *home?*

"He looked at me puzzled and said that human life probably evolved first in Africa. *Mother Africa* was the parent of the whole human species. And the next moment, I fell to the ground and dug in my fingers and lifted up handfuls, letting it fall on my head and face, like I was having some kind of *earth orgy.*

"*The earth was the parent of us all.* Not *this* earth in Africa, or *that* earth somewhere else, but the globe, itself. And everything we are, the shape of our bodies, the means of locomotion, how we ingest food, the temperature of our bodies, the form of our reproduction, our minds, our language—all reflect the *earth*, the place that begot us.

"My roots were not in one place or ethnicity. I *had* come home. To the *earth.* And the field of study related to geology and geography and all their branches, had become my passion. It led me not into a job, but into a *quest.*"

Eriot stared thoughtfully into the fire. "So," he said, "it's like the baby in Beth's womb. It's developing, and we're following how it develops until it will be born. And you've been telling us how you were, in a way, *born* into your job. How you didn't just select it, but the process was like a *birth.*"

Howard Loggat looked at him in the same way that Eriot stared into the fire. Howard slowly nodded assent.

"And," Eriot continued, "we are now like that, each in our own womb, finding out what we feel passionate about. So that employment can be not so much of a selection but a *birthing process* of our own selves."

Camel-rider had raised both hands to his head, as if holding in a thought or feeling that expanded internally and laterally. He half laughed and half sighed and lay back on the ground in slow motion, his hands still at his head. "Eriot," he said, "Take me with you."

55

There was a clue before it happened. A kind of foreshadowing. They were in the canyon country now, the arroyo leading them ever upward into the high land, toward its origin.

The clue arrived in the form of a fox. A desert fox, with alertness and personality. Not that all desert foxes did not have individuality. But this personality was *known* to some of them. The children looked, and out of whatever number of foxes roamed the wilderness, they saw, with simple recognition, not just *some* desert fox. They saw *Taco*, the individual, the unique personality that they knew.

For those in the group who did not know Taco, who saw a sandy colored desert creature as one of a generic category, they looked with surprise at the others who said, *Taco*, and dismounted to greet him as an unexpected friend.

Taco responded in kind, with almost a cat-like attitude of *I am really overjoyed to see you but I cannot show it all at once.*

So there stood the fox. And they were in the canyon country of Zoyan'qual. And where Taco appeared, could Zoyan'qual be far behind? Those clustered around the friendly fox were not thinking beyond the moment. Some of the others, sitting on their mounts watching the scene centering around the animal, neither knew the name *Taco* nor what a *Zoyan'qual* was.

But even this furry foreshadower could not have prepared any of them for what happened next. Except for Lucian. He knew. He anticipated. He waited.

For unknown to the children, to anyone but Lucian, the desert canyon menagerie of creatures that Zoyan'qual interacted with—the fox, the hawk, even a great king snake that came and sunned itself on a ledge, sometimes draping itself over Zoyan'qual's leg—that this menagerie also included a *bison*. A buffalo.

Zoyan'qual had wondered about the interaction of human and animals for transport among the ancient ones. Horses had become extinct on the North American continent before the arrival of human nomads. But there had been buffalo. In abundance. By the thousands, by the tens of thousands. In herds that had stretched their migrations from far into Canada to the lands of Mexico.

Buffalo had provided the meat and fur, the material for implements of all kinds, and had entered into the legends and myths of tribes for untold centuries. Why, he had thought, might not one of those human ancestors have looked at the buffalo for an additional contribution. Why not as a mount?

So he, the *new-ancient one*, looked at his environment and wondered what might happen if he interrelated with the buffalo in a way different from the old ones who had lived here.

He had traveled to a ranch north of the canyons where the owner kept a buffalo herd. The rancher's interest in raising them first developed in response to his own *reading* of the land, how it had once been. The spirit of the buffalo seemed to hover over him. He called himself a *cowboy of Indian ancestry*.

When Zoyan'qual had gone to meet him, the rancher had quipped that as a child, he had played *cowboys and Indians* all by himself, being qualified for both parts.

The rancher felt intrigued by this *human of the land* who had walked onto his ranch, inquiring about the possibility of acquiring a new-born buffalo, to take, and raise, and maybe ride. He felt intrigued that this stranger had no money and stood there asking what he might exchange to make such a trade.

The rancher had said, "Of course, we all call them buffalo, but unscientifically, for they are North American bison." They both had stood there and laughed. "What a tyranny of dead men," said the rancher, "that they tell us what to call the objects standing before us, the living."

"I call them *Keematan*," Zoyan'qual said, using the New Tongue term.

The rancher had at last said, "Yes. One just weaned. You take him. And in exchange, if and when you manage to ride him, come back. Come back and share the experience. Come thundering over the ridge south of the ranch, and the sight of that and the story you'll tell me will be payment in kind."

When they had parted, Zoyan'qual leading the buffalo calf, the rancher had walked with them to the edge of his property, and then said, "May the freedom of the winds accompany you, my brother."

So it was that the animal had grown up under Zoyan'qual's care. A canyon near the cliff houses had one narrow open end. This space Zoyan'qual had roped off, providing the animal ample room to roam, without leaving the area. He took it for daily walks, and then ran along beside it.

Early on, he had straddled it, and, as it grew in size, had remained seated on its back for a longer period each day. Then the riding began. It extended the range of Zoyan'qual's movement.

When the animal attained full stature, it still behaved as a calf, playful, running to Zoyan'qual, responsive to his shifts of weight and hands on the thick head and shoulder mane.

Zoyan'qual had ridden the animal back to the ranch, to see the rancher as promised. As hoped for, the man worked outside when the buffalo and rider came galloping over the hill top.

The rancher shouted, "The spirits have returned! Buffalo and rider, the spirits have returned."

Examining the buffalo after its rider dismounted, the man said, "You have done well. I am inspired to see you riding this way. The creature is a thing of such beauty. Like the other buffaloes here, yet now so different. You know, the plural can be either buffalo or buffaloes. The dead men's dictionary tells us so." Both laughed. "They also say they cannot be ridden."

The rancher asked him to return from time to time, "to bring," he said, "the spirit back to me. It feeds me to see this more than I can say."

Zoyan'qual had not told the children about the buffalo. He wanted to surprise them. He wanted the right time to introduce them to Phantom, for it was this he called it in the New Tongue.

When he knew his tribe trailed the arroyo, and that he would join them for the rest of the journey, the time to introduce Phantom had come. The homing pigeon had arrived with its message. Zoyan'qual had ridden Phantom to a bluff overlooking the arroyo in the canyon country.

When he had seen them in the distance, he readied himself behind the far side of a hill. When he knew they were in the place for the most dramatic appearance, he had urged Phantom to gallup up and over the hill into sudden and full view.

It was a wondrous sight, a sight from legend, a sight from mythology, a sight to stir the archetypal imagination.

The whole assemblage that had been surrounding Taco, the precursor, stood, or still sat mounted, and beheld the scene. Only Lucian had seen and walked with and ridden the buffalo before, and he watched the expressions of the others. The *adventure* in the faces of the children. Camel-rider's *absorption* in the totally unexpected. Dolphus' father's look of *confirmation* that he really wanted to quit his job and be a permanent resident at the Worm Farm School. Each had a response, unique and riveted.

Zoyan'qual took in all the expressions at once, with pleasure, as he came to a stop in front of them all.

"Zoyan'qual!" the children cheered.

In the New Tongue, he said, "The winds have brought me the trackers of the arroyo. And I have brought you a spirit of the earth, Phantom."

56

The appearance of the group found a kind of *completeness* with Zoyan'qual's arrival. The children in their *wild bunch* outfits, the huge horse ridden by Dolphus' father, Camel-rider in his sheik's apparel on his namesake, Howard's zebra, and the reindeer currently ridden by Eriot's mother, and now a buffalo with Zoyan'qual astride it.

"Riding Phantom," said Eriot's mother to Zoyan'qual, "you look like the picture on the cover of one of the fantasy books, with the hero mounted on some fabled creature."

Eriot could not resist saying to her, "You look like a traveler from the North Pole."

The arroyo, itself, the theme along which all this activity centered, guided them along its way into the high country.

"What is the impulse," Howard asked, "that compels us to trace this waterway? At any given point, like right here where we are, it appears only as an extended eroded depression in the land, washed away by intermittent flooding. At the moment, there is no trace of water."

"Isn't it," said Orgol, his horse trotting along without a rider, since he rode with Zoyan'qual, having his turn on the back of the buffalo, "...isn't it *not* what the arroyo is at this point, but that it goes from *here* to *there*. It has a beginning and an ending. Isn't it like a metaphor for anything we do?"

Dolphus' father said, "When you get into the *metaphor mode*, an interesting perspective occurs. That's what happens each day when Dolphus comes back from the worm farm. When he talks about all the events, when he teaches us, it's always with this idea that the items are not just isolated unto themselves. They are analogies to other things."

Essa said, "You know what I'm thinking now?"

"*Yes,*" said Normita. "That's why you like the Junk Shop so well. It's not all the *pieces of things*, but that each piece reminds you of other things. It's like a jumble of metaphors to continually sort through."

"You're like an explorer in a new continent of ideas," said Reendo, "like in the *age of discovery*. That's why it's so much fun to go through the things at the shop with you. When you attach meaning to it, it's no longer junk."

"Maybe like the bits and pieces of our lives," mused Walter.

. . .

One night, when the eating was finished, when people had walked off individually and in pairs to stand under the stars and let their minds wander on the milky way spread above them, only two remained sprawled by the campfire. Camel-rider and Lucian.

The firelight, flickering by reflection in Camel-rider's eyes, seemed to be an outward representation of inner embers. His eyes, from time to time, appeared to be trying to consume whole what they focused on. Such was the moment now.

Camel-rider felt he somehow did this *process*, this *consuming* of information, receiving this intuitive *galaxy* of impressions of people he met. Never before had he sensed anyone else responding this same way until he met Lucian. Never had he broached the subject with anyone before tonight.

Although his body remained lax, his eyes focused intently.

234

They met Lucian's unblinking chameleon gaze.

"Tell me," said Camel-rider, feeling nothing else need be said, if, in fact, Lucian's mind received the same global responses as his own.

"About...?"

"About me."

"I know so little of you."

"No, not that, not outwardly. You see globally, a whole empathic response. You've been doing it this entire venture and before. You see from the children's viewpoint simultaneous to standing outside of both you and them as if watching the interaction. You're in the specific moment and outside observing from an overview perspective at the same time. You do it with the things the children see. Now I want you to do it with me."

"But I..."

"Not your thinking. Not those pieces of information. The other part. No footnotes, no documentation. Your intuition and feeling and perceiving. No justification, no apologies. No reasoned evidence. I want you to just start talking, stream of consciousness, unfiltered, uncensored. You've probably never done this before outwardly, externally, but I see it, it's all there, just behind your eyes. Right now."

Something uncorked in Lucian. "All right."

"Go," Camel-rider starter-pistoled, rolling onto his back and facing the milky way.

Lucian looked at the same sky and spoke as if reading a star-script, already there, spread out above them, now being voiced.

"You are a genius. Your mind searches for the patterns in others' thinking. Once you have that clear pattern, you feel like you know them. You find few surprises in their future actions, and you cannot remember a time of being far afield from your first impressions. Few things ever surprise you. That's why you enjoyed the arrival of Zoyan'qual and Phantom so much. You had no inkling of their thundering arrival."

Camel-rider chuckled.

"You had few companions as a child. You absorbed whole the patterns of their behavior, while they had no idea what you were about. They plodded along doing the things that you had already understood and predicted and moved on from.

"You considered the affairs of humans as a scientist might regard the display under a microscope, and often felt as remote. You learned their ways, but not because you felt pleasure in doing so. You thought that if they lived their lives that way, and seemed to enjoy them, perhaps sometime you would understand and enjoy too. You kept waiting to *feel* something and never did. You found no more pleasure in trying to imitate their life-styles than you would have in rooting with hogs.

"For that was your challenge. You had a desperate need to *feel* something for whole patterns, for whole complicated interrelationships, rather than a single event. What made other people cry and laugh, made you *analyze*. You felt like you lived in a world of aliens and couldn't understand why.

"So you mastered their ways. Since they kept you out, in a sense, you decided to beat them at their simplistic game. They regarded money as important, although you had no feeling for it, no desire for it. But it captured *their* attention. So you decided to best them at their own role-playing. You analyzed how money was made. And you proceeded to make it. It was, for you, obvious, easy, uncomplicated, and totally unfulfilling.

"Others envied you. They thought you must have everything they wanted, as you grew rich. They treated you as a storehouse of possible reserves for themselves, and you played with them, albeit benignly. You watched them scamper after this piffle that you had no regard for. Behind your back, they called you *eccentric* and *reclusive*, and you knew it. And you didn't care.

"You had heard that every person has a price. You found it to be true. You kept wanting to find even one who had no limit, who was motivated by something else. So you created clever situations to tempt people and pushed them to their limits and watched them being *bought*. You kept hoping to find at least one person without a limit.

"You experimented with people in politics, businesses, religious groups, philosophers, academics, everyone. When you heard someone described as *unreachable*, *indestructible*, *incorruptible*, you created a plausible financial scenario, offering some kind of enticement to tantalize them. You found, after even a brief meeting, that you knew what the idol of their fancy was that they would sell out for. You knew the subtle changes of eyes and skin tone, slight muscle movement that told you worlds of information. You read humans like a transparent anatomy model.

"You are concerned with humanitarian causes but find almost no *humanitarians* connected with them. You provided money to help people, only to find them grabbing it, without a scintilla of insight of how to change their lives, habits, customs, or circumstances, to keep the problem conditions from happening again.

"You see people whose dwellings you helped to reconstruct after being flooded out, rebuilding on the same flood plain, even though they have information about how often the flooding comes.

"You can buy any entertainment or diversion that your fancy prompts. And you have tried them all, all that you could imagine. But not out of satisfaction with any of them. Only in the hope, increasingly remote, that you would find something satisfying behind the event, a satisfaction you craved and could never locate.

"You discovered companionship to be the same way. You encountered people who loved the *idea* of you and what *you could provide for them*. Who enjoyed the idea of being Mrs. *you*, or *partner of you*, or associate of you, rather than looking at and seeing *you*.

"You reached the limits of the possibilities known to you. Perhaps one of the first humans to do so. For you can travel anywhere and experience anything on earth.

"You have become one of the first prisoners of this planet. You long for something more, but suspect that whatever it may be, it is not available here. You look upward to the stars and feel your restriction to this globe as intolerable. You want to escape, to keep searching, to reach further.

"And no one around you, none of your hirelings, who may scurry about like minions, have any notion that you feel caged and weary of being caged. That your greatest pleasure is disguising yourself in denim as just another person and taking off on the dusty roads in the old truck, and hanging out at Cactus

Max, or its equivalent in whatever country you happen to be. You are weary, jaded, hopeful, innocent, all simultaneously.

"Trailing an arroyo with the children has more significance to you than any international money matters you have ever undertaken. And you still don't know why."

Camel-rider, sprawled fully on the ground, stretching hugely, as if some vast relaxation had occurred within all his muscles, all his cells, all his atoms, simultaneously.

For a long time, they both stared at the stars.

Camel-rider said, "You match me. You mirror me."

After a lull, he said, "You have *seen* me. For that, I am beyond gratitude. No one else has ever seen me."

After a moment of additional thought, he jerked upright. "But you see more of me than I can of you."

57

Dolphus father guided his horse over to the side. While the others continued onward, he rode over behind a ridge, and then he caught up with the others. Whenever anyone needed to relieve themselves, they circled off, and then returned to the group. When any of the children rode off to the side, Lucian slowed his mount, a little distance away, and then they both caught up with the group.

After one such moment, when Orgol returned to the group, he asked, "Why is it all right to *urinate* or *defecate*..." he said this with a hint of exaggerated properness in his voice, and then continued with a tough sound to say, "...but it's vulgar to *piss* or *shit?*"

The children turned toward Lucian.

"Oh," he said, "it happened in 1066. When the French Normans invaded England and conquered the resident Anglo-Saxons, you had two languages superimposed on each other. The Anglo-Saxons had used perfectly acceptable words denoting body functions. But then, the Anglo-Saxons were considered servants, even slaves, of the Normans. The Anglo-Saxon language was considered by the Normans as *low, common, unacceptable*. Their word for *common* was *vulgar*.

"But even though adults see differences of class and caste, children do not, until they are taught. So the Anglo-Saxon and Norman children, playing together, picked up each other's words for things. When the Norman parents heard their children using the Anglo-Saxon terms, they told them to stop, that such words were *common* and *vulgar*. The linguistic descendants of both groups now speak a combination of Anglo-Saxon and French Norman and call it English. And they still use *shit* and still call it *vulgar*, after fifteen hundred years.

"The Latin based words of the Normans often moved into medical language, so English had a kind of *missing middle*. Words for these functions and the body parts associated with them either moved down to vulgarity or up to technical terms, leaving no general terms for polite social use. It's about the only language in the world that lacks these generally accepted terms. People learning the language, from other countries, are mystified by their absence."

"So," said Orgol, "words are only what we make them? Words are not inherently *vulgar*, or whatever, except people agree that they are?"

"*Where* is meaning?" asked Lucian.

"In ourselves," said Normita, "and we project it into words," with a smile of insight.

"Then," Eriot said, "what they called the *vulgar* or *Vulgate* version of the Bible simply meant that it was written in the *common* language?"

"Instead of *Latin*, as it had been," said Normita, with another smile of *things fitting together*.

"So," said Essa, "Anglo-Saxons *pissed* and French Normans *urinated*. What did the child of a mixed couple do? *Pissinate?*"

"Well," spoke Eriot's mother, "whatever we call it, I've got to do it," and rode off into the sagebrush.

As she did, Dolphus intoned in a sonorous voice mimicking a documentary narrator, "And so they each, in turn, rode off into the countryside to fulfill the basic functions of all human beings, following the example of kings, prophets, astronauts, movie stars, models and tycoons everywhere, throughout the ages. Humans had found their common ground."

Later Orgol asked, "Normans—why were they called French *Normans*, and not just French?"

"Because," Lucian said, "earlier invader-settlers had come from the north down to the west coast of France and stayed there, so they were called by the locals *north-men*, or Norman."

Jhenaw said, "If they came from the north, they came from the *north-way*, is that Norway?"

"Yes."

"And isn't the northwest coast of France called Normandy, so that would mean where the *north-men* lived?"

"Yes."

"Well then," said Reendo, "since the TH sound in *north* is dropped in those words, is there some relation of the name of *Norfolk*, Virginia, to the word *north*?"

"What do you hear when you say it?"

"Nor-folk. *North-fork*?"

"Wait!" said Dolphus, "Isn't there also a *Suffolk*, Virginia, too? Same process, dropping the TH sound of the word *south*, could that be South-fork?"

"But why fork? Maybe like a fork in a road? A trail, with a north fork and a south fork?" Pica said.

"Like going around something," said Dolphus. "Swamps! When we studied swamps, wasn't that where the Dismal swamp is located? And they couldn't go through it, so maybe the trail split to go around it, one being the north fork and the other being the south fork? And maybe that's how the towns on either side got their names?"

. . .

Another night under the stars. The campfire.

"It's inevitable, you know," said Normita.

"What is?" asked Walter.

"You know. It's their time again," said Normita.

"*Their* time?" asked Essa.

"Un-huh," said Dolphus, as if his and Normita's minds conjoined. "It's time for more of *their* story."

"*Whose* story?" asked Eriot's mother.

The children said in unison, as if all their minds were joined, "The *Murlwumps*."

Lucian regarded them and knew it was inevitable. So he continued the saga to the waiting faces around the firelight in the desert night. His voice took on the dramatic flair that made Longhorn smile.

These are Murlwumps that are going to be talking. Murlwumps, in case you didn't know, are fuzzy, round little creatures, and if you haven't seen them, you can imagine them any way you wish, so long as its pleasant, and makes you feel good just to look at them.

They're expressive creatures and are always in just the right mood to make you feel best. If you're sad, looking at them makes you feel good, just to know they exist. If you're already happy, then their fuzzy smiles make you even happier, being with them to share the good time.

They talk a good deal, mostly about this and that.

One time, a long time ago, in the time of the tea-lid moon, when three of them were sitting in that thought-wandering state, one of them said, "Talk to us of friendship."

"Yes, Kahlil, do," spoke the second.

The third, passing up the second's reference, because as you know, Murlwumps have no names, and knowing it was only a literary reference of some sort, said, as he gazed into the dark sky, "Friendship...friendship...oh, of it I would speak so wisely, but I know so little."

He continued speaking much more seriously than any Murlwump had ever spoken before, "People are like a scale. Their qualities are weighed, and we choose our friends."

"But do bad qualities ever outweigh the good qualities, especially when the good ones are very good?"

"Aye, Lad," he said, a bit of a Scotch brogue slipping into his voice.

"But since there's some not-so-good in everyone, how do we ever gain friends?" And his face had a wondrously perplexed expression on it.

"Because there are those few, aye, perhaps not many, who are like ourselves, who will share their most precious commodity—life."

"But how do we know? How do we know?"

"We know them because there's understanding..."

"And honesty? And honesty?" he said twice, for that somehow seemed to be more satisfactory in his excitement.

241

"Ah, yes, and honesty with each other. They try to be nothing they're not. They accept each other's limitations as well as capacities just as they do their own, looking at them realistically."

"And just what is friendship, then?"

"Of the many ways of expressing it, how about this: the being together in silence, when nothing needs to be said, with the enjoyment of sharing life, that greatest thing we have to share with our friends."

"And are we friends like that, then?" said the first Murlwump, knowing it was so.

They put their arms about each other's shoulders and sat in silence for a long time, looking up at the tea-lid moon. Whether with silence, happiness, or tears, they shared life with pleasure and ease.

And so it was, in the time of the tea-lid moon, a long time ago.

They would go on longer, but we're all of us getting sleepy. But they feel so happy, they do, just being together.

Lucian made a gesture of completion, like an actor delivering the final line of the play, waiting for the curtain to close.

"But no," said Reendo, "it doesn't work that way. That's too short. We are all in the mood, and have the desert night before us, with no time limits."

Jhenaw added, "Make them wake up again, and continue."

Dolphus father said, "Yeah, get them back up. I like them. We need them over at the space center."

Walter said, "I'll do the set-up: Second act, curtain going up."

Lucian bowed to public pressure and continued.

But after a little nap, we all woke up, and the first Murlwump said, in much the same rolling tones that had started their last conversation, "Speak to us of love."

"Hmmm," said the second Murlwump wisely, poking around in his mind for a sage answer. "Well," he spoke slowly at last, choosing every word carefully to capture the exact meaning, "They say it makes the world go round."

And they sat in silence for some time, thinking of the world going around, for it was a very big thought.

"A twenty-four hour thought," said one of them.

"And is it hearts and flowers?" asked the second, after a while.

"Well, you remember what the poet said."

And they quoted in unison:

"What, O what, O what, what, what
    Is blood except corpuscles?
And those things there that beat within—
    O what are hearts but muscles.
And though such thoughts might
    Serve to make the new young lover quiver,
Most emotion comes not from the heart,
    But from the liver!"

"Hmmm. Biologically correct. But is this medical verse poetry?"

"No, it creates no empathy."

"Indeed not."

"We should have skipped it."

"But—Love. We really know not what it is then, do we?"

"Apparently not."

"Oh, no."

"No, indeed."

And there was a long pause, until they said in unison, "No, indeed."

"But it must be very wonderful," one said eagerly, at last.

"Apparently so."

"Oh, yes."

"Apparently so. Oh! excuse me, that was yours. I meant to say, yes, indeed!"

"Well, no harm done, for we all agree."

"Indeed, yes. Say, how's that for a variation on an old theme."

"Beethoven would be proud."

"So would Kahlil."

"I have only one more question..."

"What's that?"

"What is a tea-lid moon?"

At this, they were silent, and they smiled at each other, for though they really didn't know, they didn't care either. So they sat as oft before, sharing life and thinking Murlwump thoughts.

58

Time became connected to the sun, moon, and stars. "Our biorhythms are freer here!" laughed Grandmother, as they rested in a canyon's shade from the mid-day sun.

"I wonder how we can ever know ourselves," Eriot's mother said, "if we are not exposed to the lights and darknesses of day and night." She who had been a ballerina, now dressed in modified bull-fighter's garb, walked about the shaded area as if the desert had become her arena. "The invention of clocks and artificial lighting distance us from this. Zoyan'qual, you know this better than any of us."

He nodded.

Dolphus flicked a remnant seed from an orange he had eaten, watching it spiral upward and drop onto the earth. As he followed its trajectory, he looked in Howard's direction and suddenly recalled the special little clock he had seen on Howard's desk. "I wonder how many people there are in the world since we started this trip."

"You don't have to wonder." He reached into large utility side pocket of his pants and pulled out the device.

"You carry it with you?"

"It's within reach wherever I go." He handed it to Dolphus. "Count the population increase for one minute." When that had been accomplished, he said, "Now multiply that by sixty by twenty-four by the number of days we've been traveling."

Dolphus frowned. "It's enough for a whole town." And he started calculating how many since he had been born.

. . .

In the interval between the beginning of night and the dawn, when the wolves howled, and the hooting of the owls sounded across the spaces of the desert, the legends, new and old, myths of the ancients and of those that spoke them now, curled about them like the rising smoke from the campfire.

They developed chants that incorporated the names of the strata. They even sang from general to particular, from eras to periods to epochs. *Precambrian, Paleozoic, Mesozoic, Cenozoic,* for the broad divisions of non-fossils, early fossils, reptile fossils, and mammal fossils.

They chanted in rhythm the periods of those eras: the Cambrian, Ordovician, Silurian, Devonian, Mississippian, Pennsylvanian, Permian, Triassic, Jurassic, Cretaceous, Tertiary.

They sang the epochs of the Tertiary period: Paleocene, Eocene, Oligocene, Miocene, and Pliocene.

They ranged through the Australian periods: Wangerripian, Johanian, Aldingan, Janjukian, Longfordian, Batesfordian, Balcombian, Bairnscalian, Mitchellian, Cheltenhamian, Kalimnan, Yatalan, Werrikooian.

Scientific classification had became like an ancient song. "What is science," Walter observed, "but the newest of the ways to explain the earth. We are part of the tribe of science, and its words are the magic words of the moment, to be looked back on as the folklore and myth of the past, when replaced by the continued development in the future."

"None are primitive," observed Howard, "in their own time and place."

The naming of the rocks enabled them to discuss them in more and more detail. The more they could discuss, the more they could observe of the physical world around them. The more they named, the more they possessed. The more they possessed, the more they discussed, and the more they discussed, the more of a tribe they became, mixing, matching ideas, stimulating each other with hybrid insights that built upon themselves. Garnered during the day, these words and ideas were distilled at night about the fire, as the tribe assimilated the forms of the world around them, in patterns of rhythms accompanied by flutes and lyres.

"Why should we not celebrate the beauty of the fossil rock layers of the Egerian, Eggenburgian, Ottnaangian, Karpathian, and Badenian ages as our ancestors sang of the wisdom of Athena or the exploits of Gilgamesh?" said Beth.

Howard laughed aloud one night between such chantings. And then explained that he was thinking of his office co-workers and what they would think of these antics. "We've had some camping trips together. They left that stuff, as they refer to geological information, at the office. When they sat around the campfire, they would wash their brain cells in alcohol and have intoxicated conversations about a whole different array of subjects than these."

"I am becoming a poet," said Camel-rider, "under this influence of this other kind of *intoxication* that we experience together." He arose from his squatting position in the circle of people around the fire and began to pace in a larger circle around them all. As he walked, he said, "I will recite my creation to you in the tones and postures of a Victorian lecturer." With that, the cape of his sheiks outfit fluttering in the wind behind him and the billowing sleeves accenting his gestures, he intoned:

A fossil's that which was and is,
Yet is what it was not.
Belike a bygone bone in form
Is still, though long since rot.

For bone once gone is not here still,
Though what is not can be
In form reformed to form a form
That was, perhaps a tree.

A log that's bogged would wood be, and
Be formed before the stone;
Wood therefore would forebear its form
When fossilized, like bone.

A creature's feature's fossil
Is what was my imprint made.
What made it's not, as with a leaf's
Relief conversely laid.

If mud were pocked by rain drops dropped
And formed a mud-baked block,
And mud baked block formed pock-marked rock,
It's fossilized rock pock.

Thus patterns, wood, and bone in stone
Uncrushed by rocky jostle,
Remain the main remains in rocks.
And so you have a fossil.

Soon, the children were chanting his words, and a rhythm formed, and then a melody. Before the sequence ended, all of those who had sat by the campfire were circling it in dance gyrations led by Pica, the shape-shifter. The horses, the zebra, the reindeer, the camel, and the buffalo looked on. In the distance, coyotes sent their messages across the plateaus.

59

Howard stood like an explorer first arriving at the peak of Everest. He had brought a small flag on a stick for the occasion. He planted it firmly in the ground by the little V-shape cut into the earth where water sometimes ran its course.

"*The headwaters of the arroyo*," he announced.

"Without any water," Orgol observed.

They stood on the angular land high in a crevice of the mountains. The rains and snows that came from above drained down, and, at this point, began the cutting into the earth that became the trail of run-off water that created the arroyo, that carried the bits of earth in the torrents of water that hurled down it periodically, that was joined by a myriad other cuts in the earth and their run-off water. From above, it would appear as a pattern like the twigs of a tree joining small limbs, joining larger branches, joining the main branches, joining the trunk.

In fact, Howard pointed out, even the jargon for the water-way patterns came directly from the analogies to trees, as in the *branching* of the waterway.

Purple clouds further up in the mountains poured down rain somewhere in the distance. The group camped for a time around this *headwater* that had no water at the moment. But they were not disappointed. The clouds came closer. The rain neared. Soon they witnessed the water bouncing off the rocks, spilling over the surface of the ground, finding its way, pulled by gravity, filling the little trench, starting its long trek to the sea.

"If we could ride fast enough," said Dolphus, "and we could toss a stick in like this," and he did so, watching it swept away, downward, "we could follow the stick all the way back where we have traveled, back to where the arroyo comes near the worm farm, and all the way further, to the sea."

After the rain had passed, Howard had a suggestion. "If we trace this arroyo back, we'll be covering the ground we traversed to get here. But if we go over that ridge right there," he pointed above and beyond their present location, "we can find the beginning of another arroyo that leads through a different drainage route."

He produced his map and showed them.

"I traced this out in case we wanted another experience. If we trail the new one, we'll see some different landscapes. That one leads into the deeply eroded canyon country that exposes some of the most beautiful rock layers you've ever seen."

"Would you mind seeing them again?" asked Orgol.

"Actually I've never seen them, myself. I've seen the photographs of them, and I've always wanted to go there."

He traced his finger further along the proposed route. "Then when we get to the other end, where it empties out here, we can go across this distance and pick up the other end of our original arroyo where it empties out and trail it back to the worm farm."

Without discussion, they moved toward the origin of the next arroyo.

. . .

The afternoons and evenings might belong to geology and the wide range of associated study, but the early mornings still belonged to biology. To the baby. To Beth, the keeper of the daily progress of the child within her womb.

She had packed charts, pictures, diagrams, so they could see vividly the changes taking place in this new life, a reflection of all of their lives, a reflection of all human life, a reflection of all life on earth.

She had led the natal progression, both at the worm farm, and now on the journey, through the development of the fetus becoming established in the uterus, the interconnecting of the organ system. Even the brain had begun to play a vital part in the developments, during the third month.

"By the eleventh week, it should be about an inch and a half long," she had told them. "The spleen and bone marrow and liver took over the blood cell production provided, until then, by the yolk sac."

"So it's like an egg?" said Orgol. "What happens in an egg is what's happening in there?" He pointed toward her belly.

She had told them when the fetus had eyes and responded sensitively to light.

One morning by the arroyo, she asked Zoyan'qual for a melody, a theme, for the child. "Because now," she said, "it can hear. It is hearing my heart. And that rhythm will become the familiar beat of all the music it will ever know, after birth. Fast music will recall the increased beat of the heart under pressure and activity. Slow music, the heart beating during a resting state."

She turned to Lucian. "Do you know any of the pre-natal songs used by any cultures?"

Longhorn had no doubt that Lucian would. Lucian just *knew* such things. Had read them. Had incorporated them into a network of knowing that fascinated him. Longhorn smiled slightly to see the expression on the face of Camel-rider who looked toward Lucian, to see if this would be one request beyond expectation.

Lucian simply took out a flute from his pack and played samples of melodies from five cultures that came randomly to mind and then sang them in their original languages.

Zoyan'qual listened pensively. Then he took an instrument fashioned from the wood from his canyons. He said, "When I picture this unborn child, I hear this." And he produced what he called *dawn sounds*, a pre-natal song for the first-born of his tribe. Lucian listened with his eyes closed, then played his flute in harmony to the new melody.

While Longhorn listened, he watched Camel-rider, whose expressions reflected some deep satisfaction.

"We will play this daily," said Beth, "and when it is born, our baby will know this melody, as it will know the voices of all of us."

. . .

Morning. Early. Right after they had eaten and continued the trek downward along *arroyo two*.

There were hikers. Bedded down in their sleeping bags in the heights. Alone, so far as they knew.

Then they opened their eyes to the light of dawn. They looked at the long shadows of the high outcroppings of land. They looked over and saw the profile of a procession along the ridge.

They sat up and crawled out of their bags, adjusting to the sight. The wild bunch in miniature. The camel, its rider in flowing robes. The female matador. The giant horse. The zebra. The reindeer. And the mythic figure on the buffalo.

This *morning vision* raised their hands and waved. Slowly the watchers raised their hands in response.

"They will wonder," said Grandmother, "and with the wondering, they will grow."

. . .

The *morning vision*, in their turn that night, became the *observers*. They had formed their campfire circle, eaten, conversed about the stars, and were preparing to sleep. The embers had died. All was quiet nearby, with the far sounds of the night creatures.

Then keen-eyed Reendo whispered, "Look, on the ridge." The full moon was rising, and outlined against it, a human figure, his back to them, facing the moon.

They could hear the voice in the distance, speaking to the moon, invoking its mystery in the night, for insight, for guidance, for a sign.

"Uh-oh," whispered Reendo, "here comes his *sign*, and he hasn't seen it yet."

Along the ridge, in back of the silhouette, approaching on remarkably quiet feet, came Phantom, who roamed at will.

As Reendo had predicted, the outline of the buffalo neared the human shadow. When the gentle Phantom snorted, the human shadow turned and encountered his *vision*.

They heard his stifled sound of surprise and shock. Saw the shadow start to run. Look around. Stop. Start to run again. Stop. Look around. Walk away. Stop. And then buffalo and human stood regarding each other.

Phantom had other things to do and turned and disappeared along the ridge. The human shadow watched him go and then left in the opposite direction.

. . .

In the morning, before dawn, as the others came forth from sleep, Grandmother was riding back from somewhere.

"Where?" asked Reendo.

"Up there," she said, indicating the ridge.

"Why?" asked Reendo.

"To leave a message," she said.

"For whom?" asked Reendo, as the others listened.

"For the person we saw last night," she said.

"But he's gone."

"He will return to the scene of his vision."

"What did your message say?"

"It apologized for startling him."

"But you didn't startle him. You were down here. Phantom startled him."

"I signed it *Phantom, the buffalo.*"

In the silence that ensued, she added, "People need a little mystery in their lives. It makes them think."

60

Upon a high plain, at midday, they sat on their mounts and observed the circle of the world in all directions.

"How vast," said Essa.

"Not vast enough," said Howard, pulling out his population clock and looking at it. They all started asking him about the clock, about his study of population. He was into the subject that continuously occupied his thinking. "The people of earth are too many already. Far too many. We are breeding ourselves out of existence. Wasting the lands, building cities, destroying the species of plants and animals."

"How many is enough people?" asked Orgol.

"About the number in the mid-seventeen hundreds. Our numbers must be reduced. Overpopulation is a central cause of war, violence, stress, competition—this senseless excessive breeding. Two-thirds of every country on earth needs to be left natural, without development, for species to evolve. The other third can have managed human habitation."

"Even the farmlands?" asked Eriot.

"Especially the farmlands. Those used to be forests and plains. Now they are cultivated out of existence. At least two-thirds of these, world wide, must be returned to forest and grasslands. No roads, no development. To be explored by people as viewers only. The same with the rain forests, the jungles, the other geological zones.

"There is no value in developing more farmlands. People only eat and then breed more. The problem is not feeding the hungry. That's not the problem. The challenge is to reduce reproduction so there will not be hungry people in the first place. The same with homelessness, with refugees, with immigrants. If you build homes endlessly, the people in them breed, reproducing so many more that there are always homeless and hungry. Humans have no built-in biological thermostat to stop their breeding when there are too many, as most other species do. It has to be the fragile human thinking, reasoning, cause-and-effect insight, that now gets exercised to safeguard the human race and the planet.

"The commendable energy of those who strive to feed the hungry and house the homeless, adopt the parentless, welcome the refugees, be a haven for immigrants—that very energy needs to be aimed at least half-time to the single major cause of all of these problems, the uncontrolled proliferation of human procreation."

Orgol said, "Is the statement on the Statue of Liberty ultimately self-defeating? *Bring me* all those people but what they'll do is trash the land more?"

They rode on. The sun illumined the earth like an overexposed photograph. Howard said, "This journey, this open land, is like a frontier for us. We are exploring it. And by doing so, as Lucian said, we are discovering ourselves. Humans need frontiers. Frontiers are indispensable to human existence. That's why the space program is not just a luxury, not just an economic venture. It is an absolute necessity for the sanity of humanity."

"So frontiers change?" said Pica.

"Whatever step is next in exploration becomes the frontier," said Howard. "We, as humans, must have novelty. We have to exercise our curiosity. Even when we reduce the population and foster the continued evolution of planetary life, the major forms of frontiers that confronted our ancestors no longer will present themselves. We must look outward. Always taking the next step. The moon. The planets. The next nearest star. Its planets. New means of propulsion. Every generation, every person, must have frontiers and step across them."

Jhenaw asked, "Who will train the people on earth not to breed so rapidly and not destroy the economy, and the land, and each other? Who teaches people to regulate reproduction? To return at least two-thirds of the earth to its original nature?"

"Many people have started. I've already started, in a small way," Howard said, "collecting materials. Attending conferences. But I don't have time or resources to do much. But people who have read books of statistics know what will happen. Those who know, and care, can try to make the planet, itself, into an education center. We need to find the ways to engage every country, every government, every organization, to a form of education that will first stop the population increase, then reduce it, until it stabilizes at an agreed-on amount. The number would have to be intelligently decided by global discussion. And the space program will become a focal point for every person. We have to find the way to do it. This population project will be the major frontier of this generation. Without it, there will be no comparable *next generations*."

He pointed upward. "I hope in the future all of you will see this plain from up there, from a space ship, a space station. And when you do, you will remember the frontier down here," he pointed at the eroded waterway they were following, "tracking the wild arroyo. Up there you will see the equivalent of *arroyos in space*, trackless distances of space that will become your pathways across new frontiers."

With momentary glances at each other, the children all had the same thought and said, "Ah, the endorphins are flowing!"

Ongoing discussions about Howard's information on population study, and what he saw as solutions, and the imperativeness of dealing with it on a vast scale globally, punctuated the days and evenings. They all felt swept into the vortex of Howard's intensity and sense of urgency.

. . .

Camel-rider had shared his perch on his animal with each of the children as they wished. He began to pose questions to whoever rode with him. They took the form of *what if* questions. He appeared completely absorbed in their responses. Reendo rode on the saddle in front of him at the moment.

"What would you do," he asked Reendo, as the troupe moved single-file on the floor of the arroyo, with Beth on Rain leading the way, "if you saw a sparkle on the sides of this arroyo, investigated, found gold traces, that led you to a gold mine that became yours. What would you buy?"

Reendo's response emerged immediately but slowly, as if the answer already existed but words proved difficult to attach.

"I would..." Reendo said, "...consider what was important and start it...now."

"Important?" asked Camel-rider.

"What Howard keeps explaining about the population," said Reendo. "That sounds basic to everything else. He has a picture in his mind of what to do. I would set up a center for population..." he could not think of the next word. "...*things*. Put him in charge. Let him *do*. And as we got older we could help."

Reendo had another thought. "Actually we could help now. We have the Worm Farm Press. If it's the children now who need to be taught, we could start writing simple books, with the ideas he could explain to us. We could sort of translate it for people in school and illustrate it, like we did with Lucian's courses."

Reendo thought further and added, "Howard's center could have training classes for people from all over the world who would come to talk about those things. And plan what to do. And how to do it. Children, government people, all. "

Then Reendo tilted his head upward and back so he had a kind of upside-down view of Camel-rider's face from a below-the-chin perspective. He asked, "What would you do if you saw the

254

gold sparkling on the sides of the arroyo, and you were rich?"

. . .

They came to the deep cuts in the earth where this arroyo widened out to become a small canyon. Layer after layer of rock now revealed themselves in the eroded walls.

"A living chart," said Kayla. She could name them all, all the layers, while Pica added the *years ago* when they were formed.

As they pointed and named and dated, Eriot looked at Howard's face, Eriot said, "I know what's flowing again."

"*Besides* the water in the arroyo," laughed Normita.

Water had appeared in the stream bed at the bottom of the deep, wide cut. But this was not surface water coming from the direction they had traveled. This water flowed from subterranean layers. It now emerged into the stream bed.

"A slide time line!" exclaimed Dolphus suddenly. He turned to Longhorn. "A slide time line. Could we make one? A long slide, so we have height like these rock layers. At worm farm. A high slide, a *really* high slide, with not a steep slope. Along the side, somehow, paint the strata of rock, their ages, in order. Oldest at the bottom, newest at top, just like here. As we go down the slide, we see the sequence each time."

"Do you think," asked Normita, "that if Howard hadn't already taught us all the layers, and we didn't know them already, and we had Dolphus' slide, that we would just sort of *learn* them? Imprint them?"

Essa's eyes lit up. Those eyes that saw potential where other people saw only junk. Normita had told her once that she should call her place the *Potential Shop* instead of the Junk Shop. But Essa had replied that she never *had* called her place the Junk Shop, only the other people in town did. So Essa's eyes lit up as Dolphus' shared his vision of the slide. "I have some things at the shop," she said. Looking around at Longhorn, who seemed to be able to put together anything, "some items that would help to make the most remarkable geological time-slide ever built."

Normita said, "Probably the *only* one ever built."

Longhorn nodded. He, too, was picturing it. His hand moved to described not only a downward direction but gestured to the sides, looping around. "We could fill a half acre of land with this."

61

When they came, this band of wanderers, to the great river basin into which this arroyo emptied, they changed directions. They followed the river along its banks. Howard surveyed his maps carefully.

They journeyed until they found the mouth of *their* arroyo, the one that would take them back to the worm farm. They stood at the juncture where it emptied into the river bed. That wide, flat pathway had only a trickle of water now, looking more like a model of a river than a real one.

They began their way back from this opposite end of the arroyo that they had trailed to its highland origins. They had seen its beginning and its end, and now would traverse the remainder of its course, heading upstream.

In the course of the day they rode to a high ridge to survey the surrounding area. In the sprawling expanses, they saw a building that looked tiny in the distance. A small tavern. It stood by a dirt road leading to nothing visible.

Their descent downward from the ridge to again intersect the arroyo took them nearer to the isolated building.

"It's like a frontier place," said Walter.

"A *marginal* place," said Essa. "A place on the margin of life."

In front of the structure, at odd angles were parked a few dusty cars, motorcycles, and pickup trucks. Two people stood outside, leaning on the wood supports for the porch, drinking, squinting into the sunlit distance, spitting periodically into the dirt.

"See that too?" said one.

"Yep. You too, then?" said the other.

"Yep."

"Too much to drink?"

"Nope. Think its a mirage thing?"

"Nope. I think they're really there."

"And they're headed this way."

"Nope. Past, I think," he said, and then belched.

"Some kind of party, think?" said the one, wiping his lips on his sleeve.

"Nowhere to have a party out here," said the other, sloshing his drink and then sipping it.

" I see me some regular horses, and a big regular horse, and a bunch of funny ones." the first one said.

"Yeah, like a striped horse," the second one said.

"And one with a head and shoulders furrier and bigger than his behind part."

"And a hump-backed horse."

"And a horse with horns on his head."

"A dog following them."

"S'not a dog."

"It's a red dog."

"It's a fox."

"No way."

"It's all a mirage."

He turned, opened the door, said into the dim light. "Come out here, y'all."

Figures that looked like variations on a theme of the men on the porch slow-motioned out the door. They all had their drinks with them.

One of the original men on the porch wiped his mouth on his sleeve again and then pointed toward the mirage.

The others blinked into the light. And looked. They took intermittent swallows. Belched occasionally. Didn't say anything.

As they watched, one of the troupe passing in the distance veered her horse off from the others and circled toward the building.

Grandmother had decided Beth needed a cool drink. "Something to sip on. Your baby will appreciate it."

The men watched her coming. She rode up, dismounted, attaching the reins to nothing. She nodded to them all. "Nice day," she said, "like all days are nice."

"Yep," several said more or less together.

"What do you have, with no alcohol, no caffeine, cool?" she asked.

One man in an apron accompanied her back inside. She bought several bottles of juice used in some of the mixes.

"Enjoy," she said to the men.

"Yep," several men said, more or less together.

She mounted and rode off toward the rest of the *mirage*. They watched her rejoin the others. They watched until the group had wavered into the sweltering distance and blurred beyond their ability to see them.

One of them said, "Biggest excitement we've ever had here."

"Yep," several said, more or less simultaneously. One of them belched again. One added, "Done stirred me up s'much I gotta get me another drink."

All but the original two slowly turned and reentered the building.

The two men remained on the porch, staring off into the desert afternoon, squinting into the sunlight, and spitting into the dust.

62

"What would you do," Camel-rider asked Howard as they walked in the night, away from the campfire, scanning the stars, "if you unexpectedly had enough resources to pursue something related to population awareness and change? Obviously you can't do much now with a full-time job at the geology commission and without the necessary resources. Have you ever thought about it?"

"There's a shooting star," pointed Howard, and they both watched the greenish smear brighten and dim.

"When I get one of the clearinghouse mailings grand prizes," Howard said. "When I win a lottery for a few million. Then I picture myself setting up an office, a nerve center, a collection point. A place where first I would find out everything, from everywhere, going on now related to population. The research. The names of the people. The people in governments who are not only concerned, but focused, really focused on it.

"Then I would have a summit of these people. The *doers*. The ones already *doing* something. Or trying to. The ones who get up every morning *thinking* about it. Who ponder it. Who *feel* it. Who are passionate about it. Who hear the biological clock of all humans, of all species, on earth ticking.

"We would build a network of *who's doing what, where, when, how.* Then brainstorm. Search not for an old way. But a new paradigm. A new myth for the earth. A new way of looking at it. It can't be like anything in the past, because almost no one ever grasped the need or had the perspective to see it this way before.

"And then we would implement. Plans. Steps. Strategies. What can be done. Now. Today. And what can be done tomorrow. However small. Change. Alteration. Encourage groups to have new visions. Have new visions ourselves. Engage these children, the builders of the new paradigm. The users of the new paradigm. The new education.

"The discussion of individual rights and group survival. Does someone have an individual right to bring an explosive on a plane when all the passengers will perish from it? Earth is the plane and the explosive is the population bomb. How do we deal with it?

"How do we get to the place, worldwide, where every newscast starts with the daily report on population management progress? Every class in every school discusses it at least a few minutes daily, in relation to their subjects. Social and religions organizations make it a priority item on their agendas. Every newspaper gives daily figures and ideas on the front page. Interactive computer networks join humans in a continual planetary discussion. A permanent consortium of representatives of all governments must meet on a permanent basis, daily devising solutions and implementations for today, tomorrow, next week, next month, next year, next decade. The intellectual resources of the earth must be mustered to accomplish the goal in the minimal possible time.

"And family structure has to be examined. It might be necessary for several generations for every person to be an only child. No brothers, sisters, cousins, aunts, uncles. Families would have to be redefined. There could be clusters of families, extended families, raising children together, to give them the experience of siblings.

"After population reduction and stabilization, no more than one child per human or two per couple." His gestures had reinforced these ideas. His hands remained up in the air with the last gesture. He let them sink slowly to his sides.

He turned toward Camel-rider and, altering his voice from its former intensity, said, with an exaggerated shrug and yawning voice, "No. No, in answer to your question, I've never thought about that before."

He took out the population clock, and they watched the number increase as the seconds passed.

. . .

"I had to do some bartering to get the time from work to come, and it involves all of you," Howard said, as the caravan came over a rise in the land. "There is a little town, behind those hills. My supervisors wanted some publicity, some human interest public relations, on what geologists do. That it's not all just work at desks and maps. They remembered when you were there at the office and…"

He looked apologetically at them all. "When we get near that town, I am to contact a TV station where they will be on standby to meet us at a site up the arroyo. They just wanted to do a little piece on something like *taking geology to the people*."

He waited for some kind of confirming response. "I hope it's okay."

"Shore," drawled Lucian. "Why don't you and the wild bunch ride over and make the contact, and we'll mosey on along the arroyo until you catch up with us."

The miniature cowboys of the old west, in their long coats and flat hats galloped off with Howard toward the hills and the town. The others rode on.

. . .

At the appointed place, where a road came close to the arroyo, a camera truck, proclaiming the call letters of the station and the television channel number on its side, awaited them.

"Ah, the educational channel," said Dolphus.

One of the three people standing by the truck, watching the unusual desert apparitions approach, made some non-word sounds. "Woa! Whooee.!"

"Hey," a woman behind one of the cameras greeted them, "this is great. Don't even bother to explain who all of you are or how you came to be. Let's just focus on the children and Howard. The rest of you, just be background. Just sit around on your *whatevers*—camel, buffalo, big horse, striped thing, North Pole one. Just let the viewers figure it out."

"You see," said Grandmother, "like I said, everyone needs a little mystery in their lives."

The broadcast began with one of the interviewers saying to the children in his best educational TV voice, "Well, seen any interesting arroyos lately?"

. . .

At the bank in the little town near the worm farm, in the glassed-in office in back of the counter where Gertrude, the teller, stood, the man worked on account books. He glanced occasionally at the small TV on the wall shelf. He flipped through channels and stopped. He watched for a moment.

Then he leaned toward the door and said, "Gertrude, you better come here. I think you'll want to see this."

"What is it?" Gertrude said over her shoulder.

"On TV."

"*What* on TV?" she asked, putting some rolls of coins in her drawer.

"*Them.*" he said.

"Them, *who?*" she asked.

When he was silent, she turned around and said suddenly, "Has this got anything to do with *worms?*"

He nodded affirmatively.

She trotted toward his office.

63

The late afternoon return to the worm farm came simply. They rode along the arroyo and arrived at the location where they had started the journey. They veered off from it and arrived at the time lines, the dinosaur skeleton, their variety of personal rooms.

They sat on their mounts in silence. No one could leave. So without even discussing it, they took care of the animals, gathered wood for a fire, and prepared an evening meal.

The children realized simultaneously that, for the first time, Taco visited the worm farm. They took him over to the little addition that extended from Zoyan'qual's stone house and introduced him to it.

Zoyan'qual walked up to Beth, where she stood regarding the giant skeleton. "I know where there are ancient remains that no one else has explored yet. I can show you. Up in the canyons."

She stood with her hand on his arm. "What a pleasure that would be. An untouched site. The children could see it developed from the beginning."

She looked at him earnestly. "Zoyan'qual, if I am not able to arrange for such a dig…" Her voice trailed off in an unfinished sentence. Finally she completed the thought. "Show them where it is. Let them be the first to see it."

. . .

The campfire blazed. The cottonwood leaves on the perimeters of its light hovered like ghosts marking its boundaries with the darkness. Beyond them, the black night. Above, the stars.

Lucian said, "We return from an odyssey. Those who move from place to place and think that the outer movement is the odyssey, itself, have missed the adventure. It is the mixture of the outer with the unique inner. Like a novel set forth by the writer blends with the perceptions of the reader and becomes a new event.

"Such insights need to be shared, expressed, made available outwardly. We need this. What did we think? What did we feel? How will we move in our environment differently in the future, having made this journey? Each of us. Let us express now what we can of those thoughts, feelings, and insights to each other."

After a silence, Howard poked with a stick at the periphery of the fire. "You know," he said, "this is something like a reentry here. And going back to the office will be too. The maps will be there, but we've been to the reality the maps only refer to. The maps have no meaning without where we've been." He swirled a circle of light in the air with the ember-ended stick. "Somehow, there will be a positive difference going back, knowing where we've been."

Grandmother said, "Some people would refer to going back to their work as going back to reality. It is not that any of us are entering back *into reality*, but maybe that reality has entered more into us. And when that happens, when we go back into the surroundings we had referred to as *reality*, we see all sorts of new possibilities we had not seen before. We do not always know we have crossed a boundary until we look back on it from a new vantage point."

She looked around. "Sometimes we have what people call a kind of dream, or fantasy, or a wish that doesn't seem possible. And we cross that boundary, and look back at it and know then what to do with the dream-idea."

Howard said, "Yes. I like the way you express it. I have always wanted to go to the Mountains of the Moon. The ones in Africa. And to sail from Lake Victoria northward, along the Nile, from its inception, to the Mediterranean. Like we trailed the arroyo. I wanted to go the Nile's whole length. To stop along the way and see the evidence of six thousand years of civilization."

"And," said Grandmother, "do you already have brochures, travel information, a secret nest of things tucked away that you never show anyone else, about possibilities of doing that?"

He smiled at her. "Yes, I do. Transportation, costs, arrangements." He looked at the children. "Would you be interested...in..."

Before he spoke the rest of the sentence, they said in unison, "*Yes.*"

"There's a considerable amount of expense involved," he started to explain. "And you're all in school."

"The school is wherever we are," Dolphus reminded him.

Lucian explained, "They all have accounts for their work with the worm farm, the press, payments for assemblies they've presented. If you name the possible time and amounts, we can develop a budget projection to see what might be possible."

Lucian looked intuitively at Longhorn, who said, "Go."

The children looked at Howard's expression in the firelight and said together, "*Ah, the endorphins are flowing.*"

Grandmother said, "I know next what I want to do, too. In seeing the land, in seeing through Howard's descriptions the layers *beneath* the land, the strata beneath our feet, I want to go *down*." She pointed toward the earth and repeated, "*Down*. I know where caverns are, and I want to go to them, to go in, to go down. With all of us who want to come."

She thought for a moment and added, "They are caverns where it is said in the old legends, that people were born from the womb of the earth. I want for us to enter the earth in those places and emerge again as in a birth of the ancients."

Eriot said, "When we traveled, and we saw all of the landforms, I could *hear* them in my head. I mean, I could hear them as sounds, as music. I want us to learn to read and write music so I can put down the sounds that I hear. I have heard this music inside of me during the whole journey but I didn't realize it until Lucian asked us to say what we would now like to do."

He thought a moment. "And I have a second one, too. How is it we can know something and yet not know it at the same time? How could I hear all that music, have it all in my head, like it was just *there*, just coming out of the land, itself, along with the colors and temperature and smells, but I wasn't aware of it until now? I want us to discuss how that works."

Lucian said, "Hum or sing or play us a little."

Eriot took out a flute. "You remember when we went into the deepest canyon and began to see all of the layers? And we all felt the wind blowing straight at us? I heard it like a flute song."

He played what he called *the canyon wind.*

Orgol said, "I like that. What I'm thinking about is not something I'm going to do, but something I'm going to have to ask you to do with me. Every once in a while, I get feeling really afraid of different things and situations, and I don't know why. Can you help me explore that? I don't even know exactly what I'm asking, and I need you to help me clarify that too."

Beth reached over and placed her hand on his back.

"You understand?" he looked at her.

"More than you could possibly imagine," she said.

Normita said, "Some strange things went through my head on the trip. I mean, we were in the middle of a desert, or on a hill, or in the arroyo. I would think of *how* we were riding. And then I thought of how some people ride in sports. Like polo, and racing. And then I thought about the kinds of sports we have learned to do, but so many more I don't even know about. Well,

I would like to work on a book. I want to draw pictures, or maybe use photographs, of every kind of sport, everywhere, every country. Just to show what they all are. Everything from skiing to kinds of swimming, to hang-gliding, to even those in tribal cultures we haven't studied yet. And then," she held up her hand as if silencing a multitude, "after we have them all listed, I want us to try all of them ourselves, those we haven't done yet. So we'll each know if there's something we would particularly like to do."

Eriot's mother said, "I really enjoy this process. I'm understanding that an odyssey is a journey of visions. And then implementing them. There's something I've dreamed about, within, and have never talked about. But somehow, together as we have been, I have felt a sense of it emerging. And now that you've asked, I can try to explain it."

Her hands involuntarily positioned themselves as if above an invisible keyboard. "I have always enjoyed good organ music, with the large pipe organs. But I have always been frustrated to sit in an auditorium and see a few of the great pipes, the rest hidden in some rooms behind mesh and grills, where you couldn't see them. Most of all, when I heard the notes, I wondered which pipes were actually sounding."

Her hands raised before her as if she were seeing what she described. "I have envisioned in my mind an organ with every pipe visible. The auditorium would be like sitting *inside the organ*... Something like being in your huge model of the human body. And every pipe would have a recessed light aimed at it. When any pipe had air flowing through it, the light would illuminate it. So at every moment you would know visually each pipe that was being played. A visual borealis of sounds."

After a silence she added, "I want to find the way to plan and build that. Maybe here at the worm farm. Who knows. And then I will learn to play it. We can all learn to play it."

Dolphus said, "I have really thought about what we discussed concerning *boundaries*. I want to be part of the boundary breakers from earth. I want to know more about space and about being an astronaut. I don't know yet what I *want* to learn. But I want to go to the very edge of everything that's known, and then have us keep up with it. I want to think in terms of us going into space some day and find out how to start preparing for that now."

Kayla said, "What Beth once mentioned about there being freedom in being an orphan. I really thought about that a lot on the trip. What that meant. And it occurred to me that somehow a person with that kind of freedom wouldn't understand without knowing what the other options were."

She held up her two index fingers as if to coordinate the movements of a marching band. "I want to begin a kind of *journal of choices*. Since I can only do one thing at a time, what are the other things I also *could* be doing? A journal of choices about everything. Family alternatives. Lifestyles. Why it is that some people have *lifestyles*, and other people just have *lives*. You know what I mean? And I'm going to need everyone's help on this to work it out."

Pica said, "There were times on the trip, I would become aware that we were a long ways from where we had been when I was last aware of where we were, if that makes sense. I was just looking around, *being present* to things. I wondered if this was like a kind of hypnosis. I want to explore more about what happens at times like that. And what you can *do* with it. I mean, is it just wasted time, or is something really important going on inside the brain then?"

Lee said, "I just want to be here, a part of this, in school here. Can we do that, Uncle Howard?"

"I think we can arrange that," Howard laughed, and the children cheered.

Dolphus' father said, "Just like the outdoors became a place where we were all learning things, while we traveled—that is, the outside became a *classroom*, I thought about how we can consider *familiar* places in *new* ways. I was thinking about our house. I know Dolphus has suggested some things to do, and our walls have a lot of things hanging on them already that they never had before.

"So, what if instead of starting with the idea that a house is what we have *assumed* it to be, what if we rethought it altogether. What kind of environment would have a major impact on our emotions, our attitudes, our learning, all parts of our lives? And what if a dwelling was designed with those things in mind, another approach to living space.

266

"And I'm fascinated with your time lines now. What if a family lived in a time line? What if you assumed your major goal was *learning* and designed a house around that from the beginning? We rented the first place we could find when we moved here. But when we build a house, ourselves, why couldn't it be something no one has ever conceived of before? I want all of you to help with this. Would the Worm Farm School design me a house like—Pica, what was the word you used one day on the trip—a *chimera?*"

Reendo said, "All of us at worm farm have a room like we wanted, except Lucian, who wanted a castle. I want to figure out how to get Lucian his castle. Maybe a kind of castle that never was before."

Jhenaw said, "I want to build a robot. All along the trip, and then when you asked about it, I realized that everywhere I am, I imagine having a robot with me. I want to build one." She looked over at Essa.

"Yes," said Essa, "and I'll be your assistant. Now for mine, you're not going to believe this. This is like a *discovery*. If you hadn't asked for it, I would not have realized I was thinking about these things. Here are the several things and how they fit together.

"I love the time lines. The first I ever went through was your one with the cars. Driving through time. I learned the information along the track without even trying. And you know how I've come back and walked through all of the others. I've been concerned with how the things you have in all of your time lines are outside, exposed to the rain and wind and dust and all the elements. And the really perishable things, like books about the subjects on the time lines, you can't leave outside at all, even though you want them to be there in the sequence.

"You know how David and I get all the—ha! here's a real play on words for you—all the *junk mail*. We know all the things being sold, thrown away, given away, surplus, all of it. And we had seen this announcement about the disposal of old Quonset huts coming up. And I had thought *what a bargain*. Only I couldn't think how to use them.

"But, don't you see, that's it. I can get the huts, a whole bunch of them. And they can be attached end to end into as long a series of units as you want, opening into each other. And we could have an *indoor* time line, a *super* time line, combining all of them, and the things that go with them. Pictures, books, objects, alcoves of information all along the way.

"Until now, for example, when you wanted to read something about a poet, on your literary time line, you had to go back to the house to get a book on her. Well, now, you could have, right by the time line itself, a place for materials relevant to the period." She raised her eyebrows and hands in a gesture of waiting for a response. The response was that everyone was picturing the possibilities.

"In the light of day," she added, "this may not sound as good."

"Yes it will," said Longhorn. "Get them."

After a pause he added. "I decided on the journey, after we talked about a geologic time line in the form of a slide, probably one of the longest slides ever constructed, incorporating representations of all the layers of the earth, that we shall have our slide. I plan to start tomorrow."

"Every day," said Beth, "my concentration has to be on the baby. What a wonderful journey it has been for the little person. For me. We will continue to learn about all human development, through it, every day."

Lucian looked over at the sheik: "Camel-rider?"

Camel-rider looked pensively into the fire. "I am going to a place I know of in the dessert, where it is said that the ancient people threw sacrificial objects into a crevice that goes deep into the rock where no bottom has yet been measured. They felt it was a message carrier to the spirit of the earth, itself. By throwing their offerings into the vent, and speaking aloud the hope that some particular good would come to their people, they felt that the power of the earth would begin the process toward that accomplishment. I will take a stone I picked up at the headwater of the arroyo, valuable to me now as a representation of this journey, and drop it into that opening. Simultaneously, I will wish in some mysterious way for a process to be generated toward enabling Howard to start to implement his vision relating to world population and space frontier exploration."

Howard had been reclining on his elbow on the ground, also

gazing into the fire. He sat upright at these words and looked at Camel-rider.

"Not tonight," said Camel-rider, with a twitch of a smile, "*tomorrow*. We may call it *project endorphins*." He switched his gaze toward Lucian. "We have not heard from you. You guided us on this odyssey. You helped these things to appear. Yours?"

Lucian smiled, "Such a seemingly simple thing. I'm going to ask my parents to come to see worm farm. Even though they will probably have the current political figure they're supporting in tow when they do." He paused and said in his turn, "Zoyan'qual?"

Zoyan'qual said, "So far, in my canyon area, we have grown only plants native to the region. There must be food plants in similar climates around the world indigenous to those areas. We will secure them, grow them, and extend our potential food variety of nutrients."

Taco, who had been lying in the middle of the circle of people in the night raised his head from where it had been resting on his paws and looked around. He yawned, stretched, went over to Dolphus. Taco rested his head on Dolphus' ankle.

Zoyan'qual looked upward to the stars. "May we feel our part in the galaxy, the elements of which we are made. We, the part of the universe that makes myths."

64

The days, as always, began with the progress report of the as yet unnamed life growing in Beth's womb. The development of the ears, of the eyes, of the brain. The movement. The children feeling it, with their hands placed on Beth's expanding midsection.

In the first days back, Lucian let the mail that had accumulated during the trek lie untouched. He had little curiosity about what nested in the envelopes.

At last, one night, in the dark, in the quiet, by the flickering light of the candle mounted on the buffalo skull, he noticed again the envelopes lying there.

The Boston postmark attracted his attention. A package from Dr. Fenwicke.

He read her words. A response to what he had sent her, it seemed so long ago, when he had mailed to her a copy of the printed book, a check, his note bearing the Worm Farm Press return address.

In his mind, he could almost hear her vocal intonation of the words as he read.

To my benefactor, my gratitude. You have achieved the very pivot of balance for me. I did not want to make any effort to publish, did not want the other things that go with it. Yet, in me, as there must be within all writers deep down, a vision of the reader, the receiver of the story, hovering just beyond my consciousness while writing.

You have permitted me freedom from having connection with anything but the writing. In ways that I, too, would as soon leave as a mystery, you have somehow retrieved the manuscript, published it, even obtained reviews and growing numbers of orders. Continue as long as you wish, to do this.

I cannot tell you what an impetus this has been for me. While I would not presume upon your kindness, I am enclosing more writing. Do nothing with it, unless you find some personal pleasure in doing so. If you wish to print what I am sending, feel free to do it in the manner of the previous volume, to distribute it in any way you wish, and to keep all that may come from any sales that follow.

I feel that you are a voice in the night, a presence beyond my comprehension but not beyond my gratitude.

Lucian looked at the new manuscript she had included. The words became a vortex that pulled him into its opening section.

Prelude to the Winter of Our Discontent

It was in the October morning that they met, as they had for the past seventeen months, since the lock-horns confrontation at the Zenith Association meeting that had been an exhilarating moment for both of them.

No one, before that meeting, had ever opposed the masterful opinion of either. After all, they were critics by profession, by persuasion, by life. Their names inspired and awed.

But they had never met before that first time at Zenith. Prior to that, for years, each had held respective sway in separate literary domains. Then a newspaper shakeup, and a magazine buy-out, and suddenly, unexpectedly, they were in the same publishing pasture, the Zenith conglomerate, marking out their territories anew.

The forays in their former spaces had been mere calisthenics, a kind of warm-up for the professional exercises they displayed so nimbly, so peacockily in their respective outlets.

But that day. At that gathering of the power brokers, the editorial policy makers, all wondered what would occur when these two met. Each had always been unopposed. But then, they had never been together before.

One had spoken. Instead of the usual silence of the lesser Zenith members,who at best made a breathy sound of comprehension and respect, this time, THIS TIME, the first thunderclap was followed by another, equally loud, from the other side of the room.

It startled everyone, but, really, the most caught off guard were both of them, the first for hearing the other voice from across the chamber, with such assured profundity, and the second from receiving the shock wave of a returned volley.

The others may have been lesser characters, a Greek chorus left to comment on the Titans, to voice the commonplaces about the volleys of hubris that followed, but they were all, in their own right, editors, and publishers, and authors whose efforts, if not the outcomes, made them knowledgeable about the conflict that transpired here in their very midst.

A disaster, some members termed it, a shredding of professionalism. The Nadir of Zenith, whispered another, seeing the type-face in his mind's eye heading a page.

But for the two, it was adrenaline. The usual surrounding fog of mediocrity cleared, revealing another Titan on another mountain top. Alone no longer. A companion, albeit an adversary, as the very best in competitive societies can have no companions other than adversaries. It is an oxymoronic relationship.

So they attended these meetings with exhilaration now, instead of holding court and practicing grandeur.

But it was the between-meetings, when they decided to come together alone, just the two of them, that peaked their days. Their private wrestling on the mountain tops—for this, they came to live, preparing as they never did for a pedestrian public.

And the arena? As it had to be, a metaphor of something unspoken. A woodland glade, dappled in sunlight filtering through the leaves, a site for satyrs and Pan's clan, a place worthy of their words. A place where some park must once have been, for two marble thrones stood there in the glade, like leftovers from an outpost of Olympus, to which they brought their own cushions.

"No!" Cromson was bellowing into the isolated countryside, leaning forward on his padded marble throne, vibrating the October day. "No, it cannot and will not be by your merely saying it. The genius of that author you just named lives as no other, in fully thirty-seven of his key disciples, who have spread to no fewer than eleven major cities of the globe to practice both their own literary craft as well as to bestow it on others through their classes."

"But," retorted Limbitt, "you overlook, and purposely, I daresay, for the sake of your pitiful argument, the sixteen sub-influences I have illustrated for you already, which demonstrate conclusively the impact of three other genres, seven regional systems, as well as that of their immediate predecessors."

A rustle of leaves, a disturbance of the russet and amber that multi-wreathed the blue, blue sky and dancing puffs of clouds, little attracted the speakers. But when a voice accompanied the disturbance, and another humanish form moved into their idyllic midst, they paused, heads tilting back ever so imperceptibly and voices changing to intruder-mode.

The form, that not so much confronted them as joined them, emerged almost as a personification of the autumn surroundings and simply leaned against a tree and spoke.

"I live where I can hear you, each of these days you come here..." He did not pause to respond to their obvious question for which their mouths in unison opened, as to where he lived, but hastened on, "...and I say you have built a wall around yourselves, a wall of such proportions, that you are prisoners of your own thought. You come here, not to expand your visions of a world greater than your own, but to more solidly pack the mortar between the stones of your confining concepts."

The "wh" sound dropped from their mouths simultaneously, but the russet stranger continued before their "t" sound vibrated the air.

"You talk of worthy stories, of novels, and how do you define them? As any secondary schooler knows verbatim, it must have a plot. And a plot has a conflict, with the attending action rising to a climax and denoueing—why can't it be a verb," he interrupted himself, anticipating the potential product of their again open mouths, "denoueing into termination."

He emphasized the next word, "But..." with a branch of russet orange leaves that he raised from where it had fallen to the ground, "...what if there is no conflict? What if the shepherd,who comes to Oedipus to tell his tale, turns out to be funning, just testing the leader's mettle, and tacks on at the end, 'No, it was just a funny thought, a improbable coincidence that passed through my mind, an incredible series of really impossible coincidences that I was running through for practice, for my gaming group tonight; what a lark it will be for my role-playing team; but you—you sir, have no genetic connection to these people here, you were not the man who belted the former king at the crossroads.'

"And Jocasta returns, embraces him, their offspring come forth, making a family circle, with little terms of endearment to their parents, and the city elders find the problems of Thebes was a cyclic weather condition caused by El Nino, that now ends, and all is well. 'Gosh,' says the last chorus member to exit, 'and for a moment there we thought it was something supernatural. Goes to show you we shouldn't jump to conclusions too hastily.'"

He had their attention now. He was not thundering at them as they did at each other. They were thunder, but he was a breeze, an autumn breeze, blowing out of the yellow-russet woods. Their mouths began a unison comment again, but his voice continued.

"You have a void, you see. If the family is happy, you have no tragedy. If there is no conflict, there is no plot. If neither of these, then nothing learned, by your standards, and therefore not literature."

"Didactic..." Cromson managed to extrude.

"And," overrode the stranger, "if no literature, you both are out of a job as critics."

"Would you read Becket," Limbitt slid in rapidly, "if the king and archbishop were still friends, settled their differences, did what was good for all, politely and courteously supported each other's best interests as they pertained to the welfare of their people, sought consensus-truth from a brain-trust of the saintly—would you read that?"

"Read it," returned the russet stranger, "I would live it, do live it, welcome it, thrive on it. You have built your literature on a theory of strife, and those that don't fit into your well-built cell may remain invisible to you. Outside—OUTSIDE..."

Cromson intervened. "The other day, a manuscript, one of those unsolicited things, for no reason, came to me. I read it, I couldn't put it down, it was so bad, so happy, not syrupily so, but reasonably, yet unrealistically, for it could never be. I was scathing. It was too preposterous, too wonderful, to be considered, there would be no market...no buying public...that volume...could you..."

"Consider the possibilities," Russet said, beginning a kind of pirouetting dance among the leaves, seeming to blend with them from moment to moment in the dappling sunlight, "consider what might be outside: no plot, no story, no conflict, as we know it, because now we define life as conflict, and can see no life where there is no clash. A new perspective of life..."

"A new lease on literature," added Limbitt.

"A dream," said Cromson, "a preposterous illusion that cannot be. The narrow-minded self-righteous bigots of all ages, better-thouing their fellows with their self-serving thoughtless little tales."

"Are they not predators in their own way? And why," said Russet, continuing his breezy movements, "are we rooted in the theory of predation, that every story must be the hunt? What must you have, in order to call forth a hero?"

"A villain, of course," said Limbitt.

"For conflict, of course," added Cromson.

"So," Russet seemed to freeze in mid-leap, "villains create heroes. Without villains, no heroes. And heroes must..."

"Achieve," said Limbitt, "achieve and gain and grow."

"That they may loose what they gained," said Cromson.

"Like the building of celebrities in your culture?" asked Russet, dancing in wider gyres now.

"You build them up with stories of their poor afflicted background, how they combat it, have conflict, to gain prominence, yes, of course, and emerge to success..." said one of the critics.

"But when all is well, and the mythic everything has been attained," continued one of them, their words were rushing together indistinguishably now, so it became unclear which one said what,

274

"They have no conflict and so..."
"Enter marital breakup, drug abuse, depression..."
"In order to once again have..."
"Conflict! so they can tour the lecture circuit telling..."
"About their overcoming adversity, overcoming..."
"Conflict! But then they must face a comeback, a reentry..."
"To grandeur and attention...face a comeback, face a..."
Conflict!"
"But if conflict is not the standard..." said Limbitt in a rising voice.
"Then what lies beyond?" added Cromson.
"Banality!" shouted Limbitt. "Lackluster, dreary, never-ending..."
"Tediousness!" shouted Cromson. "Unyielding, unvarying..."
"BOREDOM!" thundered Limbitt. "Boredom! Dull and useless!"
"It is an illusion," shouted Cromson, "a dream, a nothing that cannot exist. Happiness cannot exist except as a goal. Once attained, it must be destroyed or it can never be re-attained. It can never endure. Happiness, once attained, becomes BOREDOM and self-destructs."
"That is life!" bellowed Limbitt.
"That is literature!" echoed Cromson.
"Oedipus lives..." proclaimed Limbitt.
"...by dying!" concluded Cromson.
A silence followed, broken only by the sound of wind and rustling russet leaves. The two looked around at the movement of the dappled light, now coming from an orange sun sinking into the autumn foliage.
They were quite alone. They removed the cushions from their marble thrones and prepared to leave.

65

The trailing of the wild arroyo and emergence of realizations of individual interests to pursue set into motion a series of interrelated projects.

Eriot's mother said she had found her source of energy in the *organ of her dreams* that she wanted somehow to help construct. Immediately she began to sketch her visions and prepare small three-dimensional models of what she visualized. She started brainstorming with every organist she could locate regionally, managing to entice eleven of them to the Worm Farm School to explore the matter together, in sessions that Eriot labeled as *organ-isms*.

Brigham Ekenaut, who presided over the largest organ installation in the area, became enthralled with children's systemic interrelating of fields of study. He followed them around for a week after the *organ task force* meeting, relishing his audience's appreciation as he inserted music trivia related by date, location, or theme to each of their activities. They assured him that it was not trivia once it was connected to a larger system of information. Before he could complete his question of "Who told you th..." they chorused, "Lucian told us."

Brigham introduced the concept of relating all letters of the alphabet to musical notes, thereby enabling the translating of all names or other words to melody. The place was soon adrift in strains of Orgol's theme, and that of Kayla, and the rest. Empowered with this new frame of tonal reference, they began to create *worm* melodies, *dinosaur* sonatas, and attributal tune patterns for *love*, *justice*, and *mercy*.

"Now our names have melodies as well as origins," said Pica.

"What's the origin of your name, Pica?" asked Brigham.

"It's Latin for *magpie*."

. . .

Howard Loggat sat staring at a world map adorning the wall above his office desk after everyone else had left for the day. He had not moved for minutes, except for the eyes following the contours of the continents, mentally projecting population densities on the land masses, and glancing intermittently at the population clock and its ever-augmenting number.

He startled to awareness at a knock on his already open door and turned to find a briefcase-carrying man framed in the doorway. "Excuse my intruding on your reverie, and especially after hours, but I have a matter of some importance to discuss with you."

Howard listened as the man explained in succinct sentences that he was a lawyer representing a foundation, for which the fund-donor remained anonymous. He had come to ask Howard if he would be interested in applying for a planning grant to prepare a detailed proposal of what the initial steps might be toward some

276

sort of organization to work with the prospects of population management alternatives.

The former zebra-rider sat as still while regarding the lawyer as he had been when concentrating on the map. Finally the lawyer said, "If this is a bad moment…"

"No," Howard replied, "you've made it quite a good moment."

"If you need more time…" and he reached into his pocket and removed a business card.

"No more time needed," said Howard.

"Then these forms will explain the stipulations, and this title page will need to be filled out, with the project name and…"

"The name will be *The Arroyo Project.*"

. . .

The lawyer would see no one but the university president nor would he explain his business to the secretary, office manager, or administrative assistant. "Tell him," the man said to the third tier of buffers, "that it involves a time-sensitive contribution to the university.'

Standing behind his expansive desk in the presidential chambers, the chief administrator acknowledged the visitor's presence stiffly, saying, "We will need to be quick about this since I do have a scheduled meeting in fifteen minutes, but you could have more time with one of my…"

The visitor one said, "The Foundation of an anonymous donor is positioned to give the university funds for outreach-learning opportunities for some of its advanced and graduate students in education. The specifics are listed in these papers. It is the hope of our benefactor that if you find the arrangement compatible with the university's mission, that you will see that the proper representatives fill them out and return them by the specified date."

He placed the papers on the desk in front of the President, who tilting his reading glasses to see the first page, then scanned it, reading aloud, "The graduate student education classes would be funded to observe the educational program at…" and then he paused before saying in puzzlement, "What kind of institution is a Worm Farm…*School*? And your foundation is proposing to offer the headmaster a full scholarship through our institution to enter doctoral study? What about the…"

By the time he finished reading and looked up, the visitor had already departed.

. . .

The junk shop duo came speeding up the road and dashed to find the denizens of the Worm Farm School. "Warning! Warming! Time line aproaching," they shouted. The ruckus brought all from their tasks to gather around them. Both of the *junkies*, as Orgol had started calling them, pointed toward the road where dust clouds of immense proportions signaled the arrival of something more than a car.

Trucks bearing the sections of Quonset huts rumbled in a caravan toward the house. Lucian ran out to give directions, to aim them toward large open areas beyond the farm where the rows of materials could be lined up while awaiting assembly.

Slowly, with the unloading, the area began to resemble the aftermath of a hurricane, with building pieces strewn across the land.

As the trucks, lighter than on their arrival, roared away, the worm farm crew stood in the middle of the potential-filled debris, finally ending up in a circle around David and Essa who clutched large, rolled-up pages. "They hold the secret papers," Orgol said in a movie-mystery voice. The *papers* referred to the blue-print sized documents of directions for assembling the huts.

"Why do they call them Quonset Huts? asked Kayla.

Lucian made what Reendo called his scamper gesture, which meant *go find out*, and they all ran off. Soon they returned, with Dolphus explaining, "After Quonset Point, where they were first made."

"In Rhode Island," added Dolphus.

They spent the afternoon on hands and knees over the plans, interspersed with long walks, measuring distances, hammering stakes into projected sites for what they hoped would ultimately house the long and ever-expanding time lines into the new combined *Super Time Line*.

. . .

Dr. Sydney Brummett, who Janice had once said looked something like a cross between Santa Claus and a snowman, peered with a beaming smile through the doorway into Dr. Pandra's office. "Fill me in on these Worm Farm School people. The word is *do it* from command central, straight from the chancellor's office, and I've said, *Aye captain*, without knowing what. Something about funding to take my graduate students in education there to observe and interact? Brief me."

Janice said, "I recommended you, but I couldn't tell you before you had official contact. The president called me to ask my opinion of a grant offer, I affirmed it would be of benefit, he said who should head it, I said you."

He had seated himself in front of her desk, swiveling back and forth with a need for movement that seemed perpetual.

Janet opened her mouth to begin explaining, but each time paused, and finally said, "Sydney, just go to the place, with no preparation, no preconceptions. Go without me so I won't be tempted to give you previews. You'll know what to do. You'll intuit the whole thing from your own interactions."

"That's about as clear as directions in a foreign language," he said, fingering his white beard. "Map it for me how to get there, and..." his voice broke into the suggestion of a familiar tune, "...I'm off to see the earthworms, by following the yellow dust road."

. . .

Sydney scheduled a university van and took his whole seminar class in Creative Learning Methodologies on a field trip to the Worm Farm School for his initial contact.

Guided by Janice's map, they found the place at the time appointed. When Sydney saw the looks on the faces of his students at the sights they beheld on arrival—a woman carrying an eight foot long organ pipe, a jerry-rigged cart on which was balanced a C-section of some construction material rocking back and forth pulled by several children, in the corral a zebra and a camel and a reindeer, a dinosaur skeleton peering over a building—he said, "Maybe we should just move here."

After introductions, the children each took a graduate student on an individual tour, wherever their conversations led them. Dolphus guided Sydney along with a student from Tonga. By the time Dolphus had led them along some of the existing time lines and described the plans for the Super Time Line, the doctor of education began inscribing a pocket notebook with outlines of ideas.

"Does everyone who teaches at the university make notes all the time?" Dolphus asked. "Janice Pandra does the same thing."

. . .

"Why do we have to wait?" Kayla asked around the evening campfire. "Why can't we start with what we know and write a little book asking questions about population even if we don't know the answers yet, and about, well, the future—*futuring*—now?"

Pica looked at the graduate class that had stayed later than they had projected, as they kept asking Dr. Brummett not to leave *quite yet.* "Would you like to help us on a project? You could probably find things at the university about *futuring* and population that we don't know how to access yet."

The first interactive project between a university class and the Worm Farm School began to take shape over a campfire meal of Australian outback cuisine and music of aboriginal tribal background.

66

Dr. Brummett's class opted, at their next session in their seminar room at the university, to adopt a new schedule that would permit them periodically to spend a whole day at the Worm Farm School.

They started referring to their seminar as Quonset Hut 101, as they helped with the construction. As they started to assist in assembling time line materials within completed sections, their own brainstorming accelerated, and they found themselves returning on weekends with artifacts that might be incorporated into the spreading chart of years.

Those who had children of their own began bringing them along on Saturdays, and in a ripple effect, those children reported on their experiences to their teachers, some of whom came to see how much of what they were hearing was actual.

Before one third grade teacher left, she asked Lucian about the possibility of her class making a field trip to Worm Farm

School. "Let's check with the others. We decide together," he explained, and rounded them up. Their unanimous vote was *yes*.

. . .

Before the arrival of the field trip bus, the worm farm group had decided not to plan ahead for anything except the meal. The rest they wanted to let evolve when their guests arrived.

One of the visiting students asked, "Are you the *worm farmers?*" The newly christened worm farmers each took some of those who they had in turn called *fieldtrippers*, and gave them choices of what they might first like to see.

Since Lucian's expectation of remuneration remained constantly at zero, he experienced surprise when the supervising teacher thrust an envelop in his hand with a substantial check labeled for *admission, activities, and cafeteria costs*.

The *worm farmers* decided in evening discussion to use this unexpected source of revenue to open a separate account, adding to it should more such funds come in, and earmark it for *Unexpected Opportunities*.

The deposits to this new fund did increase, as more classes came on field trips. The graduate students adjusted their visits to be there when the visitors came and took the opportunity to study the effects of *learning by teaching*, as the Worm Farm School students essentially taught mini-classes to their visitors on a variety of subjects in their guided tours of their growing exhibits and projects.

. . .

Sydney stood in back of the graduate students observing the visiting students from a field trip listening to Normita explain the new *icons-images-and-masks* room. She was in the process of describing the series of Kachinas and their use in instruction of children in tribal ways and their intertwining symbols. After she had gone down the line of traditional representations, she focused on some that the *worm farmers* had each devised to represent forces, elements, and objects not found in traditional figures. "Some," she explained, "were not included previously because they were not in the environment of that culture."

When someone asked her if she was working on any now, she said *yes*, she had wanted to do a *snowman kachina*, but had not found the proper model until recently and had not asked him yet if he would pose. She looked back at Dr. Brummett, and said, "Would you be my model?"

. . .

Howard looked at the faces of the children around the campfire. He had explained the planning grant funding he had received to develop a proposal for a center to study population management.

"One of the elements I am imagining is a board that is diverse and non-traditional. We can have the experts come in as consultants and advisors. And since the board members would have to be of a certain age legally to hold that position, I want to suggest an interlocking board of advisors, where age is no factor."

"You want *us?*" said Fenari, his mind always racing ahead of spoken words. He had come on one of the field trips and then begged his parents to transfer him to Worm Farm School. His parents had visited, telling Lucian how Fenari by four was reading the encyclopedia, sneaking copied pages of it to pre-school in his lunchbox to read behind the cover of the *Preparing to Read* series his class labored through. He was disciplined if caught for *reading non-prescribed materials.* "Maladjusted is an understatement," his mother had said. "And in his music too." She explained how he had, by age five, picked out on the piano any tune he heard, from commercials to concertos to jazz.

The day Fenari arrived, Lucian installed a piano, and the new-comer's sounds erupted periodically throughout the day. His special retreat room on campus took the shape of a piano-shaped structure, which everyone helped him to build.

So when Fenari asked his question of Howard, the *populationist,* one of the nicknames bestowed on him by Fenari, Howard said, "A trade. Let's go to your piano. I'll give you the answer, and you give us a theme for the boards of advisors."

. . .

On one of her visits to the worm farm, Janice walked with Lucian away from an Indonesian fire-dinner under the cottonwoods, while the children experimented with musical instruments from that region. She said, "Sydney is strategizing again. Among other things, the idea of children teaching children, as your students do when the field trip groups come, intrigues him. He wants you to come to his class to lecture about it."

"If the children can participate in the experience, too," said Lucian.

"I told him that already," she smiled.

. . .

The university president had given instructions that if the man who previously came with the foundation bequest for outreach returned, he was to be ushered in immediately. The man returned, and before finishing his opening sentence of, "Is the president avail…," the receptionist stood and beckoned him past the outer desks toward the inner office.

"We now have a detailed proposal for the establishment of a population management research center, resulting from a planning grant prepared by a Mr. Howard Loggat. We are disposed to follow up at this point with funding, to bring it into a working form. That, of course, requires a site. It seems appropriate to us to have it located in an educational setting. We want to investigate the possibility of such a site being housed at this university. We are ready to help finance that option."

He removed a sheaf of bound pages and placed them on the desk. "Would you wish to take under consideration the possibility of locating this project on your campus? A simple *yes* will suffice to start with, agreeing that you would at least consider it. Then details would follow. Call the number on the front page as soon as that initial decision is made. We would appreciate that call being from you personally, so that we are assured it has already passed through the necessary administrative channels for approval prior to our taking the next step."

The president scanned the top sheet, pausing over the words *population* and *futuring*. By the time he looked up, his visitor had departed.

67

"Today, system building," Lucian said in the early morning. "A word, a single word, to start with. Then we can add any terms that we want to connect to the initial one. Then we can add terms or events or dates or ideas that relate to those connections. And in this way we continue building out from the center what becomes a system of interconnected concepts."

The children rushed to the *systems circle*, a clear area in the middle of the yard. They grabbed cards and markers on the way. Eriot brought a device with a vertical roulette spinner. "Whose turn is it to spin the *systems wheel of fortune?*" Lucian asked. In unison, they remembered and said, "Fenari."

He spun the wheel, marked with the letters of the alphabet. It raced, slowed, and pinged to a stop at the letter "A." Jhenaw ran to the *reference building* and returned with the first volume of an encyclopedia. Reendo flipped it open randomly. Normita led Orgol, his eyes closed, to it, positioning his finger above the open pages.

His finger descended, his eyes blinked open, and he read, "Avalokityesuara." Lucian spelled it out with a stick, in the dirt, and transliterated it into three different phonetic systems, including *ah-wah-loh-ke-TESH-wah-rah*. Reendo, with another stick, from the musical notations they had learned for letters of the alphabet, wrote the melodic counterpart in the sand above the letters. Fenari's eyes went blurry as they did when his outer senses turned inward to hear compositions while his fingers moved, playing, as Dolphus called it, his *air piano*.

They all ran to the music building with the piano at its center, and Fenari first played the single notes in sequence of the melody translating each letter of *Avalokityesuara* into a note, and then transmuted the basic melody into variations styled, in turn, to Beethoven, Bach, Broadway, and jazz. Everyone else took an instrument of some sort and improvised with him.

When Lucian crashed the cymbals together, the musicians took flight out the door for phase two, *the search*. They were just bursting out the door, when Sydney arrived for one of his unheralded visits, a single graduate student in tow, visiting the worm farm for the first time. "We barely escaped being trampled to death," Sydney said, as the herd stampeded off to other buildings, calling after them, "What are you studying, the Big Bang?"

Clayton Wasumi, the graduate student, watched them run off

and looked at Sydney questioningly. "Just take notes," said Sydney, "you can make sense of it later."

"Systems," said Lucian, and motioned the two to follow him to *systems central*.

The children each came back clutching a book referencing some aspect of their *start word*. They were each using markers to write brief phrases on cards and then, as they placed cards on the ground next to the original word, they shared bits of information they had found.

"*Avalokityesuara* is sanskrit for *looking on, lord*." As Orgol said this, he wrote the translation on a card, placing it beside the original card.

"It refers to the *bodhisattva* of infinite compassion and mercy." Another card beside the second one.

"It shows the resolve to help all achieve emancipation."

" It's the essence which is reincarnated in each human form of the Dalai Lama." Another card.

"So it's a *compassionate gaze* on the suffering of the world."

"In Japan it's *Kannon*." Each time, another card, making visual the related ideas.

"In Chinese, it's called *Kuan-yin*."

"In Tibet, there it's a patron, and in the form of a monkey, that gave birth to the people as *Chenrezig*."

With these first relationships made with the core word, they could also now take any other word or concept from the cards that had been placed on the ground and relate to them as well. They raced off again to choose other books, and to inscribe more cards.

Pointing to a card already on the ground, Reendo said, "Japan." Next to it he added the new card. "145,766 square miles, capital, Tokyo, on four major islands, Hokkaido in the north, then Honshu, the largest, and Shikoku, and Kyushu."

Fenari quickly filling out another card. "In Japan, they celebrate September 15 as *Respect for the Aged Day*."

Normita quickly scrawled on another card, *Sydney*, and placed it next to *Aged Day*, and laughed, "Just kidding."

This made Clayton guffaw uncontrollably, pointing at his professor, as he became hopelessly hooked into the systems project, ready to run off with them on their next foray for more books.

"Bodhisattva," said Eriot, "In Mahayana Buddhism, is one who delays his own final entry into Nirvana in order to help with the suffering of others."

"Here's a coincidental interrelationship," said Normita, "only related because it happens to be on the same page as *Bodhisattva*, and it's a reference to Bode's law. This is neat! A rule for planetary distances from the sun. Take a sequence of fours. To the first add three times zero, to the second add three times one, to the next four times two, and continuing, each time doubling the number of the multiplier. Divide each by ten. The results are the approximate distances from the sun of each planet, in astronomical units."

"Okay," said Sydney, joining the card-placing group, "since you plunked my name down there, and Clayton got such a kick out of it, I'm going to make a connection to the card with my name on it, that none of you would know about—deal with this one! I once won a school science competition with the answer to the question *what is a BTU*."

Next to his newly placed card marked with those three letters, Reendo put a blank card, writing on it as he spoke, "British Thermal Unit."

Jhenaw quickly placed another card beside that, writing and saying, "The amount of heat needed to raise one pound of water one degree Fahrenheit."

Clayton, as if he were trumping it, slammed down a card with the formula, "$F=(9/5 \times C) + 32$."

The run for books continued and the cards multiplied.

Next to the *September 15 Aging Day* card, Kayla placed another card and said, "September, meaning seventh month in the old Roman calendar, became the ninth month, when the date for starting the new year changed."

"*Sydney*—Sydney, Australia, named by English Explorer Arthur Phillip, for Lord Thomas Townshend Sydney, the Home Secretary."

"Phillip's first impressions of the site recorded in a famous message dated May 15, 1788."

"The name Sydney, comes from the Old French, meaning *from Saint Dennis*."

Next to the *Sydney* card, Fenari placed a card with Clayton's name on it. "Sydney brought Clayton, that's my connection. And the name *Clayton* comes from the Anglo-Saxon, meaning from *earthy material* or *of clay.*"

"Like the story of Adam." said Orgol. "Made from clay too."

"Yes," said Reendo, thumbing through a name origin book, "Adam, Hebrew, *man of the earth,* from *red earth.*"

"*Colorado,*" burst out Kayla, "red earth, in Spanish."

"So," said Pica, "in a Spanish story, it could have been *Colorado and Eve?*"

They laughed. "Or Clayton and Eve," said Jhenaw, thumping the squatting graduate student on his back.

Eriot pointed back to the card for *September 15 in Japan,* and began to deal out a series of additional cards. "Here's what else happened on September 15. On that date in 1830, William Huskisson was the first person to be killed by a train when the Liverpool and Manchester Railway opened. 1916, the first tanks were used in battle, by the British. In the year 53, Roman Emperor Trajan was born in Spain. 1938, the novelist Thomas Wolfe died."

"Okay, let me do May 15, the day of the *Sydney Harbor message,*" said Dolphus. By that card, he spread others. "That's Independence Day in Paraguay, from 1811. And the first air mail service in the world, in 1918, between Washington and New York. Pierre Curie, the chemist, born in France, 1859. Emily Dickinson, the poet, died in 1886."

Fenari dropped in a card next to *Thomas Wolfe,* "He wrote *Look Homeward Angel.*"

"Here's a *contrast card,*" said Orgol, "instead of a place named for a person, like Sydney…" and he dropped in a card on which he had written the word *toponym,* "…this means words derived from a place name."

"Like *champaign,* coming from that region of France!" said Jhenaw, scrawling the word on a card.

"You put those cards in a *row,*" said Reendo, "so I'm relating the next one to the word *row,* rhyming with *low,* but if you got into a fight, you'd pronounce the same three letters, r-o-w, to rhyme with *now,* as *row,* and that would be a *homograph.* Two spellings with different pronunciations."

Kayla pointed to a paper clip on one of the earlier cards. "I'm relating to that. Paperclips were patented in various designs by Matthew Schooley in America, by Norway's Johan Vaaler in Germany around the year nineteen hundred."

Fenari moved back to *Chenrezig*. "Like the story that he created people, similarly the Hopi view is that *Sootukknang* is the being that brought together all the elements of nature and created the universe."

Pica pointed to the paper clip. "Paper clips were *inventions*. So I'm connecting to the idea of *inventions*. Sydney wears glasses, which were *inventions* of Salvino Armato in about 1280, in Italy, where he worked with glass."

"Eyeglasses are related to vision," said Kayla, "and this card I'm putting down has *scotopic vision* on it, which means…?" She paused for a response. "*Night vision*, being able to see in the dark."

Eriot added to the 1890s card cluster. "The same decade paperclips were being patented, basketball was being invented in Springfield, Massachusetts."

"Where the Basketball Hall of Fame is located," added Dolphus.

Jhenaw patted the ground on which all the cards lay. "We're on the worm farm land, so automatically any of our systems relate to worms. If we're looking for ways to raise more funds for our projects, then why not enlarge the worm market. How about *Vermi-composting*, which involves the use of certain kinds of worms to turn waste into organic fertilizer. There are so many cattle ranches, chicken and turkey and pig farms, that produce tons of waste that's seeping out and polluting the watershed. But these worms change it into usable fertilizer. They're called redworms or manure worms."

"Back up to *Eve*," said Kayla. "Some references say she was Adam's second wife. But that Lilith was his first, created just like Adam from the earth, making both genders equal. Then this source says that some paternalistic invaders committed *mythicide*, killing off the story by recasting Lilith as a monster in a revised myth, and then bring in Eve who was supposed to be subservient by being created out of Adam, from his rib."

"Bet there was lightning and thunder accompanying that

one," Sydney joked.

Laughing, Pica scrawled *lightening and thunder* on a card, placing it by Lilith, and said, "That's a segue into what I've been waiting to connect to something. *Boanerges.* Meaning the *sons of thunder.*"

"Jhenaw made the earth of worm farm part of our system," said Eriot, "so I'll add the Quechua or Incan word for earth, *pacha.* They used the term *pachamama* to refer to *mother earth.*"

Clayton moved forward, writing a word on a card and tossing it onto the growing system. "Wherever this goes, it will fit in. It's *Shem,* my youngest brother's name, and he's got to be in the middle of what you're doing, because his mind works this way. He just didn't know anyone else's did."

"Shem," said Reendo, placing beside the newest card another with the name *Baal Shem Tov,* "born 1698 in the Ukraine, a holy man and teacher of the Kabballah."

The process continued until Lucian called time. Now that they had done *system breadth,* he reminded them, they would go to *system depth.* He asked them to decide on one card that they each would really like to know more about in depth. Then they would look for information answering the questions *who, what, when, why, where,* and *how,* related to the subject, write it up, and describe it to the others. "This is our *research, writing,* and *speaking* component."

"I want to continue the *worm composting,*" said Jhenaw, "and see if it's actually something we could start here."

"I'll take *Lilith* and *mythicide,*" said Normita.

Orgol wanted to find out more about *Maria Mitchell,* whom one source identified as the first female astronomer in the United States.

Each in turn chose a topic. While they did, Lucian gathered up the cards into a file box. "The order doesn't matter, since everything is related to everything else. Explain for Sydney and Clayton what comes next."

"Review," said Pica. "We've got to review within an hour of going over something new to help retain it, like the material on these cards, because it first goes into our short term memory, and we have to reinforce it to help get it into long term."

"And then review again later today and again tomorrow, and then every week or so for a while after that," added Normita.

Lucian handed the cards toward Clayton. "Read them one at a time, and after each one, we'll all share what we remember." Sydney stood to the side, making notes.

When they finished their collective recollections about each card, Clayton shook his head. "I think there's still hope for me. I'm actually remembering this. Shem—I can hardly wait to get him here. His mind is going to explode!"

. . .

The next week, Shem came into the group like a long lost relative. Clayton had copied all the cards and had shared them with his younger brother. Shem had already selected a topic, the *British Thermal Unit*, and arrived with a box of materials for demonstration.

At the end of Shem's first day, Sydney, who had returned to observe the newcomer's entry into the process, said to Lucian as they waved the last of the children off to their homes, "Well, you have yet another ethnicity in your fold." Lucian looked at him with a blank stare, unable to remember outer descriptions, but recalling vividly the way Shem had *thundered* into the activity, all Lucian could think to say was, "Maybe *Boanerges* would be a good name for him."

. . .

It was time to take all of the systems cards they had generated, had reviewed multiple times, and had reported on in depth, and to place them along the time line at their appropriate dates. Each time they stopped to insert one, they talked about the other items already in place for that same date.

Onchou, a graduate student from Tibet, who had come previously with Sydney to observe, returned again. "Help me carry something," he said, and beckoned them toward his car. He pulled out bamboo poles, fitting them together to form a carrying platform that all the children could help support by holding onto of the poles. In the center of the platform, he placed an inscribed stone. "Let's carry it out together, and place it along your *roadway of learning*, the time line. To bring blessings to what you are doing." They placed it ceremoniously. "I wonder what the stone is called and what the inscription means," said Onchou, in an adult-to-children voice, as a lead-in to explaining it to them.

Reendo, taking his question as a request for information, said, "It's a *mani*, a wayside stone, inscribed with a *mantra*."

"A prayer formula," added Dolphus.

"In Sanskrit," continued Normita.

The children spontaneously chanted together, "*Om mani padme hum.*"

Onchou looked at them. "How…how did you know that?"

Eriot said, "Lucian told us, when we made one and took it to Zoyan'qual."

"And it translates as…?" Onchou tested them.

"Literally referring to *jewel* and *lotus*, between two *universe sounds*," said Orgol, "but with symbolic meaning, where each syllable corresponds to a color, or a part of the human body, or one of the realms of existence."

"Do you want to see our charts and diagrams of the colors, parts, and realms over in our Mandala Hut?" asked Fenari, pointing. Not waiting for a response, the children ran off in the direction toward which Fenari had pointed, motioning the others to follow.

Pica called over her shoulder, "*Mandala* means *disk* in Sanskrit."

Reendo turned, bowed slightly, and said, "Thank you for the *mani*." And rushed on.

Bringing up the rear, Onchou turned to Sydney who just smiled at him.

68

Dinner at the Pandras, came the invitation in mock formality from Janice. The various faculty who had traveled to Worm Farm School wanted to talk to Lucian. They agreed to the off-campus meeting place and to a Sunday afternoon for Lucian's convenience.

Lucian arrived to find a variety of cars already in front of the house. Inside, the gathering. He knew some of the people. Steve

Rutledge, Herman Brunswick, Selma Pendle, Sydney Brummett, even Isadora Ranford, the elementary teacher.

Lucian had rounded the room, greeting each of them, as Janice went to the kitchen to get him papaya juice. When Walter appeared from the hallway, Howard Loggat walked at his side.

Howard leaned close to Lucian's ear and said, "Wait until you hear what they're mulling over."

As they ate on dinner trays circled in the living room, the synthesis began. They were inviting Lucian to enter the doctorate program in education. His research efforts could focus on the on-going work with the children at Worm Farm School. The Pandras' home would become a campsite for Lucian and the children and any *assorted others* needing to come to the campus.

The university administration had approved the proposal to house a center for population study that Howard would head, *on the campus*. This in-kind contribution would free up the foundation grants from the anonymous donor to be used on *activities* rather than *property*.

They had also proposed something else. They had been moved by the children's little book on *Population and Futuring*. They saw the possibility of Lucian's doctoral dissertation project focusing on the empowerment of children to participate in the change of the world they were inheriting. The project would center around the learning experiences of working for viable means of education *for population management and earth resource allocation*, as related to Howard's proposed *population reduction and space exploration research center*.

The project would involve the development of a potential model that educational systems anywhere could make use of, to enable children, from their first educational experience on, to focus on the real issue of planetary survival and life quality, reproduction, and on space as a continuous frontier.

"Instead of *see Spot run*," Janice said, "it could *create a new planetary paradigm*."

"Your project," said Dr. Temetrias, the chair of the college of education, "will be for us a dynamic experiment of the *university without walls*, synthesizing our entire reservoir of educational principles, connected with Mr. Loggat's center as it expands.

Together you can begin to examine ways to use the world's resources to educate the world's population in a classroom that is the entire planet. Mr. Loggat has convinced me that either the generation of children you are working with, Lucian, will accomplish changes as dramatic as those he envisions, or there will be no future opportunity. We understand that more than forty species now become extinct every day. *Every day.* One every thirty-six minutes."

The chancellor of the university had sat there listening, without speaking until now. His falcon's eyes peered through round lenses. A shock of charcoal grey hair fell in abandon over his ears and forehead. "I have worked in university administration for some time now. When I took this appointment, I intended it to be my last. This institution is a blending of traditional and metropolitan education. After I did the housekeeping necessary to get my position in order, which I have now accomplished, I wanted to make this school a prototype of metropolitan institutions for the future."

He adjusted his spectacles and continued, "This project more than intrigues me. And I'm willing to put the available resources of the university behind it. The anonymous donor working through the charitable foundation that is funding Mr. Loggat's center obviously already has a passion and a commitment for something of excellence and significant potential magnitude to be accomplished.

"Lucian, although we have not had the opportunity to meet prior to this, I think even the word *extraordinary* underplays what I have learned from many of the people in this room about your resourcefulness and your inventiveness. Needless to say, thanks to the foundation's generosity, we will be in a position to offer you a full scholarship for your educational experiments with the children and full coverage of any costs for the children when they come here."

Melting. Lucian had not felt the melting away of everything beneath him for a period of time he could not rapidly reckon. Nor would he have thought of this now, had not the chair, the floor, the ground, the bedrock of the earth, all started to melt away and sink into the magma core.

Wax. It was all becoming wax beneath him, and he was slowly sinking into it.

His throat had not constricted like this for so long, he could not remember when the changes had come. By starting to sink into oblivion, he had the fleeting exhilaration of realizing that these things did not happen any more as they used to.

Until now. And he could not recall a time of specific change, only a change from when almost every moment the earth had felt like wax beneath his feet, and now, when it happened again. But in between something else had been occurring so gradually he had not realized it.

He found himself gripping, with clawed fingers, the chair arms, fearing they might pulverize in his grasp, yet even in the realization, he remained powerless to unbend his fingers. He sank further into a tomb of wax.

He wanted Longhorn here, Longhorn to buy the wax beneath his feet and trade it for hard earth.

He wanted Zoyan'qual to take him away on the back of Phantom.

He wanted to merge into an oblivion of fragrance of Beth's sandalwood and myrrh.

Previously Janice had spoken offhandedly of the *possibility* of a doctor's degree. Some of these professors had come to Worm Farm School and experimented with the *possibility* of offering courses non-traditionally. He had remotely considered these *possibilities*. But nothing had been definite. Nor urgent. Distant. Dream-like. For him, these had been merely glimmers. Hints. Possibilities. No urgency to decide. *Until now.*

Only Howard seemed to know that Lucian was decomposing. Howard stood, as if stretching, as if he had been sitting too long, and began to walk easily, by the backs of the chairs, strolling unobtrusively, appearing to concentrate on these plans that were mutating around the room.

Howard paused thoughtfully in that same full concentration, sat casually on the arm of Lucian's chair and, in a simple movement of affirmative camaraderie, rested his hand on Lucian's shoulder, which he could feel trembling beneath his touch. And Howard said to everyone else, as if Lucian were incidental, as if in response to an invitation to make home-made ice cream, "Yes, I think together we can work on this. I see us taking it a small step at a time."

Howard casually stood and moved on past the backs of the chairs around the room, where the gyrating thoughts continued. A heady hybrid of ideas begetting ideas.

Then, in an unexpected turn of mind, Lucian remembered himself dressed as Longhorn had once instructed, dark-spectacled, standing with his knees trembling before the turquoise dealers, too petrified to say anything, while the buyers took his silence for control and upped their offerings. Remembering this, Lucian almost laughed, and the process sent a little ripple of relaxation down his spine.

Again, here in this room, he sat too petrified to say anything, and the assemblage seemed to take it as deep insight and acquiescence with their plans for him.

He knew himself incapable of carrying out any of the projections circulating in this chamber. But the others seemed totally unaware of his incompetence. That he did not even know how to grow worms. That the creatures simply did it themselves.

Perhaps in his petrification, he had become a catalyst. Perhaps he had become necessary, somehow, to be dully sitting there, while they projected innovations that, because they believed in the possibilities, could have profound effects.

To his continued silence, they all responded with *don't reply now*, as if he could, *think about it*, and *we'll look forward to your response*.

Howard deflected their attention again with general statements, and the chancellor announced, "Mr. Loggat, you inspire me with your breadth of vision. We will gather an assemblage on campus next month to announce the inauguration of the center, and you can address them, and you can both be introduced."

Lucian felt the chair sinking ever more rapidly into the molten wax. It had engulfed his feet and had risen to his knees.

And then, one by one, the others all stood, as if clothed in some golden conspiratory colleagueship, and they came to shake his hand. Lucian did not stand. His legs, to the thighs, had been sucked into the wax. He did not speak. His vocal mechanism had disappeared. He had the dim awareness of nodding slightly to each.

Howard shook Lucian's hand, and in the process, grasped it firmly enough to pull him forward and upward, out of the chair, out of the wax, to a standing position.

"And I'll bet you want to get over to *that concert at the auditorium*," said Howard pointedly, though no concert had been mentioned, "and you'll just have time to drive over if you *leave right now*, without *another word*. We can all talk later." Lucian was not sure at the moment what an auditorium was or what *concert* meant, but he accepted Howard's blessedly offered window of opportunity to escape.

He felt an effusion of gratitude in some remote part of his interior for Howard's pushing him out of the room, out of the house, out of this place built on wax. Lucian did not want to stay and try to make words come out, even with Janice and Walter, who both still wore their almost visible golden aura of *possibilities*.

He wobbled on his own unfamiliar legs down the driveway.

69

Lucian felt like it took decades to negotiate with his lower limbs to the end of the Phedras' driveway, where he leaned on the car like a suspect about to be frisked by authorities, charged with impersonating a human being. As he got into the old car of Gitano's, he would have locked the doors, if they had locks, to somehow shut out the world. The dial of the radio had been turned to the university radio station and with the starting of the engine, the radio's sounds surrounded him. He headed through town, away from the Pandras, toward the road into the desert, toward the worm farm that seemed light years away.

The university radio station was broadcasting a live performance in progress from the auditorium, to which Howard must have referred. The orchestra from Louisiana had returned this year, performing again, as it had previously when he had taken the children.

They featured a cellist named Jarmon Trander. He was

introducing his own composition for cello and symphony, which, he was explaining, had been motivated by something he had read. A statement on folded pages he had found in a library book.

Lucian listened remotely, distantly, *as if through the wrong end of a telescope*, he thought, amused at the pitifulness of his impossible metaphor.

The material had so moved Jarmon Trander that he had translated his feelings and responses into music. "The idiom," he said, "of all art is a *language*. We constantly translate experiences, emotions, passions, insights, into the medium, the language, in which we personally speak. For me, music is the language. But the message came from that paper and from someone's depths."

He explained that he wanted to read excerpts from the writing he had found, so the audience could share the origin of what he had experienced and translated into music. He indicated that, as he read, selected instruments would be playing themes related to these elements of the material. And that when he finished, he would perform on the cello with the orchestra, giving full voice to the sentiments in the whole composition.

So he began reading, as the orchestra themes danced softly behind the words:

May you who read this, may you feel for a moment what I experience, if you resonate to this feeling, know that there is another who understands.

I feel at times as if I am alone on the earth, that no other human being has sentiments like mine, nor sees nor hears like I do.

I want such a simple thing. To listen and be listened to. Not judged. Not gaged as a commodity for other people's profits. Not viewed as a member of anything, or belonging to anyone or group. Just myself.

To be looked at with a real face, not a mugging mask aping sincerity and trust, but devoid of the meaning.

But sometimes I don't know what it really is I want, never having experienced it. I only imagine it. And I think I will go mad with the longing to experience what I have not. This is my last attempt to ask, is there one person who knows what I am trying to express?

I wonder at times if I am the last of some strange race or the first.

What if all the whales of the world, the leviathans that evolved to sing their songs in the world's vast oceans, melodies of communication, what if all the whales of the world but one had been pushed to extinction. And that one, not knowing of its own evolution, of a time when all whales sang, and in abundance, what if he still sang. But there existed no other whale to hear its voice, to respond. And he wandered the deeps singing, waiting, longing, and no voice ever returned the melody. The last of his race. Condemned to utter solitude, singing his ancient song, while surrounded by the noise and clutter of engines of ships, clogging the waters with their sputtering and pounding.

Am I the last of some kind of species that has lived before, and bleat my plaintive message, never to be answered in a world of tumultuous blather?

Or am I a mutant? The first of a kind, that does not yet, and may never, exist beyond me? Mysteriously split from normality by what? Spots on the sun, or the borealis? Am I one who speaks and thinks and acts unlike any other person?

And long after my departure, will whole groups of similar people evolve, but too late for me to converse with them?

Am I the first, a mutant, alone and not understood?

Or are there others, even one other, who knows what I mean, and wanders searching too. Could we find each other? That is all I am trying to do. To find another.

I write poetry. Perhaps you use other forms to communicate the feelings.

Here is one poem:

Butterfly in the City

butterfly
in the city
vainly fluttering
thrown through brick canyons
pelted with dirty wind
blown against concrete slabs
piled up and up into
the howling dusty wind
tossed by gust on gust
blowing along the gutter
with candy wrappers

298

Lucian in the car, now listened to the radio in a mesmerized state. Some non-conscious remote part of his brain guided the car out of town.

Out of town. The realization suddenly engaged his attention.

Lucian wheeled the vehicle around with screeching tires in the middle of the highway. He headed back into the city, toward the university.

Jarmon Trander's voice continued on the broadcast, reading.

I don't want to imitate whatever is the prevailing way of interacting around me. I am not a defective one of these, not something broken that needs to be fixed, to be like them.

I am not interested in medicating with prescriptions, or drugging my feelings, or forgetting with alcohol, or altering with nicotine. I want none of these things in my system. I want to find my way by who I am now. I do not want to change, but to discover.

I do not want to complain about the social system or blame ancestors. I do not want to convert anyone to a doctrine of some private version of truth. And I don't want anyone with their T-shirt slogans to try to tell me that I have been looking all my life for their exclusive movement, to follow their leader. They who bash their hierarchies against each other. Who consider victory to be converts and conquest and tribute pouring in to their administrators. Who try to franchise reality.

They have not changed anything with their imaginary triumphs, but only substituted one hierarchy for another.

And I stand back in the shadows, a non-person, a part of none of these. Alone, only seeing the results of their hierarchies, but unable to participate in them myself.

Unable to see degrees of melanin in the skin, or location of birth as having any bearing on inner individuality. I stand in the shadows, without ethnicity, raceless, ageless, genderless, casteless, wanting someone to see me, wanting to see someone like me.

I turn off the television programs with their rubber-faced announcers plying words, evangelists hawking their emotional depravity, so-called comedies of people insulting and trivializing each other. I turn off the selling of segments of grief and conflict on newscasts.

I do not belittle these. But they are other people's culture. I am simply not part of them. They are not my comedies, my news, my civilization. Who am I?

I am alone and watch the madness about me and wonder if I am not mad.

Is there not one other who will sit and talk of this aloneness, this madness, this journey, discovery, quest? One who will listen to my pathway among the stars as I will listen to theirs.

One who sat for years, that seemed like centuries, in the stifling madness of classroom-warehouses dying in boredom, wondering where life was? Classes meant for mental nourishment, where it was as if people talked about brain-food, but food never appeared, or if it did, was sneaked in by a few people who might be rebuked for it. Where life was talked about and measured with statistics and rinsed of all meaning and tested to extinction. But life was locked outside.

I cannot hire someone to listen to me. I cannot buy the time of someone who must practice professional distance. I cannot rent friends by the hour, who call themselves counselors, and who jot notations in record books and try to fix me as if I needed repair.

I want those who will listen because they want to hear, and with the hearing, be enriched. I want to do the same and listen to journeys parallel to my own.

I do not need a cult or sect, but individuals.

I want those who want to see me, who want me to see them.

I do not want to be anyone else. I do not want drugs to reduce stress.

I want to explore together. On different paths.

I sit in meetings and watch people engage in recreational argumentation as a way of life. Precluding their ever really communicating with anyone else, and who seem not to know nor care that they do this. Exchanging stories to put them on a higher rung of their imaginary ladders. While I am unable to even see such a ladder, except as a part of their mythology. I respect their right to see it. But it is not mine. I cannot climb their ladders.

I avoid using words like heart and love, because I hear the words used in sentimental manipulation by the same people who moments before were arguing recreationally. All part of the same ritual, a script written as a substitution for life.

I am alive. But I am alone. And do not know who I am. I want to see one other person who knows what this rambling message means.

When I was a child, I stood around in the sessions where people talked at each other, these adults around me and the children imitating these adults. I looked at the masks of their faces and felt they had hidden or died within, that I moved among zombies. No one seemed to see me. I would want to scream, I wasn't sure what, something like look, listen. And when no one seemed to see me, to hear me, to know I was there, I felt invisible. No one saw me. And I would quietly sneak off to the bedroom, to the full length mirror, and check to see if I was still there. If I was still visible. If I still existed. Then I would return to the gathering and wonder if the mirror was wrong.

Slowly it all turned inside. Everything raging within me. Not coming out, except in poems that no one else ever heard. In the deep nights, when I raged at the moon. All within. Contained.

I read of someone I respected once, where the biographer said that the subject could hardly have a biography written about him. Because nothing seemed to happen to him outwardly. It was all ideas, feelings, within.

I felt like that. A cacophony of symphony instruments warming up, but with no audience, no music, just noise and emotions wanting form, wanting to be heard, wanting to release themselves.

. . .

Lucian drove into the university parking lot adjacent to the auditorium, as the cellist said, "I read that message, of which I have shared with you a part, and I heard these sounds within me and have given them form. I only regret that the author of these words is unknown, for he would hear me crying out in this music what he cried out from within, through these words."

Lucian ran toward the auditorium door.

The cellist had not included the paragraph asking the reader for whom these words had resonance, to come to Buckingham Fountain on the Ides of July, holding a copy of the book in which the note was found.

Buckingham Fountain. The Ides of July. Holding the book. In the year of...

Only then, as he sprinted across the parking lot, *only then*, did it occur to Lucian that he had put no year on his message.

Lucian dashed into the lobby, flashed his last year's student card at the usher and entered the rear of the auditorium.

He stood in the back as the cellist drew moaning notes from

his instrument, and the orchestra seethed in a sound like fog over the moors with a full moon tantalizing something to be seen in the mists.

It was *inner* music, outwardly displayed. Inner feelings billowing out and made accessible. Lucian bathed in it, let it sweep over him in waves. He was permeated with it. Every cell of his body vibrated to it.

It was his melody, his song, his throbbing inner torments released in form and fullness.

The cello transmuted into an inner voice, calling in the mists, calling to others roaming in the mists, to others stumbling over the moors, grasping at shadows. Molding the noise inside the head into a song that called out for a hearer, that sent forth information into the unknown.

Lucian physically stood in the back of the auditorium while mentally wandering with the music in the fog-bound wilds.

The rear door of the auditorium opened and three figures entered, going to the edge of the last row and peering at the backs of the heads of the people in the lines of seats. Looking for someone.

Lucian, against the wall, stood behind them, and they had not seen him. When they looked around, one of them, it was Janice, suddenly focused on Lucian. She grabbed the arms of Walter and Howard, and they turned too.

Lucian saw the three vaguely familiar faces in the fog.

They surrounded him.

"Beth," whispered Janice, out of breath, "It's Beth. They just called. The baby is on its way. They need you now."

For one convulsive moment two impulses moved different sets of Lucian's muscles as half of him wanted to stay riveted there or run up on stage while the other half wanted to rush for the car.

Then he bolted out of the auditorium, past the usher and into the lobby. As he sprinted toward the door, he became aware of a movement parallel to his own, another person running toward the same entrance. He slowed so that they would not collide, and the other did the same. He glanced over but did not recognize the person who looked at him. He increased his pace and the stranger did the same. Then in vague recognition, he realized he viewed his own image in the mirrored wall.

He never had a sense of connection with the image he saw in mirrors, no feeling of reality about his outer appearance or age or background. His exterior remained a stranger, unfamiliar to the gaze of the core within. There had been occasions when he had been shown photos of a group, when he recognized all but one, and puzzled momentarily, only to realize it must be the outer image of how other people saw him, which bore no relation to himself.

He pressed his palms together toward the alien in the mirror, who did the same to him, and rushed on out the door.

· · ·

His tires screeched out of the parking lot.

The journey home included a car filled with the concert music continuing to pour out of the radio. It vibrated the car, spilling out the rhythms and harmonies into the desert.

When the symphony broadcast ended, the melodies continued sounding in Lucian's head. He could hear every note again of the piece that had embedded itself in his mind. That had always been in his mind. That had only now been released.

So dominant had been his concentration on this music, so rapid had been his sprint across the parking lot, so intense his driving alone toward the worm farm, that only in the last moments of the journey did he look in the rearview mirror and become aware of the car following him.

Janice, Walter, and Howard drove in Lucian's wake toward the birthing.

70

Calmness. Tranquillity. A fading sun on the horizon. A breeze of desert fragrance.

In unhurried elegance, Beth, herself, readied to spread the blanket, the weaving of which she had supervised for the occasion of the birthing. With Grandmother's help in design and with Longhorn's construction skills, they had made a loom. During the previous months, they, the children, everyone concerned with the coming of the child, had taken turns at the loom.

They had prepared it as a ceremonial weaving. "When the occasion is past," Beth had told them, "then it will be the child who is important. The blanket on which I will lie at that time will, the next day, be ceremoniously burned, its ashes spread, its smoke curling toward the sky. It will be a symbol to us all not to become attached in a melancholy way to peripheral things, but only to the object of our goal. It will be like a *kachina* blanket. As a kachina is burned after its lessons are learned, so will this be. When its use is finished, it will return to the elements. It will not remain as a later reminder to the child of that event. The child's life will be its own focus."

So it came to pass that with the setting sun, she spread the blanket.

Lucian had just arrived from his drive back from the city. The dust cloud of his old car had blown over the house as he leaped out and ran through the rooms and toward the back. He skidded on his heels to a stop as he leaped through the back door, remembering again that Janice, Howard, and Walter had been speeding in their car behind him.

He retraced his run through the house, met them hurrying toward the front door, the dust cloud from their car spreading over them.

Lucian started to say something in the nature of an apology about not realizing they were behind him, but Janice put her hand on his arm and motioned him to lead them on through the house.

They rapidly exited the back door. All four ran on out past the worm canisters to the cottonwoods. There, beneath the rustling leaves, the children had assembled. Beth was in the act of spreading out the blanket. Longhorn played softly an instrument of his own invention that had, as Dolphus already noted, "a sound like the wind blowing through the trees."

Grandmother helped to smooth down the blanket on the ground and then sat on its edge.

The four new arrivals felt momentarily like intrusive engines of energy bursting in from the outside world. Those sitting and standing around and arranging the blanket looked up and smiled as if they were already drugged on the desert fragrance and needed not even words of greeting. Longhorn's wafting melody had bound the mood of them all together and now gathered the four arrivals into its embrace.

"Tranquility," Beth had repeated so many times. "The world must breathe tranquilly during the transition from the womb to the wider world for this child. There will be no rushing, no hurrying, no sense of urgent orders. We will be calmly together, partaking in an age-old moment of birthing, for which the body has been developed through the ages of evolution. It will be as natural as the sunrise."

When anybody spoke, long pauses spread between one comment and the next. Dolphus said, "We know it so well, this child. We have followed its development almost every day of its life. I hope it is as ready as we are."

Grandmother rose from time to time, with herbal preparations in one hand. With the other, she rubbed small amounts on the foreheads and cheeks of everyone. "Just as there is olfactory healing," she said, "so there is mood-making that comes from the inhalation of certain potions."

Janice, now seated in the circle, breathed deeply the fragrances, inhaling the beauty of the scents.

"All we need," said Beth with a momentary expression of regret, "is for Zoyan'qual to join us. But..." Her voice trailed off as she looked out into the spacious dusk.

"Not to worry," said Dolphus.

"No," added Reendo. "We dispatched a homing pigeon with the message."

Longhorn's melody became one known to them all, and they began to sing softly together:

Hope dwells
Hope dwells
Hope dwells within us all
At one with earth
At one with sky
At one among us all.
As comes the spring
As come the rains,
As comes the newborn child

Into the circle of beauty.
Every birth
Reflects our own
Resonates with life
The cosmic life.
Hope dwells
Hope dwells
Hope dwells within us all.

As the sounds of the instrument and voices blended their last note with the air moving through the trees, they heard the thundering hooves.

He knew how they loved that coming of the galloping buffalo across the desert. So when he could first see the light of their campfire, when he could see the cottonwoods, Zoyan'qual spoke into the ear of Phantom and said, *"Thunder across the plains."*

Phantom exhilarated in running. The great muscles stretched and moved. Buffalo and rider came out of the last rim of crimson on the horizon, like a spirit visitation from the sun deity personified.

They came to the fire and halted. All in the circle rose, almost as dancers, and stood around Phantom, stroking its rough mane and grasping the hands of Zoyan'qual.

He dismounted and joined them. The buffalo seemed to merge with the coming darkness beyond the fire.

Beth embraced Zoyan'qual and said, "Peace."

He, too, had brought preparations. He opened small containers of fragrances and let her inhale the scent of each.

"Which?" he asked.

She touched the one that smelled of the lotus fragrance. Zoyan'qual stroked her hair and neck with it.

She, in turn, took it, and did the same to Lucian. Each, in turn, to another.

"Time does not measure tonight," Beth told them. She sat on the blanket. All of them were outlined in the light from the fire. "There is only tonight, but without time. Humans measure time for their events. But tonight, there is only the moon, the passing of the stars in their places, the cosmos. Birthing is not done by watches and clocks. It is done by the primal rhythms in the core of us all.

"We will all be here for the moment of birth. We will all participate in the arrival." With a voice, ever so slightly harkening back to *the instructor in child development*, she explained in a kind of *grand finale* lesson, the process of what went on at that moment within her and the preparation of the child's emergence.

71

The contractions, in the middle of the night, became more frequent.

She wanted the hands of the children on her mid-section so they would know kinesthetically the feeling of the birthing pulses.

She hummed as the baby emerged, an echo of the song *Hope dwells, hope dwells...*

She hummed as the child's head emerged. Grandmother knelt to receive the baby. Slowly it moved into view. The creature that had begun with two cells uniting, that had passed through the phases of having gills and tail and fur, that had looked like fish, reptile, amphibian, mammal, now emerged as a human child.

Grandmother cradled the child in her hands, moving it in a small circle close to all of those around.

Beth unbuttoned her garment. Grandmother laid the child on her. Beth cradled it to her breast. She continued to hum softly. Everyone joined in with her. The wind accompanied them as it rustled the leaves.

The night continued timelessly.

Beth lifted the baby and held it toward Lucian, saying, "A human is born who is a girl child. May she grow and develop as a human, not as a gender." Lucian took the baby and regarded her lying in his hands.

"She knows our voices," said Grandmother. "She knows all of us by our voices, for she has heard them every day. Our voices are recorded in the very nature of her pre-natal mind. We are already part of her in many ways."

The flames of the fire flickered in the night. Occasionally burning wood crackled. Everyone centered their gaze on the baby.

They sat as in a dream, with a baby born in the dream, beneath the arch of the milky way. Eriot gazed up at it intently. He pointed toward the galactic center and said, "That light has been traveling for thirty thousand years to arrive here tonight. The light that leaves there as our baby is born will arrive here…" His voice trailed off in contemplation.

It was Kayla who first noticed. First noticed Beth. First noticed that all was not well. Attention had been focused on the child. Now Kayla said, "Beth, *what's wrong?* Something is wrong with Beth."

They all looked and saw what Kayla saw. Beth, who had orchestrated everything about the birth, whose calmness and confidence defined the event, now lay visibly panicked. Pallid face. Hands on the verge of trembling. An expression of livid fear.

Grandmother, the midwife, took her hand, asking wordlessly, with the gesture, what was wrong.

"It should be over," said Beth. "The birth is over. All should be well." She choked back a sob. "But…but…it's like nothing has happened. The feeling is like nothing has happened. Before the birth, I understood the feeling would come. But the feeling has not gone away." She gulped several gasping sobs, at something gone wrong. "I'm coming apart."

Grandmother could be intense and tranquil simultaneously. Her hands, like sensors, moved smoothly across Beth's upper and lower body. She felt the forehead, the neck. Aware of temperature, moisture, muscle tone.

Then Grandmother, already on her knees, doubled forward, her head resting on Beth's stomach, her hands ranging in circular motions over the skin.

Beth's few choking sobs had ended. No one else had spoken. Only the wind and fire made soft sounds. Everyone's attention had joined Grandmother's unswerving focus. They waited.

When at last Grandmother straightened up, still kneeling on the ground, she held each of Beth's hands in her own. Her expression remained intense, the brow furrowed, the eyes fiercely attentive. Her gaze went from Beth to each of the others.

And then Grandmother's lips opened to speak but instead, laughed, a great rollicking laugh that echoed in the night air, humor she shared with the heavens, rocking back and forth on her knees.

Everyone leaned forward, shocked at her behavior, waiting to act out emergency directions, thinking she was, herself, becoming hysterical. The looks on their faces made her laugh all the more, until what she was attempting to say would not emerge, except in resounding laugher.

Her eyes teared now in her attempts to speak and in her reactions to the increasing panicked looks on the faces of her hearers. She put one hand to her own throat and chest as if to calm herself, while with the other, she still touched Beth.

In the midst of this display, Beth, still feeling herself *coming apart*, wondered dimly if she was hallucinating.

At last, Grandmother uttered the first word, but as she looked in their faces again, she reverted to more bouts of laughter. This time, when she could again speak, she focused on Beth.

"Our Beth of the sun-bronze hair, of course you feel like nothing has happened. Of course you feel as if the birth has not even taken place, although we hold here the evidence of that birth. For you who have never visited a doctor, who have avoided any of the machines, you have let your birthing be an event that unfolded as it would." She paused.

"Well, Beth, our daughter of the earth, that event is continuing to unfold, and is not finished yet. There is another child in there. And wanting to come out and join its sister."

With this revelation, Beth and all the others started to laugh, laughing as Grandmother had laughed, laughing at their own tension and releasing it into the wind.

And with the laughing, the birthing continued. Beth, now understanding, became calm again, though still smiling over her own panic and the explanation she had never expected.

The head of the next child came to view. Slowly it eased out of the birth passage into the starry night. Slowly it came out where the light from the center of the milky way galaxy that had left thirty thousand years ago spattered its dim vibrations upon the child.

Grandmother held the baby in her hands and placed it on Beth, saying, "May I present a boy child."

Beth held it for a time. Then she cradled it in her hands and held it toward Lucian, who received it.

Beth said, "Another human being has been born. A boy child. May he be raised as a human being also, and not as a gender."

The soft winds blew the leaves of the cottonwood. More specks of light spattered on them from the milky way galaxy.

Zoyan'qual played a quiet haunting melody on the flute and Lucian joined on another flute in harmony. The others hummed softly to the wordless song.

72

The babies had just finished feeding, as Beth carried on the next part of the *biological continuum* project. They had left the Womb Room now. "Symbolic," Beth said, "of the newborns transition to the world outside."

Everyone had moved into a newly constructed chamber of adobe built especially for the continuation of *life study*. Beth would take no time off. "Life does not stop with birth, but continues. You'll see these babies grow almost before your eyes. And we'll chronicle every step." For nothing, not even the birthings themselves, would she break stride with her sessions.

Already her diligent efforts had filled the walls of the new room with growth charts and tables of *development periods*. Prior to the births, they had researched the ways babies were treated and transported in cultures around the world. They had prepared, with Longhorn's direction, the various means of carrying children used by these cultures. Leather holders with the child in front. Board carriers with the child in back. Linen wrappings to support the child. Body holders that let the legs and arms move freely.

Some cultures isolated the child with the immediate family. Others passed it around the extended family. Some used almost exclusive maternal contact. Others shared maternal and paternal and sibling contact. "These children must have contact with all of us," said Beth. "They must see what we do, go where we go, enjoy diversity, visual and auditory stimulation, interaction, know they are a part of us. Learning by observing."

She took one child that had finished feeding and handed it to Grandmother. The other child continued to receive nourishment.

Beth took a deep breath, realizing her own tiredness but unwilling to leave what she felt needed to be done. In her symbiotic relationship with Lucian, she had but to look at him and say, "Imprinting," and Lucian began to explain from his reservoir of information.

"At this stage," he said, "the child absorbs whole and complete the experiences of the environment. The process is sometimes called *imprinting.*" He pointed to a picture on the wall of a man being followed by a trail of ducklings. "This experimental biologist hatched the duck eggs. When these hatchlings emerged, he was the first thing they saw. They *imprinted* his image, and he became like their parent. They will follow him, stay near him, later they will fly after him if he cycles off across his acreage."

"So," Lee said, "imprinting is a different kind of learning than what people usually call studying? It's like a whole and complete transfer?" He pointed at an adjoining picture that showed a dog curled up with a cat and rat, with a bird perched on its head. " What about that one?"

"I'll bet," said Pica, "that they had a similar imprinting. When they were young, did their family become whoever was there right after they were born?"

"The first four weeks are crucial," said Lucian. "These creatures were born at nearly the same time and put with each other. You're right. They are forever imprinted as *family.*"

"So," said Reendo, "as part of the family of animal life, humans have imprinting that goes on too? Like, who we're around when we're young sets up who we consider a natural part of our surroundings?"

"Exactly. We don't see group categories until we're taught them later. If we have people of diversity around us, we imprint them as family."

"*Sensitive periods*," said Jhenaw, in a moment of cross-referencing insight. "We talked about how there are time-clocks in our heads, and when they go off, we are sensitive to particular things in our environment, and imprint them. And when the time is up, the imprinting is lessened or stops."

"That means," said Normita, who now held the other child, "that these babies are imprinting all of us. Our voices in the womb, and now our shapes and sizes and colors and everything."

"Even touching them is important," said Orgol. "We read those studies about how babies that weren't touched can die."

Eriot leaped to his feet in a moment of recognition. "This chart," he patted a long paper pinned to the wall, with weeks, months and years marked on it, "shows the sensitive periods we know about for humans. Look at this one. The language sensitive period. Anything can be absorbed at first, gradually the process diminishes."

"And they can learn all the languages in the environment," said Kayla. "They just have to hear them. Just like we can speak some from several languages so far, but we've never really *studied* them."

"Just like you did for us, Lucian!" Normita leaped to her feet and pointed toward the outside. "When you put all those signs up. We never learned to read and write. We *absorbed* it. It was there and we..." she made a slurping sound. "...we *sucked* it in."

"So right now," said Fenori, "these babies are sucking in bunches of things. The kind of environment we prepare determines a lot about the *structure* they will see in the environment."

"*Order*," said Shem, peering at the long chart. "Here is a sensitive period for *order*. The way rooms and things are organized around the child at this age has an impact on the way it continues to organize from then on."

Normita stood beside Orgol now, searching the chart. "There's math sensitive periods, social sensitive periods, introspective sensitive periods—look at all of these."

"Ohhh," exclaimed Dolphus standing up with his hands over his head as if to grasp a very big thought, "then if you *go with the flow* like in the story of the Indian youth who learned to dip water *with* the current instead of *against* it—if we prepare the environment for the things relevant to the sensitive periods, we're going *with* the current, and learning is absorbed without effort."

"The whole educational process can be organized around that," said Kayla, joining in the discovery. "We've learned how to run a business, fill out tax forms, run problem-solving formats, all these things, because they're here when we're ready for them."

"Oh!" said Shem. "Then *enjoyment* happens when you're working *with* the natural biological human system as it develops. It's only when you work *against* it that becomes tedious and exhausting."

"And that can be the hope of the future," Lee said, going over to Howard, "about making the world a classroom to teach everyone about *population and birth management*, and the need for *frontiers to cross*, and all the things your center will be working on. The world already is a classroom, but what's being imprinted are behaviors that make for conflict and greed. One generation of planetary education could save the place. Really big changes can happen when you're not fighting a whole bunch of *counter-productive imprinting*."

Reendo grinned, reached up and patted Howard's head, and said, "The endorphins are flowing." Then he patted his own and added, "I think mine are too. I like the way they feel."

In a different tone of voice from those relating the series of discoveries, Longhorn said quietly, "Beth sleeps." During the discussion, she had gone from a standing position to a kneeling one, to sitting on the floor, to reclining on the floor.

Lucian stood up, walked over to Beth, lifted her up in his arms, and carried her from the room.

They all followed in procession as he took her to her circular chamber and laid her on her bed. The others stood around it. Longhorn held one sleeping baby. Zoyan'qual held the other. Beth roused enough to look at them all fuzzily for a moment and then slipped into deep sleep.

73

Every day the morning sessions continued. The *sensitive periods* wall drawings found their way into the new composite time line, within the chain of Quonset huts.

Also as part of this Super Time Line, as they had christened it, population figures appeared. They were answering the questions about how many people were on earth at any given time. How fast did they multiply? How did their expansion compare with the numbers in other species?

At a point in the time line for ten thousand years ago, they placed the sign: *eight million human population.* By 1750, more than seventy million. By 1900, more than twice that number. By 1970, more than three and a half billion, or as Kayla put it, "three thousand million." Only ten years later, more than four billion. Then in less than a decade, more than five billion. They continued placing higher and higher numbers, watching the acceleration of the doubling of the population numbers.

. . .

The day arrived for the formal announcement ceremony at the university concerning the Population Center that Howard would direct.

The chancellor had invited his list of *key people* for the public announcement. Howard had furnished him with an additional list of names of those already working regionally with facets of study about uncontrolled population impact.

The audience began assembling. The chancellor moved ceaselessly among the new arrivals. He had made his way around to Lucian, when over Lucian's shoulder, he saw a figure that captured his attention, standing alone by a wall.

The chancellor said, "That…could that be…"

Lucian turned and followed his gaze to Camel-rider.

"…that reclusive, eccentric…no one has seen or photographed him in years…but it looks something like his younger pictures…sort of…maybe…"

Then a quick thought in the chancellor's mind. "But I saw you speak to him. Isn't he…"

"That's...ah...Mr. *Camelrider*," said Lucian. "Mr. *John* Camelrider. One of the potential board members that Mr. Loggat suggested for the Center."

"Oh," said the chancellor, in a descending voice. As he watched the lone figure, a last sparkle of hope still in his glance, he saw a child approach and hug the man and move on. As Reendo moved away, the Chancellor shook Lucian's hand hastily and moved toward the child.

"Well, young man," the chancellor said, extending his hand to Reendo, "who's your friend over there?"

"My name is Reendo," he said, filling in the omission of a greeting to him. "And that's Camel-rider. He knows Cactus Max."

"Oh," said the chancellor, the flame going out of his eyes. He moved on to the next arrivals. After that, passing close to the lone man, the chancellor said jocularly, "Ah, Mr. Camelrider. *John*, it's good to have you aboard as part of the team. A friend of a Mr. *Kaktusmacks*, I understand." And he hastened on to another group.

The lone man, bemused, sauntered toward Lucian. "Hi," he said, shaking Lucian's hand, "My name's *John*. And you're Lucian *WormFarmer*?" He chuckled, leaned forward, and whispered, "Thanks."

. . .

The concert hall used for the assembly filled by the appointed hour. The chancellor described the context of the Center to the audience. Howard had asked that the Center's advisory board have seats on the stage. But not all of them stayed in their chairs. Dolphus and Normita recorded the event with video cameras. Pica took still pictures.

Beth had come, but would not sit on stage. The babies did, however. The boy baby rested in the arms of Grandmother, and Lucian held the girl baby. Longhorn stood with Beth in the shadows just off stage where they could watch the proceedings in profile. Camel-rider sat in the first row of the otherwise empty small balcony.

The chancellor introduced the *distinguished* Mr. *Loggat*. Recipient of a major grant. For a center. To deal with population management and related matters. To be housed here at the university. To place this university at the cutting edge of what a metropolitan university like this one was all about. A model for others.

Before saying anything, Howard nodded to Lee, who placed a large photograph of Abraham Lincoln in front of the podium. Howard, without mentioning the photo, began to speak.

"A few score million years ago, our biological ancestors brought forth upon this planet a new species, who conceived mightily without developing any population limitations.

"Now we are engaged in a great war with the planetary home rather than being one with it, because of unchecked population expansion, testing whether that species or any species, so conceived and still conceiving, can much longer endure. The earth has become a battlefield of that war, strewn with the pollution, conflict, overcrowding, and the annihilation of fellow species each day.

"It is fitting and proper that we should meet on this battlefield to dedicate ourselves to a resolution of this war and to honor those around the world who valiantly are trying to end this attack and to help unite in this effort.

"But in a larger sense, we cannot dedicate, hallow, or consecrate this ground, this earth upon which we walk, and which makes up our own bodies. We can only discover and acknowledge that it has always *been* hallowed, and then dedicate and consecrate ourselves to act in a befitting way as part of the system and not as a superior conqueror separate from it.

"Although people may little note nor long remember what we say here, they can never forget what people working for population reduction and management will do for all humanity, now and in the future. For currently, every month, the addition to the human population in the world equals the entire population of New York City. We must picture such an accumulation of people coming into being every thirty days, twelve cities a year, one hundred and twenty in a decade, and know it cannot continue.

"If passengers on a wooden ship found some among them chopping with axes at the bottom of the hull, perhaps with good intention to secure firewood or to find water, their action would ultimately sink the ship and all aboard could perish. It would be the common need to educate them on the larger impact of their behavior.

"It is for us, the living, to be here dedicated to the great task remaining before us. That we shall strive, through this Center, however modest its beginning, to try to make this topic the foremost of discussion for every earthly citizen by placing it first on the agenda of every school and university class, of every religious organization, of every social group, of every agency of every government, of every family, of some part of every television program, of every medical staff, of every business organization. We must continue until every citizen contributes every day to discussing and implementing what must be done; until the earth's population is reduced to and stabilized at a realistic number of individuals, until a large percentage of the land mass, of every type of terrain, is returned to its natural state, populated by our remaining fellow species.

"No longer can the past indicators of what has been termed *progress* be used, not housing starts, nor expanding sales, nor enlarged markets. The frontiers related to earthly exploration, competition for resources, and financial competition can no longer be the challenges that stimulate human beings.

"With these planetary frontiers altered, we must continue simultaneously to recognize the need for human curiosity to be satisfied on a daily basis with the exploration of space. The frontiers must be ever-present for every individual in every generation, to construct space stations, encamp on the moon, journey to the planets, with advancing means of propulsion to move beyond the solar system to the nearest stars and their planets, to the local groupings of stars, across the milky way, to the local cluster of galaxies, to galaxies beyond, across light-years of space, exploring the universe.

"We here highly resolve that those who strive for planetary population management and expansion of the multiple frontiers of space exploration shall not have exerted their efforts in vain, that this planet, as part of the universe, shall have a new concept of human freedom, and that a planet of, by, and for the people, and all other species, shall not perish from the cosmos."

Then Howard added that Lucian would explain the logo of the new Center. Lucian had not expected to do anything except to be there with the children. He rose and moved to the podium, still holding the baby.

"In the lifetime of this child…," he began, but did not finish the sentence. "Symbolically joining the ancient with the present, the logo of the new center is the Viking Rune of *Dagaz*. It looks like two triangles joined at their apex, lying on their sides, or a schema of an hourglass positioned horizontally. It is the last Rune of the Cycle of Initiation. It represents a momentous alteration in attitude. Following it, life cannot continue in the same way as before. It represents the moment which, if acknowledged and responded to, forever transforms the life course."

He added, speaking in the Norse language, "*May we make it so.*"

74

The brain. "If our brain model had a plumbing system," said Dolphus, what would the bottommost fixture be?"

Normita giggled and said, in unison with Dolphus, "A *brain drain.*"

They stood with Dr. Sydney Brummett and his graduate students, and *brain-construction supervisor* Longhorn, and the others who had come, for the moment of completion of the huge, walk-through, model of the human brain.

There it was, mighty and accessible. From the brain stem to the wrinkled surface of the cortex. A work of art and science.

Sydney pointed to parts while the children responded with various functions of those parts.

"Moves the right hand."

"Wernicke's area."

"Spatial relationships."

"A primary visual center."

The reticular formation," said Jhenaw. "The part that never sleeps and signals change in the environment."

"The one," added Lee, "that triggers the fight or flight response."

"And stage fright," included Orgol.

Sydney, the *snowman kachina* model, had been true to his word and had come back frequently with his graduate class in *Brain Development and Education*, to help build this giant representation. Two stories tall. With passages inside. And a *Brain Room*.

"First a *Womb Room*," said Kayla, "and now a *Brain Room*. We're moving up in the world."

Sydney looked at Dolphus, harkening back to his remark about the *brain drain*, and said in kind, "And what if we had three brain models and the other two were only *one* story tall—then what would we call this one?" His bushy white eyebrows arched up into his forehead as he posited the question.

Dolphus and Normita laughed in unison and said, "The *main* brain!"

"And one with an injured leg?" asked a graduate student, in the spirit of the interchange.

"A lame brain!" the children responded.

"And one from Denmark?" said Pica.

"A Dane Brain!" everyone shouted, including Sydney and the graduate students.

"And one with a stereo system?" asked Reendo.

There was silence.

"A sound mind!" exclaimed Reendo.

"One that speaks Spanish that crashed primarily in a meadow?" said Alfred, the graduate student.

Longhorn said, "The brain in Spain falls mainly on the plain!"

"Several brains traveling together on a track?" Beth joined the act.

"A brain train!" Grandmother shouted.

"Superbrain's smart girl friend?"

"Lois Brain!"

"The hair on a brain shaped like a horse?" said another graduate student, leaping up as she spoke.

They all leaped up in response, shouting, "A brain mane!"

Sydney, moving his hands like a choir director, said "Synthesis! The hair on the largest of three Spanish-speaking

Danish brains shaped like a horse on a track?"

"The Dane brain train's main brain mane falling mainly on the plain!" they all exclaimed in clamor of variations, with hands raised like gospel singers.

. . .

"They're coming," Lucian told the children out under the cottonwoods, as he read the letter by the firelight. "My parents are coming."

"When?" asked Kayla, digging a corn-husk wrapped baked potato from the soil underneath the fire over which they had cooked squash and corn bread.

"I don't know for sure," said Lucian, putting the letter away, and scooping up another potato. "They never do anything with a definite schedule."

"Just to see us?" asked Dolphus, who was spreading his corn bread with honey they had collected that day from the bee hives they had built out on the periphery of their garden.

"No, they wouldn't do that either. They have *causes* they espouse—actually political candidates who support my parents' causes. They go out and join rallies. They look so *American Gothic* that they often work their way onto platforms, are just invited there, for their *grass-roots appearance.*"

"They do this often?" asked Pica, testing the okra to see if it was done.

"They have a whole wall full, really a whole room full, actually a whole apartment full of photos of themselves with candidates. Usually inscribed with something like *to my faithful supporters.* At rallies, they're always trying to whisk candidates away for some photo opportunities with charity directors and celebrities, so they can get in the pictures too. The candidates assume the couple knows the celebrities, and the celebrities assume they are with the candidate. They collect their photos, and they always have them published back in the local papers and the newsletters of their various organizations. Then they send copies of the papers and photos to the various people in them. And carry around an album of photos, which impress the new candidates and their entourages that they're people who are supposed to be included. They've come to be known for *being known.*"

Longhorn came carrying some more vegetables for the stew pot that hung above the fire.

"Who is the candidate this time that they're supporting when they may come here?" asked Beth.

"Not a candidate anymore, though he has held different political offices. He's out doing a kind of generic goodwill ambassador groundwork for his son's probable run for some office. Visiting old cronies, calling in favors for his son, as if he's trying to start a kind of political dynasty. At this point, it sounds like he'll go just about anywhere and talk to anyone to work up any kind of backing and publicity he can for the next generation of his family."

When Lucian named the politician out doing the groundwork for the son's advancement, because everyone was looking at Lucian, no one noticed that Longhorn, at the fire, dropped the vegetables into the flames from hands that suddenly went limp at the mention of the name.

Lucian continued explaining, "My parents make up these excursions as they go along. And at some point, if or when, they will probably arrive at some airport near here, rent a car, and then they'll suddenly appear. A cloud of dust, and they'll just appear. No notice. Day or night."

Lucian smiled and ladled out more carrots onto his plate, adding, "And they're likely to have that former politician in tow when they come, enticing him off to what he thinks is some series of unexpected publicity opportunities. They have a way of doing that."

They did not notice that Longhorn was no longer with them.

75

When Sydney conducted his graduate classes at Worm Farm School, at first, during rest breaks, the graduate students just lounged doing small talk. At the same time, instead of lounging, the children turned to other projects tugging at their attention. Increasingly, the graduate students and Sydney circled about to see what the others were so engaged in.

Sydney stood with hands folded behind his back, peering over the shoulder of Pica, who in turn peered through a microscope in the science building. Pica wore a carrier on her back holding the boy baby.

"And," said Sydney, "what do you see."

"Sierozem," said Pica matter-of-factly.

After a thoughtful pause, Sydney asked, "And what is *sierozem?*"

Pica glanced up at him. "We gathered soil samples on our arroyo trip. This is one of a group usually found in arid regions." She held up the round container with the sample. "It's sort of brownish-grey at the surface but has a lighter layer beneath."

She moved aside to let Sydney take a look through the eyepiece, as she added, "It's based in a carbonate or hardpan layer."

Dolphus ran in and said, "Pica, we need the shape-shifter."

Pica went out with Sydney following. Dolphus was writing an alphabet book and was illustrating it with photos of Pica *being the letters*. It would be called the *Shape-Shifters Guide to the Alphabets of the World*. After he had started with the Roman A,B,Cs, he figured he would go ahead and include the letters of other alphabets as well.

Pica detached the baby carrier and handed it to Parvo, one of the graduate students.

The camera was positioned. "Sigmoid!" directed Dolphus.

"*Sigmoid?*" said Alfred, the lanky blond graduate student, trying to imitate Pica's stance.

"S-shaped," said Dolphus. And then he asked Alfred if he would like to be in the picture too. Alfred ambled into position behind Pica and tried to imitate her stance.

"Good," said Dolphus, "capital S and lower case."

Reendo had gone high into the climbing-bars configuration and sat there playing an instrument. Sylvia, a graduate student with three children of her own at home, hoisted herself bar by bar upward, until she sat beside him.

"Beautiful," she said, responding to his melody. "An instrument you made?"

"A *shakuhachi*," said, Reendo, "A Japanese bamboo flute."

Jhenaw arrived up in the heights to join them, with another

instrument. She held it out to Sylvia. "Like to try it?"

"Sure," Sylvia said, bleating a few notes into the air. "That should bring the goats from miles around." She handed it back to Jhenaw, who produced an exquisite minor-key melody.

"I've never seen anything like it," said Sylvia.

"It's a *shawn*," explained Jhenaw. "It has a particularly penetrating tone, basically a medieval double reed wind instrument."

"Medieval," said Sylvia, "that's a long time ago."

"Are you interested in time?" asked Jhenaw. "Would you like to see the *sidereal clock* we're building?"

The three swung down the layers of bars and proceeded to the Time Building. Inside on one wall hung calendars from twenty-seven different systems of measuring the year. On the tables stood assorted candle clocks, water clocks, hour-glasses, and a variety of other devices patterned after time-pieces from many places.

Jhenaw pointed to a work in progress spread out on a table top. "You know that we usually measure *solar days* with our clocks. But you can also measure the day by identifying star positions. We're using the first point of Aires. And that day is four minutes shorter than the solar day."

Bernard, a stocky graduate student, wandered in, trying with each break to look into another of the buildings. He was carefully carrying the girl-baby. "This is like an extensive attic, with *things*, just *things*, everywhere. What's this?" he asked the trio at the table.

Jhenaw explained again, and then pointed to a wall where the creation of a calendar hung partly completed. "See there, we're trying to coordinate the clock with a *sidereal calendar*. It works by the apparent diurnal motion of the stars. Because of precession, the sidereal year is longer than the solar year."

Bernard had gone over to look at the calendar in detail. "How much longer?" he asked.

"Twenty minutes and twenty-three seconds," said Jhenaw and Dolphus in unison.

Sylvia said to Bernard, "By the way, you were wondering aloud yesterday whose room was patterned after the lighthouse? It's Jhenaw's."

"Could I see the inside?" asked Bernard.

As they walked toward the lighthouse-room, Bernard shook his head and said, "Twenty minutes and twenty-three seconds."

Meanwhile, two adobe buildings farther, Herman Rank and Gloria Winker, two other graduate students, found themselves taking notes on their observations. They had followed Normita to the building, where she wanted to work a few minutes on her *sheelanagig*.

She put on her goggles and apron, got out her hammer and chisel, and chipped away at a block of stone. Already emerging from the rock appeared a figure of a woman. "I'm releasing her," smiled Normita.

"A shella-*what* you called her?" asked Gloria, sketching the figure on her note pad.

"A sheelanagig," said Normita. "It's a very formalized medieval carved stone female figure." She showed them photographs she was using as her guide.

"That's from a long time ago," said Gloria.

"Not as far back as Kayla's working on. "Have you seen her plans for the new year celebration?"

Gloria's *no*, brought Normita to her feet. She removed her goggles, laid down the equipment, and led them to another building. Kayla sat at a table with star maps laid out.

"Happy new year," Normita said as she entered. She and Kayla both laughed.

Kayla showed them a particular sky map where she had circled a particular star just appearing over the horizon. "That's Sirius also known as....? She looked at Gloria, who shrugged. "...as the Dog Star," continued Kayla. "When it rose in ancient Egypt, the festivals began for their new year, about our July twenty-third. I'm researching as much as I can find so we can celebrate, too, when that comes around. Hope you can come."

"Wouldn't miss it," said Gloria. "What about these?" She pointed to stacks of other materials on other tables.

"Each of those are studies for other new years of other tribes and cultures. We want to find out why each group of people chose the time of year they did to start their annual calendar, how it fitted into their worldview. Then we want to celebrate them all, doing some of the same things they did."

"Sirius," said Gloria, going back to the circled spot on the star map.

Kayla said, "Its rise signals the start of the *dog days*, when the dog star rises and sets with the sun."

"Al Pacino," added Normita.

"*Al Pacino?*" questioned Gloria, missing any connection.

"*Dog Days Afternoon*. A movie he made."

Gloria looked at her. "You've just connected Al Pacino with the ancient Egyptian new year?"

During another break, when storm clouds rumbled on the horizon, Orgol casually commented, "*Shango* is angry again." And Eriot had agreed.

"Who?" asked Sydney, squinting at the distant purple cloud mass punctuated by lightning.

"Ah!" said Steepen, the Nigerian graduate student who had heard the word and came jogging up behind them. "Yes! My friend *Shango!* He's the god of thunder and lightning in our Yorubas region of western Nigeria."

"You want to see his *relatives?*" laughed Eriot.

He led them to his room, patterned after a sod house. One wall held a world map with names pinned all over it. Beside it were Eriot's fantasy drawings of mythical beings, all sharing the common elements of clouds and lightning bolts.

"Thunder and lightning really intrigue me," Eriot said. "I study everything I can about how people depict them." His hand swept around the room. "These are the lightning and thunder deities of the world. And there..." he pointed at a drawing.

"...is Shango!" Steepen finished Eriot's sentence. "I would recognize him anywhere. He is beautiful." He swept Eriot up in his arms and gave him sort of a *rocking-back-and-forth* hug. "Oh, how I miss my children while I'm in this country as a student. Eriot, be my son while I'm here," he laughed, "and I'll take you back with me for a few weeks when I return home." He looked past Eriot's head at Orgol watching them, and shifting Eriot to one arm, picked up Orgol with the other. "You too," he said. He set them down. Then he saw Lee and said, "And you too."

"A letter," Steepen continued. "I will give you the names of my children, and you can write them a letter and I'll send it with mine. I want them to get to know you. Tell them what you're doing. Tell them about Shango and his thundering family." He had another idea. "A picture! Send them a picture of your room, too."

During one presentation, Sydney had made passing reference to "the four oceans." Fenori had involuntarily held up his hand with all fingers extended, indicating *five*. As break started, Alfred counted aloud on his fingers, "Let's see. Four oceans. Atlantic, Pacific, Indian and..." he hesitated.

"Arctic," added Steepen.

"So...*four*," said Alfred, looking at Fenori, "there's no fifth."

"The *Southern Ocean*," Fenori said, "sometimes called the Antarctic Ocean, surrounding that continent." He beckoned them on to the Oceanography Hut, where they were building small wave machines. He pointed to the charts they were making, to one headed *Southern*. "It has a different food chain or food net than the others do, and different conditions. Actually, it's one of the shortest food chains anywhere." He got out a chart from the shelves labeled *Food Chains* to show them.

When they returned to start the next session, Alfred said to Sydney with mock formality, "Dr. Brummett," and he held up five fingers as Fenori had done before, "five. There are five oceans."

"All right," said the ever quick, sparkly-eyed Sydney, "name the *Seven Seas*."

While Alfred was thinking, Shem hastily wrote them down and slipped the note into his hand.

· · ·

Sydney and his students, sitting around the campfire at night under the cottonwoods, after eating supper, enjoyed comparing notes on the experiences they were having with the children. They looked over to where Jhenaw and Reendo and Lee were working together on carving a mask.

"It's a *shenemalula* mask," said Jhenaw, "worn by the Congolese tribe of Kuba. We have a Mask Building where we keep all the masks we make, patterned after those of different tribes in Asia, Africa, the Americas, Europe, Australia, the islands, everywhere we study about."

"Haven't you seen them yet?" Kayla said. She ran off with

Orgol and Shem and came back carrying boxes of colorful countenances.

They handed around the masks, and the children told the stories of each, the myths that matched people to their environments through millennia.

Later Kayla brought forth several more masks that she arranged on the ground around her. "The making of myths and masks are a living process, Lucian explained to us. So all of these stories live when we participate ourselves. These masks I made to represent the seven major moods of Kayla," she said, patting herself on the chest. She placed each in sequence before her face and turned her head, looking through their eye-holes at the people circled around the fire. "If you want, during break tomorrow, you can start to work on some of your own."

76

"I'm Sigma. Sigma Norstrund." She stood, with her earth-toned squaw dress blown by the wind. She waited for the man kneeling on the ground, building a model of a mountain, to look up. His mountain stood at the edge of a vast three-dimensional, miniature map of geologic formations.

Longhorn stared intently at his task. "In a moment," he said. "This must be right. This slope. This ledge below the summit. The summit, where the ceremony will be."

"I'm the one who does the newsletter. From the university," she offered. She had been assigned to follow up the chancellor's announcement of a new center exploring options in managing population and space exploration with an article in the alumni magazine.

"I graduated last year after doing an internship in the alumni office. And they kept me on to do the newsletter, full time."

Longhorn did not ignore her but had a rhythm of his own in completing this mountain. The one that Zoyan'qual had selected for the *naming* of the babies. The *middle mountain*.

"Now." He stood, and they beheld his work together.

"I tried at the house," she pointed far in the distance, "and no

327

one was there. Someone was driving away with what looked like a pot of dirt?" She said this last as a question, to which Longhorn did not reply.

So she continued, "And then I came out back when I saw the big skeleton of the dinosaur. And then I just kept on walking past all these things," her arm extended toward them, "until I found you. I'm supposed to interview..." she looked at her notes, "...Lucian? Are you Lucian?"

"I could be if you want," Longhorn said, "or you could wait until he returns with the children. They went to a talk by five people who have been in space. One from India, one from Russia, one United States, one from Japan, and I don't remember where else. You know there's an international organization of all the people who have actually journeyed into space. Our worm farm group is going to see if some of them can come here and help us determine where to start in developing a space exploration perspective for schools."

Although she had come to fill in her report, her attention had been diverted on her way to where she encountered Longhorn by what looked like an unbelievably long Quonset hut, by a lighthouse, a stilt house, by a zebra and a reindeer in the corral—Zee and Rain had come with Lee to visit for a few days—by this solitary workman who had produced a masterpiece of miniature landscape and now talked about *space exploration*.

So she followed him about as he moved next to the in-progress work on the what Fenori had christened *the world's longest slide through time*, with the strata of the earth represented and labeled.

She looked upward trying to identify the layers of earth and their years in geologic time. "So, what do *you* do here?" she asked.

"I make geological-slides and mountains," said Longhorn.

"My photographer will be here in a few minutes," she said. "What do you suggest we get pictures of?"

"What do you want to convey?"

He capped off a screw-top with a plastic mounting and removed a rope that had closed off the stairs that went alongside the slide. He started walking up the stairs, inspecting the slide as he went. A slide that did not just go down, but sideways, and back, and around, looping and turning.

"So," she said, "you can *walk* it or *slide* it. Slow or fast. Study it slowly…" her voice drifted off as she became involved in the layers, the years, the markers, the descriptive plaques, the representation of different fossils projecting from the layers.

Remembering her task, she said, "There was something Lucian apparently said at the university in a talk he gave, that I needed to ask him about. Someone said he had mentioned something about *roles* that people play being, I don't know, *limiting* or something. And wanting him to clarify it. But how would a society function without them? Roles. Wouldn't it be some kind of hippy commune, where no one does anything? Everything drifting and getting nothing done? No organization?"

They had worked their way to the top of the stairs. Longhorn removed the rope from the slide now. He gestured toward it and the meandering path it took, curving around through his constructed canyons of rock layers.

"This is enormous," she said, just grasping the dimensions of the work.

"Please," he said, gesturing for her to try the slide. "Be the first."

"Me? *Now?*" she said.

He waited, and she got in place, clutching her note pad, and began the prolonged descent. She looped past the most recent layers, took a sweeping turn by the time she reached the Mesozoic levels, slid through the age of dinosaurs, on to the Paleozoic, on and on. "A videotape!" she shouted over her shoulder. "We need a videotape of this from the sliding-down perspective!"

When she slowed at the mound representing the oldest rock layers on earth, at the bottom, and stood, she found herself surrounded by children, Beth, Lucian, and two babies, who had just returned.

"It's completed," Eriot shouted and started up the stairs, followed by the others, with Shem and Normita carrying the babies. On their way up, Longhorn passed them on the slide, on his way down.

As he stood, Longhorn said without explanation, "She wants to know how society could function without roles."

Beth plunged in with feeling, as if it was a topic that simmered below the surface all the time, just waiting for a conversational space to erupt through, "Lucian is so *clear* about that. A person who becomes a *role* tries to live it all the time and gives up his *individuality*. Yet society needs *functions* performed. An individual can perform a *function* and keep his *individuality*, without becoming a *role*. He can interact with other individuals performing functions and not treat them as a *category*. *Roles* and *functions*. There is a world of difference between social organization by *roles* and social organization by *functions*."

Sigma stared at Beth.

The children were coming down the lengthy, leisurely ride, with prolonged sounds of "Ooooh," and "Ahhhh." As they alighted, they clustered around the discussion and joined in.

Orgol said, holding the boy-child, "When you're an individual doing a function, you're flexible and can experiment with doing other functions as well. But if you're a *role*, there are prohibitions on what is appropriate or inappropriate for that role. Lucian explained that."

Pica said, "Lucian had us play out the same scene in two ways. First, as if we were a rigid role-category. The CEO, the Mother, the out-caste, the *ingenue*, the defender of the faith."

Sigma echoed, as if to convince herself that this child had just said , "...*the ingenue, defender...?*"

"And then," Pica continued, holding the girl-child to her shoulder, "second, as if we were individuals performing functions, those functions can change, and we can be flexible."

"It's sort of," added Eriot, "as if we were not *to the manor born* nor *to the serf's hut born*, but *in* the manor house or *in* the hut born. And could walk away and into other dwellings.

"...*to the manor born...?*" Sigma was repeating again.

Kayla held one hand way up and the other as low as she could, as if she measured a long imaginary fish hanging by its tail, straight up and down. "Roles make people feel they are in a vertical formation, with those at the top being better, with more power and control than those below them. People show different behavior to those above them than to those beneath them. They scramble to get higher, some at any cost."

"And call that normal living," interjected Orgol.

Kayla changed her hand positions, stretching as far right and left as she could reach. "But with *functions*, you have a horizontal structuring of society. Individuals are not inferior or superior that way. But certain *functions* being performed are more or less important to whatever task is being undertaken at the time."

"...*task being undertaken at the time?*" Sigma was mumbling again.

"Yes," said Dolphus, "you wouldn't want a stone-carving sculptor, however beautiful her work, to perform your brain surgery. But the brain surgeon is not a brain surgeon when he's ice-skating."

"...*sculptor...brain surgeon...ice-skating...?*"

One of the babies was hungry and Beth started breast-feeding him.

Normita said, "See, there's a function none of the rest of us can fill in the same way at the moment."

Sigma listened and jotted notes. In a lull, she gestured toward them all, "Don't you people believe in introductions? We haven't even been introduced, and we're having this *intense* conversation? And you all quote *Lucian.*"

She turned toward him. "And if I may presume, since no one has been introduced, that you may be Lucian? I presume that you're the person they're all quoting, but you haven't *said* anything. If you don't *say* anything, how can they all quote you?" She smiled as she finished. "Huh?" Adding, "And why do you spell your name that way?"

Dolphus said, "I guess being a reporter for an alumni newsletter is a pretty dead-end job. And frustrating."

"*What?*" she said. "Are you psychic as well? Without introductions, how do you know *what* I do?"

Reendo said, "Easy. When we came in, your photographer was knocking on the front door looking for you."

"Where is he now?" she said, quickly turning around.

"Last we saw him, he had taken a picture from inside the rib cage of the dinosaur, and then had reached about 1700, going backward in the Super Time Line."

She took a deep breath, closed her note pad, stuck her pencil behind her ear, cleared her face of all expression, as if she were starting this all over again, turned to Lucian, extending her hand and said, "Hello, my name is Sigma Norstrund. I'm—" and here she did a raised-eyebrow look at Dolphus "—the reporter, writer, editor, in fact the entire staff of the university alumni and public relations newsletter, a dead-end, frustrating, underpaid job, tolerated until I can be *discovered*, and I'm here doing a story…"

As she was speaking, the children watched behind her, where Lee and the photographer, on a reindeer and a zebra, came riding toward them.

77

Of all the excavations on which Beth had worked, there was one to which she wished to return with some urgency, before the naming ceremony of the babies. They had traveled, all of them, to the site, by horseback.

"This was my favorite *family*," Beth told them. "I know these people who lived here, by their artifacts."

She deployed the children in separate segments of the dig, which lay neatly divided by cross-grids of string. They each brushed away thousands of years of dirt and revealed fragments of the past.

"How expert you have become," Beth told them, observing, while holding a feeding baby at her breast. The other slept on a papoose rack in the shade near where Normita dug. "You show as much care with the past as with the present."

. . .

At night, at the dig site, they sat about the fire that illumined them and talked of the people whose artifacts they unearthed. Then Beth looked at Lucian and asked. "Please, a story of the Murlwumps. It has been a long time."

The children settled back. Dolphus held one of the babies. Pica held the other. "How easy you are with them already," said Beth. She had begun earlier to supplement the breast milk with bottled formula, so everyone could have the opportunity to share the feeding times.

"I want the babies to imprint with all of you," Beth told them, "as being significant in providing for their needs."

The children had been taking turns staying overnight at worm farm and keeping the babies with them, feeding them or walking with them when they awakened at night.

So now the babies joined with them at the excavation, beneath the starlight, around the fire, for the *Murlwump impromptu* that Beth, with unusual intensity, had requested.

Lucian, after looking at the faces illumined by the flames, spoke in a strangely distant way:

For a long time the Murlwumps were gone. I expected them to pop up at any moment. Then late one night I heard their voices once again. I know not what they had encountered during the period of their long wanderings, but there appeared a new look about their faces I had not known before.

"I think we must go away," said one Murlwump.

"Yes. I know we must," said the second.

Added the third, "But let's take this moment for a bit more talk, this calm before the great whirlwind."

"You mean, where will we go, don't you, dear friend?"

"Yes."

"If we were part of imagination, must we not go where imagination ends; is that not true?"

"Of course. And then the great imagination that created all our social world will end?"

"No, the world, the—how shall I say it—cycles, coiling their way through existence, these will continue. The elements, the parts, will continue, veering off into new cycles. But we may not be in the same cycle together."

"But there is no sadness."

"No."

"Perhaps a cup of hemlock juice for us, hmmm?"

"No, for thus it is not written."

And so saying, the first Murlwump wandered into a bed of flowers and plucked several long stems of fragrance. He slowly walked back.

After a long silence, the third Murlwump said, "But we never talked of the moons of Mars and Jupiter."

"No. But there will be others to do that."

"For we are weary."

And so saying, they sat back to back, and began to fade away.

They all sat in silence, watching the fire. Longhorn looked penetratingly at Lucian, after this different mood of the usually lighthearted stories. Whatever it was that Lucian was feeling, Longhorn had been experiencing it as well.

After a time, Beth said quietly, "Even if they have gone, may we have a memory story of them? Just one more?" She asked with a sense of sadness in her voice.

Lucian commenced again:

Lonely, I sit here tonight. The moon has circled many times since last speaking with my furry friends. I miss the voices of the Murlwumps; silence, only, greets my ears. But while I sit here, fancy, in its own soothing way brings back to mind with such clarity that my ears and eyes feel the memory strongly of the time and events that the Murlwumps called the Great Adventure.

I remember how, late one night, sitting on the window sill, tossing a prune seed back and forth, they made hand shadows on the moon-lit floor and spoke all the while with great urgency.

This, I later learned, was the beginning of the Great Adventure.

"If I were huge, and the world were small and somewhat flatter than at present and pointed at one end and brown in color—in a word—shaped like this prune seed—" and he held it between his furry fingers so that it shown in the light of the moon, "—then I would hold the world between my fingers."

"Throw it here," said Murlwump two. He similarly held the seed in his hand and closed his eyes. A brief second later exclaimed he, "The very truth, indeed."

"Now," said Murlwump three, "what would be, of all adventures, the very greatest?"

A long quiet ensued, until Murlwump one exclaimed, "I have it! I have it!"

"Good. And shall we, then, begin the Great Adventure?"

"Yes, let's commence the Great Adventure."

And so they did. But they haven't told us what it was yet.

The story had ended, and the late night called them all to their tents and pallets scattered out away from the site. Beth and Lucian, each carrying one of the babies, walked toward the tent sites with the children. Then the two of them, carrying the babies, wandered in the night as if to some melody in a minor key that they could hear and feel in unison.

They walked back to the central excavation and stepped down into it. Beth handed the baby she held to Lucian, who then sat on the ground, a child in each arm. Beth knelt opposite them and absently picked up a brush used in removing dirt from artifacts. She began brushing at the earth, dim at her fingertips, as if her memory needed no daylight to know where her hands moved. The sky of stars filled the circle above them, formed by the sides of the pit.

Beth, with her brush, gradually revealing a buried piece of pottery as she unearthed it from the soil in the shadows.

Lucian reclined against the wall of the dig. For a long time, they spoke no words as the revolving earth made the stars seem to move above. Framed as the two of them were by the edges of the excavation, some stars could be seen appearing over the edge at one side while other stars disappeared over the other edge. Twinkling into and out of view. The babies slept, and Lucian looked up from their faces to see Beth regarding the three of them.

Lucian looked at her face and had the sensation that it was fading even as he watched. Not gone, but shimmering like a mirage, becoming transparent. Not that the whole person faded, for someone seemed to be there underneath. But Beth seemed increasingly transparent.

The transparent-seeming face looked at him. Long. As if drinking in the sight before it might disappear. She had put down her brush with a finality that discarded it rather than placed if for further use. As if the hand was fading too. Though there was another hand, beneath it, while the hand that held the brush began to fade.

She said, not looking at him now, but focused on the stars, "Tell me just one more story. Of the Murlwumps. Once more."

Even the voice, the voice of Beth became wispy as if it struggled to speak, to be heard before it faded.

"Please," she added. A soft pleading resonated in that *please*. She took one of the babies, still asleep, and sat leaning against the wall opposite Lucian.

Lucian, his head tilted back, his eyes roving the milky way, holding the other child, responded by beginning a story.

The spinning earth marked off the rapid succession of days. Immersed in many activities, my time hastened by, and with it fled my hope of ever seeing the Murlwumps again.

Walking up a desert hill late one afternoon, I saw the skies darken threateningly and rapid successions of lightning exploded on the horizon. Bending against the fierce wind and watching my footing on the slippery rocks, some time passed before I chanced to glance upward again.

And there I saw three Murlwumps leaning into the wind, riding on the foremost crest of the thunderhead. The mighty mass ran with legs of lightening that chopped the shrieking air and left a trail of thunderclaps rumbling in its wake.

"What a rouser!" shouted Murlwump one.

"To the left! To the left!" screamed Murlwump three above the gale.

Murlwump two leaned his body in the direction indicated and the mighty mass of purple veered to the left to roar through another portion of sky.

As in the children's game of crack the whip, the last members of the line cannot turn with the rest and thus speed straight ahead, so it was with the the thunder-rumblings at the rear; unable to follow the circular path, they sped straight forward, coming to rest at last in a peaceful, cloudless valley, which they filled with their sputterings and rumblings until the local inhabitants were sore afraid.

The crackling tumult of the Murlwumps' stormy stallion's hooves swept from the ground dust billows, which the fierce wall of water prodded back to earth.

The small three figures sat upon the foreword billow of the cloud, their fur dripping with the spray, their eyes narrowed against the driving wind. They guided the huge mass this way and that; they scraped the cloud's belly on the mountains and left the shrubs bending in the wind;

they roared across a valley and left the creeks as torrents; they spun boulders off of cliffs and sent them reeling to the valley. Their steed's sharp hooves split trees and clove rocks.

What portent this—what has transpired?

"What portent, indeed!" cried they. "Tis one to use when e're you choose. Perhaps for..."

But here the thunder sounded and the wall of rain swept by and we lost their words.

Beth knew he had finished as the silence ensued, and they both gazed upward at the stars. He knew she would speak, and he waited. Both babies slept now.

Beth breathed in a great intake of air. She tried to speak, but the voice made dry sounds.

She managed on a second attempt to say softly, "I will go soon."

After a pause, she continued, "I will go from here where I am Beth, to a place where Beth does not exist, where I do not exist."

She gestured toward their surroundings. "You know how we refer to these long-ago people, those who lived in this place, in this room, whose bones we've been excavating from this floor? The husband, the wife, the children. The *categories*. Well, I go where I am the *wife*, to one who is the *husband*."

She seemed to focus all her energy to get out the story. "My mother was a socialite. The daughter of a family of great wealth in this country. When my grandfather died, my mother inherited holdings vast and widespread. She had no idea how to direct them, and was lonely and sad and confused. She wanted only to write her poetry and be taken care of, as she had always been.

"An enterprising person from another land, who had more ambition than wealth, courted her. He discovered little by little what she wanted him to be, and became the seeming embodiment of that. Kindness, thoughtfulness, compassion. He took care of all her affairs. Buffered her from pain. She was so grateful. He had ended her confusion. He married her and ran the family fortunes. She let everything be transferred to his name, without realizing what was happening. Then he transferred the wealth back home, his home, and her with him, pregnant then, with me.

"There she was, the red-haired wife of a living embodiment of ambition, who traded wherever he could for more wealth, power, and control. She was never *herself*, a *human* to him, but only another commodity to be bartered and traded. For his traditions taught him that he was master of us all, literally, and could make decisions of our lives and deaths. He begot children, other children by my mother and his other wives, for such was the custom of the land, training the boys to be his underlings, the girls were sold into alliances that connected him to other families of influence. *Sold*, I say, because they had no voice, no protest could be made. For they, we, all learned his ruthlessness, and that if any one of us objected, we would see the others treated in a way we could not endure.

"My mother closed her eyes to this, *all this*, and played her part. She became *herself* when we were alone, talking of the things that made life *real* but returning to her submissive role when he was around."

While Beth's one arm held the baby, her free hand made a futile gesture toward the stars, then dropped at her side. She stared downward toward the floor of the pit.

The stars moved further before she continued, "I was *promised*, Lucian, promised, given, allied, *married*, at the age of four, to a husband who was ten. If the words paternalistic, dominating, authoritarian, extended family patriarch mean anything to you, you can begin to understand.

"My one release was school. As a token to the liberalizing influence, to the international business connections, I was permitted to be schooled, although by tutors, then a private school, and then, so I could be the dutiful wife, subservient but able to communicate with liberated wives from other countries where these men did business, I was permitted to come back to this, my mother's country, to go to university.

"I have parlayed that opportunity to a thin attenuation as far as it will go. Convinced them that the ancient heritage of their land could be benefitted by my pursuing archaeological studies, perhaps to give advice on how to build the tourist industry, to spread cultural good will, to show the long lines of our patriarchal civilization.

"I have three women, *watch-women*, if you will, guards, keepers, who are to oversee my safety. Who are to see that I do not consort with decadent ways." She voiced Lucian's unasked question. "Where are they?" Her free hand gestured to the surrounding space.

"I discovered early on that they hated digs. Hated the heat and sweat and boredom and inconvenience. They wear the coverings, the degrading coverings to hide their shapes and looks from men, so as not to tempt males to wayward thoughts.

"Have you ever heard so perfect a description of *projection?* The *men* have wayward thoughts, so the *woman* are to blame and must be shrouded in cloth and entombed in homes. They hated the digs and the outdoors and finally stopped coming with me at all. Stopped accompanying me anywhere. They eat their rich foods and watch television and grow fat and send the messages back that all is well in my pursuit of education. And my long desert digs extended from days to weeks, to months, while I call in from time to time, to affirm that all is well.

"I escaped into this oblivion of land here, to dig with archaeologists, to dig alone, to piece together the fascinating lives of skeletons and their potsherds. And if I have any claim to being known at all, it will be millennia hence, when someone digs me up, and stretches out my bones, and labels me *the wife*.

"Not *the* wife, actually, but *one* of the wives, for he, my betrothed, already has more, plus assorted concubines. Other alliances, that bind him to political power. And if I would refuse to return, if I would run off and try to hide, my *loving* father and my *loving* spouse, and all their clan would render such horrors on my mother—she still lives in some twilight life, her money, property, everything all transferred to his name—such horrors on her and my siblings, for which I would be responsible.

"It is one thing to purposely pursue a status, a position, and then *become* it and endure the consequences of giving up what *could have been*. It is another to be *born* into a rank, so rigidly an entombing one, that real life is never possible. Being born into a rank is being born into slavery, the slavery of a role.

"I am a theater child, born upon the stage, the actors all in place and playing out their parts. They created my part. I had no

339

say in it. And I must perform it from the first unto the last. In their testosterone-and-adrenaline-driven scenes of mayhem of a drama, they have no remote inkling that their whole lives are lived on stage in these absurd roles. No inkling that there is a place outside the theater. That there is…. "

She did not complete the sentence, but leaned back against the side of the pit opposite Lucian. She again breathed in deep lungfulls of air.

She said, "But what do I know, except for *this*. This, my uneventful archeology. My peaceful digs. I have gone off stage for just an instant, out the stage door, and gulped the air, and…

"Now I hear my cue to return to stage, or else I'll hear the cries of anguish of those who depend on me, and I will be responsible for their ruin. It is a subplot of the script, an alternative written in.

"Every time I see a king or queen, a prince or princess, the first-born of someone claiming to hear messages from God, who demands his lineage obey, or the hapless child of inherited wealth and position, I cry for them."

She rose and said, "And yet, we kings and bartered brides are immortal, for *positions* never die. Only individuals do. Long live the pharaoh, king, and tribal chief and his wives. Those who fill those posts are not alive. They became the part. The part is immortal. And others envy them. They stand and envy the living-dead. And strive to be like them."

She moved to Lucian and placed the second sleeping baby in his arms beside the other. She knelt on the ground, her arms around all three. Her head rested on Lucian's shoulder, the warmth of her cheek against his. Her fragrance of myrrh and sandalwood blended with his of lotus.

For a long moment they remained within the pit beneath the swath of stars.

She stood at last. As she walked away, she added, "May none who see the bones or portraits of these people exhibited in museums along with their gold regalia feel anything but pity for the lot."

Lucian watched the retreating shadow disappear into the darkness.

340

He looked down at the babies that he held and wondered at their future, wondered at their also fading into that darkness about to engulf their mother.

78

The day of *naming* had come. The very time appointed by Beth on that night of their birth. She had asked Zoyan'qual to select the place. He had chosen the remote site he called, in the New Tongue, *the central point, the middle mountain.*

They prepared to travel to the mountain, that *central point* between the four directions and the four mesas—*the pillars holding up the sky.* The babies would be named there.

They began to gather under the cottonwood trees at worm farm for the journey out into the desert. Normita came carrying the boy-baby. She had kept it overnight in her worm farm room. Dolphus came out of his dwelling with the girl-baby whom he had cared for during the night. Longhorn had prepared the horses, had packed the provisions on additional mounts. Grandmother came galloping out of the desert to join the others. Howard arrived by car and came around the house to the trees. Each in turn arrived, until only Beth remained to emerge from her circle house for this day she had orchestrated for the naming of the children.

Longhorn went from the waiting group to get Beth. He returned from her round adobe room with an envelope.

"She is not there. But this envelope with your name on it, Lucian, says *read it now.*"

Lucian nodded to him to do so.

Longhorn read aloud: *Lucian can explain to all of you what he wishes of my circumstances.*

Longhorn looked at him, and he briefly told them of what Beth had revealed to him in the archaeological dig.

Then Longhorn read again.

Only know this, all of you. Never, under any conditions in this world, can any contact be made by anyone with the part I now must play, the script that I must perform. Nor have any thought, however momentary, that there is any relation between that part and Beth. The role I go to has another name you do not even know nor must ever know. Be assured that Beth is no more. There is nowhere to look for her, for she no longer will exist when this pen is put down and this message is concluded.

Know that Beth is mother of these children, and not the person that may resemble her, who is gone. Beth would not abandon them, but then, Beth will be no more. Only the role of second-wife, given at the age of four.

Know that the man who plays the role of husband to this role of second-wife, is not the father of the children. Know that the role I must become again is to return to him now for the purpose of bearing him heirs. He and she, the second-wife, have never been together intimately. That was to begin on her return. Will he assume no one has yet known her, that she was active in cycling and other sports here and that her seeming non-virginity is from that? What will he conclude? Can he tell she has borne children? There are subplots if such suspicions become too strong. But Beth will never know. She will be no more. What happens to the other role is of no importance.

Know that this man who is her husband will never father children by her. She goes now to have a doctor undo that ability to give that husband-role children like himself. And when in time he casts her aside for her prolonged sterility, there will be no repercussions on the others for her insufficiency. There are yet other subplots awaiting.

Know that when we at worm farm studied the biology of reproduction, and we peered into microscopes at Lucian's sperm, that we used but a small part of the samples for that purpose. The rest, Beth introduced into herself. And we watched Beth grow large with child, with children, and they entered into the light at birth.

Know, Lucian, you are the father of the children, as is certified on the enclosed documents. Actually, you are the parents, and I mean that in the plural, both parents, of these children. Beth only carried them for a time and gave them back to you. Beth gave two eggs. She donated them to you. And now the role that will replace Beth will have that womb made void of any other eggs.

Lucian, you deserve them, and they, you. Beth came like a mirage from the desert, was real long enough to give two eggs and the hollow of her womb. And then she evaporated back into the desert, from whence she came and is no more.

342

Let nothing, not this letter, not your feelings, not your thoughts, nothing, interfere with the naming ceremony for the children. It must continue exactly as planned, at the arranged time. Beth is dead. Mourn her if you will, though I have already mourned enough for all of us. But do not flinch for a moment in getting on with life, the life of the babies and yourselves.

In the new tongue—Talwa. Talwa haysu. Hamba walera bagmay. Sigda ba-at rom heglu. Meenma spalsay. Ante promu Zwentokaneemay. Ante promu lelwa siquine.
Beth

And Longhorn, who for himself had never wept, now wept for her.

79

Longhorn suggested the others begin as scheduled for the ride toward the middle mountain. He said he needed some time alone with Lucian following the revelations in the letter. The others journeyed onward, out into the stream beds and the ridges, out into the vastness of the desert.

The naming ceremony would proceed as planned.

Longhorn pointed to the ground and Lucian sat there cross-legged. With colored powders, Longhorn made a large circle on the earth, intersecting it from the four directions to the center where Lucian sat. Longhorn slowly moved around the circumference of the circle, chanting softly, calling upon the healing of the winds, of the powers of the sky, of the power of the sun, of the richness of the earth, of the energy of the plants, of the interlocking realms of animal life. He called upon the hidden powers to be unleashed to heal Lucian, to bring him inner focus and strength.

He then made a motion that Lucian understood to mean a repeating of the ceremony for him. They traded places, and Lucian circled, chanting in the new tongue, the evocation of the life force.

Then placing Beth's letter in the middle of the circle, they both moved in opposite directions around it, pausing at the ends of the directional points, raising their hands to the sky, and chanted for the one now gone.

. . .

Longhorn told Lucian to ride on, beginning his journey toward the middle mountain. Saying that he needed to remain longer, Longhorn began a slow movement and chanting in ever wider arcs to encompass more of the land.

. . .

Alone amid the canisters of worms, Longhorn stood and pondered the impact of the letter.

When, at last, he walked toward the corral and sat astride his mount, ready to ride away alone, to follow Lucian, to follow the others, he saw a dust cloud on the roadway in the distance, coming closer, and he paused to see its destination.

. . .

Zoyan'qual had ridden Phantom from their hidden canyon, traveled across the desert to the middle mountain, arrived two sunrises before the others. He had walked the circuits around its varied levels, knowing all the textures with his footsteps, seeing all the life that stirred upon its slopes.

From a flat outcropping below the mountain's summit, he had seen the horses and the riders in the distance, coming far across the plains.

They dismounted, leaving their steeds at the juncture where the mountain's base broadened, sloping outward until it joined the lowland. They found their way up the sides, moving toward the heights, past the boulders and the caves, past the plants that flowered following the rains.

All stood on the outcropping there with Zoyan'qual. They watched the single rider in the distance. Lucian coming far across the plains.

When he had joined them there beneath the summit, Lucian told Zoyan'qual of the letter, told him of the message, told him of the contents.

The two sat cross-legged facing one another, the distance of the desert spreading out below them. Zoyan'qual took Lucian's hands and placed his palms against them. The two of them raised their hands pressed together skyward. The others joined round and placed their hands around the upraised ones. Zoyan'qual said in the New Tongue, "*Let paining nourish all the roots, drawn upward in the stems and the leaves, mixed with power of the sunlight be transformed into energy for growing, blooming, and fructifying.*"

There they stood, circled on the summit of the mountain, as the orange sun lowered toward the horizon. On the opposite edge of the world, storm clouds billowed upward. Distant lightening shafted across and down within the purple colors. A partial rainbow shivered into being.

Zoyan'qual chanted and threw dust from the four mesas into the wind. They all sang in the New Tongue. Normita read verses she had written.

Lucian held one baby high, upward above his head, firmly cradled in his hands. Grandmother held the other similarly.

Focused as they were on their ceremony of the sunset, five figures, unseen by them, had come to the flat outcropping, below and behind them. Five stood looking up at the sight above them. One was Longhorn. With him were four others.

80

When Longhorn had seen the dust cloud on the road at the worm farm, he had met the car that hesitatingly drove up, three occupants emerged, asking for directions. Two explained they were looking for their son. His name was Lucian. He had some kind of ranch here. They would not bring themselves to say the words *worm farm*.

"Synchronicity," said Longhorn.

"What? said the mother. "Is that some local greeting?"

"A concept of Jung," he said softly. He added with the hint of a smile, "Or an album by Sting."

"What?" said the mother.

Longhorn told them Lucian was *elsewhere*, but if they wished he could take them to him. They agreed, indicating they had rerouted their flight to the nearest airport, rented this car, and followed various directions to this place. Their visit would be a surprise, since they had not informed Lucian of their coming at this particular time, although he had asked them to come *sometime*.

The third person was a former politician, building up goodwill, in behalf of his son's future bid for higher office.

"Synchronicity two," said Longhorn, piercing the man with his gaze.

"What?" said the mother again, tilting her head in perplexity.

"Another song by Sting," said Longhorn, softly, still penetrating the man, without turning to the mother.

"Sting?" the mother squinted, turning to the father.

The father said with curt authority, "It's a sword in *The Hobbit*."

"Why would these people use the Hobbit's sword for a greeting?" said the mother.

"Don't pay any attention. It only encourages them," said the father. "They want you to react."

Longhorn smiled faintly at having become part of a *they*. Again.

The politician was on a low-key, flexible, informal *grass roots tour of the heartland of this great country, testing the waters*, visiting orphanages, speaking to civic leaders, having his picture taken with potential supporters for his son's potential campaign, and training his grandson to learn the family trade in the process.

Lucian's parents had supported his informal rallies, where he projected that his son could continue the work he had started in offering a *return to traditional values and long cherished principles of decency and justice*. Local citizens were escorting him off to informal gatherings in unscheduled places, where he shook hands, cradled babies, and smiled, his substantial jaw firmly set, his eyes looking to the future, toward the *next generation of leadership*. He was using commercial airlines rather than private transportation, so that *the common people will know I, just like all the rest of my family, including my son, am just one of them, with their interests at heart*, as he curried the favor of *ordinary citizens*.

So when, at his most recent rally, these two supporters had offered to take him to the airport for the same flight they were taking for the next phase of his journey, he had graciously, in front of the press, accepted *this humble, sincere offer of two more of the multitude of constituents in a growing army of supporters for my son.*

The parents had convinced him that the *slight detour* might offer additional publicity. Their mention that they would use an airport layover to stop at a school their son operated registered with him only as another chance for publicity *in rural America.* He could not understand why, inexplicably, flashbacks of the war years in the Pacific started coming back to him at this farm.

Their car door opened again, and a fourth figure emerged from where he had been listening through the open window and wanted to get closer to the conversation. He was the politician's grandson, being groomed, following his recent university graduation, on this cross-country tour by his grandfather, to learn the tricks of the trade, to train him to continue the hoped-for dynasty for a third generation.

"Get the maps," the grandfather said without looking at him. The youth moved as one used to receiving orders. Then to Longhorn, "Now, you, show us the route to this next location…"

Before he could finish, Lucian's mother was fumbling with her camera, saying to the youth, "Take our picture here with your grandfather in front of some of these outbuildings of our son's ranch. Why it's so large we can't even see the main buildings from here, just these little outbuildings."

"Do what she says, boy. You have to learn to listen to the voices of our faithful constituents." He emitted a practiced laugh. "And bring our camera too. Note down the location in the record. Put up that car window so it won't be filled with dust. Hurry up."

Lucian's parents positioned themselves on either side, while the politician reflexively postured into a statuesque pose and smile.

"Perhaps you should let the gentleman guide us as he offered since he already knows the way," the grandson suggested.

They let Longhorn drive their rental car, the recent college graduate sitting in the front seat with him, the other three in back. He headed out on desert roads and dirt trails to get them as close as possible to the mountain location. The mother chattered about this trackless wasteland. The father interspersed statements about the government needing to do something to make this useless area productive. The politician made extravagant claims about his own son's *outstand qualifications*, and the potential of the *next generation* as if rehearsing his next speech.

In the midst of these, Longhorn said, "Tell me, what do you think will be the role of the aboriginal American from a postmodern perspective?"

The remark caused a momentary hush and then remained ignored by the backseat passengers who quickly resumed their loud pronouncements, while the politician's unexpected flashbacks suddenly intensified.

Under their noise, the young man began asking Longhorn about his *aboriginal* question, and a conversation in *sotto voce* continued between them in the front seat. Longhorn, in turn, questioned him about his feelings for being the *heir apparent* of the *family business* and what he might want to do under other circumstances. The youth also asked him about *Sting* and *Jung* and *synchronicity*.

· · ·

Reaching as close to the base of the mountain as possible, Longhorn led the four on foot along its flank, as the elder three became increasingly reluctant to continue walking upward along the steepening grade.

By the time they achieved the outcropping, the three were sweating, winded, and not at all happy. And from there, they beheld the sight at a distance above them.

The woman whispered, *"Who are those motley children? Who is that naked man? What is that ethnic woman doing with that baby? Dear heavens! Surely that is not our son, holding up that baby up in the air that way? Why is he doing that?"*

"That baby," Longhorn told them, "is your grandchild. So is the other."

"I will endure no more," the mother wheezed as if her whole body had been seized in a systemic asthma attack. She turned, followed by her husband, heading downward.

"We disown him," the father said. "And his out-of-wedlock children of god knows what ethnicity they may be."

Longhorn said softly, "How can you disown what you have never owned?"

The politician's grandson took in the scene as if seeing a vision.

"Take us back," the father ordered Longhorn.

"I am remaining here with them," Longhorn said, nodding upward.

"Then we'll find the way back ourselves," said the father.

"The way may be difficult to remember. There were few markers," Longhorn said.

"We secured regional maps before we came," the father said.

"Some places are not on maps," Longhorn said softly toward the descending pair, who were already picking their way down among the rocks and plants. "Perhaps where Lucian has come to, there are no maps."

The politician had not yet moved. The man's eyes were squinting as one who sees phantoms mixing with the reality before him, as Longhorn stared unblinkingly back at him.

Longhorn took something from his pocket. They were spent bullets. He held them in his open hand toward the man.

"You gave these to me some time ago," Longhorn said. "I have no more use for them now. Perhaps you do."

He grasped the other's hand, dropped the bullets into the palm, and pressed it closed.

For a time, the politician's figure seemed to have petrified. Then, still clutching the missiles of destruction in his fist, he stumbled downward, not as if he were seeing and walking on this mountainside, but as if he navigated some inner landscape of his own, rumbling with an earthquake.

The young man quickly penned something on a scrap of paper and handed it to Longhorn, whispering, "Contact me." He ran after his grandfather, who stumbled onward, staring at his own closed fist which he held out in front of him.

Longhorn turned and started climbing the rest of the trail that curved on upward.

81

Longhorn arrived at the summit and joined the circle. He briefly touched, in turn, each of the babies.

Zoyan'qual gave them New Tongue names. He said, as he and

Grandmother held the babies, "They are made of the same elements as the glowing sun. The fire of the lightning electrifies their nervous system. All of the minerals and chemicals in every one of their cells also exists in the soil beneath our feet. The composition of their blood that nourishes their cells is a mixture like the fluids of the oceans. They are a form composed of the matter of the galaxies. They are a fragment of the universe, made of its materials, shaped by genetic message codes of life. May they walk the earth of which they are made, knowing that this planet, and the sun, the stars, the galaxies, and universe are both their parents and themselves. May they know beyond the words that say these things that we all are unitary, single, one."

Far below, a dust cloud of a departing automobile fanned out in the winds and disappeared.

The children all now beat the drums and played the flutes, to music Lucian had taught them. Its four parts alternated multiple-flute melodies and harmonies with the words the children sang.

They played and sang the first part:

> *Wander with me in the desert*
> *Just behind a springtime shower.*
> *Inhale the fragrance of the wildflowers*
> *Spread throughout the desert valley.*
>
> *Dip your feet in turquoise rain pools.*
> *Lift your hands unto the sunset.*
> *Chant the mantra of the desert*
> *From the mythic depths within you.*

The flutes again played the second melody, and then they sang:

> *We can fly*
> *Through the sky*
> *Where the wind spirits sing*
> *We can rest*
> *In the nest*
> *By the eagle's wing.*

We can plummet
From the summit
Of the mountain heights,
We can glide
By the side
Of the rainbow's lights.

The flutes and drums again changed their melody and rhythm.
The children sang:

The floods sweep down the wild arroyos.
The spirits of the clouds and rain survive.
Here we feel at one
With all their mysteries
And know they are alive.

They began a deep, flowing new melody.

Again the storm clouds come with lightning,
Firebolts from clouds to the earth.
Feel the liberation
With each reverberation
Of the thunder of our birth.

As they prolonged the singing of the word *birth*, Zoyan'qual
said, "Our awareness now expands to the *seven* directions." He
gestured toward the *east*, *north*, *west*, and *south*. And then *below*
toward the earth and *above* toward the heavens, and finally *within*
as the fingers of both hands touched his own chest.

The sun had set on one side of the horizon. The *fire-bolts*
flared on the opposite side. The rumble from the lightning in the
distance rolled across the arching sky, around the mountain,
around them all, as they repeated once again:

OF THE THUNDER OF OUR BIRTH.

About the Author

Dr. Allan Ward is Professor Emeritus of Communication Studies at the University of Arkansas at Little Rock, and a consultant in Intercultural Communication and Diversity Training. He has traveled to all continents exploring diverse worldviews. The personal stories from these explorations are included in his book *Beyond the Visible Spectrum*.

He has spoken in Africa, Asia, Europe, and North and South America on communication and the postmodern perspective. Requests for him to apply this perspective to a distillation of worldviews and the universal journey of those who seek to expand their insight resulted in his book *Postmodern Zen: A Path of Paradox and Process*.

He speaks on these subjects, and on "Life As a Novel Experience," utilizing the themes from his novel, *Lucian*, for book clubs and other organizations, and may be contacted at alward@ualr.edu. Copies of all three volumes are available by phone order from 1-800-880-0122.